Praise for
and *USA TODA*
Bren

C000147061

"Brenda Jackson writes romance that sizzles
and characters you fall in love with."
—*New York Times* and *USA TODAY* bestselling
author Lori Foster

"Jackson's trademark ability to weave multiple
characters and side stories together makes shocking
truths all the more exciting."
—*Publishers Weekly*

"There is no getting away from the sex appeal and
charm of Jackson's Westmoreland family."
—*RT Book Reviews* on *Feeling the Heat*

"Jackson's characters are wonderful, strong, colorful
and hot enough to burn the pages."
—*RT Book Reviews* on *Westmoreland's Way*

"The kind of sizzling, heart-tugging story Brenda
Jackson is famous for."
—*RT Book Reviews* on *Spencer's Forbidden Passion*

"This is entertainment at its best."
—*RT Book Reviews* on *Star of His Heart*

Dear Reader,

It is hard to believe that we are celebrating the tenth anniversary of the Westmorelands. It seemed like it was only yesterday when I introduced you to Delaney and her five brothers. I knew by the time I wrote Thorn's story that I just had to tell you about their cousins. Now twenty-three books later, we are still going strong.

It has been an adventure and I appreciate sharing it with you. Thank you. I've gotten your emails and snail mails letting me know how much you adore those Westmoreland men and I appreciate hearing from you. Each Westmoreland—male or female—is unique and the way love takes control of their hearts is both heartwarming and breathtaking.

In this story, Riley Westmoreland is willing to take a chance on love with a woman who has a past she'd rather not deal with. But this Westmoreland man shows her that true love can conquer all.

I hope you enjoy this story about Riley Westmoreland and Alpha Blake.

Happy reading!

Brenda Jackson

ONE WINTER'S NIGHT

BY
BRENDA JACKSON

All the characters in this book have no existence outside the imagination of the author, and have no relation whatsoever to anyone bearing the same name or names. They are not even distantly inspired by any individual known or unknown to the author, and all the incidents are pure invention.

All Rights Reserved including the right of reproduction in whole or in part in any form. This edition is published by arrangement with Harlequin Enterprises II B.V./S.à.r.l. The text of this publication or any part thereof may not be reproduced or transmitted in any form or by any means, electronic or mechanical, including photocopying, recording, storage in an information retrieval system, or otherwise, without the written permission of the publisher.

This book is sold subject to the condition that it shall not, by way of trade or otherwise, be lent, resold, hired out or otherwise circulated without the prior consent of the publisher in any form of binding or cover other than that in which it is published and without a similar condition including this condition being imposed on the subsequent purchaser.

® and ™ are trademarks owned and used by the trademark owner and/or its licensee. Trademarks marked with ® are registered with the United Kingdom Patent Office and/or the Office for Harmonisation in the Internal Market and in other countries.

To the love of my life, Gerald Jackson, Sr.

Happy holidays to all my family, friends and
dedicated readers.

A very special thank you to event planners
extraordinaire—Shikara Linsy, Sandra Sutton, Tammy
Griffin, and Tracy Hale.

My interview with you regarding the life of an event
planner and your patience in answering all of my
questions was most appreciated.

Pleasant words are a honeycomb, sweet to the
soul and healing to the bones.
—*Proverbs*, 16:24

Brenda Jackson is a die "heart" romantic who married her childhood sweetheart and still proudly wears the "going steady" ring he gave her when she was fifteen. Because she believes in the power of love, Brenda's stories always have happy endings. In her real-life love story, Brenda and her husband of forty years live in Jacksonville, Florida, and have two sons.

A *New York Times* bestselling author of more than seventy-five romance titles, Brenda is a recent retiree who now divides her time between family, writing and traveling with Gerald. You may write Brenda at PO Box 28267, Jacksonville, Florida 32226, USA, by email at writerbjackson@aol.com or visit her website at www.brendajackson.net.

THE DENVER WESTMORELAND FAMILY TREE

Raphel and Gemma Westmoreland

Stern Westmoreland (Paula Bailey)

Thomas (Susan)

Adam (Clarisse)

Dillon (Pamela) ①

Ramsey (Chloe) ②

Zane

Micah (Kalina) ⑥

Jason (Bella) ⑤

Riley ⑧

Canyon

Stern

Brisbane

Adrian

Aidan

Bailey

Derringer (Lucia) ④

Megan (Rico) ⑦

Gemma (Callum) ③

① Westmoreland's Way
② Hot Westmoreland Nights
③ What a Westmoreland Wants

④ A Wife for a Westmoreland
⑤ The Proposal
⑥ Feeling the Heat

⑦ Texas Wild
⑧ One Winter's Night

One

A blistering cold day in early November

It had snowed overnight and a thick white blanket seemed to cover the land as far as the eye could see. The Denver weather report said the temperature would drop to ten below by midday and would stay that way through most of the night. It was the kind of cold you could feel deep in your bones, the kind where your breath practically froze upon exhale.

He loved it.

Riley Westmoreland opened the door to his truck and, before getting inside, paused to take in the land he owned. *Riley's Station* was the name he'd given his one-hundred-acre spread seven years ago, on his twenty-fifth birthday. He had designed the ranch house himself and had helped in the building of it, proudly hammering the first nail into the lumber. He was mighty pleased with the massive two-story structure that sat smack in the center of his snow-covered land.

He was probably the only one in his family who welcomed

the snowstorms each year. He thought the snow was what made Denver the perfect place to be in the winter and why his home had fireplaces in all five of the bedrooms, as well as in the living room and family room. There was nothing like curling up before a roaring fire or looking out the window to see the snowflakes fall from the sky, something he'd been fascinated with even as a child. He could recall being out in the thick snow with his brothers and cousins building snowmen. These days he enjoyed moving around the mountains on his snowmobile or going skiing in Aspen.

Riley got into the truck and after settling his body on the leather seat he snapped the seat belt in place. There really was no need for him to go into the office since he could work from home. But he had wanted to get out, breathe in the cold, fresh air and feel the chill in his bones. Besides, he did have an important appointment at noon.

Since his oldest brother, Dillon, had slowed down now that his wife, Pam, was close to her delivery date, a lot of the projects on Dillon's plate at their family-owned business, Blue Ridge Land Management, fell on Riley's shoulders since he was the next man in charge of the Fortune 500 company. The next thing on the agenda was the planning of the employees' holiday party next month.

The event planner that had handled their social functions for the past ten years had retired and before Riley had taken over the project, Dillon had hired Imagine, a local event planning company that opened in town less than a year ago. The owner of Imagine, a woman by the name of Alpha Blake, had put together a charity event that Dillon's wife, Pam, had attended over the summer. Pam had been so impressed with all the detailed work Imagine had done that she passed the woman's name to Dillon. As far as Riley was concerned, you couldn't come any more highly recommended than that. Dillon trusted his wife's judgment in all things.

Riley was about to start the ignition when his cell phone buzzed. He pulled the phone off his side belt. "Yes?"

"Mr. Westmoreland?"

He lifted a brow, not recognizing the ultrarich, feminine voice but definitely liking how it sounded. He figured this had to be a business call since none of the women he dated would refer to him as "Mr. Westmoreland."

"Yes, this is Riley Westmoreland. How can I help you?"

"This is Alpha Blake. We have a noon appointment at your office, but I have a flat tire and had to pull off to the side of the road. Unfortunately, I'm going to be late."

He nodded. "Have you called for road service?"

"Yes, and they said they should be here in less than thirty minutes."

Don't count on it, he thought, knowing how slow road service could be this time of the year. "Where's your location, Ms. Blake?"

"I'm on Winterberry Road, about a mile from the Edgewater intersection. There's a market not far away, but it didn't appear to be open when I drove past earlier."

"And chances are it won't be open today. Fred Martin owns that market and never opens the day after a bad snowstorm," he said.

He knew her exact location now. "Look, you're not far from where I am. I'll call my personal road service company to change your tire. In the meantime, I'll pick you up and we can do a lunch meeting at McKay's instead of meeting at my office, since McKay's is closer. And afterward, I can take you back to your car. The tire will be changed by then."

"I—I don't want to put you to any trouble."

"You won't. I know you and Dillon have gone over some ideas for the party, but since I'll be handling things from here on out, I need to be briefed on what's going on. Usually my administrative assistant handles such matters, but she's out on maternity leave and this party is too important to hand off to anyone else."

And what he didn't bother to say because he was certain Dillon had done so already was that this would be the fortieth anniversary of the company his father and uncle had founded. This was not just a special event for the employees, but was important to everyone in the Westmoreland family.

"All right, if you're sure it won't be an inconvenience," she said, breaking into his thoughts.

"It won't be, and I'm on my way."

Alpha Blake tightened her coat around her, feeling totally frustrated. What did a person who had been born in sunny Florida know about the blistering cold of Denver, especially when it had snowed all night and the roads and everything else were covered with white?

But she was so determined to keep her noon appointment with Riley Westmoreland that she'd made a mess of things. Not only would she be late for their appointment, but because of her flat tire they would have to change the location of the meeting and Mr. Westmoreland would be the one driving her there. This was totally embarrassing when she had been trying to make a good impression. Granted, she'd already been hired by Dillon Westmoreland, but when his secretary called last week to say that she would be working with the next man in charge at Blue Ridge, namely Dillon's brother, Riley, she had felt the need to make a good impression on him, as well.

She turned up the heat in her car. Even with a steady stream of hot air coming in through the car vents, she still felt cold, too cold, and wondered if she would ever get used to the Denver weather. Of course it was too late to think about that now. It was her first winter here, and she didn't have any choice but to grin and bear it. When she'd moved, she'd felt that getting as far away from Daytona Beach as she could was essential to her peace of mind, although her friends thought she needed to have her head examined. Who in her right mind would prefer blistering cold Denver to sunny Daytona Beach? Only a person wanting to start a new life and put a painful past behind her.

Her attention was snagged when an SUV pulled off the road to park in front of her. The door swung open and long, denim-clad, boot-wearing legs appeared before a man stepped out of the truck and glanced her way. She met his gaze through the windshield and couldn't help the heart-piercing moment when she literally forgot to breathe. Walking toward her car was a man who was so dangerously masculine, so heart-stoppingly virile, that her brain went momentarily numb.

He was tall, and the Stetson on his head made him appear taller. But his height was secondary to the sharp handsomeness of the features beneath the brim of his hat. There was the coffee-and-cream color of his skin, his piercing dark brown eyes, a perfectly shaped nose, his full lips and a sculpted chin.

And she couldn't bypass his shoulders, massive and powerful-looking. It was hard to believe, with the temperature being what it was, that he seemed comfortable braving the harsh elements with a cowhide jacket instead of a heavy coat. It was in the low teens, and he was walking around like it was in the high sixties.

Her gaze slid all over him as he moved his long limbs toward her vehicle in a walk that was so agile and self-assured, she almost envied the confidence he exuded with every step. Her breasts suddenly peaked, and she could actually feel blood rushing through her veins. She didn't have to guess about what was happening to her, but still, she was surprised. This was the first time she'd reacted to a man since her breakup with Eddie.

The man made it to her car and tapped on the window. She all but held her breath as she pressed the button to roll it down. "Riley Westmoreland?" She really didn't have to ask since he favored his brother, Dillon.

"Yes. Alpha Blake?" he responded, offering her his hand through the open window while looking at her with what she thought was cool and assessing interest.

"Yes." She took his hand and even through her leather gloves, she thought it felt warm. "Glad to meet you, Mr. Westmoreland."

"Riley," he corrected, smiling, and she felt her insides melt. He had a gorgeous pair of eyes. Dark and alluring. "The pleasure is all mine," he added. "I've only heard exceptional things about you and your work. Both Dillon and Pam speak highly of you, Alpha. I hope it's okay for me to call you Alpha."

"Thank you, and yes, that's fine."

"I've made all the arrangements with my road service. Keep your emergency lights on and leave your car keys under your seat," he said, taking a step back so she could get out of the vehicle.

She nervously gnawed her bottom lip. "Will it be safe to do that?"

He chuckled. "Yes, days like this keep thieves inside." He opened the car door for her. "Ready to get inside my truck?"

"Yes." She placed her key under the seat and then grabbed her purse and messenger bag. Tightening her coat around her, she walked quickly to the side of his truck. He was there to open the door and she appreciated finding the inside warm and cozy. It smelled like him, a scent that was masculine and sexy. She blushed, wondering why she was thinking such things, especially about a man she would be working for.

He closed the door just seconds before his cell phone rang, and she looked at the outside mirror as he spoke on the phone while moving around the front of the truck to get in the driver's side.

Opening the door, he climbed inside and proceeded to adjust the seat to accommodate his long legs before snapping his seat belt in place. The call had ended. He put his phone away and glanced over at her with a smile. She thought she would melt right then and there. "Warm?" he asked in a voice that was throatier than anything she'd ever heard.

If only you knew, she fought back saying. Instead her response was a simple "Yes. Thanks for asking."

"No problem." He then glanced into the rearview mirror before easing the truck onto the road.

The ensuing silence gave Riley the impression the woman was shy. And with her wrapped in a bulky coat and standing no more than five foot three, he figured she was probably short and stocky. He preferred tall, slender and curvy, but she had a pretty face that was eye-catching. She was definitely a looker. That had been the first thing he'd noticed. He was a sucker for a pretty face each and every time.

Deciding he didn't like the silence, he reached out and switched on the CD player. Immediately the soulful sound of Jill Scott filled the air. After a few moments, he concluded the music was not enough. To get a dialogue started, he asked conversationally, "I understand you're from Florida. What brought you to Denver?"

She tilted her head to look at him, and the first thing he noticed was her eyes. They were a chocolate brown and oval in shape. Then he was drawn to her hair, a beautiful shade of brown. The thick strands touched her shoulders and curled at the end. The coloring, whether natural or from a bottle, was perfect for her smooth, cocoa-colored complexion. And then there was that cute dimple in her chin, which was there even when she bore a serious expression.

"I've never been the adventurous type, but when my godmother passed away and left me enough funds that I could make a career change without going broke, I took advantage of it."

He nodded. "So what were you doing before you became an event planner?"

"I was a veterinarian."

"Wow. That was some career change."

She smiled. "Yes, it was."

He looked ahead, thinking that if she thought she would not have to explain why someone would stop being a veterinarian to become an event planner, she could think again. "How does a person go from being a vet to becoming a party planner?"

She pushed a lock of hair from her face and said, "Becoming a vet was my parents' idea, and I went along with it."

"Why?" He couldn't imagine going to college for anything other than what he wanted to do in life. He did, however, know how a person could get their dream career waylaid, as in the case of his cousin, Ramsey.

Ramsey had always wanted to be a sheep rancher, and he'd gone to school to study agricultural economics. The only reason Ramsey had taken a CEO position at Blue Ridge Management after school, instead of going into farming, was to work alongside Dillon to keep the company afloat when their parents had died in a plane crash. But once Ramsey and Dillon had made it into a million-dollar company, Ramsey had turned full management of Blue Ridge over to Dillon to become the sheep rancher he'd always wanted to be.

Riley's truck came to a stop at the traffic light, which gave him the opportunity to glance back over at Alpha just in time to see her gnawing her lips again and fidgeting with a sterling silver Tiffany bracelet on her wrist. *Umm, it seems "why" was another uncomfortable question,* he thought.

"I became a vet mainly to satisfy my parents. They own a veterinary clinic and figured I would join them and make it a family affair. I did so for a year, but discovered my heart just wasn't in it. They knew it, but still, they weren't happy when I decided to switch careers. However, they accepted that being an event planner was my calling when I put together their thirtieth wedding anniversary celebration."

"Did a good job of it, huh?" he asked.

She looked over at him and the smile that touched her lips extended from one corner of her mouth to the other and was simply breathtaking. "Yes, I did a bang-up job."

He laughed. "Good for you." He paused a second and asked, "Are you the only child?"

It seemed to take her longer than necessary to answer. "No. I have a sister."

He didn't say anything for a long moment and decided to change the subject. "So what do you have in mind for our employees' holiday bash next month?"

He listened as she went into the details. Some he was able to follow and some he could not. He was a visual person and couldn't use her words to produce mental images. He needed to see actual photographs to get the full effect.

She must have detected such from the expression on his face. "I had prepared a PowerPoint for today. But since we're meeting at the restaurant instead of your office, I—"

"Can still show the presentation. I called ahead and asked for a private meeting room."

"That's great. I have everything I need in here," she said, tapping lightly on the messenger case in her lap.

That caused him to glance down. She was wearing over-the-knee boots, a cute, dark brown leather pair. He glanced back up to her face and saw she was looking out the window, studying the scenery they were passing.

"I never come this way when going to McKay's."

He returned his gaze to the road. "It's a shortcut."

"Oh."

She got quiet again, and this time he decided to let the silence rule. He figured whenever she had anything to say, she would say it. In the meantime, he was perfectly satisfied to sit back and listen to Jill sing her heart out.

Alpha couldn't stop the fluttering in her stomach as she continued to look out the truck's window, trying hard to ignore the man behind the steering wheel. She would have to deal with Riley Westmoreland soon enough when they got to McKay's. She should have known he was drop-dead gorgeous, given Dillon wasn't bad on the eyes. And he seemed to be full of questions. At least he'd already asked two that she wished she could have avoided answering. The reason she had left Daytona was still too painful to think about and after the heated conversation she'd had with her parents last night, she preferred not to think of them right now, either.

Forcing thoughts of Daytona from her mind she saw that they were pulling into the parking lot of McKay's. It seemed the weather was not a deterrent for people wanting to dine at the popular restaurant. The parking lot was full, and Riley had to drive around back to find a spot.

She flexed her hands, liking how the gloves were keeping them warm, and tightened the coat around her as she prepared to get out of the vehicle and confront the cold again. She glanced over at Riley. He wasn't wearing gloves and it seemed the jacket was all he had. She couldn't help asking, "Aren't you cold?"

He smiled over at her. She wished he wouldn't do that because every time he did, he reminded her how long it had been since a man had smiled at her without her questioning his motives.

"Not really. Unlike most, I enjoy cold weather. For me, the colder the better."

She sat there and simply stared at him. He had to be kidding. "Why?"

He shrugged his massive shoulders. "Not sure. I guess I'm too hot-blooded to be bothered."

"Evidently," she said under her breath. If he heard her, he didn't let on. Instead, he opened the door to get out and she released her seat belt and opened her door to do the same. That's when she went sliding and would have fallen flat on her face if Riley hadn't acted quickly to catch her.

"I should have told you to be careful. The ice on the parking lot makes things slippery."

Yes, he should have told her. But if he had, there would have been no reason for his arms to be wrapped around her or for her to be holding on to him for support, feeling the heat of a hot-blooded man so close to her. And that same male scent that had nearly driven her crazy on the ride over wouldn't be doing a number on her.

"I think I can make it now," she said, releasing her tight grip on him.

He kept a firm hand on her arm. "I'll make sure of it." He then swept her off her feet and right into his arms.

Two

Riley entered the restaurant carrying Alpha in his arms. The place was packed with a lunchtime crowd, and Alpha was certain she would die of embarrassment when a number of people watched them.

One man, who was on his way out the door, patted Riley on the back, chuckled and said, "You're still sweeping them off their feet, I see, son."

Riley grinned and replied, "Seems that way, Mr. Daniels." Riley then glanced down at her. "You should be okay from here," he said, putting her on her feet.

"Thanks." She refused to look up at him, but out of the corner of her eye she saw him take a step back. He was probably wishing he was someplace else since she hadn't cost him anything but trouble today.

"Welcome, Riley. The room you requested is ready," the hostess said, smiling, in a way that was a little too friendly, Alpha thought.

"Thanks, I appreciate it, and make sure we aren't disturbed, Paula."

Alpha shouldn't be surprised that the woman knew his name and that he knew hers.

"No problem," Paula said, gesturing for them to follow her. "We gave you the best room in the house." She looked over her shoulder, gave a dismissive glance to Alpha, then looked at Riley directly and said, "Because you deserve the best."

Alpha tried not to frown, wondering if that had been a deliberate dig. Didn't the woman know they were holding a business meeting? So why had she extended her claws?

Alpha felt a thrumming heat in the center of her back when Riley placed his hand there. Even through her coat and all the clothes she had put on to stay warm, she felt his touch and wondered if there would be a permanent handprint on her back.

She blinked when the door closed behind them, and it was then that she glanced around. The room was nice and spacious with a table for two in one corner. There was also a pull-down screen, a projector, speakers and everything else she would need to provide visuals of her plans for the party. And then there was the wall-to-wall window that provided a beautiful view of the mountains. How was anyone expected to work in here with such a gorgeous view?

"Do you want to do it first or eat?"

She swallowed deeply and drew in a deep breath, certain he hadn't meant "it" the way it had sounded. "Whichever you prefer—it's your call."

"In that case, I'll let Paula know we'll eat first. I'm starving."

She nodded, getting distracted watching him slide his jacket off his shoulders. Those massive shoulders were even more broad and powerful than she'd thought. At that moment, she saw firsthand how well his jeans fit his body, especially his tight, masculine thighs, and how they tapered down to his booted feet. He was definitely a hunk if ever there was one, a fine specimen of a man, hands down. He was a sample of pure masculinity, as raw as it could get.

Following his lead, she unbelted her heavy coat and shrugged it off. Then she peeled off her thick, wool sweater, unwrapped the scarf from around her neck and removed another bulky sweater. She had worn as much clothing as she could in order to stay warm.

Walking over to the coatrack to hang up everything she had taken off, she worked the kinks out of her neck and shoulders. Putting on so many garments had weighed her down and stiffened her muscles. She was flipping her hair back off her shoulders when she turned around to find Riley staring at her with an odd expression on his face.

She swallowed, feeling a bit uncomfortable at the way his penetrating dark eyes nearly swallowed her whole. She nervously licked her lips. "Is something wrong?"

Suddenly, a guarded look appeared in his gaze before he glanced out the window. When he switched his gaze back to her the look was gone. "No, nothing's wrong," he said in a brisk tone. "Excuse me for a minute while I let Paula know we'll eat first."

Alpha watched him leave while wondering what that had been all about.

Unnerved to the core, Riley closed the door behind him and leaned against it, releasing a deep breath. Every muscle in his body was thrumming with a need like he hadn't felt in a long time. He was glad the room he'd been given extended off a corridor for privacy...because at that moment he needed it.

Where in the hell had that curvy figure come from? He'd heard of a woman having an hourglass shape, but in all actuality, he'd never truly seen one. Until today.

He couldn't believe what Alpha Blake had been hiding underneath all those clothes. He'd almost dropped his chin to the floor when she started taking off that coat and those sweaters and then stood there in a pink, formfitting sweater dress belted at the waist, with over-the-knee boots. She looked so damn feminine that he'd been jolted with a degree of lust he'd never felt before.

Not only was she a looker, the woman had a body with luscious curves that could make a grown man weep. Lust, as sharp and keen as it could get, was taking over his senses, and the thoughts running through his mind were totally inappropriate, undeniably unacceptable and definitely X-rated.

Her waist was so small that if he blinked he might miss it. And her chest was a perfect size with nice perky breasts. The way the top portion of her dress pressed against those breasts had almost made his eyes pop out of their sockets. And then there was the way her hips flared from her small waist. They were smooth and shapely.

When she had walked over to the coatrack, he had taken it all in. He heard the heel of her boots clicking on the wooden floor and watched with deep male interest how her hips swayed with each step. He was convinced he'd never witnessed anything so sensual. And the shape of her backside filled his mind with all sorts of ideas.

Then she'd turned around and caught him staring. The look in her eyes had been unsettled, and he was sure the look in his had been cautious. That's usually the way it was with him when he'd been caught off guard and had to rebound. He was a man who, under no circumstances, mixed business with pleasure. But he'd wanted that rule to go rolling out the window the moment she'd taken off the coat and those sweaters. Okay, he would admit that it was a physical thing for him, but he couldn't help it. Westmoreland males enjoyed the physical.

"Need help with anything, Riley?"

Paula's question immediately snatched his thoughts back to the present. His gaze roamed up and down the short black hostess outfit she was wearing. Paula Wilmot had a nice body, but even hers couldn't hold a light to Alpha Blake's.

He and Paula had dated a couple of years ago. When it was time for him to move on, she somehow thought some injustice was being done. He had explained up front—as he did with all women he became involved with—that he didn't do long-term flings. Sex with no commitment. One month, six weeks at the most, was all the time he would put into an affair. Not enough time to get sentimental and clingy. That's the way he operated. He called it Riley's rule. Women knew up front what to expect—or not to expect—from him, and he liked it that way.

And the one thing he wouldn't tolerate was someone who agreed to his terms and then decided somewhere along the way to make getting a ring on her finger her number-one goal. All it had taken was a month with Paula to see what her intentions were. For some reason, she'd assumed she would be the woman capable of changing him. It wasn't happening. He'd wasted no time ending things and placing her on his Never Date Again list.

"Yes, please tell our server that my lunch guest and I have decided to eat before getting down to business."

Paula tipped her head to the side as a frown creased her brow. "And I can just imagine what kind of business you intend to get down to, Riley," she said curtly.

His gaze held hers intently. "Can you?"

"Yes. Do I need to remind you that I've been there with you and know just how you operate? So tell me. What does Ms. Frumpy have going for her? Good grief, Riley, I'm sure you can do better."

Frumpy! A vision of the ultrafine body of the woman he'd left in the room floated through his mind. He doubted he could do better. "First of all, this is a business meeting, Paula. Blue Ridge has hired Alpha to handle our holiday party. Secondly, none of my affairs, business or otherwise, are any of your concern." The only reason he'd told her the former was because he knew better than anyone about that vindictive tongue of hers. He refused to have her tarnish Alpha's reputation in any way.

Paula placed her hands on her hips. "One day a woman is going to come along and break your heart. I hope I'm around to see it."

Riley rubbed his hand down his face. Where was all this drama coming from? And why today? Hadn't he woken up in a good mood? "Fine, you've put a curse on me. I guess that means I won't sleep most nights worrying about it," he said, reaching out to open the door.

She quickly reached out and grabbed his hand. "Sorry, Riley, I shouldn't have said that, but you never returned my calls," she said in a frustrated tone.

He stared at her. "No, I haven't, and it's been almost two years, right?"

"Yes."

He nodded slowly, lifting a brow before turning to open the door, hoping she got it that time.

Alpha looked up from her laptop when she heard Riley returning. He glanced around and saw that she had set up the room for the presentation. "I thought we were going to eat first," he said.

"We are. I thought it would save time if I had everything ready so I can move right into my presentation."

He nodded as he sat down at the table. She was about to ask if he could see the huge screen from where he sat when the door opened and a waiter entered, carrying a pitcher of water and menus. Deciding she had wasted Riley's time enough for one day, she moved toward the table when the waiter began filling their glasses with water.

She took the seat across from him and was glad when the waiter handed her a menu. She needed something else, anything else, other than Riley to occupy her attention. She might be wrong, but he seemed upset about something. Was he upset with her?

She placed her menu down. "I'm sorry, Riley."

He glanced up from his own menu and arched a brow. "For what?"

"For getting off to such a bad start with you—having a flat tire, taking you out of your way to come get me, and then having our meeting place changed to accommodate me."

He gave his head a little shake. "No apology necessary. You haven't gotten off to a bad start with me, Alpha. I'm fully aware there are days that don't go quite as well as you'd like. You didn't ask for that flat tire, did you?"

"Goodness, no."

"Then don't worry about it. I'm just glad I was able to help. And as far as having to change our meeting place, McKay's is a favorite of mine, and I'll think of any excuse to get some of their chicken noodle soup. Have you had any?"

She shook her head. "No, I've only eaten their burgers and fries."

He smiled. "Then you don't know what you're missing. You need to try it, if for nothing more than a cup as an appetizer."

He had her curious. "Okay, thanks. I think I will."

She picked up her glass of water to take a sip and then she said, "So you come here often?"

"Yes. Tony McKay and I were good friends all through high school. We went to different colleges and he ended up taking a job in Phoenix. When his father died, he returned to Denver to help his mother close down the restaurant, but decided to stay and run it instead. He wasn't crazy about the job he'd landed after college and his management degree gave him plenty of ideas on how to take this place to a whole new level."

He paused to take another sip of his water. "Old man McKay would not have approved of the changes Tony made, especially with the expansion and keeping the place open until midnight. He didn't believe in change and fought it tooth and nail. Tony and I tried to convince him for years that the only constant was change, and so he might as well get used to it. We told him to embrace it like everyone else so he could stay competitive."

He chuckled. "Tony not only embraces change, but he's implemented a few precedents. Such as convincing our school board to add a culinary class to their high school curriculum and then giving students jobs to gain firsthand experiences while getting class credits."

"Smart move."

Riley smiled. "We thought so."

She glanced back at her menu. "So what else would you suggest other than my usual burger and fries?"

"Umm, you can't go wrong with their chicken. It's covered with the best gravy you can eat and comes with mouthwatering scalloped potatoes and hot buttered yeast rolls."

She couldn't help frowning. "That sounds like a lot of food."

"It is, but if the forecasters are right, you might be snowed in for the next day or two and leftovers would come in handy."

Was that excitement she heard in his voice? "You really do like it, don't you?"

"Like what?"

He glanced over at her, and the moment he did so she felt a zing in the pit of her stomach. Why was her body reacting so much to him? She was twenty-seven and knew all about chemistry between a man and a woman, but she'd never in her life experienced anything so potent. "The cold weather. I thought you were teasing about liking it, but apparently you weren't. Here I was, all bundled up like I was living at the North Pole, and you were wearing a lightweight jacket as if you could barely feel the cold."

He shrugged, and she couldn't help but admire the undulating movement of his shoulders beneath his shirt. "I guess I'm immune. I've been here all my life and was told I was born during one of Denver's worst snowstorms. I've always enjoyed playing in the snow."

He chuckled and the sound floated around the room with such a rich octave it made Alpha draw in a charged breath. "February is my favorite month because that's usually when Denver is the coldest."

Riley leaned back in his chair and her gaze was drawn to his hands. For a quick second, she recalled how those hands had felt when he'd picked her up and carried her into the restaurant. She had felt the warmth of them through the thickness of her clothes.

"Today is nothing compared to how things will get later on," he said, breaking into her thoughts. "Surely you understood what you were doing when you traded sunny Florida for Denver?"

Alpha drew in a deep breath. No, she hadn't fully understood. The only thing she'd known was that she needed to put as much distance between her, Eddie and her parents as she could. "I didn't expect it to be this cold so soon. I figured I would prepare myself for January and February, but it's still November."

"Yes, and Thanksgiving is right around the corner. Are you going back south for turkey and dressing?"

Not on her life. "No. I plan on spending Thanksgiving here since I have a couple of projects during that time." And they were projects she could have gotten out of doing had she wanted to, but she hadn't.

The waiter returned to take their orders, and she was glad for the interruption. She was getting too comfortable with Riley and had to admit that he made such a thing easy. He came across as a nice guy. Down-to-earth. A real gentleman, respectful. It was nice to know that for some men, sex wasn't the only thing on their minds.

Three

Riley shifted in his seat, thinking that if Alpha knew all the things that were going through his mind, she would think he was as low as low could go. He had met her less than two hours ago and all he could think about was jumping her bones. No, jumping her bones was too quick and raunchy. He would love easing between those legs and then…

When he heard the sound of her lightly clearing her throat, he realized the waiter standing beside him had poured cups of coffee and was waiting to take his order. He glanced up at the waiter. George. The seventy-something man had worked at McKay's for ages and had waited on him plenty of times before with many of his other dates. Was that a smirk on George's face because the old man had finally caught him being taken with a woman?

"And what can I get for you, Mr. Westmoreland?"

"The usual, George."

"All right," George said, taking the menu from Riley.

Riley glanced over at Alpha and saw she was absorbed in

the beauty of the mountains that could be seen through the windows. "It's beautiful, isn't it?" he asked, studying her more so than the mountains he'd seen all his life.

"Yes."

Sitting this close to her, he could see just how beautiful, how stunning, she was. That wasn't a good thing. How was he supposed to concentrate on whatever presentation she was giving when he wanted to concentrate on her?

She broke eye contact while reaching for her coffee to take a sip and he did likewise. "So, other than the cold weather, how do you enjoy living in Denver so far?" he asked her.

"I like it. I'm grateful that the people here have been so kind. I didn't expect my business to take off like it has."

"I understand your work speaks for itself. My sister-in-law was definitely impressed."

She smiled. "Pam is super nice."

Their conversation was interrupted when George returned with their appetizers, still wearing that smirk on his face.

Alpha drew in a deep breath. She had done presentations quite a few times and knew there wasn't a shy bone in her body, but standing in front of Riley had butterflies floating around in her stomach.

She looked over at him to find him looking back at her. She forced a smile. "I promise to have you out in fifteen minutes."

"Take your time."

He would say that, she thought. Their waiter had cleared the table and filled their cups.

"The first thing we need to decide on is a theme for that night. These are the ones I came up with while trying to stay away from holiday themes. Because of diversity in the workplace, the last thing you want to do is offend anyone."

"So what do you suggest?" he asked her.

"A winter theme always works. These are a few that I've come up with," she said, clicking the remote in her hand to bring the screen alive. "As you can see, I have Winter Wonderland, Winter Delight, One Winter's Night and Winter Around the World."

She watched him study each suggestion. He shifted his eyes back to her, and she felt her stomach stir from the intensity of his gaze. "What's your favorite?"

"It's really your decision."

He nodded. "I know, but which one do you like the best?"

She glanced up at the screen. "Based on the fact that this year there will be a nighttime party in the ballroom of the Pavilion Hotel, instead of the daytime party you usually hold at the office, I like One Winter's Night. There's a sort of magical ring. I like it."

A smile curved his lips. "So do I. Let's go with it."

Alpha nodded, excited that he'd liked the same theme that she did. "All right. And as far as the ballroom at the Pavilion Hotel, I took a tour a few days ago. It will hold up to two thousand people," she said, showing an aerial view of the huge hotel, which was located midway between downtown and the airport.

"And it's a definite we have it for that night?"

"Yes," she said, smiling. "They were happy to accommodate us. The Westmoreland name carries a lot of weight."

Deciding to move on to the next point, she said, "I thought it would be nice to set the mood by having it be a dressy affair."

He lifted a brow. "How dressy?"

"Black tie." At the grimace on his face, she smiled and quickly said, "Not as bad as all that, Riley. I think your employees will appreciate it. It will make them feel special. Other than your family's annual charity ball, your employees probably never have anyplace to go where they can dress up and feel as if they're stepping out on the town."

He nodded slowly, and she knew he was thinking about the idea. She just wished she didn't feel that sexual chemistry between them even while discussing business. "Let's table that for at least a week," he suggested.

"All right," she said. "But I'll need a decision on the attire in order to determine what sort of decorations will be appropriate."

"I'll keep that in mind."

"Last but not least," she said, switching off the screen, "is the discussion of the budget. That handout I've given you breaks everything down. I inflated the expenses to allow for decorations. I'd rather operate on the high end versus a low one."

She paused a moment and then said, "Those are all of my ideas and suggestions. Is there anything you want to add or change?"

He shook his head. "No, I think you did a thorough job explaining things."

"Thank you," she said, crossing the room to place the remote near the television screen. That's when she dropped her ink pen and leaned down to pick it up.

For the second time that day Riley was slapped with a case of lust so thick he wondered how in the hell he was going to stand without giving away his body's reaction. She had leaned down to pick up her pen, and the way the material of her dress stretched snug across that gorgeous backside, he'd almost swallowed his tongue. Drawing in a deep breath, he used his hand to wipe away the perspiration forming on his forehead.

"Need help with anything?"

"No, thanks," she said, flicking a quick glance in his direction before returning to what she was doing. He continued to sit there, almost willing her to glance back at him, hold his gaze, feel his heat and not deny the potent chemistry flowing between them.

At that moment, he made a decision. "We'll need to meet

again next week, after I've reached a decision about the attire for the event."

He knew she was probably wondering why they needed to meet to discuss that when it was something they could cover over the phone. Instead of questioning him about anything, though, she simply said, "That's fine. Do you know when and where?"

"I'll call you."

She met his gaze and held it. He knew at that moment that if she hadn't felt the strong undercurrents flowing between them before, she did now. "All right."

Now that was where he disagreed with her. It wasn't all right, but he didn't know a way to change the path he seemed determined to take where she was concerned.

He watched as she re-dressed in her two heavy sweaters, scarf, huge overcoat and gloves. Was all that necessary? Evidently to her they were. If she wanted to stay warm the best thing she needed was body heat. Namely, his.

"I'm ready to go."

Glad he had gotten his body under control and that there was no sign of the lust that had overtaken it earlier, he stood. "Do I need to carry you out?" he teased.

Her eyes rounded and it amused him that she'd assumed he was serious. "No, and I'm sorry you felt the need to do so before. I'm usually not clumsy," she said apologetically.

"You weren't clumsy, Alpha. You aren't used to walking on icy, slippery surfaces and that's understandable. Will you do me a favor?"

She tilted up her head to look at him. "What?"

"Stop apologizing. You haven't done anything wrong."

"Thanks."

"Doing that must drive your boyfriend crazy," he said, deliberately fishing for information.

"I don't have a boyfriend."

"Oh." He placed his hand in the center of her back as he led her out of the room. So she didn't have a boyfriend. Hmm.

An hour or so later Alpha entered her home and immediately shrugged off her heavy coat and began peeling off her sweaters and gloves. It was then that she missed her scarf and figured she must have left it in Riley's truck.

During their ride back to her car she'd noticed he no longer seemed to be on guard with her, the way he had been at the restaurant earlier, and she took advantage by keeping the conversation going about the holiday party—One Winter's Night. The more she talked about it the more excited she got.

Once they reached her car, she saw her tire was fixed and her car keys were back where she'd left them. He wouldn't accept any money for having her tire taken care of, so she thanked him for lunch. After assuring him she would follow up with him in a week to discuss the attire for the party, she hurried off to her car. He had sat in his truck, watching her drive off.

Now she was home, inside the house she'd fallen in love with the first time she'd seen it. The last house in the cul-de-sac of a street where all the backyards faced the mountains, it was smaller than her place in Daytona but she'd always thought her condo on the beach had been too large for her anyway. Now she didn't have any wasted space, and the windows facing her backyard provided a gorgeous view of the mountains. However, there were days she missed the beach, until she remembered she had given up the beach for a reason.

Sitting down on the sofa, she began removing her boots. The first thing she'd done after buying the house was carpet the majority of the tile floors. The thought of getting out of bed and letting her feet touch cold tile had sent chills up her body. Other than that she hadn't changed a thing. Definitely not the extensive woodwork trim or the custom cabinets.

Moments later, taking her shoes in her hand, she walked

in bare feet to her bedroom while thinking about what had driven her here to Denver.

Eddie Swisher.

At one time, she had thought he was everything she had wanted in a man. In the end, she'd discovered he was nothing more than a puppet with his parents pulling the strings. She would never forget the day, a mere week before her wedding, when he had shown up at her place and dropped the bomb. A family meeting had been called and his family had voted. It had been decided that he couldn't marry her unless she vowed to disown Omega, her twin sister—the former porn star. After all, he had pointed out, her own parents had turned their backs on Omega. He couldn't understand why she wouldn't do the same. It had meant nothing to him that Omega was no longer in the business or that she had met a man who'd adored her regardless of her past. It was a past her parents and Eddie just couldn't get beyond.

At least he hadn't stooped to the same level as LeBron Roberts, the guy she'd dated before Eddie. When LeBron had learned of her twin's occupation, he'd assumed Alpha would miraculously transform into Omega in the bedroom. When she had dashed those hopes, he hadn't wasted any time in dropping her.

Her thoughts shifted back to Riley. He was a fine specimen of a man, definitely a threat to the peace she was trying to find. It didn't take much for her to remember those beautiful dark eyes, long lashes and the way his jaw curved whenever he smiled. She'd never been drawn to any male with such intensity. He took the word *sexy* to all new heights. She had been attracted to LeBron and Eddie but not to the same degree. It was something about his voice, the way he looked at her, his entire presence that made her think of long winter nights—with him.

She tossed the hair from her face, thinking she had truly gotten her drool-on today, whether he knew it or not. And it was best that he didn't know since it couldn't lead anywhere. She had definitely learned her lesson. When her relationship with Eddie ended she had vowed not to get seriously involved with another man. It wasn't worth the pain and hassle.

She dropped her boots in the closet and, leaving her bedroom, moved on to her family room. It was small and cozy. At the moment, she wanted cozy. She would curl up on her sofa and find something interesting on television. Or better yet, she could just relive her time with Riley. For just a little while, she would wallow in fantasies and then, later, she would get up and try getting some work done.

Riley sat on the sofa in his living room in front of his fireplace, drinking a cold beer while replaying in his mind his encounter with Alpha. Now that he had satisfied his curiosity about her, knew she was competent and could handle what Dillon had hired her to do, he could easily delegate any one of his supervisors to work with her. But he didn't want to do that, and for the life of him he couldn't understand why, especially when it was obvious the woman posed a lot of problems for him.

He knew that she had the ability to drive any man to distraction, which was the last thing he needed. No other woman had been capable of doing such a thing to him, but after meeting her today, he believed that she could, physically and mentally. The thought that he was even considering mixing business with pleasure was the first sign that he had messed up somewhere. He'd allowed her to get under his skin. But with single-minded determination, he intended to get her out.

He had learned his lesson by watching how obsessed his youngest brother, Bane, had been with Crystal Newsome and the heartbreak Bane had suffered when the teenage lovers had been forced apart.

Riley released a deep sigh. Bane had been the last child born to his parents, and everyone had assumed Bane would be a girl, the daughter their parents didn't have. Things didn't turn out that way. They'd gotten Bane. Personally, Riley had been happy about it. Who wanted a sister anyway? He had his girl cousins, Megan and Gemma, and as far as he was concerned, they were enough. So he'd become Bane's protector while growing up, or at least he'd tried. But he hadn't been able to foresee the pain Bane would suffer when, at eighteen, he fell in love with sixteen-year-old Crystal. Her parents had been against the match from the start and had separated the teens by sending Crystal away to parts unknown.

Riley would never forget that day for as long as he lived. A heartbroken Bane had ridden his horse out alone. When he hadn't returned at a reasonable hour, Dillon had gotten worried and sent Riley looking for him.

He had found Bane in an old abandoned shack that had been on the Westmoreland property for years. The moment Riley had entered the place he'd known it had been Crystal and Bane's love nest. But what had really gripped Riley's insides was the sound of Bane howling like a tormented and wounded animal.

Riley had actually felt his brother's pain and heartbreak that day. The sound had pierced something deep within him, and he'd wondered what there was about love that could torture and torment even a badass dude like Bane. On that day he'd vowed never to find out.

Without letting Bane know he was there, Riley had backed out of the shack and left, allowing his brother to grieve privately for the love he'd lost. That had been several years ago, but Riley's vow to never fall for a woman hadn't changed. That's when he had implemented Riley's Rule.

Reaching out, he picked up the wool scarf Alpha had left in his truck and brought it to his nose. It smelled like her. Sweet. Womanly. Enticing...so damn enticing. And the scent reminded him of all the heated desire that had warped his senses during the time he'd been with her. It was heated desire that was still slowly driving him insane.

He placed the scarf aside and picked up his cell phone to redial the number that had come through that morning. He felt his stomach tighten when he heard her soft voice.

"Hello?"

"Alpha? This is Riley. You left your scarf in my truck, and I want to get it back to you. Will you be home tomorrow?"

There was a slight hesitation and then she said, "Yes, but you don't have to come out of your way to return it, Riley. I have several of them."

"No problem. I want to make sure you get this one back. You live in the Arlington Heights area, right?"

"Yes."

"I'll be out that way tomorrow around two. Is it okay for me to drop by?"

Another slight hesitation. "Yes, I'll be home."

"Fine, I'll see you then."

Riley clicked off the phone. He was doing the decent thing by returning the scarf and nothing more. The thought that he was itching to see her again had nothing to do with it.

He brought the scarf to his nose once more. Yes, he definitely wanted to see her again.

Four

"I should have been more forceful about him not returning that darn scarf," Alpha muttered as she glanced at herself again in the full-length mirror in her bedroom. "I guess, considering the layers of clothes I was wearing to keep warm yesterday, he figured I must need every piece."

Drawing in a deep breath, she licked her lips, wondering if she should put on lipstick. If she did, he might assume she'd gotten pretty just for him. She frowned, knowing that, in essence, she had. Wednesday was the day she usually did housework and seldom put anything on other than her sweats. But not today.

She had awakened and quickly straightened up, eaten lunch, baked her favorite cinnamon rolls, showered and dressed in a canary-yellow buttoned shirt that tied at the waist and a denim skirt that hit above the knee. A pair of striped, black-and-white ballet flats that she had purchased before leaving Daytona were on her feet.

"I look cute, if I have to say so myself," she said softly and then threw her head back and laughed. When was the last time she had gone to a lot of trouble to look good for a man? Why was she doing so now?

Okay, she thought, deciding to put on lipstick after all, she would answer the first question. The last time had been for her parents' anniversary party a year or so ago and the man had been Eddie. In all honesty, she had stopped thinking of her and Eddie as a couple long before he'd given her that ultimatum about Omega. They had begun drifting apart. Once she had gotten serious about becoming an event planner they had found excuse after excuse to not spend time together. It hadn't bothered her, and she had a feeling it hadn't bothered him, either. Yet neither of them had made a move to call off their wedding for those reasons.

Her thoughts drifted back to the second half of the question she'd asked herself. Why was she going out of her way to look good for Riley? It could be that a part of her wanted to feel like a woman—a woman any man could be interested in, a woman a man could and would notice.

He *had* noticed the other day, which surprised her when she'd caught him staring. She hadn't expected him to display as strong a reaction to her as she had to him. And she was certain she hadn't imagined it. It had been there in his eyes when she'd turned around. Although it had been quickly replaced with a guarded look, it had been there.

"Okay, for the first time in a long time I feel like a desirable woman, and I like it," she said, after applying her lipstick and pursing her lips to see the effect.

Even before they'd broken up, Eddie had stopped going out of his way to make her feel like she could rock his world. But with Riley the sparks had been there, and they were sparks that sizzled. They had both tried to downplay it, but hadn't been successful. And that was one of the things that concerned her. Would the sparks be there when she saw him again today?

She was about to take the comb and work with her hair some more when she heard the doorbell. Riley was early. A good five minutes early. Looking at herself in the mirror one last time, she tied her hair back from her face before quickly leaving her bedroom. She headed for the door, not sure if those five minutes were a good thing or a bad thing.

Riley glanced around. Nice house. The stucco structure with an A-line roof and carved columns on the porch suited her. The Arlington Heights area was one of the oldest in Denver, but he could tell her home had been added within the past ten years or so. She had a pretty nice neighborhood. Quiet. Serene. Mountains as a backdrop and snow-covered yard. It had snowed again overnight and was slow in melting.

On the drive over, he kept asking himself what he was doing. He could easily mail the scarf to her, return it when they met again next week or keep it for a souvenir. But here he was, standing on her doorstep like a lust-craved addict eager for one glimpse of her.

Okay, who was he kidding? He wanted more than a glimpse. He wanted *her*. In his bed. There was no reason for him to deny it because it was true. He had tried talking himself out of wanting her all through the night but had failed miserably. In the end, he'd figured that as long as he applied Riley's Rule he would be safe. And as for mixing business with pleasure, technically, she was on contract and not a real employee of Blue Ridge. Now, if he could get her to go along with his proposition, then an affair would be a surefire way of taking care of this desire before she had a chance to get deeper into his system.

He heard her at the door and knew she had looked out the peephole at him. He had felt her checking him out, which was fine since he planned on checking her out, as well. Chances were she wasn't covered in all those coats and sweaters today. Hell, he hoped not.

The door opened, and she stood there. He had to clamp his jaws together to stop them from dropping. If he'd thought she looked good yesterday then he was totally unprepared for how stunning she looked today. His gaze roamed over her, and he quickly decided that he loved her outfit. It emphasized her figure.

"Riley."

"Alpha."

She licked her lips, and his stomach tightened. Not for the first time, he thought she had a nice-looking tongue. He couldn't wait to taste it.

"You brought the scarf?" she asked, intruding into his thoughts.

"Yes." Did she expect him to hand it over to her right here and now and then leave? Did she not expect him to hang around for a few minutes? He hadn't thought of that possibility.

He pulled the scarf out of his jacket pocket. "Here's the scarf."

She took it. "Thanks." And then she asked the question he'd been waiting for, the one he had begun to fear she wouldn't ask. "Would you like to come in? I just made a fresh pot of coffee and was about to have a cup with some cinnamon rolls I made earlier."

He forced his feet to stay put and not rush past her. "Sounds good. Yes, I'd like a cup of coffee and rolls."

She moved aside and he walked in, inhaling her scent as he brushed by her. It was the same scent on the scarf. He glanced around her home, admiring the furnishings, crown moldings, spindle staircase and beautiful light fixtures in the ceiling. She had a great room with a huge fireplace, and he loved that a blaze was going inside of it, throwing warmth into the room.

"Would you like to give me your jacket?"

He glanced over at her. "Sure," he said, shrugging off his

jacket and handing it to her. She walked over to the coatrack, and he watched her every move. He had to clamp down on his lips to not let out a whistle. The woman had the most gorgeous legs he'd ever seen. When she turned around, there was no need to act innocent. He'd been caught red-handed checking out her legs.

He cleared his throat. "Nice shoes."

"Thanks."

"Different." Although he hadn't been concentrating on her shoes, they *were* different. Striped.

She glanced down at them. "Different but comfortable. Do you want your coffee out here or in the kitchen?"

He shoved his hands inside the pockets of his jeans. "Where do you usually take yours?"

"In the kitchen."

"Then lead the way."

And she did. He deliberately stayed a few paces behind her to check out her legs, waist and backside. And no, he had no shame. She had more sensuality in her walk than some women had in their entire bodies, and the male in him felt the need to take the time to appreciate it.

She was wearing flats, but with her shapely calves he could just imagine those legs in a pair of stilettos. Her skirt was a decent length, but if it had been just a tad shorter he would probably have already had a heart attack. At that moment, he felt blood rushing straight to his groin.

He walked into her kitchen and stopped, equally impressed by the custom maple cabinets, granite countertops and stainless-steel appliances. The high-top café table was facing a huge window overlooking her backyard, which included a view of the mountains.

"How do you take your coffee?"

He glanced over at her. "Black and as strong as you can get it."

She smiled. "My dad drinks his the same way."

"Does he?" he asked, sliding onto a bar stool.

"Yes. My mom prefers hot chocolate and so did I."

She brought the coffee to him with a tray of sweet-smelling rolls. They looked fresh, hot and delicious. Just like her. He took a sip of coffee. It was good, just like he figured she would be. He bit into a roll and closed his eyes. It was delicious.

He opened his eyes and found her smiling at him. "Hit a sweet tooth, huh?" she asked.

If only she knew. "Homemade?"

"Yes, one of my mom's old recipes. She likes to bake."

"It's delicious," he said, taking another bite and then gobbling up the rest of it while thinking he would love gobbling her up in the same way.

"You can have another. I ate a couple earlier."

"Thanks." He didn't waste time taking her up on her offer, grabbing another one off the plate and biting into it.

"Thanks for bringing my scarf back, but like I told you, you didn't have to do it. It could have waited."

Riley glanced over at her, thinking that, no, it could not have waited. He was one of those men who, once he made up his mind about something, there was no turning back, no hesitation and no stopping him. He hadn't been in an affair for about four months now, mainly because he'd had a lot on his plate at the office while taking over for Dillon. Now that he had things at a level where he could work without too much stress, he had time for some of the finer, more enjoyable things in life. All work and no play wasn't good for anyone.

"The reason I brought the scarf back, Alpha, is because I wanted to see you again. And I would have found any excuse to do so."

He watched her expression. She probably hadn't counted on him being so in-your-face honest. But he always was at the beginning of his affairs…and at the end.

She licked her lips. He was beginning to recognize that as a sign that she was nervous. She held his gaze for a moment and asked after taking a sip of coffee, "Would you have... found any excuse?"

"Yes. We're adults, and I don't like playing games. I believe in being up-front with any woman I'm interested in."

"And you're interested in me?"

He heard the surprise in her voice. "Yes, but you should have known that after yesterday. There is chemistry between us. A lot of it. I could barely watch you while you gave that presentation without getting turned on."

Maybe he'd given her too much information, but he wanted her to know just what he was dealing with. What they were both dealing with, because although she hadn't admitted anything yet, he had a gut feeling she was as attracted to him as he was to her.

She looked down and nervously began toying with her paper napkin, but he preferred that she look at him. He needed to know what she was thinking. "Alpha?"

She glanced up, and the look he saw in her eyes made his stomach quiver all the way to his groin. That same potent chemistry, that electrical sizzle, they had shared yesterday was present today whether she wanted it to be or not. It was just as strong and powerful...but he could tell she was fighting it tooth and nail. Why?

"We just met yesterday," she said softly.

He nodded. She had to do better than that. As far as he was concerned meeting just yesterday didn't mean a thing. People were into one-night stands. He'd done a number of those himself. "And?"

"And I'm working for you."

Okay, now she was trying to play the "it's not ethical" card, but it wouldn't work. "No, you're not working for me, at least you're not my employee. You're on assignment for Blue Ridge Land Management for a project that ends next month. As far as I'm concerned that has nothing to do with what's going on between us."

"There's nothing going on between us," she said, taking another sip of coffee.

Now she wanted to be in denial and he wasn't going along with that, either. He leaned back in his chair and stared at her. For a long moment he didn't say anything and then he said, "I want to know why you're sitting there denying what is so blatantly obvious."

Her lips began quivering, in anger or desire he wasn't sure, but neither curtailed the electricity sizzling between them. "And just what do you think is so blatantly obvious?" she asked in a quiet tone.

He reached out and placed his hand over hers. The moment he did so, he felt what she wanted to deny. A heated spiral of desire flowed between them, and she gasped softly. He wanted her to feel it. He needed her to feel it. And he knew by the look in her eyes that she had.

"What is so blatantly obvious, Alpha, is that I want you and you want me."

Alpha couldn't stop the chaotic fluttering in her stomach. Nor could she slow down the beating of her heart. What was Riley doing to her? What was he making her feel? All these incredible sensations that she'd never felt before were swamping her all at once.

She tried to force herself to think logically. She needed to make him understand something about her. "I've never been a woman to engage in casual relationships, Riley."

"There's a first time for everything, isn't there?" he asked, still holding her gaze as if he was looking deep into her very soul.

Yes, there was a first time for everything, but she wasn't sure she was ready for what she knew would be nothing more than a fling. But another part of her was demanding to know *why* she wasn't ready. She had moved from Florida to Colorado to start a new life. It wasn't that she hadn't gotten over

Eddie, because she had. So what was the holdup? Riley was ultrahandsome, much too sexy, and he was attracted to her. Why was she afraid to go with the flow?

He leaned in close to her. "In that case, I propose we take some time to get to know each other, but..."

She'd known there was going to be a *but* in there somewhere.

"But that we enjoy each other while doing so."

Her pulse quickened. She didn't have to ask how they would enjoy each other. The man was pushing all her buttons, in ways she hadn't known existed. He was making her consider doing things she'd never thought of doing before.

"With all of my affairs there are rules so we have a good understanding from day one," he added.

She lifted an arched brow. "What rules?"

He smiled. "First, there needs to be a time limit on how long the affair will last. Definitely no longer than six weeks."

She nodded. "What else?"

"There has to be exclusivity. I'm not into sharing. Neither am I into clinginess. This affair doesn't give us the right to crowd each other. We need to respect each other's space."

Evidently he'd had issues in the past. Well, he wouldn't have to worry about those issues with her. "Okay."

"And if, for whatever reason, the rules are broken by either of us, the affair ends," he said.

His rules were reasonable, but still... "I need to think about it," she said. At least he was being honest by letting her know up front what he wanted out of a relationship. She could appreciate that.

"That's fine. Since we need to meet next week to discuss some things regarding the party, you can give me your answer then. What about Monday? Hopefully the weather will be better and we can meet at my office. Let's say around ten. Is that time okay for you?"

"Yes, ten o'clock will work."

"Good." He stood. "I'm sure you have a lot to do today, so I'll be going. Thanks for the coffee and rolls."

She stood as well, thinking how his height seemed to dominate the room. She never thought her kitchen was small until now. "You're welcome."

He took her hand and held it gently in his while they walked through her great room back toward the door. Hand-holding was something she'd always craved but something Eddie had never delivered. He wasn't a touchy-feely type.

When they reached the door she turned to Riley, to again thank him for returning her scarf, but the words died on her lips. He had the most irresistible smile, one that showed his dimples. To distract herself, she looked over his shoulder at the picture hanging on her wall, but Riley lifted his hand to cup her chin and return her gaze to him. Then he softly trailed his fingertips along the lines of her jaw.

In that heated moment, when their eyes connected, she felt a sensual connection to him all the way to her toes. She wanted to take a step back but couldn't. Like he'd said, she couldn't deny what was taking place between them.

"I want to leave you with something to think about."

She didn't have to ask what that something was because she knew. The rippling of coiled anticipation in her stomach spelled it out for her. He was about to stamp his presence all over her, and she would do more than think about it, she would fantasize about it for years to come.

Her heart skipped a few beats when he released her chin to ease his arms around her waist and settle his hands right above her backside. Then he took a step closer while their gazes remained connected. There was a heated resolve in the dark depths of the eyes staring into hers. And when she saw him lowering his head, her feet—of their own accord—arched on tiptoes so she could meet his lips. All those amazing and incredible feelings she'd encountered since meeting him totally obliterated her senses.

The man had all but admitted the only thing he wanted from her was sex, but she hadn't decided whether or not he would be getting what he wanted. All she cared about for the time being was locking her lips with his, taking in more of his scent and acquiring his taste. She was tired of dealing with all these crazy emotions and sensations. She wanted relief, and she knew one place where she could find it.

Right here, she thought, the moment Riley's mouth aimed straight for hers.

His tongue entered her on impact, and she responded on instinct. Reaching up, she wrapped her arms around his neck and pressed her body closer to his. No kiss had ever made her feel like this. Riley was a master at using his tongue, and he was doing so with a skill that nearly brought her to her knees. He explored first one side of her mouth then the other. And he was doing it with such intimacy that she felt it deep in her bones.

He was taking her mouth greedily, as if this was his one-and-only chance. He was giving a whole new definition to French-kissing, and she moaned with every lick, every suck and every blatant stroke.

Alpha was certain she would lose her mind if Riley didn't let go of her mouth, and he seemed in no hurry to release it. Instead, he continued to take it in an even deeper kiss, stroking his tongue in a way that sent high degrees of desire spreading all through her. The hard bluntness of his arousal pressed like steel into her belly, and she moved her body to cradle it in the juncture of her thighs.

She knew he was intentionally driving her mad, branding her and leaving his mark. The heat flaring in her midsection was sending her hormones—which were getting his name stamped all over them—raging out of control.

And then he slowly pulled his mouth away. Heavy-lidded dark eyes remained steady on her. She tried to stop the way her stomach was quivering and found she wasn't able to do so. Nothing was capable of bringing a halt to the sensations stampeding through her.

"Now, a promise to you, Alpha. If you agree to what I suggested," he said in a low, throaty voice, "I'll make sure that we enjoy each other in a way no two humans have ever done."

He then leaned down and lightly brushed the tip of his tongue across her lips before opening the door and walking out of it.

Five

Riley thought this had been the longest week of his life. Now the day had finally arrived when he would be seeing Alpha again. More than once he'd been tempted to come up with any excuse to pick up the phone and call her to see how she was coming along in her thought processes regarding the affair he'd proposed.

He would find out in a couple of hours at their scheduled meeting. He'd even arrived to work early, had advised the receptionist covering the lobby to send Alpha in as soon as she arrived. There was no need for her to wait. He was tired of waiting.

There was a knock on his door, and he knew from the three repetitive knuckle raps that it was his brother, Canyon. Dropping by Riley's office at the start of the workday was the norm for both Canyon and his other brother, Stern. Riley was eleven months older than Canyon and almost two years older than Stern. The three of them had been close while growing up, and although they didn't always agree on everything, they had deep respect for one another. Working for the family firm after college had always been their goal in life, and they enjoyed working alongside Dillon to preserve the legacy their father and uncle had begun. All his brothers worked in some capacity at Blue Ridge except for Micah, who was an epidemiologist with the federal government; Jason, who, along with cousins Zane and Derringer, was in the horse training and breeding business; and Riley's youngest brother, Bane, who was in the navy.

"Come in."

Canyon, who was one of the firm's attorneys, quickly walked in with his briefcase in hand. "I need to run something by you, Ry. It's that dispute we're trying to settle out of court with Shade Tree Developers. We're holding our initial meeting tomorrow."

Riley looked at his watch. "Okay, I have less than a half hour to spare, so make it quick."

Canyon lifted a brow. "And just what fire are you going to?"

Riley tossed aside some papers on his desk. "No fire, just an important meeting at ten."

"With who?"

If Riley didn't know of his brother's penchant for being inquisitive, he would have been annoyed with Canyon's questions. "I'm meeting with our event planner, Alpha Blake, about the holiday party next month."

"Oh," Canyon said with a smirk on his face. He took the chair in front of Riley's desk. Riley knew why the smirk was there. Dillon had tossed the responsibility to both of them and neither had wanted it. In the end, they'd drawn straws. Riley hadn't been happy that he'd been the one to lose, but now he was more than glad that he had.

"Okay, Canyon, what's going on with Shade Tree Developers?" he asked, deciding to steer his brother away from the subject of Alpha.

"I talked with one of their new attorneys today. She was brought on board a couple of weeks ago and you won't believe who she is."

"Who?"

"Keisha Ashford."

Riley scrunched up his face, remembering. "Is that the same Keisha you had that affair with a few years ago?"

Canyon shifted in his seat. "One and the same."

"Ouch." Riley remembered the affair hadn't ended well.

"Yes, that's what I said. However, she sounded pleasant enough."

Riley chuckled and leaned back in his chair with his arms raised and resting against the back of his neck. "They always do, even when they're about to cut off your balls. I told you to always be up-front with a woman. You set the parameters and the rules. Then there'll be less drama on the back end. That's why I have Riley's Rules. That's the only way I operate."

While Canyon rambled on with nonsense about not all women agreeing to rules, Riley's thoughts shifted back to Alpha. He had already spelled out his terms and she could take them or leave them.

He was hoping like hell that she took them.

Alpha stepped off the elevator onto the fortieth floor of the Blue Ridge Management building where the executive offices were located. She recalled the first time she'd come here, last month, to meet with Dillon and how impressed she'd been with the plush surroundings the moment she'd walked inside the building.

First, there had been the huge, beautifully decorated atrium with a waterfall amidst a replica of mountains, complete with blooming flowers and other foliage. Seeing all those flowers had reminded her of a spring day in Daytona when flowers sprouted everywhere. They were the first sign that the city

should prepare for spring break, when all the college students
would hit the beaches.

She liked the feel of the thick, luxurious carpet beneath
her shoes. The first thing that caught her eye today, just like
the last time, were the huge portraits of two couples that
hung on the main wall in the lobby. They were Riley's parents and his aunt and uncle, who'd all perished in an airplane
accident. Four beautiful people who had died young and left
behind offspring who loved them. And speaking of love, the
photographer who'd taken the photographs had captured the
essence of love in both portraits. The way the two women
were leaning in toward their husbands, the smiles they wore
and the way the couples held hands showed that they'd truly
loved each other. She would like to think that seeing these
photographs gave the Westmorelands the strength to go on
when others would have given up. She couldn't help but admire the way they had bonded together in a crisis, a response
which had been so unlike her own family's.

She glanced at her watch and saw she was ten minutes
early. The weather was a lot better than last week now that
the snowstorm had passed. However, she knew that it was
just the beginning and forecasters had already predicted a lot
of cold weather ahead.

Alpha tried ignoring the stirring in the pit of her stomach
when she approached a bank of offices. She drew in a deep
breath when she reached the one with Riley's name elegantly
carved in bold gold script. She had no reason to be nervous
since he had given her enough time to make a decision and
she had. It was one she would live with and not regret making.

She would have an affair with him because, whether she
understood why or not, she wanted him. It was as if he had
cast some spell on her and even when she'd tried talking herself out of wanting him, she couldn't. So against her better
judgment, she would follow the cravings of her body. For
once in her life, she would give in to her wants. Besides, after

Eddie had told her he wouldn't marry her, she had pretty much known she wouldn't set herself up for that kind of heartbreak again. A serious relationship with any man was totally out of the question. And she was curious about all that pleasure Riley had talked about.

Another thing she had taken into consideration was that she knew, at some point, she would date again. Although she was certain there were a lot of single men in Denver, she wasn't sure just how decent they were. She considered Riley both decent and honest. He'd demonstrated that by being up-front with her. He hadn't tried sugarcoating an affair or making it out to be more than what it would be. He wanted her. In his bed. Just like she wanted him in hers. No excuses. Just bald facts.

She let out another deep breath. Thinking that way was one thing but actually doing it was another. Growing up, Omega would tease her about talking a good talk, but when the time came to back it up, that was another story. Alpha hoped to do things differently this time around.

She opened the door to another elegant-looking lobby. A young woman sat at the receptionist desk and smiled when she walked in. "Ms. Blake?"

Alpha was surprised the woman knew who she was. "Yes?"

"Mr. Westmoreland has been waiting for you."

Alpha lifted a brow before glancing down at her watch. "But I'm not late."

The young woman chuckled. "Yes, I know, but he's checked three times to see if you've arrived, although I assured him that I would send you in the moment you got here. I guess this meeting is pretty important." The woman then picked up the phone and announced her arrival to Riley.

No sooner had the last word left the woman's lips than Riley's office door was snatched open and he stood there. This was the first time she had seen him in business attire. The transformation left her speechless. He was dressed in a gray suit and a white shirt. The printed tie brought both together and all three complemented the brown coloring of his skin. The cut of his suit did everything to emphasize his masculine build. He looked so handsome standing there, dominating the doorway in such a way that she had to force her breathing to slow. But she could do nothing about the way her blood was rushing through her veins.

The corners of his mouth curved in a heart-stopping smile. "Ms. Blake."

She released the breath she hadn't known she was holding. "Mr. Westmoreland. I have all the information we discussed last week," she said with professional decorum, for the benefit of their audience of one.

He nodded. "Good, I'm anxious for us to get started since we have a lot to cover." He averted his gaze from her to the woman sitting at the desk, who was watching them with interest. "Make sure we're not disturbed until our meeting is over."

"Yes, sir."

He then shifted his glance back to Alpha and stepped aside. "Ms. Blake, please come in."

The thoughts running through Riley's mind when Alpha passed him by were too dangerous to think about at the moment. Why did she always have to smell so darn good? Fresh, sweet and all woman.

She moved to stand in front of his desk and turned around. He remained standing with his back against the closed door with his hands shoved into his pockets. He studied her, thinking every single thing about her spelled *SENSUOUS* in capital letters.

"I've researched more information on the party and have a proposed budget for—"

"You look nice, Alpha," he interrupted her spiel to say. When she began nibbling on her bottom lip, he knew that he was making her nervous but he couldn't help it. He was obsessed, and at that moment he offered no excuses for being so. There was just something about seeing a woman in a business suit with pumps on her feet. Had she assumed her attire would make him want to get down to real business, without thoughts of making love to her? If so, the intent failed miserably.

"Thank you. Now can we get down to—"

"Business?" He gave a negative shake of his head said. "No, not yet."

He slid his hands from his pockets. She was right; they should get down to business. He could go even further and say there was really no reason they should be meeting today at all. The information she was here to give him regarding the party could have been done over the phone. He knew that and figured she knew that, as well.

"What have you decided?" he asked, tempted to walk over to her but knowing if he did he wouldn't be able to keep his hands to himself.

She averted her gaze momentarily and when she looked back, she said, "Maybe we ought to discuss this at another—"

"Alpha."

The menacing tone of his voice probably pretty much told her she could forget that suggestion. "All right, then," she said, placing her messenger bag on his desk. She then glanced over at him. "You were right about there being this strong attraction between us. I've thought about it and considered all aspects of what you've suggested, although, like I told you, I've never engaged in a casual affair—sex with no commitments—before."

"But you've reached a decision?" he asked, noting her expression wasn't giving anything away.

"Yes."

Both hope and despair flooded his stomach at the same time since he had no idea what her decision was. He said nothing, just waited for her to go on. When she didn't, he asked simply, "And?"

She nervously licked her lips again before lifting her chin. "I agree to it, but I have a few rules of my own."

That surprised him. No other woman ever had. He moved from the door to stand beside his desk. "Do you?"

"Yes. First of all, I don't want us to rush into anything."

"You mean not rush into sharing a bed?" he asked for clarity.

"Yes. Like I told you, I'm not used to engaging in casual affairs so it's not anything I can just jump into. I'm going to need time to get used to this."

He wondered how much time she would need. The affair was only supposed to last six weeks at the max. But then the last thing he wanted was a reluctant woman in his bed. Besides, there were ways of breaking down her defenses. "I can agree with that."

She nodded. "And another thing."

"Yes?"

She paused, as if she needed the courage to say her next words. "It's about that promise you made last week, right before leaving my house."

He knew what promise she was referring to and remembered it well. "What about it?"

"I'm holding you to it."

Riley said nothing. He only stared at her. But he wasn't *just* staring at her, Alpha thought. He was doing so in a way that was tantalizing her senses and sending electrified sensations all through her pores. Omega would never believe Alpha was letting any man affect her this way. Or that she was drawn to a man who was leading her down a road Omega knew well and had traveled down plenty of times. One that was naughty as sin.

"Now, can we get down to business and discuss the details of the party for next month, Riley?"

He shook his head. "No."

She lifted a brow. "No?"

He shook his head as he unbuttoned his coat to remove it and loosened his tie, tossing both on the chair across from his desk. "Not yet." Then, closing the distance between them, he pulled her into his arms.

She went to him willingly, opening her mouth the moment his lips touched hers. And when he slid his tongue inside, the memories of the last time they'd kissed magnified tenfold. She was convinced that no other man kissed the way he did. No other man could fill a woman with as much longing and desire as he could. Heat sizzled along her nerve endings, and her stomach tightened with each meticulous stroke of his tongue.

It was almost too late when she realized he had been walking her backward. Barely breaking the kiss, he eased her up by the hips to place her on top of his desk. He didn't let up, continuing to take her mouth with a hunger she felt in every part of her body. In response, she tightened her arms around his neck and moved in closer, needing the contact of his chest against hers, liking how her nipples were hardening in need.

"Mr. Westmoreland, I'm leaving for lunch now."

The sound of the receptionist's voice over the intercom seemed to boom across the room. Riley pulled his mouth away but kept it within inches of hers. "I hope you liked that," he whispered against her lips, tipping her chin up for better access.

A smile curved the corners of her mouth. "The kiss or the fact that your receptionist is taking lunch?"

He chuckled. "The kiss."

There was no reason to lie, so she said, "I did.'"

He traced her lips with his tongue before saying, "Good. Just thought I'd get a little head start on all that pleasure I plan on giving you."

She thought he'd gotten more than a head start. "Do you mind getting me down off your desk now?"

"Not at all."

And just as easily as he'd placed her up there, he had her

back on her feet. They were standing close. She could feel the heat of him all over her. "I've got a suggestion, Alpha," he said in a deep, husky tone.

She lifted a brow. "What?"

"I suggest we move our meeting someplace else, and I know just the place. Go home and change into something comfortable—like jeans and boots—and I'll pick you up in an hour."

"And just where are we supposed to be going?"

"Riley's Station."

"Where?"

"Just do it, okay?"

"And this is a business meeting, right?"

A smile touched the corners of his mouth. "Both business and pleasure."

When she opened her mouth to remind him of her rules, he quickly spoke up and said, "I know, you want to take things slow and not be rushed. I got it."

She was glad he got it. Now if she could only get her traitorous body on the same page.

Six

Alpha tried keeping the butterflies from her stomach as she quickly dressed, knowing Riley would be there to pick her up in less than thirty minutes. "This is crazy," she muttered, pulling a burgundy V-neck sweater over her head. "All he had to say was 'let's go' and I'm going."

She stood sideways to look in the mirror at her perky breasts pressed against her sweater. It had been Omega's idea for her to wear a push-up bra with all her sweaters, and she would admit it made her girls look bigger than they really were.

She was about to put on lipstick when her cell phone rang. She grinned as she answered it. "Speak of the devil."

"Hey, and you were talking about me to who?" her sister said with laughter in her voice.

"No one, just thinking about what you told me, about ways a woman can make herself look sexy."

"Umm, you're trying to look sexy? Sounds like you've made some decisions about a few things."

Alpha leaned against the bathroom counter. When Omega had called last week she had spent over an hour on the phone telling her twin the latest about her meeting with Riley, how fine he was and his suggestion that they indulge in an affair. Of course Omega had been all for it, saying Alpha needed to rev up her love life. "Yes, I agreed to do it, and he's agreed not to rush me into anything."

"But no climax control, right?"

Alpha lifted a brow. "Climax control?"

"Yes, you plan to let the orgasms rip."

Alpha threw her hand to her mouth to keep from screaming with laughter. Her sister could be so outlandish at times. Um, in fact most of the time. "Behave, girl. And how is that book coming along?" Omega had decided to write a book about her experience as a porn star.

"Great. It's wonderful therapy for me."

Alpha didn't say anything for a minute and then asked, "Do you miss the business, Omega?" She'd always wondered but never asked. Nothing her parents said or did had made Omega give up her line of work until Omega had been ready to do so herself.

"I know it's hard for most people to understand, Al, but for me it was nothing more than a job—a job I needed while going through that rebellious period in my life. I don't want to think about where I'd be or what I'd still be doing if Marlon hadn't come along. He reminded me of who I was before I made those decisions, and he was willing to love me, no matter what."

Alpha loved her brother-in-law because she knew he loved Omega, no matter what her past had been. He didn't give a damn what others thought. He treated her sister like his queen.

Omega had been out of the business less than a year when she met Marlon. Alpha knew Omega was happy and could hear it in her voice every time they talked. The only dark cloud in her sister's life was their parents and their holier-than-thou attitude.

"The only thing I regret," Omega was saying softly, "is hurting you and the folks. Maybe one day they will forgive me. You never turned your back on me, even when the folks tried getting you to do so…and even when I cost you the man you loved because you wouldn't choose him over me."

Alpha nearly dropped the phone. "Who told you that? How did you know?" she asked, going back into the bedroom to sit on the edge of the bed. "I told you—"

"I know what you told me, and you lied. You and Eddie didn't just decide to call off the wedding because the two of you felt like you were drifting apart. I ran into Eleanor Sloan, in New York of all places, when Marlon took me there on a shopping spree. She approached me, thinking I was you, and you know Eleanor," Omega said of their high school friend. "She told me how sad she was for you now that Eddie had made you call off your wedding because of me."

Alpha tilted her head back and looked up at the ceiling. "When was this?"

"Last Christmas."

Alpha brought her head back down to gaze out the window and frowned. "And you've known all this time and never mentioned it," she accused. "Why *didn't* you mention it?"

Omega paused a minute before responding. "I couldn't say anything because I was feeling your pain. After the way I had lived those three years, here I was, about to marry the best man any woman could have, and there you were, you who'd always been the good girl and did everything the folks told you to do…even going to college for a career you didn't want to please them. I was the one who ended up with the fairy-tale marriage and getting a real prince and you ended up with a toad. It didn't seem fair. Life sucks."

A smile touched Alpha's lips. Life did suck at times, but a part of Alpha wouldn't change a thing. Because thanks to

Marlon, things were the way Alpha had always dreamed they could be for her twin.

Determined to get her sister back in a good mood, mainly because she didn't want Omega feeling sorry for her, Alpha said, "Yeah, must have been rough being a porn star."

"Oh, Alpha, you didn't have to go there."

She knew she'd succeeded in changing the mood when she heard the giggle in her twin's voice. Alpha laughed. "Yes, I did. Besides, had I been married to Eddie I wouldn't be having this fling and doing the no-climax-control thing."

Omega chuckled. "Okay, sis, you got me there. Is this Riley Westmoreland as hot as you make him out to be?"

Alpha remembered how he'd looked when she'd been to his office earlier that day. Yummy. "Trust me, he is. And I'll find out just how hot he is soon enough."

Omega went silent for a moment and then asked, "Will you tell him about me?"

She could hear the seriousness in her sister's tone. She had tried doing that with LeBron and Eddie and both men had ended up showing their true colors.

"Why would I tell him anything? It's not that kind of relationship. It's about sex and nothing more. Besides, at the point when we begin sleeping together, I doubt we'll have time for much pillow talk. Remember, no climax control. And I want to find out if multiple orgasms are real or something you porn stars just try to make look real."

Omega chuckled. "Oh, you're bad, and trust me, they are real…with the right man in control."

"We'll see. As far as being bad, I'm finally going to live a little, have some fun and enjoy myself. And I have a feeling Riley is just the person to make sure that I do so."

Brrr. I can't believe the temperature has dropped five degrees already."

Riley smiled as he watched Alpha tighten her coat around

her when he escorted her to his truck and opened the door. "What are you complaining about, woman? It feels good out here."

She glared at him over her shoulder before easing into the truck's leather interior. "I can't help but wonder what kind of blood is running through your veins. Look at you."

He glanced down at himself. Okay, so he'd left his jacket in the truck. He looked fine. He felt fine. No sense reminding her he was hot-blooded. She would find the truth of that soon enough. He kept smiling as he closed the door and then rounded the front of the truck and opened the door to climb in on the driver's side. "I guess I've developed some sort of tolerance to Denver's cold weather."

After buckling up he smiled over at her and said, "My tolerance to Denver's cold weather drives everyone in my family crazy. They're convinced I'm going to die of pneumonia at an early age."

"I have to agree with them."

He tilted his head to look at her. "And you've been living in Denver for how long now?"

"It will be a year in April."

He grinned. "No wonder you're whining. You missed all the real good days."

"Lucky me. I'm not complaining," she said, chuckling. "If I had come any earlier I might have been tempted to head back south."

He glanced over at her. "You don't come across as a quitter, Alpha."

She chuckled. "I've thought of heading back south more than once, trust me."

As he was driving, he had to stop for a school bus. "I remember those days," he said thoughtfully.

"What days?" she asked.

He gestured with his head to somewhere outside the windshield. "When my brothers, cousin and I used to ride the bus to and from school. Either Aunt Susan or my mom would be there at the stop to get us. My parents had a van we all called Crazy Horse. It was blue and huge and could hold all of us."

"Sounds like a lot of good memories."

"They are."

"I admire you and your family, Riley," she said softly.

He looked over at Alpha. "Do you?"

"Yes. I heard about your parents and your uncle and aunt and how they died together in that plane crash. It must have been awful for all of you."

He stared straight ahead as his hand gripped the steering wheel and he watched the kids continue to unload from the bus. "It was, especially when there were so many of us still under sixteen. Seeing those kids reminds me of so many things. Kids think their parents are going to be around forever. I'll never forget the day I realized mine would not."

"How old were you?"

He glanced over at her. "Fifteen. Just a few months shy of my sixteenth birthday. Mom had promised me a party that year, and I was so looking forward to it. I had gotten my learner's permit, which meant I could start sharing Dillon's old truck with my brother, Jason. Life was good. Even Bane was good. He was my mom's baby. Spoiled rotten and a tattletale."

Riley was quiet for a second, remembering. "And then, suddenly all of it came to a crashing end, literally, when their plane went down. We lost them. Bane couldn't handle it and became a badass. He was hard for anyone to handle. Dillon was the oldest and then Ramsey. They had just finished college. Dillon was going pro in the NBA and Ramsey was on his way to Australia to learn about sheep ranching. They both gave up their dreams to keep our family together."

He felt her touch. Knew the moment she'd reached out and touched his arm. He needed the contact right then. Sad memories seldom came his way and when they did, they were too painful to dwell on. He'd been close to his mother, close to his father and aunt and uncle.

"Hey, you okay?"

He glanced over at Alpha. "Yes. Memories can be a bummer at times."

"Yes, I know."

He wondered if she was talking from experience. He had noted the indention on the third finger of her left hand where a ring used to be. Had she been married at one time? Deciding to change the subject, he said, "I thought about it and ran it over with the family. We're cool with the party being a black-tie affair. The reason I hesitated in making a decision was because I didn't want any of the employees to incur any unnecessary expenses if they didn't have to. But Dillon reminded me that this will be the company's fortieth holiday celebration so we need to be classy about it."

A huge smile touched her lips. "I was hoping that would be your decision. I like class and already have a lot of ideas on how to make the night special."

He nodded. "And they like the theme—One Winter's Night."

"That's great!"

When they came to a traffic light she opened her messenger bag to pull out several documents. "I have another presentation for you when we get to our destination. Now that you've decided on the attire, the menu can be planned accordingly. I'm working with Foods by Jerlon as the caterer."

"I've attended several parties he's catered, and everything he's prepared is delicious."

For the next half hour they covered more details about the party. It was only after discussing the budget that she lifted her gaze from her notes to look out the window. "We're a long way from town, aren't we?"

He glanced over at her. When had the sight of a woman with her hair in a ponytail ever turned him on? "Not too far."

He slowed the car to make a turn off the highway onto a two-lane road. A huge marker said Westmoreland Country.

She glanced over at him after reading the marker. "Westmoreland Country?"

He chuckled. "Yes. My great-great-grandfather settled here eighty-something years ago on over two thousand acres. Dillon, being the oldest, inherited the family home and the three-hundred acres it sat on. The rest of us got a hundred acres each once we turned twenty-five."

"So all of you stay around here, close together?"

"Close enough. Being on a hundred acres gives you privacy, at least most of the time, but there's still Bailey."

She raised a brow. "Bailey?"

"Bailey's my cousin and was the youngest Denver Westmoreland when my parents, uncle and aunt died. She likes to think she can boss all of us around. She hasn't reached twenty-five yet so she figures she can bum sleeping space wherever she wants. Usually she hangs out at Gemma's place since it's vacant now that Gemma is living in Australia."

"Is Gemma another cousin?"

"Yes." He decided it probably would be beneficial if he gave her a rundown of everyone. "On my parents' side there's Dillon. Then Micah, who works as a scientist for the federal government. He got married in June, and he and Kalina are expecting. Right now they're living in Alexandria, Virginia."

Riley slowed down when they reached another school zone. "Then there's Jason who's married to Bella." He chuckled. "She's from Savannah, and her first winter here was hard on her, too. Then there's me and my younger brothers, Canyon, Stern and Bane."

She lifted a brow. "No sisters?"

"Nope. I think my parents were hoping Bane was a girl, but it didn't turn out that way."

He then told her about his cousins, naming each one individually and the spouses of the married ones. Usually the last thing he talked about whenever he was on a date with a woman was his family. But he felt comfortable talking about them with Alpha.

He turned onto the road for his place and she glanced over at him and smiled. "Riley's Station?"

He chuckled. "Yes, Riley's Station."

Alpha was spellbound when they pulled into his yard. As far as the eye could see, she was surrounded by mountains and streams. Tucked away in the center of it all was a stately two-story house with a wraparound porch. Floor-to-ceiling windows covered the entire front of the house with a huge bay window facing the mountains on the side. A portion of the land close to the house had been cleared for a small waterfall and birdbath.

"All this is yours?" she asked, getting out of the car. He gripped her shoulders lightly when he placed his arms around her.

"Yes, one hundred acres. Isn't it beautiful?"

Beautiful? Words couldn't describe how soul-touchingly magnificent the view was. The one thing she had fallen in love with when she'd first visited Denver had been the mountains. Aside from the cold weather, Denver was a beautiful place.

"Now I understand about Riley's Station," she said, looking up at him.

"Do you?"

"Yes. On the way here I saw the markers—Ramsey's Web, Dillon's Den, Derringer's Dungeon, Zane's Hideout, Gemma's Gem.... Where on earth did those names come from?"

He threw his head back and laughed as he led her up the steps to the house. "Bailey. She figured all our places needed names and came up with them for us. She even designed the markers. At the time it was her pet project and we all gave in. We would have done anything to keep her out of trouble."

"I take it that she used to be a handful."

"If only you knew."

She stepped aside so he could open the door for her. "Welcome to my home, Alpha."

"Thanks," she said, passing him, stepping inside. For the second time that day her mouth almost dropped open. She moved from the foyer and glanced around at the open-concept room. His home was beautiful, the furnishings gorgeous and the decor breathtaking. The entire place was simply immaculate.

"Okay, although this is definitely a man's place, there's no way the decorating and coordinating of the furnishings was done by you. You hired an interior decorator, right?"

He moved away from the closed door. "Right. My cousin, Gemma. She owns an interior decorating company and insisted upon doing her thing in here."

Alpha continued to glance around. "Insisted."

"Yes, for the most part. I would have been satisfied just to have a kitchen table and a bed, but she'd made up her mind, after going into business for herself out of college, that her brothers and cousins would be her first clients. And none of us got discounts."

Alpha chuckled. "But I like that. Keeping it all in the family. Supporting one another."

"That's the Westmoreland Way." He moved across the room to open the blinds to a huge window that had a gorgeous, picturesque view of the mountains.

"And how do you keep it all clean and everything in place?" she asked, not seeing a speck of dirt or smidgen of dust anywhere.

His eyes glinted as if insulted. "Are you trying to insinuate I'm a slob?"

She waved off his pretended insult. "You're a man, Riley. Not too many tidy up after themselves. I'm impressed."

"Thank you, but I'll admit to having a weekly cleaning service. A woman drops by and takes care of the houses for all the single Westmorelands. It's an annual birthday gift from the ladies in the family for the single male Westmorelands."

He glanced at her messenger bag, which she was still carrying in her hand. "You can set up things in my office. I even have a pull-down screen in there." He glanced at his watch. "And while you're doing that, I'll start dinner."

She arched a brow. "You cook?"

He chuckled softly. "Yes, sweetheart, I learned how to fend for myself when I discovered the women inviting me over to their place to eat all had ulterior motives."

She tried ignoring the fluttering in the pit of her stomach caused by his term of endearment as she eyed him up and down. He had removed his jacket and tie and was standing in the middle of his humongous living room, looking at home and oh-so-sexy.

"Can you?"

"Can I what?"

"Cook," he said, opening blinds to another window.

"Yes."

"The kitchen is around that bend in the wall," he said. "After getting things set up, you can join me and we'll see how well you can cook."

When was the last time he'd whistled while cooking? Riley wondered as he pulled all the spices he needed out of the cabinets. He glanced to where Alpha stood at the island making dessert—sugar cookies. She had come up with the idea after discovering that he had all the ingredients she needed.

This wasn't the first time he'd ever invited a woman to his house by any means, and this wasn't the first time one had shared space in his kitchen. But he would admit, although he didn't want to do so, that she was the first whose presence felt totally right.

He pushed the thought to the back of his mind, not wanting to ponder why he felt that way. All he knew was that he enjoyed glancing across the way and seeing her there. She was wearing a pullover sweater and a pair of skimmer jeans, and he liked the short leather boots on her feet. He thought the outfit was perfect for what he had in mind later. They were going horseback riding around his property after dinner.

A thought then entered his mind. "You do ride, right?"

She glanced over at him. "Ride what?"

"A horse."

She chuckled and the sound echoed around his kitchen. "Yes. I went to school to become a vet, remember. One year I spent the entire summer on a horse ranch in Ocala, Florida, working as a ranch hand. It was definitely a learning experience. I'm no jockey, but I can hold my own."

He stopped what he was doing and turned around. "Glad you think so because we're going riding later."

"We are?"

"Yes."

She shrugged. "Okay." She then returned to what she was doing.

"How are you coming along over there?" he asked, curious. She had been quiet, concentrating on the task until he'd interrupted her just now.

"Fine. You did preset the oven to 350 degrees, right?"

"Yes."

"Good. I haven't made sugar cookies in a long time. What are the odds that you would have everything I need?"

"Only because Bailey likes my kitchen and keeps it equipped."

She glanced up and around. "I can certainly see why she likes this one. It's a cook's dream. Beautiful oak cabinets, granite countertops, stainless steel appliances and—"

"Hey, you have all those things in your kitchen, except your cabinets are maple instead of oak."

"Yes, but I can place my small kitchen in here three or four times over. Most men would see this much square footage in a kitchen as wasted space."

"I'm not most men."

She glanced over at him and moved her gaze up and down. "Yes, I can see that."

He smiled and shook his head. "You know those kinds of looks can get you into trouble."

An innocent smile touched her lips. "I'm not doing anything."

Instead of disagreeing with her, he turned back around to the sink to start peeling the potatoes that he planned to stew on top of the stove with pork chops and his special gravy. The dish wasn't as good as McKay's, but he didn't think it was all bad.

Out of the corner of his eye he watched as Alpha opened his oven door to slide the tray of cookies inside. "These are slow-baking, so an hour should do it."

"I can't wait," he said, turning toward her. "Once I get this started it will be on simmer for a while."

"All right. Do you want me to cover the rest of the info for the party before or after dinner? The only thing left to cover is the budget."

He nodded. On the drive over she had covered a lot, being detailed and precise and, not surprisingly, he had liked all of her ideas. "Let's do it before dinner."

"Okay, I'll go get things set up in your office."

He watched her walk off with his pulse hammering and his erection throbbing. She looked good all over but had such a curvaceous backside that seeing her in jeans was a total turn-on for him.

Riley drew in a deep breath as the rush of blood seemed to hit him right in the groin. At some point they would share a bed, but he had promised not to rush her and he wouldn't, even if it killed him. Alpha was not a one-night stand, nor would she be a one-and-done. She would have her six weeks.

More importantly, he would have his six weeks. He doubted he would want less than that. And he'd taken the time earlier that day, while in his office, to figure out the exact ending date, and wouldn't you know it, it would be the night of the holiday party.

So it would be one winter's night in more ways than one.

Seven

"Well, what do you think about the pork chops?"

Alpha glanced across the table at Riley. It hadn't taken long to go over the budget and wrap up all the other minor details she needed to finalize in order to move ahead with her plans. All her people were ready and in place and now that he had approved her suggestions and the budget, it was full steam ahead. She'd be putting on a party that she knew would impress him and everyone attending.

She smiled ruefully. "I think if push comes to shove, you can quit your day job and become a chef. Everything tastes wonderful, Riley." And she meant it. The pork chops were so tender they all but melted in her mouth and the gravy and potatoes were better than any she'd ever eaten…even those at McKay's.

From his smile she knew her compliment pleased him. "Thanks. Wait until you taste my shrimp and lobster casserole. It's going to knock you off your feet."

Hmm, was that an invitation? Sounded like one to her. "I'll look forward to it."

"And I'm looking forward to eating your cookies. They smell good."

"Thanks."

She continued to eat and when she glanced up he was watching her with a strange look on his face. She tilted her head and arched a brow. "Something's wrong?"

"No," he said rather quickly and continued eating. Moments later, after taking a sip of his wine, he said, "I looked at a calendar earlier today and if we both agree to go the full six weeks for our affair, then it ends the night of the company party."

"Sounds good to me."

She saw something flash in his eyes. "So we understand each other?" he asked.

She smiled. "Perfectly." She then picked up her wineglass and took a sip, not sure why he was still sitting there staring at her. Had he expected her to request more time or something?

She glanced at her watch. It was getting late. She darted a look over at him. "Do you still want to go riding?"

"Yes.

"Then we need to get going if we want to take advantage of the daylight."

He stood. "I agree."

She stood, as well. "I'll help clear the table."

"You don't have to."

"I want to, and it's the least I can do for such a great meal. You outdid yourself."

He chuckled. "For you, any day."

She didn't say anything as she helped him clean off the table and load up the dishwasher. The heat was on, and it was getting to her already. And she had a feeling things would be getting hotter.

* * *

An hour later Riley stood at the window and looked out, waiting as Alpha used one of his guest bathrooms. He had enjoyed his time with her and now it was close to seven. It was hard to believe she had spent five hours with him today. And he had enjoyed every second of those hours. After dinner she had helped him clear the table and load the dishwasher. Then they had gone riding, and she'd pulled one over on him when she'd given the impression she wasn't good when it came to riding a horse. The woman was an excellent rider.

When they returned they had eaten the cookies she had baked and drunk cold glasses of milk. He shared more stories about his family and she had listened attentively, asking questions and laughing when he told her all about Bane's, Bailey's and the twins'—Aiden and Adrian's—escapades and how Family Services had threatened to separate the youngest Westmorelands from the family if their bad behaviors didn't improve.

But the one thing he noticed was that she hadn't talked a lot about herself or her family. He knew she was from Florida, that her parents owned a veterinary business and that she had a sister. But there was the issue of the missing ring on her finger. Had something other than a career move driven her to Denver?

"You even have a beautiful powder room, Riley. And it's so big. I probably could roll a bed in there and take a nap."

He turned around slowly. "Glad you—"

Whatever he was about to say died on his lips when their gazes connected. Suddenly, from across the room he held her in focus. His stomach tightened and his nerve endings sizzled. "Like it," he said, finishing his sentence.

She'd done something to her hair. It was no longer pulled back away from her face in a ponytail, but was now loose. A mass of brown curls were hanging around her shoulders. He'd seen her hair that way before, earlier today in his office.

But for some reason, at that moment, restyling her hair made her look incredibly beautiful.

His feet began moving toward her with a purpose ingrained in every part of his body. He met her gaze, held it, and when he came to a stop in front of her, he reached out and traced a finger across her chin. He then slowly moved his finger down the length of her neck before touching a lock of her hair. "You're wearing it differently," he said in a deep, husky voice, liking how the silky tresses felt flowing through his fingers.

She nodded slowly. "The clamp came loose while out riding and I thought I'd play it safe and take it off. The clamp was a gift from my sister and means a lot. I don't want to lose it."

"I like your hair this way. It's a stunning shade of brown. The color is perfect for your skin tone. It's beautiful. You're beautiful."

"Thank you."

He lifted her hands to his lips and kissed them while gazing up at her. "I promised not to rush you, but just so you know, I have no qualms about making love to you tonight. I'm tempted to do just that."

"Then I better move temptation out of your way by letting you take me home. Then you can concentrate on other things."

His lips curved in a smile. "Even if you weren't here, I would think about you, Alpha."

She chuckled softly. "I bet you say that to all the ladies."

Riley shook his head as he continued to kiss her hand. Now he was using the tip of his tongue to taste her skin. He liked hearing how her breathing sounded forced. "No, I don't say that to all the ladies."

And he meant that. He would admit to throwing out a convincing line or two when it served his purpose. That was to be expected when he was a man on the prowl. But that's not what he was doing here. With Alpha, he was being totally honest. He had thought about her over the past week more than he'd thought about any other woman. He had dreamed about her, waking up with a need and desire he'd never felt for any other woman.

Since he didn't know why his experience was so different with her, he intended to be cautious in whatever he did, whatever they shared. He had to be realistic enough to admit there had been something between him and Alpha from the first. She had been wearing gloves, yet when their hands touched he had felt the intense heat. He had felt the chemistry. An electrical charge had zinged through him. At first he'd thought it was a fluke, nothing more than an overreaction. But then, when he'd picked her up in his arms in McKay's parking lot to carry her into the restaurant, it was as if something had exploded between them, a connection he couldn't describe. And that was before he'd even seen what she was hiding under all those clothes.

He straightened and reached up to touch her chin again, coaxing her to meet his gaze. "Go out with me this weekend. We can do dinner and a movie or a play."

He studied the shape of her lips. Heat stirred his groin, making several ideas flow through his head and prompting him to add, "Or better yet, after dinner we can come here or go to your place and play a game."

Her brow arched. "What game?"

"The Pleasure Game. Have you ever played it before?"

He saw how her eyes darkened with desire when she shook her head. "Can't say that I have."

"Then let me assure you that you're going to enjoy it. It's easy to play, and there are not a whole lot of rules to follow. You can let me know that night if you want to play. How about if I pick you up for dinner around seven? There's this restaurant near the airport that I've heard nice things about, and I want to take you there."

"Okay," she said, smiling softly.

"And the Pleasure Game will require you staying overnight here or me staying overnight at your place. No pressure.

No rush. If you don't think you'll be ready to play Saturday night just let me know."

She nodded. "I will."

He leaned in close and slanted his mouth over hers, needing to taste her and leave her with something to think about. When she opened her mouth to return the kiss, he pulled her into his arms and deepened it, knowing he would be counting the days until he spent time with her again.

Eight

"Wow, the invitations will be simply beautiful," Lindsey Hopkins said. The twenty-something stay-at-home mom assisted Alpha on a part-time basis. As she looked at the computer screen over Alpha's shoulder, she had a huge grin on her face. "And you're the one designing them?"

Alpha smiled, too, pleased that Lindsey liked them. "Yes, after coming up with what I thought would work for our theme, One Winter's Night, I thought the idea of a country house in a light snowstorm would be perfect."

And she knew just the house she would use as a model. Riley's home. It would be picture-perfect. She had mentioned using a picture of his home on the invitation when he brought her home the other night. He said he had no problem with it and had given her the green light to do it.

"Do you know whose house you're going to use?" Lindsey asked her.

She turned her chair around and met Lindsey's inquiring

gaze. "Yes, it belongs to one of the Westmorelands. Riley Westmoreland."

Lindsey's face lit up. "He's one of Bane's older brothers. I met him once, and I bet the house is as gorgeous as he is."

Alpha threw her head back and laughed. "Well, yes, I guess you could say that."

"Trust me, I do. Every woman in town knows how good-looking those Westmoreland men are. Some of us are married, but we aren't blind. Any woman can appreciate a good-looking man."

Alpha grinned. "True." She turned back to the computer. "So you think Riley's house might work as a backdrop?"

"I've never seen it, but I don't see why not. I've been to Westmoreland Country once or twice, years ago with my father when he did the landscaping for the main house. He took me and my brothers along to help. You know, free labor," she said, laughing. "The main house was huge and majestic. I heard all the siblings have built their own homes now."

Alpha switched her computer to another screen, one that showed an example of some of the decorations she contemplated using. "Yes, that's what I heard." None of Riley's rules had governed publicizing their affair, but she didn't feel comfortable broadcasting it to anyone.

An hour or so later, Lindsey had left to pick up her baby from her mom and Alpha was on her way to the kitchen to fix a sandwich—her favorite, peanut butter and jelly—when the doorbell rang. Wondering who could be calling on her, she crossed the living room to the door. A quick glance out of the peephole indicated a florist deliveryman.

Pursing her lips thoughtfully, she opened the door. Who would send her flowers? Perhaps the man was at the wrong house. "May I help you?"

The older man smiled. "Alpha Blake?"

"Yes."

"These are for you," he said, handing her the huge, beautiful ceramic vase of pink roses. A dozen of them.

"Thanks," she said, accepting the flowers.

"And the tip has been taken care of."

"Oh, thanks," she said, stepping back and using her toe to close the door. The roses filled her house with a sweet-smelling scent. As soon as she set the vase down on the table, she pulled off the card, eager to see who'd sent them.

Two days left. Riley

She threw her head back and laughed. She had thought about everything he had suggested for Saturday night, especially the Pleasure Game, and felt she was ready. There was no need to put off the inevitable. Besides, she'd never played games with a man in the bedroom. Eddie hadn't had an imaginative bone in his body. LeBron had been full of ideas but only with the pretense that his bed partner was Omega. Alpha shook her head at how he actually hadn't seen anything wrong with wanting to make love to her while pretending she was her sister.

Moments later, Alpha was still standing in front of the table and gazing at the roses when her cell phone rang. She pulled it out of her pocket and saw it was her father. She and her parents talked at least once a week, but usually at night. She was surprised he was calling her in the middle of the day.

"Dad?"

"Yes, Al, how's my girl?"

She couldn't help but smile. "I'm fine. What about you?"

"Great. Look, I just had to call you and tell you I saw Eddie today when he brought Cleo into the office."

She frowned. "Is Cleo okay?" she asked, inquiring about the beautiful Labrador retriever that Eddie owned. She had fallen in love with the dog and had begun considering Cleo as hers, too.

"Yes, Cleo's fine. He brought her in for her annual visit."

"Oh. You didn't have to call to tell me that, Dad."

"I know, but I figured you'd want to know that he asked about you."

Like she cared. "Did he?"

"Yes. He even asked if you've mentioned anything about moving back home." There was a pause. Alpha knew she wouldn't like what was coming next but decided to let her father have his say since he would do so anyway.

"Look, baby, I know Eddie was the one to call off the wedding and all, but understand it from a man's point of view. He didn't want your reputation tarnished."

Alpha gritted her teeth. "He wanted me to disown Omega."

"But your sister chose the life she wanted. None of us were happy with it. Even your mom and I haven't been able to forgive her for embarrassing us that way."

And to this day Alpha felt her parents were wrong. She'd told them so more times than she could count. Regardless, Omega was their child and her sister, and nothing should have slid a wedge between those relationships. But her parents had succumbed to their friends' gossip and whispers. "I know, Dad, and you know how I felt about that. No matter what, she's still your daughter and my sister."

"Well, one day you're going to face up to what she did to us, what she did to you. You had men looking at you funny, thinking you were her."

"It was only one man, Dad." She had heard all this before and wasn't in the mood to rehash this with her father. "Besides, that was three years ago. Omega is now a happily married woman."

"With a past."

She rolled her eyes. "We all have one. Some a little naughtier than others."

"Naughtier? What your sister did was a disgrace."

"What Omega did has nothing to do with Eddie."

"Had you and Eddie married, the two of you would have been one, so it did have something to do with him. And as far as I'm concerned, he's a good man. All he wanted was to protect you."

"No. He was trying to control me."

There was a pause on the other end. "So you're saying the chances of the two of you getting back together are slim to none?"

"I'm leaning heavily on none."

There was another pause. "I hope you're not making a mistake. What about the next man you meet who might find out what your sister used to do for a living?"

"Any man I become seriously involved with, Dad, is going to have to accept me as I am. Omega has nothing to do with it."

"You're wrong, Al. She's a part of your past that you can't get rid of."

"No, Dad. She's a part of my present, and I can't imagine it being any other way."

When he heard the brisk knock on his office door, Riley knew who it was without looking up. "Come in, Canyon."

His brother entered, letting off steam. "Keisha Ashford is not the same woman I was involved with three years ago. Do you hear me, Ry? She is not the same woman."

Riley leaned back in his chair. "Yes, I hear you. In fact, I'm sure everyone on this floor heard you. I take it the meeting didn't go well?"

"Go well? That woman deliberately tried to make me look as if I didn't know what the hell I was doing."

A smile touched the corners of Riley's lips. He seldom saw his brother hot under the collar and just to know a woman was responsible was somewhat amusing. Especially since the Canyon he knew would never let a woman get under his skin. "And did you?" he asked, watching his brother angrily pace back and forth in front of his desk.

Canyon stopped and glared. "Did I what?"

"Know what the hell you were doing?"

At first Canyon appeared to have been taken aback by the question. But then he lifted his shoulders in a defensive stance. "Hell, yes, I knew what I was doing, but she deliberately tried to make me look bad."

Riley forced the smile off his face. "And why would she do something like that? Was it because she found out you were seeing another woman behind her back, when the two of you were supposed to be dating exclusively? Hmm?"

Canyon glared. "I was not seeing that other woman and you know it. Bonita Simpkins set me up, and Keisha fell for it."

Riley opened his mouth to say something but the receptionist's voice on the intercom stopped him. "Mr. Westmoreland, Ms. Alpha Blake is on line two for you."

"Thanks." He then glanced over at his brother. "I need to take this call."

His brother shrugged. "Go ahead."

When Canyon just stood there, apparently still fuming over his encounter with Keisha, Riley cleared his throat and said, "It's a private call."

Canyon lifted a brow. "With the company's event planner? What could be so private about that?"

When Riley didn't respond but continued to sit and stare at his brother, waiting for him to leave, something flickered in the dark depths of Canyon's eyes. "Please don't tell me you've got the hots for the event planner."

"Okay, I won't tell you. Close the door behind you on the way out."

Canyon stood there and gaped at him. "I don't believe it."

Riley rolled his eyes. "What don't you believe?"

"What happened to your policy about never mixing business with pleasure?"

"It's still in place. I'm not mixing them. When we conduct business, we conduct business. And when we want pleasure, we'll have pleasure. Solely separate entities that aren't being mixed."

Canyon threw his head back and laughed. "You sound like a damn politician who's breaking the rule and then trying to find a way to make the situation work for you."

"Goodbye, Canyon. If I were you, I would focus on a way to make peace with Keisha Ashford."

The amusement on Canyon's face immediately vanished to be replaced with a glare. "You take care of your business, and I'll take care of mine."

It was on the tip of Riley's tongue to tell his brother that he was the one who sought him out and not the other way around. "Whatever."

It was only after Canyon had left and closed the door behind him that Riley clicked on the second line. "Alpha? Sorry for the wait."

"No problem. I'm just calling to thank you for the flowers. They are beautiful."

So are you. "I'm glad you like them."

"I do. I truly do."

He leaned back in his chair and did something he hadn't done in a long time—propped his feet up on his desk. "So, what have you been doing with yourself since I last saw you?" *Which was only two days ago.*

"Designing the invitations, picking up items for decorating and finalizing the menu with the chef. However, I did take time out for my dance classes."

He lifted a brow. "You're taking dance classes?"

She chuckled. "Yes, twice a week at the high school at night."

Why didn't he know that? And just as quickly as he thought it, he was reminded that their connection was about sex without commitment. There was no need for him to know what she did every hour of the day. "Sounds like fun."

"It is. Well, I don't want to hold you up. I just wanted to call and thank you for the flowers and to let you know how beautiful they are."

"You're welcome and have a good night." He paused a moment and then said in a low tone, "Think about me tonight."

"I will. We have two more days."

He drew in a long and deep breath, already feeling frustration settle within his bones. Two days was too long in his book. "Yes, we have two days."

It was hard not to suggest they shorten that time. He could drop by later. But he would hold fast and not give in to temptation. He had offered this time before their date on Saturday because he wanted it to be special for her. However, he decided to say, "I can't wait to see you again. I've thought of you often."

"And I've thought of you often, as well."

That was good to hear, but he doubted she had thought of him as much as he'd thought of her. It had been hard to concentrate on all the reports that had come across his desk and not on the memories of her and that night they'd dined together at his place. Whether it was the dinner they'd shared, the conversation between them or the horseback ride they'd taken, he had enjoyed his time with her, and there hadn't been anything sexual about it. Just sitting across from her, admiring the soft and smooth skin of her face, the stunning bone structure that made her such a gorgeous woman, the pair of lips he could get addicted to if not careful...

"Goodbye, Riley."

"Goodbye."

He eased his legs off his desk to stand and walk over to the window. He and Canyon had tossed for this office, mainly because of the view. There was snow on the top of the mountains and already he felt the urge to go skiing. He had a trip planned to Aspen in January and wondered if Alpha could ski.

He shook his head, chuckling at the foolish thought. She couldn't stand cold weather so chances were she would never venture anyplace where snow was waist-deep and you could feel the cold all the way to the bones.

But the most important thing he had to remember was that his affair with Alpha would be over by then.

For some reason that thought bothered him.

Nine

Saturday night hadn't come quickly enough, Alpha thought, standing in front of the full-length mirror to give herself a final once-over. She had appreciated the good weather yesterday since it had given her the chance to go shopping. This was her first official date with Riley and she wanted to wear everything new—from the inside out.

This is when she missed Omega the most. As teens, and even while in college, they would go places and do things together, especially shopping. They'd shared some of the same taste in clothing and shoes, but when it came to undergarments, Omega was always more daring.

Alpha looked down at her legs. It would get colder later so she'd decided to wear a pair of boots, a new black suede pair she had bought yesterday. She liked the way they fit her legs, but more importantly, she liked how they looked with the outfit she was wearing—a printed kimono top with an elastic belt that emphasized her small waistline and a black sateen pencil skirt that highlighted her boots.

Her hair was styled slightly differently after her visit to a salon yesterday morning. She knew Riley liked seeing her hair around her shoulders, since he'd said as much that night at his place. So she had enhanced the look by making her hair appear fuller. She'd gotten it layered around her shoulders. A number of people had complimented the new style and said it was perfect for her face.

Riley had suggested that they either spend the night at his place or here, and either one was fine with her. She was so looking forward to tonight and a part of her felt giddy. Omega had called earlier that day and suggested she have an overnight bag packed just in case.

And because there was a chance this is where they would end the evening, her bedroom was ready. She had even bought silk sheets for her bed and scented candles had been placed all around. She liked the way her bedroom looked and although it wasn't nearly as large as Riley's, it would serve their purpose.

As she moved away from the mirror, she recalled the tour Riley had given her of his home. Why one person would need that much space she didn't know. But she had to admit there was something about every room that suited him.

Even his entertainment room suited him. Or should she say *rooms,* since there were two. There was a state-of-the-art theater with power-operated reclining seats. His music room held a white oak entertainment system with a sophisticated stereo, and a beautiful white Steinway baby grand piano sat in the middle of the floor. According to Riley, his mother, who had been a music major in college, had taught each of her seven sons how to play the piano. After she'd died, Dillon had made sure the lessons continued by hiring a private music instructor.

Alpha's heart kicked up a notch when she heard the ringing of the doorbell. A quick glance at her watch indicated Riley was fifteen minutes early.

She glanced around her bedroom one last time, liking what

she saw. Her queen-size bed was covered in a beautiful blue comforter and she'd added additional shams and decorative pillows. She'd changed the wattage of the lightbulbs in the lamps on both sides of her bed to soften the lighting in the room. Her bedroom had been transformed into a romantic haven.

She liked it. She liked it a lot. And she hoped that if Riley got the chance to see it, he would like it, as well.

"I hope I'm not too early, but I wasn't sure how traffic would be coming this way," Riley said, once he'd been able to regain control of his senses. He had almost lost them when Alpha opened the door. She looked absolutely stunning, from the new hairstyle she was sporting to the outfit she was wearing. Sexy enough to devour. She hadn't called to say she wasn't ready for the Pleasure Game later so he could only assume that she was.

Raw need, mingled with potent lust, consumed him. His body hadn't wasted time getting aroused. This was one time he was grateful for the long leather coat he was wearing. But his full concentration was on what *she* was wearing. Her outfit was designed to articulate every curve on her body and was doing a great job.

"No, you're not too early at all. It will only take a second to grab my coat," she said, stepping aside so he could enter her home.

"Take your time, Alpha."

"Thanks."

And then, with deep male appreciation, he watched her walk off, getting even more aroused by the sway of her hips with every step she took in that pencil skirt with the slit in the back. When she was no longer in sight, he drew in a deep breath, knowing it would be one of those kinds of nights. The only good thing about knowing it was being fully aware of how it would end.

He would let her decide whose bed they would sleep in tonight. It didn't matter to him since he didn't intend for them to get much sleep. That was why he intended to feed her well because she would definitely need all her energy for later.

"I'm ready, Riley."

That made two of them. He was ready, as well.

"I guess now is the time to ask whether I'll be coming back here tonight," she said. He saw the flash of color that appeared in her cheeks and knew the topic of what they intended to do later made her blush. He smiled thinking that she would be doing a whole hell of a lot of blushing later, if she had any shy bones in her body.

He shoved his hands into his coat pockets. "It's your decision. It doesn't matter to me where we make love."

His bluntness caused the color in her cheeks to deepen, but that did nothing for the heated look she gave him from beneath her silky long lashes. He knew it was unintentional, but nobody informed his erection, which was beginning to throb like hell. When she nervously licked her lips, he knew that if he didn't get her out of there now he would be initiating a roll on the floor in the next few minutes.

"I'd like to come back here," she said softly, holding his gaze.

"Then we shall. Ready?"

She nodded and led him to the door for them to leave. As far as he was concerned, it wasn't a moment too soon.

"Welcome tonight, Mr. Westmoreland. Your table is ready."

"Thanks, Pierre," Riley said, handing his coat to the manager of the restaurant.

While Riley assisted Alpha in removing her coat, she thanked the older man, who had a deep French accent, a Maurice Chevalier reincarnated. He gave her a brilliant smile, leaned in and lifted her hand to kiss the back of it. "Welcome to *Les' Amores, mademoiselle.* You are most beautiful."

She smiled at the compliment. "Thank you."

He straightened and then grabbed a couple of menus from a nearby rack. "Please follow me."

Alpha glanced at her surroundings as they followed their host. She had been quite taken with the French restaurant the moment Riley had turned into the courtyard of fine shops and boutiques. Since moving to Denver she had heard about *Les' Amores* but had never had the opportunity to dine at the plush brasserie.

As Pierre led them through the main dining area, she took note of the adobe brick walls lined with ornamental racks filled with fine wine and crystal glasses. The tables were adorned with red silk tablecloths and candle lanterns. Authentic French artwork hung on the walls and a large fireplace with a roaring blaze was in the middle of the room.

Instead of seating them at one of the vacant tables they passed, Pierre escorted them to a room in the back that had a table set for two. The room was quaint with wooden beam ceilings and a huge brick fireplace. Cozy and private.

Riley moved to pull out her chair before Pierre had a chance to do so and leaned close to her ear to whisper, "I love your outfit, but I can't wait to take it off you." She couldn't help the blush that crept into her features. She knew he was telling her that the seduction of Alpha Blake had begun.

He took his chair and Pierre handed them menus and proceeded to offer his recommendations for that night. That done, he asked about wine and Riley named a brand she'd never heard of. When she looked at him, he turned sensual dark eyes on her and said, "It's a magnificent blend. You'll like it."

She nodded, swallowing deeply and wondering if she would need something stronger to get her through the evening. "I'm sure I will."

Pierre left them and within minutes was back to pour their

wine. "I'll give you time to look at the menu," he said, easing from the room and leaving them alone.

Alpha glanced down at the menu. "Everything looks good, Riley. What do you recommend?"

"About you or what's on the menu?" he asked with a flirty wink at her.

She gave him an admonishing smile, wondering if this was how it would be for the rest of the night. "The menu, Riley."

He smiled. "In that case I would recommend the…"

She listened while he rattled off a number of dishes, pronouncing each in a deep French accent that stirred her nerve endings. She gazed deep into the eyes staring back at her. In the depths of his dark gaze was a promise of what would come later. A hot, lusty night filled with pleasure. And heaven help her, she was looking forward to it.

"So what do you think, Alpha?"

She knew he was asking about the menu and the dishes he'd just told her about, but though she had heard, she hadn't listened. "I'll let you decide."

He nodded and gave her a smile, one that told her he knew why she was taking the easy way out. Pierre returned with the wine and poured some into their glasses and then took their orders. When he left, Alpha glanced around.

The room was small and intimate. They had been given a table with a view of Pikes Peak, and it was breathtaking. Music was flowing into the room through hidden speakers, and the tunes were romantic. She hadn't realized how secluded the room was until she recalled walking through the restaurant to get to it. Not only did the fire blazing in the fireplace provide warmth, but it also set an intimate tone. On the drive over, she'd tried bringing him up to date on the party plans, but Riley had reached out, touched her hand and said tonight was not about the party but about them.

"This is a nice room," she said.

"I'm glad you like it. So tell me, Alpha. Do you ski?"

* * *

Why was he asking her that? Riley immediately wondered. It had to be for the purpose of conversation, nothing more. The inquiry certainly couldn't have anything to do with his ski trip to Aspen in January since their affair would have ended by then.

"No, I don't ski."

He wasn't surprised. "Would you like to learn how?"

She shook her head. "That would mean being out in not just cold weather but super cold weather, so I'll pass."

He should let it go, but couldn't. "What if I promised to keep you warm?"

She chuckled. "I don't think you can keep me *that* warm, Riley."

"But if I could?" he inquired further, taking a sip of his wine.

"You can't."

He didn't say anything but, deep down, he saw it as a challenge. He held her gaze. "We'll see."

She tilted her head and looked at him. "Tell me. What do you get out of skiing? I heard it's not really a form of exercise."

He watched her take a sip of her wine. The way she closed her lips around the mouth of the glass sent flutters off in his stomach. "Not true. Any time you use muscles you don't normally use, you're exercising."

He took a sip of his wine as he told her about the first time he'd put on a pair of skis. "I was all but seven and my father and uncle took their sons on a ski trip for the sole purpose of providing us with professional ski lessons."

He chuckled. "I guess they knew their sons and figured if they didn't make sure we were taught by a professional then we would learn the wrong way and risk our lives. Being on the slopes with my family was special to me and I consider those memories some of the best ones of my childhood. Maybe that's why I enjoy skiing so much."

He saw the wistful look that shone in her eyes, so he added, "I'm sure you and your sister did things with your family that you hold as special memories, too."

She shifted her gaze from his to pick up her glass of wine. "Yes, of course."

Not for the first time, he thought she was deliberately not sharing information about her family. It shouldn't bother him, but it did, mainly because he didn't have any problem telling her about his family. The only thing he knew about her parents was that they had wanted her to go into veterinary medicine but had accepted her decision to change careers. She seldom mentioned anything about her sister, and he could only assume the two were not close. And he was still curious about the ring that used to be on her finger. He was about to question her on the topic when Pierre returned with their appetizers.

Pierre, efficient as ever, was in and out in no time, leaving them alone once again with a basket of hot buttered rolls, a platter of imported French escargots sautéed in a creamy, garlic butter sauce and steamed artichoke. He'd even taken the time to refill their wineglasses before breezing out.

Riley glanced over at Alpha. He should have used the time during Pierre's interruption to rethink pursuing his interest in the man who'd put a ring on her finger, as well as the reason she didn't talk much about her family, but he didn't. For some reason, he felt the need to address it. "Can I ask you something?"

She was reaching for an escargot and glanced over at him with a smile. "Just as long as what you want to ask has nothing to do with these. They look delicious."

He chuckled. "Not at all, please help yourself," he said, glad she was enjoying his choice in foods.

"Okay, then, ask away."

"I have two questions, really. I noticed you used to wear a ring. Were you married before?"

Her hands stilled. "Does it matter?"

He held her gaze and shook his head. "No. I'm just curious."

"No, I've never been married, but up until a year ago I was engaged."

"What happened?" he asked, as if he had every right to know.

She didn't say anything for a minute and then, "It was decided that marriage wasn't the right move for us after all."

She was being somewhat evasive so he couldn't help wondering who had made that decision. The guy? Her? Had it been mutual? Why did he care? It didn't matter, and he only cared if she'd gotten hurt by the decision. But, in a way, he was glad the marriage didn't take place because if it had she wouldn't be here with him tonight.

"And your second question?" she asked, returning to eating.

He smiled. She was letting him know there wouldn't be any further discussion on the first question. "Why don't you like talking about your family?" Her hands stilled again, and he could tell she was about to freeze up on him, but he refused to let her do that.

"I told you about my family, Riley."

"Not enough."

"I told you my parents were veterinarians in Daytona and that I have a sister."

"Is she still alive?"

She lifted a brow. "Who?"

"Your sister."

"Yes. Why do you ask?"

He shrugged. "Because you never talk about her. Where does she live? Is she married? Does she have any kids?"

Something, he wasn't sure what, flashed in her eyes before

she lowered her head to slowly bite into an escargot. "Omega lives in Paris. She's married to a wonderful man and they are trying real hard to start a family."

"Are the two of you close?"

"Yes, very close. As close as any two sisters can be."

His curiosity had been appeased. He decided that, in the future, the subjects of her ex-fiancé and her family were closed unless she brought them up. "You like that?" he asked, motioning to the escargot she had gone back to eating. He was getting turned on as he watched her chew a few times and then lick her lips.

"Yes, it's delicious."

A trickle of butter was running down her chin. "Come here and lean close," he told her, picking up his napkin to wipe away the butter. But when she leaned in toward him, he changed his mind and swiped the butter from her chin with the tip of his tongue.

"There," he said huskily. As he drew back, he met the surprised look in her eyes and smiled. "It's all gone now."

"Thanks," she murmured softly, drawing back in her chair.

"Anytime. I like the way you taste," he responded huskily. She took a sip of her wine. "It was the butter."

A doubtful smile curved his lips. "Umm, the butter tasted good but you tasted better. Makes me anxious to taste you all over later."

Riley watched as a blush touched her cheeks and she took another sip of her wine. "Don't drink too much of that, baby. I want your mind completely functional for later."

"Will that be all, Mr. Westmoreland?" Pierre asked after he and another waiter finished clearing the table. He had already asked if either Riley or Alpha wanted dessert and they had both declined.

"No, Pierre, that will be all. Just make sure we aren't disturbed for the remainder of the evening."

"Yes, sir." The older man quickly left with the other waiter trailing behind him.

No sooner had the door closed than Alpha swore she heard the distinct sound of a lock clicking in place, and Riley turned his full attention to her. His dark, piercing eyes held her within their scope and she all but squirmed in her seat, feeling sexual currents flow from him. Suddenly, an electrical charge seemed to vibrate through the air causing blood to rush through her veins.

Blood was rushing through another area of her body, as well, the one located at the juncture of her thighs, which made her cross her legs. She drew in a slow breath when he stood and rounded the table. Holding out his hand, he said, in what sounded like a deep, husky growl, "Dance with me."

Alpha felt her stomach quiver with each word he said. Earlier, she had heard music flowing into the room but the sound had been rather faint. At that moment, as if on cue, the volume increased. She slipped her hand into his, feeling his heat immediately. Uncrossing her legs, she eased from her chair and he gently pulled her into his arms, right smack against his hard, masculine body.

The song being played was perfect, just the right tempo for the way their bodies melded together as they swayed to the lyrics and melody. With her hand on his shoulder and her head lying on his chest, she could feel the rapid beat of his heart, which was somehow keeping time with hers. Being this close to him, bodies locked as tightly as they could be, stirred something elemental in her blood and reminded her of just how potent the chemistry was between them.

Pressed against him, she felt every inch of his lean strength. And when his hips moved, so did hers, slowly, methodically, magnetically. Heat sizzled through all parts of her when she felt his hard erection against her middle. The pressure triggered her nipples to harden. An ache began in her loins and branched upward, filling her with an indescribable hunger, a sexual need she didn't know she was capable of feeling.

"You okay?"

The sound of his voice ignited rampant sensations within her. She raised her eyes to his and inwardly moaned when she connected to the dark depths. "Yes, I'm okay." *But barely,* she held off saying. Never before had dancing with a man caused this much havoc on her emotions. Never had it driven her to want things she'd never wanted before.

They continued to gaze into each other's eyes as they swayed to the music. When one song moved to another, they stood in the same spot, feet firmly planted, bodies barely moving while his hand spanned her backside, making a slow ache throb there. She reveled in the feel of him holding her in his arms.

When she couldn't take looking into his eyes any longer, she placed her head on his chest again. The heat from his gaze was unnerving her, making it hard for her to breathe. What was there about him that made her not want to fight the heat but to wallow in it? She wanted tonight. She needed tonight—and all the nights he wanted to give her…for six weeks. And when it was over, it would be over. Final, with no regrets, no worrying about a lost love that should last forever or a love that never was. She was going into this affair with her eyes wide open. She was not the naive woman who'd thought she was the luckiest female on earth when Edward Swisher, of the prestigious Daytona Swishers, had asked her out. She had learned her lesson. She should have learned it with LeBron. But it had taken Eddie to make her vow never to give her heart to another man.

The song melded into another and they continued dancing. He tightened his arms around her and held her closer. Her breath caught each and every time he would deliberately slide his leg between hers, letting her feel the length of him through his pants. She could feel her panties getting wet with each moment of contact.

Almost overwhelmed in desire, she tilted her head back, met the dark, penetrating gaze staring down at her and asked, "What are you doing to me?"

He didn't even pretend not to know what she was asking. "Prepping you for later."

Who needed to be prepped? She opened her mouth to ask him that very thing when he lowered his mouth to hers, slid his tongue inside and proceeded to kiss her in a way that sent powerful surges through her. He began toying with her tongue, feasting on it like a hungry man getting his last meal.

She was just as greedy when she tightened her arms around him while they devoured each other's mouths. Nothing else mattered at that moment. It meant nothing to her that they were in a public place and there were people on the other side of that door having dinner. Nor did it matter that Pierre and that other waiter probably had a good idea what she and Riley were doing in here. All that mattered at the moment was the way he was kissing her, stirring a need within her that was nearly making her lose it.

Riley pulled his mouth back, and she was able to draw in a much-needed breath. He was able to do the same and rested his forehead against hers.

"Baby, I should be the one asking what *you* are doing to me," he whispered softly against her lips that were still moist from their kiss. "All I want to do at this moment is put you on that table and spread you wide and take you like I've been dreaming of doing for the past couple of weeks."

Her heartbeat kicked up a notch, knowing he wanted her as much as she wanted him. She refused to play games about this. She wanted to experience it all, and she wanted to experience it with him. She wanted several nights of hot, mind-blowing sex with no strings attached and no guilty conscience to deal with afterward.

She would go into the affair as the consenting and mature adult she was. She was the one paying the bills on Noble Lane, and what she did there was nobody's business, certainly not her parents', who lived thousands of miles away. They would frown upon an affair between her and anyone. Her father was hoping that she and Eddie would get back together even if it meant she would have to cut ties with her twin sister to do so.

"Are you ready for me to take you home?"

His question gave her pause. Now would be the perfect time, if she wanted to change her mind about anything they planned to do later. But her mind was made up, and she wasn't changing it. "Yes, I'm ready."

He pulled back slightly and looked at her, those dark eyes locked with hers, refusing to look away, as if her very soul was laid out for him to read like a book. "Are you sure you're ready, Alpha? I intend for it to be one hell of a night."

And she was counting on just that. She nodded, deciding right then and there to shed her inhibitions once and for all. She countered his question with one of her own. "Maybe I should be asking you the same thing, Riley. Are you sure you're ready?"

He reached down, took her hand and led it to the crotch of his pants. "What does that tell you?"

Oh, he was ready all right. What he'd done by letting her touch him was a bold move, one Eddie would never have taken. Eddie would never have encouraged her to cop a feel. And since Riley put her hand there, she saw no reason to move it...at least not yet. She was simply amazed how large he felt behind his zipper. She moved her hand around to take in the length, shape and feel of him.

"If you keep it up, Alpha, I just might be tempted to take you here and now."

Something, she wasn't sure what, drove her to utter her next words. "Do it."

"What did you say?" he asked, his voice deep and throaty, his eyes steady, mesmerizing and hungry.

She could play it off and pretend she hadn't said anything. But she didn't want to do that. What would be the point? She wanted Riley, and she wanted him now.

Alpha leaned in close to him and whispered, "I said, do it. Do it now."

She could tell from the way his breathing changed that he got the message. "Then take it out," he whispered against her lips. "You want it, then go in and get it, baby."

Her heartbeat kicked up another notch. His gaze held hers as she slowly eased down his zipper and then reached inside the opening. She tried releasing him but found his briefs to be in the way.

After a few failed efforts, he asked, "Need help?"

She didn't see amusement in his gaze, just gut-wrenching need. "Yes. Please."

He took one step back, and she watched as he pulled himself out of his pants. She sucked in a deep breath when she saw him and her mouth nearly dropped open. He was huge and had a condom in hand.

"Don't tempt me with an open mouth, baby," he said, easing on protection.

She closed it, and before she could think about anything, he moved back toward her. "Now lift up your skirt for me, Alpha."

She slowly inched up her skirt, giving him a view of her silk thigh-high stockings and lacy black panties. She wasn't sure what he'd planned to do next, but she hadn't expected him to reach out and tug her panties past her knees and down her legs.

"That's what I want to see," he said, staring at the throbbing flesh her panties had been hiding. "It's just like I thought it would be. You look beautiful there, and your color is natural."

Alpha swallowed hard. "Yes, of course. I've never dyed my hair."

As if seeing that part of her bared wasn't enough, he reached out and touched her, trailed fingers through the curls and all around her feminine folds, slipping one finger inside as if to test her wetness. Her legs automatically parted to give him better access. And he took it, penetrating his finger farther inside of her.

She heard him draw in a deep breath before he said, "Your scent is killing me." And when he removed his finger from inside of her and inserted it between his lips to suck on it, she got weak in the knees.

"And you taste good, too. I'm having you for breakfast in the morning."

Before she could figure out if he was serious or teasing, his hands went to her waist and he lifted her off her feet. "Wrap your legs around me," he instructed huskily.

She did so and the moment he lifted her body, she felt the head of his erection touch her. Easing her legs apart a little more, she sucked in hard when he thrust inside of her, clutching tight to her hips until he was fully embedded within her. She wasn't aware a man could go that deep.

"Now we dance this way," he said against her moist lips.

And they did. While the music played, he held her in his arms with her legs wrapped around him, supporting her weight while he was fully planted inside of her. She tightened her arms around his neck, swiveling her hips against him in tiny circles, keeping a sensuous beat with the music. Never had she danced with a man like this before. Rocking his body hard against hers and reminding her of just how buried he was inside of her. The intense penetration combined with the moves of their bodies to stimulate her with searing intensity. She closed her eyes as her nerve endings became more and more charged. Electrified. Intensified.

And then there was the scent of him, clean and masculine.

Whatever cologne he was wearing was a fragrance meant to drive a woman over the edge, and it was definitely doing a number on her. His hold on her thighs tightened even more, and the next thing she knew there was a hard wall against her back. She hadn't been aware they had moved away from that spot in the center of the room.

"I can't take you slow anymore," he growled seconds before he began thrusting in and out of her hard and fast, working his hips back and forth and side to side. She tightened her legs around him, convinced he was trying to drive her insane.

When she felt her body about to explode, she moaned his name and was just about to scream when his mouth lowered and planted firmly on hers.

But that didn't stop her body from splintering into a thousand pieces. And she knew the moment his detonated, as well. He thrust deeper, harder and she felt him, all the way to her womb. Her muscles squeezed him, were driven to hold him hostage inside of her.

This was incredible. He was incredible.

She reveled in the feel of his body in hers, the hardness of his chest against hers and how his firm, muscled thighs felt while keeping her propped up against the wall. She fought not to scream again but couldn't retain it, and once again his mouth was there to silence her.

Moments later, when he pulled his mouth away, dark eyes stared into hers and she read what his eyes were saying. *I want more.*

She mouthed her response. *Get all you want.*

He remained inside of her, staring down at her, until they were both able to breathe normally again. It was only then that he lowered her feet to the floor and leaned down to pull up her panties before rearranging her skirt, smoothing it over her hips and thighs. She then watched as he proceeded to tuck himself back inside his pants.

After rezipping, he glanced over at her. "Ready to go play Pleasure Games?"

"I'm more than ready," she said, as a satisfied smile touched her lips, although she wasn't sure just where she would find the energy to do such a thing.

He returned her smile. "I'll instruct Pierre to bring our coats. The sooner I get you to your house, the better."

Funny, she'd been thinking the same thing.

Ten

Riley had a tough time maintaining his self-control on the drive to Alpha's home mainly because she was deliberately making it hard for him. Instead of using his truck, he was driving his Lexus sports car. It was sleek and smooth and perfect for the classy woman sitting beside him. However, the car's intimacy was almost more than he could handle, especially since her scent was all over the place.

He glanced over at Alpha, knowing he should be keeping his eyes on the road. But he was finding it hard to do so when she was deliberately inching up her skirt to show a pair of luscious brown thighs. It didn't take much to remember how it felt being between those thighs, which made his erection hard with the anticipation of getting between them again.

He had enjoyed sharing dinner with her, had loved sitting across from her and watching her mouth move as she ate. Not for the first time, his head had been filled with thoughts of all the things he would love to see that mouth do to him.

But he would also admit he had enjoyed their conversation. Although he had pretty much gotten the hint that her past was not open for discussion, and he had told her early on that he didn't want them to discuss anything about the party, they had managed to find other things to talk about. Mainly movies they had seen, their thoughts about the ongoing war, the recent election and Hollywood scandals. He had been surprised to discover they had the same tastes and opinions about a number of things.

He'd also told her about his cousins in Atlanta, Texas and Montana, and how excited the family was about his cousin Megan's upcoming wedding in June, which meant the family would all be getting together again. And he shouldn't have been surprised when Alpha told him that Megan was considering her as a wedding planner and had interviewed her last week. Megan would be making her decision in a couple of weeks.

He told her about his great-grandfather, Raphel, and how Megan had hired a private investigator to find information about him, and how the two traveled to Texas to discover Raphel had a child before marrying Riley's great-grandmother, which meant the possibility of more Westmorelands somewhere.

He glanced around when traffic slowed down. He had decided to drive through town to hit the interstate, figuring there wouldn't be much traffic tonight. But that assumption had turned out to be wrong when he got caught up with people leaving a concert.

To get out of the mad rush he had taken another shortcut that carried him through another part of town known for its boutiques. Thanksgiving was just a few weeks away and already storefronts were all decked out for Christmas.

Riley glanced over at Alpha's thighs again. She had hiked up the hem of her skirt another inch or two. He loosened his tie when he brought the car to a traffic light and frowned over at her. "Be forewarned, Alpha. If tempted badly enough

I wouldn't hesitate to pull this car to the side of the road and take you again, here and now."

She threw her head back and laughed as if she couldn't imagine such a thing. The sound flowing from her throat stirred his blood and sent it straight to his groin.

"That should make interesting reading in the newspapers tomorrow morning if the sheriff or one of his deputies stumbles upon us," she replied smartly.

He held her gaze intensely. "Trust me, it won't make the papers. Dillon is best friends with Sheriff Harper and it wouldn't be the first Westmoreland he's come across on the side of the road."

She tilted her head. "Do tell. Is it something that runs in the family?"

He chuckled. "Only with Bane. I can't tell you the number of times Sheriff Harper brought Bane home after coming across him and Crystal parked somewhere."

"Crystal?"

Riley frowned. "Yes, Crystal Newsome, Bane's obsession. Maybe I should say they were equally obsessed with each other."

He decided to keep talking, figuring it would take his mind off getting under her skirt. "Crystal and Bane have been under each other's skin since they were kids. It would drive Mr. Newsome bonkers, not just because Bane was four years older than Crystal but because Crystal told anyone who wanted to listen—and even those who didn't—that she wanted Bane and vice versa, even when they were too young to think about wanting anyone. Mr. Newsome was totally against a union between his daughter and a Westmoreland."

"Why?"

He shrugged. "Something that happened years ago with our grandfathers, resulting in a grudge that ran deep. It was unfortunate for Crystal and Bane."

"What happened?" Alpha asked curiously.

"Carl Newsome got tired of Crystal climbing out of her bedroom window in the dead of night or cutting school just to be with Bane. Since Crystal was a minor, at fifteen, and Bane was nineteen, old man Newsome got a restraining order against Bane. If Bane came within a mile of Crystal he would go to jail. Well, Bane, being the hardheaded badass that he is, shrugged off the old man's threat and he and Crystal would sneak around. They did it for years, and then one night when Bane was twenty-two and Crystal not yet eighteen, they eloped."

"Eloped?"

"Yes, but they were found before they could tie the knot." At least that's the story Bane had told them. Riley often wondered if that was the case.

"Anyway," Riley continued, "they returned home and old man Newsome sent Crystal away to live with some relative, and Dillon talked to Bane about getting himself together by making something of himself instead of being a troublemaker."

Riley paused a moment and then said, "Losing Crystal almost destroyed Bane since he didn't have a clue where she'd gone. Her father made sure of that. We were able to talk Bane into not going after Crystal...at least until he made something of himself and both he and Crystal matured. Bane eventually joined the navy and is working toward being a SEAL."

"Do you think he'll eventually go after Crystal? Find her?"

Riley's frown deepened. "There's no doubt in my mind that he will."

She arched her brow. "You don't seem too happy with the thought of him doing that."

He thought she was very observant. "To be quite honest, I'm not. That whole Crystal thing, with her leaving Denver for parts unknown, nearly destroyed Bane. It's like Crystal is in his blood and he refuses to purge her out of it. She's a part of him that he can't let go of."

He didn't say anything for a long moment. "So yes, Bane will go looking for her one day and he *will* find her. What worries me is the possibility that he will get hurt all over again when he does. For all any of us know, Crystal might have moved on with her life and Bane is just a memory."

As he continued to drive, he decided not to talk anymore for a while. He didn't want anything to ruin his night and thinking of Bane and Crystal would do that for him.

But then maybe he should think about them and, more specifically, recall his brother's agony. Doing so would reinforce the reasons why he would never fall in love with a woman. He refused to ever go through that much pain.

He glanced back over at Alpha. She was quiet, as if she was thinking hard about something. He hoped like hell she wasn't having second thoughts about tonight. He eased out a deep breath when he turned on her street. His overnight bag was in the trunk. When he walked into her house, he intended to stay.

Thoughts of what she and Riley had done back at the restaurant filled Alpha's mind. That had been some dance. She doubted she would ever forget it. While in his arms and connected to him that way, it was as if nothing or no one else existed but the two of them. She'd felt as though the two of them were in their own little world. Never had she done anything so impulsive and spontaneous, so scandalous and wild.

And when they had made love, against the wall of all places, she'd felt sensations take over her body that she'd never felt before. Was this a sample of what she should come to expect from Riley? Anything but the norm? She had a feeling that with him there would never be a dull moment. He had promised her pleasure, and more pleasure, and so far he was right on point.

No man had ever made love to her that way, with such intensity and completeness. And just to think, there was more where that had come from. A lot more.

She blinked when she saw they had arrived at her house already and looked over at Riley when he brought the car to a stop in her driveway. She saw dark, penetrating eyes staring at her. She wondered if there would ever come a day when she would look into his eyes and not get turned on, not feel those incredible sensations flowing through her body.

Without saying anything, he leaned over, unbuckled her seat belt and then reached up and cupped her chin in his hand. "I enjoyed making love to you, Alpha. And I won't apologize for how it happened or where it happened."

She held his gaze. Did he assume the reason she had gotten quiet was because she'd begun having regrets? She held his gaze. "I don't want you to apologize. I asked for it." She chuckled. "You definitely gave me what I wanted, Riley." *What I needed,* she thought.

"Happy to please you, sweetheart."

She didn't have time to think about how easily that term of endearment had rolled off his lips before he was kissing her with an intensity that set her loins on fire. What was there about him that could arouse her so easily, to the point where he had her not only throwing caution to the wind, but also flying in the wind? He had her wanting to try things she'd never thought about doing before.

He slowly ended the kiss, pulled back and stared at her. She felt the intensity of his gaze all the way to the bone. "You had me worried for a minute, when you got quiet on me," he said.

She smiled. "I was merely relishing those moments."

He seemed pleased with what she'd said. "Then let me give you even more of them." He opened the car door and trotted around to her side of the car.

Alpha had a vague memory of him walking her to the front door. And then there was the moment when she'd found it difficult to insert her key into the lock until Riley had eased the key from her nervous hands.

He opened the door and moved aside for her to enter. When she crossed the foyer to the living room, she removed her coat and hung it on the rack before placing her purse on the coffee table. She glanced across the room and saw the fire still kindling in the fireplace, giving the room a warm, toasty feel. She was about to turn to ask Riley if he wanted something to drink when she felt his heat directly behind her. He wrapped his arms around her and pulled her back toward him. Immediately, she felt his aroused body pressed against her backside.

His heated breath touched the side of her face when he whispered, "I want to make love to you in front of the fireplace."

He eased his hold on her so she could turn around in his arms and she stared up into his face. "Sounds like a good plan to me." She leaned forward on tiptoes and slanted her mouth across his.

She wanted to initiate this kiss, master it the best way she knew how, and she figured if she let her tongue do the work that she would be fine. So she kissed him, trying to recall the ways his tongue had driven her crazy. She wanted him to see just how it felt to be on the receiving end this time.

So she feasted on his mouth and he stood there, rock solid, legs braced apart with his arms around her waist, and let her have her way with him. Never had a man's mouth tasted so good. She was enjoying herself so much that she couldn't help moaning in pleasure.

Then, suddenly, she found herself hauled against his hard chest as he took over the kiss, plundering her mouth with his demanding tongue. Desire took over her senses and sent fire through her, blazing hotter than the one in the fireplace.

After that, she couldn't recall how her clothes were removed. The only thing she recalled was being naked while watching in fervent anticipation as he removed his clothes.

When he had taken off the final stitch she couldn't do anything but simply stare. She had seen his erection at the restaurant, but now she was getting a view of the entire picture—the curly strands of dark hair covering his broad chest, rock-hard biceps, lean hips, sinewy thighs and muscled shoulders. But still, her gaze returned to his middle and she couldn't move her eyes away.

She could clearly see that he'd put on a new condom, and when he moved his powerfully built, masculine, naked body toward her, she couldn't help asking, "You do that often?"

"Do what?" he asked coming to a stop directly in front of her, easing his thigh between hers and wrapping his arms around her waist. His action caused her to lose her train of thought for a moment.

He leaned in close, brushed his lips across hers and asked again, "Do what often?"

"Carry a condom with you all the time."

Riley chuckled. "I don't carry one *all* the time, just when I know how the night's going to end. But in some cases, making love might very well be the beginning. I almost lost my head once and messed up and figured I would never come close to letting something like that happen again. It's better to be safe than sorry."

She could arrest his concerns and admit to being on birth control but she knew that with some men it wouldn't matter. They had to have their own form of protection as well, since pregnancy wasn't the only thing a person had to be concerned with.

He leaned in close and nuzzled his nose in her hair. "Mmm, you smell good all over."

His words reclaimed her attention and she lifted her head so she could meet his eyes. "Thanks. So do you."

Riley took a swipe across her lips with his tongue. "You taste good, as well…and I intend to taste you all over, starting now."

Then he claimed her mouth again, just as greedy as before, demolishing any and all of her coherent thoughts. Each and every kiss they shared was more powerful, commanding and potent than the one before it and this one was no different. His mouth ravaged hers, and she couldn't help the moans of pleasure coming from deep within her throat. The man was a great kisser, and he definitely knew how to use that tongue of his.

Being so enmeshed in sharing this heated kiss with Riley, she wasn't aware that they had sunk to their knees in front of the fireplace until he pulled his mouth away and she saw the room beyond his shoulders.

But that observation was short-lived. His mouth left hers to trail kisses along her lips and nibble the sensitive flesh around her mouth. She slid her hand up and down his chest, liking the feel of the curly hair beneath her fingers. She threw her head back when he began sucking her neck then moved slowly down to her shoulder blades. On instinct, she arched backward to rest on her elbows, which caused her breasts to rise upward and her hips to lift off the hearth rug.

His warm breath caressed the side of her face when he whispered, "I love you in this position, and I'm about to show you why."

Riley was convinced he had never wanted any woman this much. Everything about Alpha was perfect, from the smooth slope of her chest, which held two of the most beautiful breasts he'd ever seen, to her firm stomach, curvy hips and thighs and long, shapely legs with gorgeous calves.

Not holding back, he swooped a nipple into his mouth and began sucking on it intensely, hungrily, displaying the voracious sexual appetite that he had for her. With his mouth still clamped to her nipple, he began moving his hand, letting it roam everywhere, but definitely making a path toward the juncture of her thighs. His finger slid inside, finding her not just wet but drenched. Her hum of pleasure drove him to penetrate deeper and massage her clitoris with circular strokes.

"What are you doing to me, Riley?"

He figured he could ask her the same thing. The womanly scent emanating from her tempted him to eat her alive. It was such a luscious, feminine fragrance.

He released her nipple and before moving to latch on to the other, he glanced up at her and said, "I'm giving you pleasure. I also intend to pay you back for tempting me in the car."

"What did I do?"

"You deliberately flashed me some thigh. Not that I mind. But it was a hard drive back to your place. No pun intended."

Deciding he didn't want to talk any longer, he began giving her other breast the same ardent attention. He felt her hand on his head, rubbing gently. And she was shoving her breast deeper into his mouth. He didn't have a problem with either movement.

The more he devoured her breasts and inhaled her scent the more he was thrown into a sexual frenzy. He pulled back, smiled up at her flushed face, the heavy-lidded eyes staring back at him. Seeing her so stimulated plunged him into primitive desire, as raw as it could get.

He began licking his way down her body, liking the feel of his tongue on her skin. And when he dipped his head between her legs and replaced his fingers with his tongue, she cried out riotously while digging her nails into his back.

He ignored the pain as he lapped her up, using his tongue to pleasure her the way he'd done in his dreams. He held tight to her hips when she moved them from side to side, gyrating against his mouth. He heard her moans, and they were sensual music to his ears.

The trembling of her thighs was the first sign that an explosion was on the horizon, and when she released a deep, throaty groan followed by a hell-wrenching scream, his tongue penetrated deeper within her womanly folds. She pushed her hips upward even more, calling his name.

By the time she lay whimpering softly, he had stretched to settle between her legs. "Alpha?"

She slowly opened her eyes and gazed up at him. A shiver of some unknown force passed through him, gripped him within its clutches. The reflections from the blaze in the fireplace danced across her naked skin, making her even more beautiful. Desirable.

Alpha reached up and cradled his face in her hands. "That was incredible," she whispered.

He wanted to tell her no, that she was incredible. But instead, while still gazing into her eyes, he lifted her hips with his hands and entered her with one smooth thrust.

"Riley!"

"I'm here, baby, and tonight I intend to ride you hard all over the place."

And then he began moving, thrusting within her like the demented sexual maniac that he felt like tonight. The room was filled with the sound of flesh slapping against flesh, moans and groans, and with him whispering words to her that were erotic and wicked.

Then, for the third time that night, he felt her body explode as her inner muscles clenched him hard. He threw his head back and growled her name as he continued to plow her with deep, hard strokes.

He felt his own body shatter and fought to hold it together and couldn't. No orgasm should be this powerful, this mindblowing, this dominating.

That's the one thing he couldn't let happen. He couldn't let any woman dominate him in any way. He refused to be another Bane. He forced the thought from his mind, deciding no domination would be taking place tonight. He was getting paranoid. He figured over-the-top sex could do that to a man. And this definitely had been over-the-top. She had blasted them off the Richter scale, hands down.

He continued to ride her hard while she wrapped her legs tightly around him. He took her mouth and kissed her with more hunger than he'd ever felt for a woman. His tongue was commanding and demanding as an orgasm continued to rip through him, flinging him to a universe unknown.

The fire roared in the fireplace when a short while later he settled on his back and pulled Alpha into his arms, trying to get their breathing and heartbeats back to normal. He wrapped his arms around her, needing to hold her this way. Not fully understanding why, but just knowing that he did.

She raised her head and looked over at him. "Riley?"

"Hmm?"

She opened her mouth to say something and then, as if she thought better of it, closed her eyes and shook her head. "Nothing."

He lifted a brow. "You sure?"

She nodded. "Yes." She then settled into his arms, snuggling close.

He entwined her legs with his and tightened his hold on her, wondering what she'd been about to say. He glanced down and saw she had dozed off already, breathing gently. Reaching up, he pulled the afghan off the sofa and draped it over their naked bodies.

They would sleep awhile and then wake up and make love some more.

Eleven

"Hey, what did you do this weekend, Alpha? You can barely keep your eyes open. I don't ever recall you being so exhausted."

Alpha took a sip of her coffee as she looked across the table at Lindsey. Her assistant was right; she'd never been this exhausted. But then she'd never had to deal with the likes of Riley Westmoreland before, either.

It had been one heck of a weekend. He hadn't just spent the night with her on Saturday, but had stayed Sunday night, as well. To say it had been wild was an understatement. No matter how many hot baths she'd taken, she couldn't completely work the soreness out of muscles she hadn't used in a long time, if ever. And her hair—for crying out loud, ever since Riley had said he liked it down, that's how she'd worn it. It had been down all weekend, even when it had begun looking tousled and disheveled. When she had mentioned how crazy she must look, he'd said she didn't look crazy, just wildly sexy.

She was convinced Riley had a mental manual in his head

of every sexual position known to mankind and some he probably conjured up himself. He had names for all of them. There had been the Electric Slide, the Ball Game, London Bridge and Sweet Seat, just to name a few. And after kissing her, before leaving this morning, he had assured her with that sexy smile of his that there were plenty more where those had come from.

Needless to say, in one single weekend, the man had given her more orgasms than she'd gotten in her entire life. There had definitely been no climax control. How he stayed up she wasn't sure, but at no time did he go soft on her. He was always forever-ready.

"Alpha," Lindsey said, popping her finger in front of Alpha's face. "Come back down to earth. And why the heavy breathing? Are you all right?"

Alpha set her coffee cup down and smiled at Lindsey. "I'm fine but I admit to feeling tired."

Lindsey scooted back. "You might be coming down with something, so if you don't mind, I'd rather not catch it. With three little ones at home, that would be disastrous."

Alpha nodded, deciding not to tell Lindsey what she had wasn't contagious…unless your bedroom was invaded by the likes of Riley Westmoreland.

Besides, as much as they needed to go over the decorations they'd decided on for the party, she wasn't fully concentrating anyway. "Yes, maybe I need to go back to bed and get some rest after all."

"Sure, but just so you know, I think your decoration ideas are going to wow everyone that night. When do you meet up with Riley Westmoreland again to go over everything?"

Alpha drew in a deep breath. She hadn't a clue. Riley had decided that unless it was a scheduled business meeting, their time together was not about discussing business. Their time was strictly used for pleasure. "I'll probably meet with him in a week or so."

A half hour later Alpha was preparing to take a nap when her phone rang. Her heartbeat kicked up a notch at the thought that the caller might be Riley. She picked up the phone and tried to hide her disappointment when she saw the caller was not Riley, but was, of all people, Eddie. Why was he calling her? It had been more than a year since they had spoken last. She was certain he had gotten on with his life like she had gotten on with hers.

She started not to answer but curiosity had her clicking on the line. "Yes?"

"Alpha, this is Eddie."

"Yes, I know. Your name came up on Caller-ID. This is a surprise."

"Yes. I ran into your father the other day when I took Cleo in."

"Okay."

"I asked your dad about you. I'd heard you moved to Colorado."

"Yes, I'm living in Denver. I love it here."

He chuckled. "But I'm sure you hate the weather. You and I both know you don't like anything cold."

He was right. So why had she tolerated *him* for so long? It had taken spending time with Riley to realize Eddie had been as cold as a dead fish. "Yes, well, sometimes we learn to tolerate things that aren't good for us."

He didn't say anything for a moment and then, "I'll be in Denver on business next week and I'd like to see you while I'm out there."

She lifted a brow. "Why? Nothing has changed, Eddie. I didn't go along with your ultimatum, and there was nothing left to be said."

"I'm beginning to think that's not the case."

Not the case? She held the phone away from her ear and stared at it. Was she really talking to Eddie? The man who hadn't hesitated to dump her a week before their wedding because she wouldn't let him control her? "Well, I know that *is* the case. You made your decision."

"Yes, but since you and your twin aren't on speaking terms…"

Not on speaking terms? Where in the world did he get such erroneous information? "That's not true. Omega and I are closer than ever. Where did you hear such a ridiculous thing?"

He didn't say anything for a minute. "From your father. And even if it isn't true, I think that it should be."

Anger flared up within her when she heard the sharpness in his voice. "And what if I told you that I don't give a royal damn what you think? Now, goodbye and please don't bother calling me again."

She hung up the phone, furious with herself for answering Eddie's call in the first place. He hadn't changed. He still expected her to adhere to his wishes like a good little girl. The man just didn't get it.

As she crawled on top of the bed for her nap, she couldn't help but recall that the last time she'd been in it, Riley had been with her. Shifting, she pushed a wayward curl from her face as she lay on her side with her head resting on her hands, wondering how long it would take for the soreness to work itself out of her body. When she picked up Riley's scent, which was entrenched on the pillow, she closed her eyes, remembering the weekend. As desire gripped her… of all places…between her sore legs, she knew she couldn't wait to see him again.

After his meeting, Riley made it back to his office with both Canyon and Stern on his heels. He went straight to his desk, sat down and sent both brothers a questioning look. They were standing in the middle of his office with smirks on their faces.

"Okay, what's going on with you two?" he asked.

Stern crossed his arms over his chest and chuckled. "We

should be asking you what's going on. You could barely keep your eyes open during that meeting with Dillon. We expected him to call you out for dozing."

Riley rubbed a frustrated hand down his face. Had he really dozed off in one of Dillon's meetings? Especially one that Dillon had specifically come into the office to hold with them?

"You must have had one hell of a weekend, Ry," Canyon said, eyeing him curiously. "I dropped by Riley's Station a couple of times and it was apparent you weren't home. That means you were gone *all* weekend. Must be some hot number you're seeing."

Straightening in his seat, Riley picked up a file off his desk. Instead of responding to Canyon's comment, he said, "Don't you guys have other things to do? Because if you don't, I do."

"Will you be able to stay awake long enough to do any work?" Stern asked, grinning.

He was about to tell his brother where he could go…in not-so-nice words…when there was a quick knock at the door just before Dillon walked in. He smiled when he saw his three brothers. "Good, all three of you are here. I just got a call from Mack Owens. He's ready to sell that piece of land we've had our eyes on for a strip mall in Memphis. The trip will last until Sunday since Mack and his wife are hosting a dinner party Saturday night. Which one of you wants to go and close the deal with Mack?"

Riley could see both Stern and Canyon easing toward the door. Evidently they had hot dates for the weekend. But then so did he. He had invited Alpha to the movies Saturday night. He was about to tell Dillon he had plans but quickly changed his mind. Dillon was depending on them to keep things running smoothly while he was away from the office. And if Canyon and Stern had other plans that meant things fell on his shoulders. Going to Tennessee wouldn't be so bad if he could talk Alpha into going with him.

"I'll be able to go to Memphis, Dil. When do you need me to leave?"

"Thursday, if possible."

Riley nodded. "Okay, I don't see a problem." He glanced over at Canyon and Stern and took note of their relieved expressions. They owed him big-time.

"Good." Dillon headed for the door but then suddenly turned back around. "You're evidently keeping late hours someplace, Ry. I suggest that you get some rest."

Ignoring the "we told you so" grins on Stern's and Canyon's faces, he said, "I will."

When Dillon left, Riley glared at his brothers. "The only reason I decided to go to Tennessee is because the two of you evidently had important plans for this weekend."

Canyon waved off his words. "We do, and we appreciate you being the sacrificial lamb this time. Mack Owens has a tendency to bore you to tears."

"Whatever. Now will the two of you leave so I can get some work done?"

Moments later, after his brothers had cleared out of his office, Riley leaned back in his chair, finding it hard to believe he'd actually dozed off during one of Dillon's meetings. There was no excuse for that. However, he would be the first to admit he'd experienced one hell of a weekend. It had been simply incredible. He closed his eyes as erotic memories flowed through his mind.

First, he and Alpha had made love in front of the fireplace, then when they'd gotten hungry they went into the kitchen for a snack and ended up making love in there, as well. He had introduced her to the Courting Chair position. Never before had he enjoyed making love to a woman who was not only open to trying different things but was as exciting, energetic and beautiful as any woman could be.

He reached for the phone, but then hung it up before the first ring. He would wait until later tonight to call her when he could be assured there would not be any interruptions.

He opened the file in the middle of his desk, hoping that Alpha would agree to go with him to Tennessee. If she did, he would certainly make the trip worth her while. He would guarantee it.

Later that night, Alpha sat on the sofa going through her book of party favors. Since this would be the fortieth anniversary of Blue Ridge, the Westmorelands wanted each attendee to leave with a favor that would remind them not only of the significance of that night, but also of the party theme. She had marked a few items she thought would be perfect and still within the budget. The vendors she'd spoken with had pretty much guaranteed everything would arrive well in advance of the party date.

A log broke in the fireplace and the pop made her look up. It was then that she remembered making love to Riley, right there in front of the fireplace on the hearth rug. It had been simply amazing, and the memory caused flutters in her stomach. But then, she thought, every time they'd made love had been off the charts.

She stood and stretched, feeling well rested after her nap. She wasn't as sore as she'd been that morning, which she thought was a good thing. Tomorrow she had an eleven o'clock appointment with the granddaughter of a couple who would be celebrating their seventieth wedding anniversary on Valentine's Day. And on Wednesday she would be meeting with a woman who was giving herself a fiftieth birthday party in April.

Omega had called a few hours ago, wanting to know everything about her weekend with Riley. Of course Alpha hadn't told her sister every little detail, but she'd shared enough for Omega to draw her own conclusions about how well her weekend had gone. She hadn't mentioned Eddie's call, since she didn't want to upset her sister. But Alpha intended to talk to her father, who apparently had encouraged Eddie's call.

She was about to head to the kitchen for a cup of hot chocolate when her cell phone rang. She leaned down to pick it up off the table. "Hello."

"You've really done it this time, Alpha. The only reason Eddie called you was because I talked to him that day and told him you would love hearing from him."

Alpha drew in a deep breath upon hearing her father's voice. "You had no right to tell him Omega and I weren't speaking when you know that is not true, Dad. Things are over between Eddie and me. Why can't you accept that?"

"He'd take you back if you got your act together and did what he's asking. You shouldn't let your sister come between you and the man you love."

Alpha gritted her teeth, trying to hold back from telling her father just how wrong and unfair he was, and had always been, to his other child.

"I'll let you go so you can think about it, Al." She then heard a click in her ear. She shook her head. Not for the first time, her father had hung up on her.

Her phone rang. And not for the first time he would call her right back to give her more of an earful, but she had news for him. She clicked on the phone. "Listen, Dad. No matter what you want, Eddie and I are not getting back together. I'm seeing someone else now, and he's more of a man than Eddie will ever be."

There was a moment of silence and then a deep, husky voice said, "I'm glad you think so."

Alpha closed her eyes. *Ah, hell.*

"Alpha?"

She had gotten quiet on him, Riley thought. He didn't know what had prompted her to pick up the phone and say what she had, but evidently she and her father had been having quite an interesting conversation before he'd called. And evidently her father was a huge supporter of her ex-fiancé.

"Yes?"

"Are you okay?" he asked with concern in his voice.

"Yes. Sorry about that. I thought you were my father calling back."

"I see." He waited to see if she would expound on that. Instead, she changed the subject by saying, "I'm surprised you called. I hadn't expected to hear from you until the weekend."

"Yes, that had been my plan but something has come up. I'll be leaving town on Thursday for Memphis and won't be back until Sunday."

"Oh."

Was that disappointment he heard in her voice? "I was calling to let you know and to see if you wanted to go to Memphis with me."

There was a pause and then, "You want me to go out of town with you?"

"Yes. I have a meeting Friday morning and will be attending a social event Saturday night. I'd like you to be there with me. However, if you can't clear your calendar on such short notice, I understand."

"No, I'd love to go."

Riley released a breath he'd just realized he'd been holding. "That's great. We'll fly out around noon on Thursday. Have you ever been to Memphis before?"

"No."

"Then I'm going to enjoy showing you around. I've been there a number of times."

"Sounds like fun. I look forward to going."

There was another reason he had called. One that had concerned him since leaving her. "Are you okay? When I left you this morning you were quite sore." He, of all people, had been aware of the intensity of their lovemaking, but it was as if they hadn't been able to get enough of each other.

"Yes, I'm fine."

"Good." For some reason, he wasn't ready to end the call yet. "So what did you do today?"

He listened as she talked, liking the way she sounded. He had come home, showered and was sitting in his living room on the sofa with his legs stretched out in front of him, alone in the dark, talking to her. He had stopped by his brother Jason's place for dinner, and had enjoyed the time he spent with Jason's wife, Bella, and the twins.

"I'm glad you were able to take a long nap," he said, wishing he could have been there to take the nap with her. He had ended up leaving the office earlier than usual to go to the gym. It had taken a good workout to get his adrenaline flowing again. And talking to her now was a definite boost. There was nothing else he'd rather be doing. *Monday Night Football* couldn't even compete.

They talked for a while longer, and she did sneak in information about the favors she'd come across that she thought would be perfect for the party. They continued talking about some of everything, including which NFL team they thought would make it to the Super Bowl.

All too soon he glanced at the clock on the table and saw it was after midnight. "Sorry," he said, standing to stretch.

"What are you apologizing for?"

"For the third night straight I've kept you up late." He was certain he didn't have to remind her of what they'd been doing those other two nights around this time.

"No apology needed, Riley."

He liked the way she'd said his name just now. He liked it even better when she screamed it in the middle of an orgasm. And she'd done that a lot over the weekend. "Well, I'm not going to keep you. I enjoyed talking to you tonight. And I'm looking forward to our trip to Memphis."

"I enjoyed talking to you as well and can't wait until we leave on Thursday."

By the time he had ended the call, Riley knew the one thing was happening that he hadn't intended to happen.

Alpha Blake was getting under his skin.

Twelve

"Welcome to the Peabody, Mr. and Mrs. Westmoreland."

Alpha tried to keep a straight face when she heard the hotel clerk's erroneous assumption. She glanced over at Riley, who was standing beside her, and wondered if he would correct the man. He didn't. Instead, he smiled and winked at her.

"Thank you," he said, accepting the passkey.

"I hope your stay here is a great one," the man added.

"I'm sure that it will be."

Taking Alpha's hand in his, Riley led her to the bank of elevators. As they waited, he leaned in close and whispered, "He made an honest mistake."

She nodded, not saying anything because she didn't see how the man could have made that mistake when neither she nor Riley had rings on their fingers. When the elevator arrived, they stepped inside along with several others. Every aspect of the hotel was gorgeous, even right down to the spacious and elegantly designed elevator car. She tried concentrating on the small television screen mounted above the door. Everyone's attention was glued to the commentary. Everyone's except hers and Riley's.

Their attention was on each other and had been since he'd picked her up to take her to the airport. He'd carried her luggage out to his truck, but not before kissing her in a way that had made her panties wet.

Now, the elevator stopped on the fifth floor and she moved aside to let a couple off. She immediately felt the warm rush of blood that flowed through her veins when Riley placed his arms around her waist and pulled her closer to his side.

When the elevator reached their floor, he led her out. Holding her hand, he walked beside her down the beautifully decorated corridor to their room. Although there hadn't been a discussion about it, she and Riley would be sharing a room. She hadn't thought of staying anywhere else.

They came to a stop and Riley let go of her hand to open the door. With an efficiency she wasn't surprised he had, he opened the door and then stood aside for her to enter.

She walked into the room and looked around. It was a beautiful suite, almost as large as her home. She was about to tell Riley just how beautiful the room was when strong arms encircled her waist and turned her around.

The eyes staring down at her were so full of need and desire that it sent a sensuous shudder through her. It didn't take much to recall all they'd done the last time they were together. A replay of those vivid erotic images had done a number on her mind all week.

"I missed you this week," he said huskily.

She couldn't help the smile that touched her lips. It was nice knowing she was missed. She had definitely missed him, as well. "You know where I live," she said teasingly.

He chuckled softly. "Yes, and trust me, not paying you a visit was one of the hardest things I've ever done. But your body needed a time-out. It had quite a workout last weekend."

"Now that's an understatement," she said, her smile widening.

He didn't say anything and she could have sworn she saw a guarded look in his eyes, but then he leaned in closer and asked, "Have I told you how much I like you?"

"No, I don't believe you have."

"Well, let me go on record by saying, I like you, Alpha Blake. Probably more so than I should."

She was about to ask what he meant by that when he quickly said, "Come on, we need to get out of this room. Let's do dinner and then a night of blues on Beale Street."

A few hours later, while walking down Beale Street, Riley couldn't help glancing over at the woman walking beside him, the woman whose hand was firmly held in his. When was the last time he and any woman had walked down a street holding hands?

Never.

So why was he doing so now? Sex with no commitment was just what it sounded like. No strings attached. No reason to lie and promise the moon, the stars or the sky. And no drama, since he'd laid out the rules. Why weren't they up in the hotel room making out since that's all their relationship was supposed to be?

He drew in a deep breath. And when was the last time he'd gone barhopping? Yet here he was, strolling down Beale Street, going from club to club, bar to bar, while holding hands with a woman he'd confessed to liking.

But what really riled him up was that he'd gotten angry when he'd seen a couple of guys checking her out at one of the clubs. He would be the first to admit she looked damn good in her jeans, but still. Why had he gotten jealous? It wasn't as if he had a serious relationship going on with Alpha. She was merely his sex partner for six weeks.

"This place is wonderful," she said, breaking into his

thoughts. Excitement and gaiety shone in her eyes. "I've really never appreciated the blues until now. Thanks."

His hand tightened around hers. "I should be thanking you. If you weren't here I would be up in my hotel room on my laptop getting a start on next week's work. You've turned what probably would have been a boring trip into a fun one."

She threw her head back and laughed before arching a perfect brow. "Truly you don't want me to believe that Riley Westmoreland would not have had fun without me?"

Yes, he wanted her to believe it because it was true. Yes, he would have had some degree of fun, but not like this. They had enjoyed some fabulous foods, had taken over the dance floor a few times and he'd even talked her into karaoke, a Billie Holiday number.

He stopped walking, reached out and lifted her chin with his fingertip. "I never say anything I don't mean, Alpha, and this is the most fun I've ever had with any woman."

She slid her hand up over his chest. "I'm glad."

He was tempted to kiss her but held back. There would be plenty of time for kisses when he got her back to their hotel room. Tightening her hand in his once more, he began walking again.

He glanced over at her. "So what are your plans tomorrow while I'm in my meetings?"

She leaned up on tiptoe, nuzzled her nose in the side of his face and whispered, "Depends on how well you wear me out tonight. If I'm up to it, I plan to go shopping. Christmas is next month, you know."

Yes, he knew, and they would have ended their affair by then. "You got a lot of people to buy for?" he asked.

"Umm, just the usual."

She was being evasive again. "You plan on going home for Christmas or staying in Denver?"

"Haven't decided yet."

"Does your family get together for the holidays?" he asked

her, holding tight to her hand and looking both ways before they crossed the street.

"No, not everyone." Then, as if she wanted to get a question of her own in, she quickly asked, "What about with your family? Will everyone be home for Christmas?"

"This Christmas, yes, mainly because of the holiday party, with it being the fortieth anniversary and all. I believe our parents, aunt and uncle would have wanted us all together, celebrating something that major. Bane won't be able to make it since he's on assignment someplace, but Gemma and her family are coming from Australia."

"Sounds like the Westmorelands will be having a fun time. And as the event planner for the holiday party, I intend to make it a night to remember." She smiled over at him.

He returned her smile. "I believe it." And he did. On the plane, she had gone over her decorating ideas with him and he could tell she was a person who was on top of every single detail.

"So what about it?"

He blinked, aware that Alpha had asked him something. "Sorry, what did you say?"

She smiled and the warmth of that smile filled him with something he couldn't name. She leaned closer to him. "I suggested that we call it a night and head back to our hotel. Are you okay with that?"

Instead of answering her, he stepped off the sidewalk and pulled her into the shadows where two buildings connected. They could still partially be seen but he didn't care. He pulled her body to his, lowered his mouth and kissed her—long, hard and deep, tangling his tongue with hers.

Moments later, he released her mouth and pressed his forehead to hers. "Did you get the answer you wanted just now?" he asked slowly, trying to catch his breath.

He felt the curve of her smile against his lips. "Most definitely."

* * *

There was no doubt in Alpha's mind, as she watched a naked Riley stride out of the bathroom, that he was what any woman would consider a hottie of mega proportions. And speaking of proportions... Her gaze lowered to his middle. He was aroused and had already sheathed his thick erection in a condom. Her gaze stayed glued to that part of him as he approached the bed.

He caressed the side of her face with his finger.

"Why are you staring at me like that? You don't think what I'm packing is real?"

She looked up at him. "Oh, I know it's real. I'm just wondering how it tastes."

She saw the flash of intense desire fill his eyes, making them dark orbs of heated lust and her heart started racing wildly. She'd never been so bold with a man before. It was almost unbelievable how comfortable she felt with Riley, to the point where she would say just about anything.

He held her gaze and then said in a low tone, "Then I guess I'll let you find out."

He moved his hand from her face, and she watched as he slowly, methodically, removed the condom and dropped it in the wastepaper basket near the bed. He then looked at her. "Now what do you want me to do?" he asked.

She scooted over in the huge bed and patted a spot. "I want you here. On your back."

The bed dipped beneath his weight as he joined her, lying flat on his back as she'd instructed. She then eased between his thighs, lifting them up so his knees braced both sides of her head. On her knees, she smiled down at him. "I'm sure there's a name for this position already, right?"

He swallowed deeply before nodding. "Heels Over Head."

Alpha nodded. "Sounds appropriate." She then eased her head down to his aroused shaft. He was huge. Gigantic. And the veins running along the engorged head were so eas-

ily visible that she swore she could see the blood rushing
through them.

She touched him and appreciated the solid weight she held
in her hand. He was so large it took both hands to hold him—
definitely a handful—and she figured that he would be a
mouthful, as well. She was about to find out.

Alpha opened her mouth over the head of his penis and
her tongue swiped across it before fully taking him in. And
once her lips locked down on him, she went to work, licking
every inch of him, loving his taste. His masculine moans of
sexual gratification made her feel totally feminine.

He gripped several locks of her hair but she felt no pain,
only pleasure. He had a unique way of educating her and
satisfying her needs at the same time. Describing what he
would be doing to her in vivid detail was just as arousing as
him actually doing it.

That was one of the reasons she wanted to make this special for him. He probably could tell she was a novice, but
hopefully he would see that at least her heart was in it. And
the thought that his heavy shaft was fully lodged in her mouth
was a total turn-on for her. From the sounds he was making,
he apparently liked everything she was doing. Encouraged
by his response, she closed her eyes and turned up the heat,
intent on satisfying her man.

Her man?

Where had that thought come from? But instead of dismissing it totally, she accepted that for all of six weeks, he
would be her man. And then on the night of the holiday party,
her fantasy fling would come to an end.

"Alpha…"

Her name, growled from deep within his throat, filled her
with intense desire. She knew every long lick of her tongue,
and the deep suction she was applying, was sending him over
the edge just the way she wanted.

She opened her eyes when she felt a hard tug on her hair,

as he tried to get her mouth off him, but she held tight. He finally gave up and let go. She tasted the essence of him as he filled her mouth.

Moments later she released him and before she could say how tasty he was, he rolled over, pulled her down to her stomach and straddled her back. With his legs tucked between hers, he lifted her hips. In one smooth thrust, he entered her, going as deep as he could. He then leaned down close and whispered against the back of her neck, "This is called Inside Out."

She soon found out why when he began thrusting in and out of her hard, extending as far as her womb and then back again. She felt him in every stroke, and it was only then that she realized he wasn't wearing a condom.

"Riley, the condom!"

He went still. But she didn't. At least not on the inside where her muscles continued to clench him, milking him hard. His deep growl sent sensations through her pelvis, electrifying her spine. She expected him to pull out immediately but instead he leaned down so close that she felt his heated breath against her ear. "Please tell me you're on the pill or something, baby."

His plea was tortured and she was more than happy to erase his concerns. "Yes, I'm on the pill."

As if that was what he needed to hear, he began moving again, with even more urgency than before, stroking her deeply, growling like a primitive animal performing his last mating ritual. She felt him in every muscle of her body and shivers of pleasure rammed up and down her spine with every hard thrust. Then she felt him explode deep in her womb. His hand cupped tight to her bare bottom, tilted it at an angle that hit a spot that sent her screaming. She buried her head in the pillow to smother the sound, but it did nothing to the sensations ripping her apart. On top of everything, she felt his mouth on her back, nibbling her skin, licking it, nibbling some more. Branding her.

"Riley!"

Her body began quaking, all the way to her toes. Sensations overtook her. Pure feminine satisfaction tore through her, and she shivered with an intensity that shook the entire bed as pent-up passion was released from deep within her. When she collapsed, totally drained, he flipped her on her back and lifted her hips. Using the missionary position, he reentered her. She looked up at him, amazed, although, if the truth be known, she shouldn't be astonished. She had found out last weekend that Riley Westmoreland had the stamina of a bull.

And although she didn't think it was possible, a moment later he brought them both to yet another orgasm, and she knew this was only the beginning.

There would definitely be no climax control tonight.

Thirteen

"I'm glad you're going to be my wedding planner, Alpha."

"And I'm glad you chose me for the job."

Alpha sipped her tea as she studied Megan Westmoreland—Megan Claiborne in six months. She thought Megan, who was a doctor of anesthesiology at one of the local hospitals, was a beautiful woman. And Alpha could see the Westmoreland similarities in the dark eyes, perfectly arched brows and cheekbones.

Other than Dillon and his wife, Pam, Alpha hadn't met any other family members. Due to the nature of her and Riley's relationship, there was no need for him to introduce her to his family and she was certain that none of them were aware they were having an affair.

Alpha's thoughts shifted back to the bride-to-be. Megan's engagement party had been held earlier in the month. With that out of the way, Megan was ready to plan her June wedding. Alpha had gotten the call on Monday, the day she had returned to Denver from spending four wonderful days in

Memphis with Riley. Goose bumps formed on her arms whenever she thought about just how fantastic those days had been.

"So you like the wedding colors I've selected?" Megan asked.

Alpha's attention was pulled back to the business at hand. "Yes, I think buttercup and lime are wonderful colors together. They give me a lot to work with."

Megan seemed pleased with that. "I'm glad."

They were in the middle of discussing the food items Megan wanted as part of her menu when Megan's front door opened and a man, who Alpha knew immediately had to be one of Riley's brothers or cousins, stalked in with a furious expression on his face.

A calm Megan glanced over at him and asked, "What has you so riled this morning, Zane?"

So this was Zane Westmoreland? Alpha thought, sipping her tea, trying not to let it be so obvious that she was checking him out. Since arriving in town, she'd heard a lot of feminine whispers about him. Women thought he was hot and she could see why. But then, Riley was hot, as well. Even hotter, in her book. But she would be the first to admit she was biased where Riley was concerned.

"This is Alpha Blake. She's helping me plan my wedding," Megan added, introducing them.

The man gave a quick tip of his Stetson in Alpha's direction before returning his full attention to Megan. "What's this I hear about Channing Hastings being on your invitation list?"

Megan smiled sweetly. "Yes, what of it?"

"I don't want her at your wedding."

Megan put her teacup down and gave her brother her full attention. "Why? No matter how your relationship with Channing ended, if you recall, she and I worked together at the hospital long before the two of you met. I've always liked her and still consider her a friend and—"

"I don't want her there, Megan."

Megan frowned. "It's my wedding, Zane, and she's invited, so if you have to get yourself together before seeing her again then I suggest—"

"That's not it," he snapped.

"Sounds like it is," Megan countered.

Instead of saying anything else, Zane Westmoreland turned and stormed out the door with the same turbulent gust of wind that had brought him in. When the door slammed shut behind him, Megan glanced over at Alpha with an apologetic smile on her face. "As you can see, not all the Westmorelands are civilized."

Alpha took another sip of her tea before asking, "Are you sure you don't want me to remove Ms. Hastings's name from the invitation list?"

Megan smiled. "I'm positive. It's time my brother comes to terms with his true feelings about some things."

An hour later, Alpha had wrapped up her meeting with Megan and stood, ready to go, when there was a knock at Megan's door. Alpha wondered if Zane had calmed down and was returning.

"Come in," Megan called out.

The door opened and Alpha's heart almost fell from her chest when Riley walked in.

Megan glanced over at her cousin. "Riley, if you're here on Zane's behalf to talk me out of inviting Channing to the—"

"No," he interrupted. "Channing is Zane's issue. He has to deal with it. You have the right to invite who you want."

His gaze shifted from Megan to Alpha. "But he did mention you had company, your wedding planner, so I thought I'd drop by to say hello."

Megan looked curiously from Alpha to Riley. "You two have met already?"

Riley nodded. "Yes, I'm working with Alpha on the holiday party at Blue Ridge next month."

Megan tapped her forehead. "That's right. How could I

forget you're coordinating that? Last time I heard you were doing it grudgingly, Riley. Evidently that has changed."

Megan would be surprised to learn just how much things had changed, Riley thought. "Yes, that has changed."

Megan smiled. "I'm glad to hear it."

When Riley didn't say anything but continued to look at Alpha, in a way that probably seemed like he could eat her alive, Megan cleared her throat. "Is that the only reason you dropped by?" she asked.

He shifted his gaze from Alpha back to Megan. "Not really. I wanted to ask Alpha something."

He glanced over at Alpha again. "My family is doing their monthly out-on-the-town dinner Wednesday night at McKay's. I wanted to know if you'd like to come? That way you can meet the rest of the family. I think they'd like to get acquainted with the person putting the party together."

Out of the corner of his eye, he saw Megan raise a brow, because in truth, there was no need for the family to get to know the person putting the party together. He knew it and she knew it, as well.

Luckily Alpha didn't know it. She smiled and said, "Yes, I'm available Wednesday night to meet the rest of your family."

"Good. I'll pick you up at six."

He glanced over at Megan, who was still staring at him. She was probably wondering why he offered to pick up Alpha when anyone living in Denver clearly knew the directions to McKay's.

"That will be fine and I'll be ready," Alpha said.

He began backing out of the house before Megan felt the need to ask him anything. "Great, I'll see you again later, then." And he meant that literally because he planned to drop by her place tonight.

"All right."

He turned and headed to the door in quick, powerful

strides. She'd looked good in her dark brown slacks and peach-colored pullover sweater. The coloring was perfect for her complexion. And her hair was loose and fanned around her shoulders, just the way he liked.

He told himself to keep walking to the door, to open it and not look back. But for some reason, he couldn't do that. When he opened the door and glanced back over his shoulder, he looked directly at Alpha. She was holding his gaze and he felt that sensual chemistry that had his body tingling with the same powerful awareness he felt whenever he was around her. He smiled at Alpha and she smiled back.

There was no way his perceptive cousin hadn't picked up on the exchange, which was probably the reason she kept looking back and forth between him and Alpha. She would have questions, he didn't doubt that, but he would deal with his cousin's nosiness later.

"Ry?"

He switched his gaze from Alpha to Megan, aware that Megan had said something. "Yes?"

"Either come in or go out. Holding the door open is letting out the heat," she said with an amused expression on her face.

"Oh. Okay, I'm leaving." He firmly closed the door behind him.

Riley smiled as he headed for his truck, but once he got inside, buckled his seat belt and saw his reflection in his rearview mirror, he frowned. What the hell was wrong with him? As soon as an angry Zane mentioned Alpha was at Megan's, he hadn't wasted time getting over there, leaving Zane staring at him like he'd lost his mind.

And, in a way, he was afraid that he had.

The first of the craziness had been making love to Alpha without a condom. Since the first time he'd made out with Emily Parker at the age of fourteen, he'd always used a condom. His father had had "the talk" with all his sons when they turned thirteen, and Dillon had reinforced those talks over the years. Since no form of birth control was 100 percent, it hadn't mattered one iota if the woman claimed to be on the pill or any other kind of birth control. His rule was to use a condom.

Why had he broken that rule for Alpha?

Granted, being inside her—skin-to-skin, flesh-to-flesh, feeling the way her inner muscles had clamped on him—had felt out of this world. Totally awesome. Even so, there was no reason for him to take chances, and he'd continued to take chances. He hadn't used a condom with her since they'd arrived back in Denver yesterday morning.

He leaned back in his seat. It didn't take much to remember the four days he and Alpha had spent together in Memphis. Words couldn't describe how much he had enjoyed the trip, and it had nothing to do with him signing off on that business deal. It had everything to do with Alpha being in Memphis with him.

He had finalized the contract early and had returned to the hotel room to find she'd gone shopping. He had paced the floor like an obsessed man, and the moment she had returned, he had swept her into his arms, making all her shopping bags go flying.

He'd never known he could undress a woman so quickly. Within moments they were both naked and back in the bed again. Saturday, they had done a tour of the city, including Graceland and the hotel where Martin Luther King Jr. had lost his life.

Then on Saturday night they had gone to Mack's dinner party. She had looked fantastic, and he'd known she would wow everyone just like she'd wowed him. He'd actually regretted packing up and leaving Memphis yesterday.

Drawing in a deep breath, he straightened and started the ignition. Now he'd done the unthinkable and invited her to share dinner with his family. He could just imagine what all of them would think when he arrived at McKay's with Alpha on Wednesday night.

He was beginning to act real crazy with her. That wasn't a good thing.

The best thing to do would be to put distance between them until the family dinner.

The last person Alpha expected to see when she opened her door later that evening was Riley. "Riley," she said, moving aside to let him come in. "I was just about to grab something to eat. Do you want to join me?"

"I'd love to."

She closed the door behind him. "You're not going to ask what's for dinner?"

"Doesn't matter. I came to see you. Dinner is an extra."

He'd come to see her, and she didn't have to guess why. The man had a ferocious sexual appetite that was contagious. But she had no complaints. He'd unleashed something within her. She would admit that she wanted him as much as he wanted her.

"And, if you're in the mood, after dinner I thought we'd grab a movie."

She glanced over at him. "A movie?"

"Yes."

"I'd love to but…"

He raised a brow. "But what?"

"I've already made plans for the evening."

"Oh," he said, and she could tell by his expression that he was surprised. "I apologize. I should have called first."

"No reason for you to do that. I figured it was time for me to organize my junk room and planned to spend the evening doing just that."

"Your junk room?"

She smiled. "Yes. Whenever I'm out and about and see anything that captures my interest, anything I feel just might work for a future party theme, I bring it home and stick it in my junk room. Needless to say, the room is pretty disorganized now."

He chuckled. "Need my help?"

She was surprised by his offer. "You want to help?"

"Yes."

She thought of all the other things he could be doing tonight. "Are you sure you want to do that?"

"Positive. Besides, it's the least I can do to thank you for inviting me to dine with you."

Alpha waved off his words with her hand. "No need to thank me. And if you're sure about helping, then thanks. I can certainly use it. It's been a while since I got things organized in that room, and I was determined that tonight would be when I started on it."

"Then count me in."

"Every time I eat a meal you prepare, I'm impressed," Riley said, leaning back in the chair as he used a napkin to wipe the corners of his mouth.

"You've only eaten two meals prepared by me," Alpha said, grinning.

"Then I've been impressed twice."

She threw her head back and laughed. He loved the sound. It was rich, feminine and genuine. It didn't matter at that moment that earlier that day he'd sworn to put distance between them. All it took was him being home alone with a deep craving to see her again. It was a craving that had him taking a shower, changing clothes and driving over to see her like a demented fool.

They sat and talked about her plans for Megan's wedding and then he helped her clear the table before assisting her in loading the dishes in the dishwasher. For no reason, other than he wanted to kiss her, he took her hand and pulled her to him. The feel of her hardened nipples pressing against his chest made him draw in a deep breath and fill his nostrils with her scent.

"I need to kiss you," he whispered against her lips before leaning in closer and claiming them. He maneuvered his arms around her waist to bring her closer to him. He enjoyed being inside her mouth, licking her from corner to corner, tasting her deeply as their tongues tangled passionately. And he definitely loved the sounds she made, those sensual moans of pleasure that made his mouth even hungrier for hers. He could lock lips with her for hours, days, weeks…well past six weeks.

He broke off the kiss but continued to hold her in his arms while inwardly chastising himself for even thinking such a thing. He would admit it was a novelty to want a woman this much, but he would eventually get over it. However, he would be the first to admit she wasn't making it easy. When she peered up at him, it was the most natural thing to brush his lips across hers.

A number of other women had been eager to say or do whatever was needed in the hope that he would extend his six-week rule. It hadn't happened. Yet he knew he would make Alpha the exception, if she was interested. But he had a feeling she wasn't. Why did it bother him that she wasn't interested in going beyond the six weeks like the others?

"Hey, don't think a few kisses will get you out of helping me," she said, placing her hands on his shoulders.

Tempted, and giving in to it, he leaned down again to trace a kiss along the nape of her neck. "Let me assure you, I'm not trying to get out of anything. Although I'll admit a few naughty thoughts have crossed my mind."

"There's always later," she whispered.

He wondered if she knew how much that promise made his erection throb. He went back to her lips, loving the feel of how they quivered beneath his. "Actually, I was hoping…"

She threw her head back. "Now, why doesn't that surprise me?" She took a step back. "Come on and let's tackle that room before we're tempted to get into something else."

He followed her from the kitchen to where her bedrooms were located. She passed her sleeping quarters and opened the door of another room.

He walked in behind her and glanced around. He'd seen junkier rooms, but her collection of items intrigued him. He walked across the room and picked up the For Sale sign and looked back at her. "Moving?"

She shook her head and smiled. "No, I kept that because you never know when I might have a moving party for someone."

He nodded and picked up another item. "Boxing gloves?"

She shrugged. "You never know when they might come in handy, as well, for one of my future events."

He picked up several other items, and she provided her reasons for grabbing them either from a store or a yard sale. "Okay, Ms. Blake. Tell me what we need to do to get this show on the road."

She rubbed her hands together as he rolled up his sleeves. "Okay. I've already named those huge plastic tubs over there by traditional party themes—birthday, wedding, anniversary, retirement and new baby. All we have to do is put them in the designated tub."

That sounded easy enough. "And if I'm not sure which one will fit?"

"Then remember the name of my business, Imagine, and let your imagination go to work. If you're still in doubt, then just drop it in the miscellaneous tub for me to sort through later."

"Okay."

He quickly went to work, knowing what was on the agenda for later. She had turned on a radio and, except for the music floating around the room, the only other sounds were those they made moving around while putting items in order. Using his imagination like she'd said, he put every item he picked up into what he felt was the appropriate tub. He tossed a few items in the miscellaneous tub when, for the life of him, he could not figure out what she'd had in mind when she'd bought it.

He thought they worked well together and within an hour he could definitely see them making progress. He glanced over at her. She had removed her pullover sweater to uncover a T-shirt that said Look at Me and Imagine. He smiled, thinking he could definitely do that.

At that moment, he could imagine her without a stitch of clothing, spread on top of the table where they'd eaten earlier. He could see her long legs dangling off the sides as he stepped between them after removing all his own clothes. He could further imagine taking his favorite jam—strawberry—and smearing it all over her body, then taking his time licking it off. He could imagine the tip of his tongue covering every inch of her and—

"Taking an unscheduled break, Riley?"

Her voice sliced into his daydream. He blinked, realizing he had been standing there staring at her, for no telling how long. Swearing under his breath, he shook his head. "No, I was just checking out your T-shirt."

"My T-shirt?" she asked, looking down at herself with a quizzical expression on her face. "Oh," she said, in a tone that let him know she'd forgotten about what was written on her shirt.

He couldn't hold back the smile that crept into his features. "Nice."

She shrugged. "It was a gift from my sister and meant to be funny."

He hadn't seen anything amusing about it. It had the opposite effect. Those had been some serious musings stirring his imagination. Pretty damn hot musings, in fact. "Really?"

"Yes, sometimes she has a warped sense of humor."

He would take her word for it since he'd noticed how she would change the subject when any discussion of her family came up. "Well, I think it's nice, and it's time to get back to work. We're almost finished."

She nodded and went back to folding up tablecloths of just about every color you could name. He latched his attention onto one of the last items he needed to put away, one of those bouncy exercise balls. It was bright yellow, reminding him of the sun. He wondered what she had in mind for it. He started to ask, but decided he would just use his imagination. The only problem was that the thoughts going through his mind were probably way off from what she'd intended.

He looked back over at her and saw she was pretty absorbed in what she was doing. He glanced back down at the ball, then back at her again. *Imagine.* He could see her naked, with her back on the ball. She'd be spread across it, facing him. Thighs open, her femininity wet and ready as he straddled her. And when she arched her body upward, he would lower his downward to connect. It would be a joining he would savor as he fought not to push too hard nor too fast inside of her. Sensations would take over and pleasure would seep into their pores, sink hard into their bones and—

"If the reason you're standing there staring at the ball is because you're trying to figure out where it goes, don't bother. It's not supposed to be in here. I use it to exercise."

He glanced over at her. "I was just imagining you working out on it." He shifted his gaze back to the ball and then returned it to her with a lazy smile. "So, what do you say, Alpha? Do you want to play ball?"

Fourteen

Two days later, Alpha tried to downplay both her nerves and her excitement as Riley escorted her into McKay's to meet his family. Although she kept reminding herself that her purpose for being here was mainly to bring everyone up to date on the holiday party, she could barely contain her enthusiasm.

Riley had ended up spending Monday night with her and had dropped by for dinner last night, as well. She'd had that couple's seventieth anniversary party for Valentine's Day to work on, and while she sat at the kitchen table taking care of the details for that event, he had stretched out on her living room floor in front of the fireplace, watching a cop show on television.

He had pretty much left her alone to hammer out the details for the February party, but, from where she sat at the kitchen table, she could see him. She had been fully aware of each time he'd moved, whether it was to stand to stretch his legs or to shift his body into another position on the floor.

When she had finally finished her work, she had joined

him in front of the fireplace with glasses of wine. Later they'd stripped each other naked and made love before he left at midnight.

She was well aware that time was ticking. They had less than three weeks before their affair would end. Since the finale was the night of the party, she was reminded of it each time she worked on the holiday celebration.

"Well, hello, Riley. Welcome to McKay's," a feminine voice said. Alpha glanced up at their hostess and saw it was the same woman from before.

"Paula," Riley greeted. "I believe my family is here already."

"Yes, they are," the woman said, in a cheerful mood, deliberately not looking at Alpha. "Must be an important business meeting going on with your family."

"No, just our usual get-together," Riley said, handing Paula his leather jacket and then proceeding to help Alpha out of her coat to hand over to Paula, as well.

Alpha wondered why the woman blinked and stared at her so hard, roaming her gaze up and down Alpha's outfit. The ankle-length, formfitting dress Alpha was wearing had been one she'd purchased while shopping in Memphis. She could tell from the way Riley had looked her up and down when he'd picked her up, and the low whistle that had eased from his lips, that he liked the way she looked. So what was this woman's problem? Why was this Paula checking Alpha out with venom in her eyes? It wasn't hard to figure out there was history between Paula and Riley. Alpha had picked up on that the last time.

But then a part of her understood any woman giving Riley a second glance on any night. But especially tonight. The man looked so jaw-droppingly, potently sexy, so robustly masculine, in his Armani jeans, herringbone blazer and white shirt.

She was tempted to tell Paula to pull back her fangs. In a few more weeks, Riley would be on the eligibility list once again. That meant this woman might be the next woman in his bed.

As Alpha studied the woman's reaction further, she saw Paula turn her stunned expression to Riley, who merely smiled. Alpha couldn't help wondering if there was a private joke somewhere, and if there was, why it seemed to involve her.

She glanced over at Riley, who broke eye contact with the woman to glance over at her. A different smile touched his lips when he slid his hand in hers and asked, "Ready?"

She drew in a deep breath and tried dismissing from her mind the interaction she'd seen pass between Riley and Paula. She returned his smile. "Yes, I'm ready."

He then looked back at Paula. "Please show us to our table."

Alpha saw the stiffening of the woman's spine as she moved forward to do as Riley had asked. Paula might be ticked off, but that didn't stop her from deliberately swaying her hips in her short black waitress outfit as she led them toward the back of the restaurant. Alpha was sure Paula's saucy walk was for Riley's benefit.

When they reached the room, Paula opened the door and stepped aside. The look she slanted Alpha would have cut her to the core had she thought the situation was that serious. To her, it wasn't. Alpha thought it was simply pathetic for any woman to get pissed off at another woman over a man neither of them had any right to claim.

They stepped into the room and all the conversation between the people at the long table suddenly ceased as all eyes shifted toward her and Riley. The men stood and the women eyed her and Riley curiously. She knew Megan was expecting her, but she hoped her presence wasn't a surprise to everyone else. Surely Riley had told his family he had invited her. Therefore, Alpha could only assume the reason they were

staring with such intensity was because Riley was still holding her hand and didn't seem inclined to release it.

Seizing the moment when they had everyone's attention,
Riley said, "Hello, everyone. I'd like for you to meet Alpha
Blake."

Alpha waited for him to continue the introduction, expecting him to say something like "Alpha is the event planner handling our company's holiday party." But he provided
no further clarification as he tightened his hand on hers and
moved around the table, making individual introductions.
Because he had talked about his family so much, she felt like
she knew them already.

Everybody shifted places and she found herself sitting with
Riley on one side of her and his brother, Canyon, on the other.
To say the Westmoreland men favored was an understatement.
Because she knew Dillon and Pam already, she felt comfort-
able being included in the conversations. Other than being
asked where she was from—which led to a discussion about
Florida beaches—no one inquired about anything concern-
ing her family and she was grateful for that.

Riley helped tremendously by being so attentive. At some
points, she wondered if he was overdoing it, since more than
one of his brothers and cousins took note of it. When he
asked her to try what he'd ordered for dinner, he had fed it
to her with his fork and then used that same fork to finish
eating his meal.

"Are you excited about planning the party, Alpha?" Riley's
cousin Bailey asked from across the table.

Alpha smiled and nodded. "Yes, definitely, and I think all
of you will be pleased." Bailey had been making conversation
with Alpha off and on during the meal and it was hard to believe the young woman was the same one Riley had claimed
was once a holy terror in the Westmoreland family.

It was later that evening, when Riley was taking her back
home after dinner, that she decided to bring up that very thing

with him. Although he didn't take his eyes off the road, she saw the way his lips curved in a smile.

"Don't let the sweet act fool you. I would be the first to admit that Bailey has matured in a lot of ways, but if rubbed the wrong way, the old Bailey will resurface in a minute. I'm surprised she took to you so easily. Usually she's very stand-offish with those who aren't family."

"Then I guess I should feel special."

The car came to a stop at a traffic light and he turned his dark, piercing gaze toward her. The moment their eyes connected, she almost forgot to breathe. The kind of heat she was beginning to get accustomed to around him curled around in her stomach, making her nipples stiffen and her pulse rate increase.

"You are special, Alpha."

She had to draw in a deep breath, wondering why on earth he had to go and say something like that. Why had he spoken in that husky voice that could make her panties wet on impact? And why did she want to believe he actually thought she was someone special?

"Thank you," was the only response she could make. Her heart was beating a mile a minute. Riley had the ability to make her want things she shouldn't. Believe in things that she couldn't. Hadn't she learned her lesson with LeBron and Eddie? But still, she wished she could ask Riley to explain what he meant. Why he thought she was special. Heaven help her, she really didn't want to put too much stock into what he'd just said.

Riley turned his attention back to the road and she let out a deep sigh. No matter how many times he looked at her or touched her, her body responded in a way it had never responded to a man before. Her affair with him was supposed to be just a fling that meant nothing. Sex with no commitment.

She swallowed with difficulty. But she was beginning to

feel emotions that she shouldn't be feeling, especially when she knew the score.

That wasn't good.

Riley settled between Alpha's thighs and gazed down at her as he lifted her hips to ease unerringly into the essence of her. They stared at each other, looking deeply into each other's eyes, as he guided his throbbing erection right through her heat.

He released a low growl the moment her muscles began clenching him, pulling him deeper inside of her, sending frissons of pleasure rippling all through him. What was there about how she made him feel, the emotions making love to her evoked?

Riley closed his eyes as he began moving, slowly thrusting in and out of her. He didn't want to rush. He wanted to savor the moment. His body felt alive, free. Tension began flowing out of him, unwinding and easing away to allow sexual gratification to come in to such a degree that he flexed his toes in time with his strokes. This was what real lovemaking was about, the kind that made you realize what you'd been missing, and what you could only have when you loved a woman.

What the... He snatched his eyes open to look down at her and was grateful to find her eyes closed as a deep moan escaped from between her lips. Something made her open her eyes and her sultry gaze connected to his. He knew there was no way he could deny what he was feeling at that moment. Emotions he didn't want to feel. And he was certain they were the same kind of emotions that had torn Bane's heart in two.

But he was feeling them nonetheless.

There was no way he could deny that he had fallen in love with Alpha.

He had felt himself falling hard in Memphis, probably even before that. And each time he'd tried fighting it and denying it, he was drawn to her even more. He knew his family had

questions since he'd never invited any woman to their little
family gatherings before. By arriving with her tonight, he
had made a statement. He was taking a chance with his heart.

A part of him wanted to believe Alpha was different. She
would never hurt him the way Crystal had hurt Bane. But
what about those family secrets she was obviously trying
to keep? He brushed the thought aside. Whatever they were
didn't matter. He loved her anyway.

His body kept moving inside of her, boldly claiming what
he deemed, at that moment, would always belong to him.
Starting tonight, he would be a Westmoreland in pursuit. He
knew there were things she wasn't ready to share with him
and that was fine; he would use his time to break down her
defenses and prove to her that no matter what had happened
in the past, he was a man worthy of her love.

Overcome with emotions he couldn't contain, he tightened
his hold on her and leaned down to capture her mouth with
his. It was either that or confess words she was not ready to
hear.

She locked her legs tighter around him and he heard her
deep groan at the same time as sensations burst within him,
releasing spasms of pleasure that ripped all through him. Shot
to every angle of his body.

He broke off the kiss to throw his head back. "Alpha!"

And then he exploded, spurting his release all through
her as he encountered an out-of-body experience that connected him to her in a way that tested the bedsprings. He felt
vibrant, alert, alive, and now he also knew how it felt to be
a man in love.

As his tremors subsided, he eased off Alpha, lifted her
in his arms and snuggled her head to his chest. Their bodies
were wet with sweat and their limbs entwined as he gathered
her closer. They were connected heart to heart, soul to soul.
He knew that no matter how long it took to convince her, Alpha's place in his life was permanent.

Fifteen

"Are you excited about the party this weekend?"

Alpha glanced up from her inventory list and smiled over at Lindsey. Her question was bittersweet. Yes, Alpha usually loved the day an event she'd worked on finally arrived, but since this event also meant the end of her affair with Riley, she was torn.

She decided to give Lindsey the answer her assistant probably expected to hear. "Yes, I'm excited."

She immediately glanced back down at her list so Lindsey wouldn't see the tears threatening to fall whenever she thought about what this weekend entailed. It was hard to believe it had been three weeks since her trip with Riley to Memphis. So much had happened since then. First, it had been his invitation to McKay's to meet his family. She was certain that is what had prompted Pam to call her two days later to invite her to the Westmorelands' Thanksgiving dinner.

Every one of the Denver Westmorelands had been there except for Bane and his cousin Gemma who lived in Australia. The twins, Aiden and Adrian, had schooled her on the family's after-Thanksgiving-dinner game of snow volleyball. Lucky for everyone, except for her, it had snowed that morning and a sufficient amount was still on the ground after dinner. After the players divided into the Reds and the Blues, she found her and Riley on opposite teams.

It had been the most fun she'd had in a long time, and she'd seen just how down-to-earth the Westmorelands were. For a little while, they had made her feel like she was a part of them. That was one of the reasons breaking up with Riley was going to be so hard.

Then there was also the fact that she had fallen in love with him.

As she continued to check items off her list, she couldn't help but feel the pain in her heart. Omega had warned her that such a thing could happen as soon as the flowers began arriving. The day after she'd had dinner with his family at McKay's, he had, for no reason at all, begun sending her flowers. The flowers would arrive practically every two to three days and when she asked why, he would merely smile and say it was because he was thinking about her.

Then there were those other habits they had started that would be hard to break—like sharing dinner practically every day, either at her place or his; his spending the nights with her more often than not; and their Friday date-nights. They would take in a movie or go to a play or roller-skating. More than once, he had mentioned something about her going skiing with him and she would change the subject, not having the heart to remind him that they wouldn't be together for the trip to Aspen that he had planned for January.

An hour or so later, after Lindsey had left, Alpha was busy making last-minute adjustments to the menu for this weekend's party when her phone rang. She smiled when she saw it was Riley.

"Hi. Thanks for the flowers. You are spoiling me."

"You deserve to be spoiled. I just want to make sure we're still on for tonight."

"Most certainly. I always enjoy any meals you cook." They would be dining at his place and, as usual, she would be spending the night.

"I have a special dish for you."

She chuckled. "What is it?"

"A surprise."

She liked his surprises. "All right."

"Good. I left work at noon today to come home to get things together, so I'll come and get you—"

"There's no need for you to do that, Riley. I can drive over to your place…unless you have a problem with my car being seen by anyone."

"Why would I have a problem with it?"

"I'm staying the night, remember. I wouldn't want your family to—"

"What I do is my business. Trust me, they know we're involved and have probably seen your car here overnight before. Do you have a problem with them knowing?"

"No, I don't have a problem with it, not at all," she said.

"Good. In that case, I'll see you when you get here."

She hung up the phone, thinking that even if she had a problem with it, it was too late. Time wasn't on her side and she wanted to spend as much of it with Riley as possible.

Riley had just finished everything and had put the stew on to simmer when he heard the sound of his doorbell. He glanced at his watch. He wasn't expecting Alpha for another hour or so and hoped it wasn't one of his relatives dropping in without calling first. Some of them could smell his stew from miles away and thought it was their God-given right to invite themselves over for a free meal.

As he walked out of the kitchen toward his front door, he couldn't help but smile. He was looking forward to Alpha coming over because, at some time before she left in the morning, he wanted to tell her just how he felt. The holiday party was in three days, and he needed to hear from her that although she might not have fallen in love with him yet, the idea was possible.

Without checking to see who his caller was, he snatched open his door. A deep frown settled on his face when he saw Paula standing on his porch. "Paula, what are you doing here?"

She smiled brightly. "I came to see you, of course. I have some information that I think you need to know."

Riley doubted it and was about to tell her so when she quickly slid by him to enter his house. Closing the door behind him, he crossed his arms over his chest and watched her look around like she'd never been here before, and then he remembered she hadn't. He had broken things off with her before the affair had gotten that far. "What information do I need to know?"

She turned to face him and threw her hair back from her face. She was wearing knee-high leather boots and a light blue mini sweater dress that was so tight it appeared glued to her body. "Mmm, something smells good. Don't you want to invite me to dinner?" she asked, placing her hands on her hips to draw attention to her small waistline.

At that moment, he admired Alpha even more. During the time they'd spent together, she'd never found any reason to flaunt her attributes. They were noticeable without her having to show them off. "Sorry, I'm expecting company in a few hours."

He saw the frown settle on her face. "I take it that you're still involved with that party planner," she said with a sneer.

He tried keeping his anger in check. "What of it?"

"You must like her a lot to include her in one of your family dinners. Not too many women get that privilege from Riley Westmoreland. I didn't. And I know how much you pride yourself on your reputation and the family's name and all that."

He wondered what she was getting at. "If you have something to say, Paula, just say it."

"All right, then." She paused a moment and then slid down to sit on his sofa uninvited, crossing her legs, deliberately showing plenty of thigh and said, "I'm sure you've heard I'm seeing Samuel Porter."

Not that he cared, but he wasn't surprised. Sam was and always had been a party animal, and Paula liked having a good time and getting wild and crazy. And he'd heard Sam was into over-the-top stuff in the bedroom, like group sex and all that. "And?"

"And I was going through Sam's collection of special videos one night to pick out one I thought we would enjoy watching together. Get my drift?"

Riley did get her drift and didn't have to ask what Sam's special videos were. He'd heard the rumor years ago that Sam had a cabinet filled with porn. He drew in a deep breath, still not sure where she was going with all of this. "And?"

"And…" she said, smiling, pulling something out of her purse, "I came across one, and the woman looked so familiar that I took a second look. You might want to take a look, as well. I'm sure you'll recognize her."

He took the DVD she offered and glanced at the picture of the couple, mainly the woman who was stretched out spread-eagle on a four-poster bed very naked. His heart nearly stopped beating, and he forced his hand to stop trembling. He looked at Paula, fighting to keep his teeth from gnashing together in anger. "What are you trying to insinuate?"

"That your girlfriend used to have a naughty past."

He tossed the DVD on the sofa next to her. "I think you're about to set yourself up for a lawsuit you can't afford. This is not my girlfriend on this DVD jacket, just someone who favors her."

Paula lifted her chin dubiously and smiled. "You sure of that?"

Riley's gaze narrowed. Yes, he was sure. The porn star on the DVD jacket was not Alpha.

"Positive. In fact I'm so positive that if I hear about this from anyone else, I'm going to assume you're the one spreading vicious lies and malicious gossip, and I will sue you myself for slandering her name."

The smile quickly disappeared from her face. "You wouldn't do that."

"Try me."

She drew in a deep breath. "I know what I see."

"And I know what I know, but if you want to play your hand, go ahead, I dare you. I won't stop until I make you not only a laughingstock but destitute. Now, I want you to leave and not come back. And remember what I said. If I get wind of any lies you're spreading, I will make sure you regret it."

She jerked up off the sofa and angrily headed for the door, opened it and slammed it shut behind her with enough force to make his windows shake. It was only then that he noticed she'd left the DVD behind, whether accidentally or intentionally he wasn't sure.

Picking up the DVD he headed for the bedroom to take a shower. His dinner guest would be arriving within the hour. And he knew just as sure as the forecasters had predicted snow for the weekend that at some point during the course of the evening, he and Alpha would have a long talk.

"We need to talk, Alpha."

Alpha glanced over at Riley. Something was wrong; she could feel it. Although dinner had been great and she enjoyed his company as usual, she was chilled by the feeling that something just wasn't right. More than once during dinner she had caught Riley staring at her only to quickly look away. What was going on?

A part of her didn't want to know, but still she couldn't stop the what-ifs from swimming through her head. What if he wanted to bring a date Saturday night and had decided he wanted to end his affair a few days early? He had been so adamant about her having dinner with him this evening and now she couldn't help wondering if it was one of those break-up meals. Men had a way of thinking a woman preferred to get dumped on a full stomach. Hadn't Eddie taken her to dinner the night before he'd given her the ultimatum about Omega?

"Alpha."

She took a sip of her wine before placing her glass down on the table. She was a big girl and could handle anything that came her way. But she didn't want to do it now. If he wanted to make this their last night together then she wanted it to be special.

Easing up off the sofa, she slowly crossed the room to where he sat in a leather wingback chair. With his legs stretched out in front of him, he was sipping his own wine while his dark, penetrating gaze watched her every move. And with good reason, she thought, since she was discarding her clothes, piece by piece. His attention was definitely being held the way she wanted it to be. They would have their talk but it would be later. Much later.

By the time she had reached his chair she was totally naked. He pulled her down in his lap and cradled her in his arms. "You like tempting me, don't you?" he asked huskily, leaning close to her lips.

"Umm, it wouldn't be any fun if I didn't." And she wanted him to remember all the times she had tempted him and he had tempted her. She wanted him to remember everything, especially when they were no longer involved. Because she would. Her memories would sustain her when she buried herself in her work to forget him.

It would be hard being involved with Megan's wedding.

She expected to run into him, but hopefully, she would have gotten over him by then.

Yet how could a woman get over a man she truly loved?

"Baby, we need to talk."

She leaned in close to him, and swiped the tip of her tongue across his lips. "And we will talk, Riley. Later. Now I want you to take off your clothes so we can have fun," she said, easing off his lap and pulling him up from the chair.

"Fun?" he asked her, reaching out and running his fingers across the tips of her breasts while letting his gaze roam all over her body.

"Yes," she said, looking up at him as she pulled his belt through the loops of his jeans and then began unbuttoning his shirt. "What do you say about that?"

He reached out and swept her off her feet and headed toward the stairs to his bedroom. "Then I'd say, let's get started."

Alpha stretched out her legs in bed the moment she opened her eyes. It was daylight, and through the window she saw it was lightly snowing. Just her luck, what with those last-minute details she had to handle to get ready for the party tomorrow night.

She turned over in the empty bed, wondering where Riley was. It was then that she saw the note pinned to the pillow where his head had lain the night before.

Didn't want to wake you, but I had an eight o'clock meeting at work. I know you probably have a ton of things to do today to get ready for tomorrow, but make yourself at home until you're ready to leave. Riley.

She held the note to her chest, thinking that at least he hadn't mentioned anything else about them talking. She flopped back down in bed as a smile touched her lips. She'd deliberately made him forget. All it took was for her to glance around at the rumpled bedcovers to know just where Riley Westmoreland's concentration had been last night and during the early hours of this morning. She hadn't gotten much sleep last night, which wouldn't be bad if she didn't have a million things to do.

She looked around the room for her clothes and then remembered she had removed them last night in the living room. The last thing she intended to do was parade around Riley's house naked. He mentioned that he never locked his doors and his brothers or cousins were known to just drop in. Easing out of the bed, she knew he had a robe around here someplace. When she didn't see one, she figured one of his T-shirts would have to do.

She recalled just where he kept them and opened the top drawer to his dresser. Her breath caught. Lying on top of his stack of T-shirts was a DVD, but not just any DVD. It was one of her sister's, titled *Time to Play*. Where did he get it? How long had he had it?

Alpha stood there staring at the DVD as a thousand questions flowed through her mind. Did Riley assume like Le-Bron had at first that it was her on the DVD and not Omega? Or did he figure like LeBron had later that if he couldn't have his ideal porn star then her twin sister would do?

She angrily shoved the drawer closed as fury ripped through her. No wonder he had wanted an affair with her.

But then why was she getting angry anyway? She'd known it was nothing but sex with no commitment all along. Nothing more.

Not caring anymore if anyone saw her naked, she raced downstairs and saw Riley had picked up her clothes off the floor and placed them on the sofa. She quickly dressed, grabbed her purse from the table and left. For the first time since moving to Denver, she didn't notice the cold.

What she noticed more than anything was how deep her heart was hurting.

Sixteen

Riley walked into the ballroom of the Pavilion Hotel and stopped short. Wow! Alpha had miraculously transformed the room into one winter's night, just as the theme declared.

The color scheme was silver, blue and white. Large white columns had been erected, connected by swathes of white netting. The ceiling looked like a midnight sky with the moon and dots of stars. Miniature mounds of snow lay in one area and props of snow-covered mountains were strategically placed around the room.

"Welcome." A hostess dressed as a snow maiden greeted him. "And here's your gift from Blue Ridge Management," she said, handing him a snow globe with a replica of the Blue Ridge Management building inside.

"Thanks." He couldn't resist shaking it up and watching snow float all around. A huge smile touched his lips. His woman had definitely outdone herself. *Imagine.*

"Your girlfriend did a bang-up job, didn't she?"

He turned and looked into Bailey's smiling face. He could tell she was equally impressed. "Yes, she did."

Bailey tilted her head. "So, she is your girlfriend?"

He paused, thinking that Bailey was the second person in two days who had referred to Alpha as his girlfriend. He hadn't denied it then, and he wouldn't deny it now. "Yes, she's my girlfriend."

She stared at him. "Of all the women you've been involved with, I've never known you to claim any of them as anything other than a sleeping partner."

He grabbed a glass of wine from the tray of a passing waiter. Everything, including the outfits the waiters and waitresses wore, looked festive and right in keeping with the party's theme. "She's different."

"In that case, I hope you intend to treat her differently."

He already was, and would continue to do so. In fact, starting tonight, he intended for them to take their relationship to a whole new level, but first they needed to talk. He had left several messages, but she hadn't found time to return them. He knew how hard she had worked and planned for the party tonight, often staying up late and getting up early. But tonight she had to be proud of her accomplishments. He was, and was certain the rest of his family would be, as well.

"You look good, by the way," Bailey said, giving him a once-over. "You Westmoreland men clean up well."

He couldn't help but laugh. "So do Westmoreland women." He glanced around again. "Have you seen Alpha?"

"Yes. She's around here someplace, making sure everything is running smoothly. At some point, I hope you make sure she slows down to enjoy herself. She's worked hard for tonight and it shows."

It was a half hour later before he got a chance to see Alpha, and it was from across the room. He had been standing in a group talking to Morris Caper, one of the oldest employees at Blue Ridge, along with the man's wife, Canyon, Stern and two other couples, when Alpha came into his line of sight. His breath caught when he saw her. She was wearing blue, the same shade being used at the party.

He nodded a few times, trying to pretend to listen to the speaker, when in reality his attention was on Alpha. He began wondering why she wouldn't look his way. Surely she knew he'd arrived. However, he had to remind himself that tonight wasn't about him. She had a job to do. But he had a niggling discomfort that something wasn't right.

He was about to look back at Mr. Caper when Alpha finally glanced his way. He was about to give her a smile and a thumbs-up when the look she gave him made him go still. What was that glare all about? He lifted his brow, and she quickly turned to head toward the room where food was being prepared.

"Excuse me for a minute," he said to the group before walking off in the direction Alpha had gone. Something was going on, and he intended to find out what.

He walked through several rooms and was stopped by a number of people before he finally came within a few feet of her. She looked up, saw him and was about to walk away when he increased his pace and touched her arm. "Everything is above my expectations, Alpha, but I'd like to talk to you for a second."

He was very much aware that with others around, she couldn't deny his request. After all, his family was the one paying for this affair.

"All right."

To anyone else it would appear she was acknowledging his request, because, unless you were standing as close to her as he was, you couldn't see the sharp daggers in her eyes or the tightness of her lips. *What the hell?*

"Privately, please," he said, taking her arm and leading her to an empty room in the back, far away from her staff, his employees or his family members.

He closed the door behind them and then turned to her. She was looking at everything in the storage room but him. And he could feel her tension. Her anger. "Now. Would you like to tell me what's going on?"

Her brows furrowed, and she lifted her chin. "There's nothing going on, at least nothing you should be concerned about. This is our breakup night anyway, right? What did you say when we started out, that you didn't stay with any woman past six weeks? Well, your six weeks ended today, no sweat."

Riley gritted his teeth. "What's this about, Alpha?"

"Nothing, and if you don't mind, I have a party to run and—"

"Your assistant can handle things until you get back. And I intend to keep you here until you tell me what's wrong, even if it takes all night."

She placed her hands on her hips. "I don't owe you any explanations."

He crossed the room to where she stood in a furious stance with her gaze flaring, spine straight and head thrown back. "Yes, you do. When I left you in bed yesterday morning it was with a smile on your face, so what's with the venom tonight? Are you mad because I left without waking you?"

"Is that what you think?"

He rubbed his hand down his face. "I don't know what to think, so tell me."

Alpha tried not to give in to the plea she heard in his voice and turned her back to him. For two solid days she had tried putting thoughts of him out of her mind. She had tried to concentrate on what had to be done for this party. It hadn't been easy, but she had managed to get through it somehow, and every single Westmoreland here, including him, had complimented her on her work. Tonight should be a night of celebration and excitement for her. Instead it was one of heartbreak.

She heard him move and could feel his heat, breathe in his

masculine scent and knew he was standing directly behind her with little space between them. The thought of what he'd done and what he'd thought of her hit low and hard, and he had the nerve to act like nothing happened. In essence he had no idea what she'd found in his drawer. Maybe it was time for her to tell him.

She turned around and met his inquisitive gaze. "Yesterday morning after you left, I needed a T-shirt to put on before going downstairs to get my clothes."

"Go on."

"I thought you wouldn't mind if I looked in your drawer to get one."

Something in his gaze let her know that he knew what would come next and he spoke before she did. "And you found that DVD Paula gave me."

His words nearly sucked the breath from her lungs. "Paula?"

"Yes, Paula, from McKay's."

Her head began spinning. Now she understood the looks that had passed between him and Paula that night. "So that was the private joke between the two of you," she said, barely getting the words out, forcing them beyond the tears she refused to let fall.

"What are you talking about?"

"Nothing. The main thing right now is that you had that video and you thought it was me, didn't you? That's why you initiated an affair with me, isn't it? I played right into your hands—and into your bed."

Riley felt a sting to his cheek, thinking her words were like a slap to his face. He struggled against the need to lash out at her the way she was lashing out at him. How could she assume something like that? "What are you accusing me of, Alpha?"

"That you and your ex-girlfriend thought you had things

figured out. You both thought that I'm the woman on that porn DVD."

At that moment he felt angrier than he'd ever felt in his life because the woman he loved didn't trust him. She had a lot of nerve. He had been up-front with her about everything. She was the one keeping secrets yet he had fallen in love with her anyway, against his better judgment.

Risking the kind of pain he'd vowed never to feel.

"I knew you were not the woman on that jacket," he said through gritted teeth.

She took a step closer to him, got in his face. "How could you have known that when Omega is my identical twin? You wouldn't be the first man who thought I was her."

"I don't give a royal damn what other men thought. I knew it wasn't you the minute I looked at that DVD jacket. You might be identical twins but a man who has made love to you as often as I have, who has touched you, tasted you, got up close and personal with you, could tell the difference. I know every mole, crevice, indention and mark on your body. I knew that wasn't you and figured it had to be your twin…a twin you never told me you had."

He paused a moment and added, "And if you recall, I did mention we needed to talk and intended to bring it up on Thursday night, the same day Paula brought that DVD over for me to see. I told her then it wasn't you. So who's the victim here, Alpha? It seems pretty clear to me that I trusted you a whole hell of a lot more than you trusted me."

He then turned and walked out of the room.

Alpha drew in a deep breath the moment she heard the door close behind Riley. Was it really true? Had he known the woman on that DVD jacket wasn't her? If so, then she had done him a grave injustice, especially when she hadn't told him about Omega.

What had been lacking between them was trust and communication, more on her part than on his. He had told her about his family, introduced her to them, but she had told him hardly anything about hers. And he hadn't been quick to believe the worst about her like she had about him.

And he *had* wanted to talk Thursday night, but she'd assumed he wanted to break things off with her. Had she let him have his say, none of this would have happened, and if she hadn't jumped to conclusions and assumed the worst then she wouldn't be standing here filled with so much remorse. But after dealing with the likes of LeBron and Eddie, she had been too afraid to trust another man.

There was a gentle knock on the door. "Yes?"

Lindsey stuck her head in with a concerned look on her face. "Is everything all right?"

"Yes, why do you ask?"

She came into the room and shrugged. "I saw Mr. Westmoreland request to talk privately and wondered what could be wrong since everything seems to be going all right. Everyone I talked to thinks you outdid yourself. Everything is beautiful."

Alpha swallowed deeply. "I had a lot of help, and no, Mr. Westmoreland wasn't complaining about anything. He wanted to discuss another matter."

"Oh."

Deciding the best thing she could do now was to get back to work and stay busy, she said, "Come on. Let's make sure everything continues to stay impressive for everyone." She checked her watch. "It's almost time for the snow to start falling."

As part of the theme, she had decided to have fake snowflakes swirl from the ceiling, and with the special lightning she had installed, it would give the illusion that the entire ballroom had been transformed into a beautiful winter wonderland.

As Alpha left the room with Lindsey, she knew what she should do but had no idea how to go about it.

* * *

"You sure you don't want to come to dinner, Riley? With that huge snowstorm headed this way it might be the last good home-cooked meal you get for a while," Dillon said.

"Yes, it might be at that," Riley replied as he stood at the window and looked out. It hadn't started snowing yet but according to the forecasters a snowstorm was headed their way. "But I'll still pass. I wouldn't be much company anyway."

Dillon didn't say anything for a minute. "So Pam and Chloe were right. There's trouble in paradise."

Riley didn't have to figure out how they knew. He had found out a long time ago that the women in his family were too observant for their own good. "I guess you can say that."

"Then take it from someone who knows, people in love have spats sometimes."

Riley lifted his brow and said in a defensive tone, "Who said I was in love?"

"I did. And don't try denying it. I watched you and Alpha at the party trying to avoid each other. It's been over a week. Don't you think the two of you need to kiss and make up?"

Riley rolled his eyes. "Too complicated to kiss and make up, Dil."

"Not if you really love her. If I can forgive Pam for coming within seconds of marrying another man, then I'm certain you can forgive Alpha for whatever the transgression."

A short while later, after his conversation with his oldest brother had ended, Riley stood in the kitchen pouring a cup of coffee, replaying in his mind what Dillon had said. He appreciated the pep talk but there were times when it was better just to count your losses, move on and not look back. Instead, he was going to take the same advice he'd given to Bane— advice Bane had refused to follow. Now, his brother was *still* hurting and, more than ever, Riley refused to be another Bane.

He was about to walk over to the refrigerator to pull out a microwave dinner when he heard his doorbell. He didn't have to wonder who was probably at his door. Bailey. She'd called twice already and if Dillon had mentioned Riley planned on skipping a meal with the family, she wouldn't hesitate to come and grill him about things he'd rather not talk about.

He thought about not answering but decided if Bailey had braved the blistering cold to come to his place then he would see what she wanted. But he would not let her stay long. Although the snowstorm hadn't hit yet, it was cold as the dickens outside. He would send Bailey on her way, and he would eat his meal alone and get in bed early. The mayor had already predicted that most of Denver, including the airport, would be shut down tomorrow.

Riley opened the door to find this furry white thing standing in front of him. He leaned in the doorway, trying to make out just what or who it was when the person tilted her head and moved away all the fur. "Alpha?"

She nodded. "May I come in so we can talk? It's cold out here."

He quickly moved aside. "Get near the fireplace," he ordered, wondering what in the world she was doing out in this weather. It was in the low teens. He thought it was pretty damn cold and he was used to it. It would be murder on someone like her.

He stood back and watched as she peeled off a long white coat trimmed in fur with a matching hat and gloves. She then pulled a white knitted ski mask from her face before pulling off another coat and two sweaters. When she stood trembling in front of the fireplace in a pair of winter-white stretched slacks and a pretty winter-white pullover turtleneck sweater, he just stared. The outfit looked good on her. Too good.

And when she ran her fingers through her hair to fluff it out, he felt heat on his skin. He swallowed hard and said, "I'll pour you a cup of coffee while you warm up. And then you can tell me why you came here in all this bad weather."

He quickly walked away, to the kitchen, and tried to

breathe calmly while he poured her coffee. He hadn't seen her or talked to her since the party, but that didn't mean he hadn't thought about her, because he had—every waking minute as well as when he should have been sleeping. She hated cold weather, yet she had come here, on what would probably be the coldest day they'd had since last winter.

Trying to keep his hand steady, he walked back to the living room and found her standing with her back to him, in front of the fireplace, staring down at the flames as if she was in deep thought. He wondered what she was thinking about and knew he would soon find out.

"Here you are," he said, claiming her attention. She crossed the room to meet him. She took the cup from his hand and the minute their fingers touched, a frisson of warmth flowed through him. He took a step back and watched as she immediately took a sip.

She glanced up at him. "Thanks, I needed that."

"I'm sure you did. So why are you here, Alpha?"

"I was hoping we could talk. I considered calling but figured you would refuse."

She had figured right. "What more is there to say? I trusted you more than you trusted me."

"It's not just about trust, Riley."

He crossed his arms over his chest. "Then what else is there?"

"An understanding between us. And I would be the first to admit I didn't tell you everything, but I had a reason for keeping my family secrets to myself. All we were sharing was an affair."

She glanced over at the sofa. "May I sit down so we can talk? I think it's time that I tell you everything."

A part of him was tempted to tell her no. It was too late to tell him everything. He preferred that she leave.

But he knew he couldn't say any of that. She had come over in the cold weather, which meant whatever she had to say was important to her. So the least he could do was listen to what she had to say. "Yes, you may have a seat."

She sat down and he took the chair across from her and wondered why she hadn't been able to decipher when his feelings for her had changed and he'd wanted more than sex without a commitment. What had she thought those flowers were all about, the amount of time he had spent with her compared to all the others?

He watched her and knew she was trying to gather her thoughts. Why? Was he such a hard guy to talk to? He had shared more of himself with her than with any other woman. Too bad he couldn't say the same about her.

She looked over at him, met his gaze and he knew he had lied to himself.

He'd awakened that morning with a firm resolve that he no longer wanted her or loved her. But seeing her here at Riley's Station only confirmed that he still wanted her in a way he'd never wanted another woman. And, more than anything, he still loved her.

She finally began talking. "My identical twin sister, Omega, dropped out of college our first year when she met this older guy at some club near campus. The man convinced her she should be a model."

She paused a moment and took another sip of her coffee. "Omega was always the more outgoing of the two of us and always wanted that sort of thing—the limelight, recognition, stardom—so her decision didn't surprise me. And, in a way, I doubt that it surprised my parents. At least it shouldn't have, since she was the one who defied their every order while we were growing up.

"Anyway, my parents were livid about her dropping out of college. When she left they didn't hear from her for months, but because she and I are close, I knew her whereabouts. I knew before anyone when she discovered the man hadn't propositioned her for a real modeling job but for a job as a porn star. He didn't twist her arm or hold her hostage. Omega could have walked away at any time. It was a choice she made. She thought she had a beautiful body, and she didn't mind flaunting it. She considered what she was doing a job. She was a well-paid entertainer and nothing else."

He nodded. "Did your parents know what she was doing?"

She shook her head. "No, and Omega and I both figured that they wouldn't find out, either. She was living out in California and had become popular on the West Coast; whereas my parents lived in Florida, the Bible Belt. We thought good churchgoing people would never find out about stuff like that. But we were wrong. It seemed a few men who knew my parents were getting porn off the internet, so you can just imagine how they couldn't wait to spread the word. Soon it got back to my parents. Someone even sent them a DVD in the mail."

"That was kind of low," he said.

"Yes, it was, and it led to a full-blown scandal that embarrassed my parents. Some of their so-called friends stopped socializing with them and, for a while, they lost business at the vet clinic. Mom and Dad tried to talk to Omega. Of course they went about it the wrong way, by making demands, and that only made her defiant. In the end, they threatened to cut her off if she didn't quit what she was doing and return home. They also forbade me to have contact with Omega, which I refused to do."

"I'm sure they weren't happy about that."

She shook her head. "No, they weren't. They finally just left me alone and requested that I not ever mention anything about Omega to them. The embarrassment was too much, and in the end they made a decision to disown her until she came to her senses."

She took another sip of her coffee. "A few years later, I met this guy name LeBron, who moved to Daytona with his job from Ohio," she said softly. "LeBron and I dated for six months, and I thought everything was going great until one night he presented me with one of my sister's DVDs and said he'd been a fan of hers for a couple of years. He even said what had drawn him to me was that he assumed I was her. And when he found out I wasn't, he figured he had the next best thing. He wanted me to imitate what she did on the DVD. He even wanted to call me Omega whenever we made love."

Riley tensed and anger flowed through his body. "He actually wanted you to pretend you were your sister?"

"Yes. I refused to do so and left. The next day he called, breaking things off with me."

She didn't say anything for a long minute. "A year later, I met Eddie when he brought his dog into the clinic. We hit it off immediately. He had moved to Daytona from his family's home in Palm Beach. They owned a slew of electronics shops, and he'd moved to Daytona to open a new store there. It was hard for me to trust anyone, and after we'd dated awhile, I told him everything. I confided about Omega and told him about LeBron. He was angry that LeBron could be such an ass, and he said what Omega did for a living meant nothing to him. It was her life and he could understand me wanting to keep a relationship with my sister."

"Sounds like a nice guy."

"I thought so, and when he asked me to marry him, I agreed. Everything was going along fine until someone, not sure who, sent his parents a copy of Omega's DVD. They were appalled and demanded that he end things with me. He refused, but they put pressure on him to at least get me to agree not to have anything to do with Omega."

She took another sip of coffee. "I refused, and he called off the wedding a week before it was to take place."

She paused, as if remembering that time. "That was another embarrassment for my parents, especially when they thought I should have given in to Eddie's request. I decided to move as far away as I could, which brought me to Denver."

He leaned forward. "So when you saw that DVD in my drawer, you assumed I was another LeBron or that I could be another Eddie?"

She held his gaze. "Yes."

Her single answer gave him pause. "Is that the reason you didn't talk much about your family?"

"Yes. I know all families have issues but to this day my parents have not forgiven my sister. If they had their way I wouldn't have any contact with her. My mother is softening somewhat. She at least asks about Omega. But my father is still being hard-nosed."

"Is your sister still in the business?"

"No, she quit making porn movies a few years ago, but some people have long memories, especially since she was once very popular. I've been on business trips when men have approached me asking if I was Omega and could they have my autograph."

She paused again. "I still don't understand it. You say you knew immediately it wasn't me, but that's hard to believe when most people can't tell me and Omega apart."

He nodded. "The first thing I noticed was the dye job."

She lifted a brow. "The dye job?"

"Yes, you once mentioned you'd never dyed your hair and it was obvious the woman on the DVD jacket had. And then when I looked at it further, I noticed she had a mole on her inner right thigh. You don't. And you don't have a tattoo near your navel."

She nodded. "I'm sorry about jumping to conclusions, Riley, but we had agreed on a sex-only relationship because the last thing I wanted was to get seriously involved with someone. I had before—twice— and things didn't work out."

"What is your sister doing now?"

"Omega is living in Paris and is happily married to a wonderful guy who knows about her past and loves her regardless. Marlon is a successful businessman and the two of them travel a lot. With his encouragement, she returned to school and now has her graduate degree. But even with her marriage and her other accomplishments and achievements, my parents still haven't forgiven her."

"And I take it your father wants you and Eddie to get back together."

Her eyes widened. "How do you know that?"

"If you recall, I happened to call you one day and you thought I was your father. You said something that let me know he was trying to get you to reinstate your relationship with your ex-fiancé."

"Yes, but only because Eddie thinks he still has a chance to convince me not to have anything to do with Omega. But like I told him, my sister and I are closer than ever."

"I'm glad."

She looked surprised. "You are?"

"Yes, and I'm disappointed you would think that I wouldn't be. I love family, Alpha. I told you about Bane, the twins and Bailey and the reputation they had around town. Not once did any one of us think about disowning them. You don't disown family, and I think it's sad that your parents are doing that to your sister. Nobody is perfect."

"Yes, but having a bad reputation around town for things you did while growing up is one thing, Riley. Being a porn star is another, and Eddie's family let me know that families with good names wouldn't want to have theirs tarnished by such a scandal. Why would I even assume your family would be any different?"

"Because you met them. We aren't judgmental nor do we place ourselves on any type of pedestal. There are skeletons in every family closet. I told you all the stuff we're uncovering on my grandfather Raphel."

He paused a moment and then asked, "Have you ever heard of the Chamberlain gang?"

She nodded. "Yes. Father and two sons did a rash of bank

robberies across the country some years back. I was in high school, and one of my classmates brought in an article about them. We all found it fascinating how they were able to pull things off, zigzagging across state lines and evading the FBI for as long as they did before finally getting caught."

"What they did was pretty scandalous, wouldn't you say?"

"Yes, of course."

"Well, I happen to know one of their family members. Brooke Chamberlain. The Chamberlain gang consisted of her father and her two older brothers. They're still serving time, and I doubt they will be getting out anytime soon."

"You actually know someone related to them?"

"Yes, in fact I know her very well because she's married to my cousin Ian Westmoreland, who owns a casino near Lake Tahoe. All of us know about Brooke's family but none of us hold it against her. We're also aware she keeps in contact with them and find no fault in that, as well. Family is family, Alpha. I would never have judged you by what your sister did. Nor would I have pushed you not to have any contact with her."

"I see that now, but because I wasn't sure, I didn't want to take the chance."

"Do you believe me?" he asked, holding her gaze steadily, with single-minded focus. He knew at that moment how much he wanted her to believe him. To believe in him.

"Yes. I didn't know then," she said softly. "But I do now."

He nodded, satisfied with her answer. "Now that we've cleared up your issues, let's discuss mine."

Dread rippled down Alpha's spine. She wondered just what kind of issues he could have. "All right."

He slowly stood from the chair and paced a few times in front of the fireplace. The glow from the fire reflected on him. In jeans and a pullover sweater, he looked too sexy for her senses. She watched him move and her stomach tightened with each step he took. Moments later, he stopped and turned to face her. "I told you about Bane and Crystal, right?"

She nodded. "Yes."

"What I didn't tell you was how much their fiery relationship affected me. Bane loved Crystal with the passion and soul of a man beyond his years. I felt the love whenever he mentioned her or when he would look at her. We all did, and that worried us. In a way, I felt sorry for Mr. Newsome. The more he tried keeping them apart, the more they were determined to stay together at any cost."

He was silent for a moment. "I saw the pain Bane went through when he and Crystal were forced apart. I can still see that pain whenever he comes home and asks about her or mentions her name. A love that fierce scared the hell out of me. I never wanted that kind of love for myself. Our lives were shattered when we lost our parents and uncle and aunt in that plane crash. I could not imagine falling in love with a woman and going through that sort of pain due to death or any other kind of separation."

He went back and sat down. "So my issues were making it hard for me to ever consider a serious involvement with a woman. Until you. With you, it was hard to keep my emotions in check, and I found myself wanting things I felt I shouldn't have."

Alpha could barely breathe. Was he saying what she hoped he was saying? That at some point it had become more than just sex with no commitment? That he had been fighting his emotions for her like she had been fighting hers for him? "What are you saying?" she asked softly.

"I'm saying that as much as I wished otherwise, it stopped being just sex for me during our trip to Memphis. I wanted to tell you then but didn't want to push you into anything. So I decided to give you hints about where I wanted our relationship to go. That's why I started sending the flowers. Why I invited you to meet my family. They took the hint but you were slow. It angered me when Paula showed up at my place with that DVD. How could you have thought it had been a private joke between her and me?"

She tried to get her heart rate to slow down. Had he kind of said, in so many words, that he loved her? "I saw the exchange between you two that day at McKay's, when I took off my coat and she saw my outfit."

He smiled. "Oh, that. It wasn't a private joke. It was egg on her face. The last time she saw you, you were overdressed because of the cold weather. She made a comment about me dating a frumpy woman. She got to see just how *not* frumpy you were and was almost rendered speechless. I liked the fact that she had to eat crow."

"Oh."

"I think we both had misgivings about allowing our relationship to go beyond anything other than just sex. So now I want to make it clear what I want. I want you, Alpha, and not just in a physical way. I love you so damn much it scares me. But I'm willing to take a chance on love and believe it was meant for us to be together, no matter what."

Alpha tried to fight back the tears that filled her eyes. "Oh, Riley, I love you, too, but I had promised myself never to let anyone come between me and Omega. When I saw that DVD in your drawer, I thought the worst and I'm sorry."

He eased from the chair and crossed the room to sit down beside her on the sofa. Reaching out, he wiped away her tears and then took her hand in his and held it tight. "So what do you think we should do about our issues?"

She was filled with so many emotions, she almost couldn't speak. Then she said, "What do you suggest?"

"I think we need to communicate more when it comes to things that threaten the love we have for each other. The thought of losing you for any reason is my worst nightmare and something I won't let happen."

"Oh, Riley."

He leaned down and brushed a kiss across her lips. Then he pulled her into his arms and kissed her with all the intense emotion that he was feeling. When he finally released her mouth, he softly caressed her cheek. "Will you marry me?"

She reached up and caressed his chin. "Only if we can have a long engagement. We owe it to ourselves to build our relationship, develop open communication and trust. And besides, there's no way we can marry before Megan's big day in June."

He nodded in agreement. "Then you decide when and I shall be there. I love you, and I want to spend the rest of my life with you."

"I love you, too." She stood. "Now I need to get back home before the storm hits."

He stood, as well. "If you think for one minute I'm letting you go back out in that weather, then think again. It's hard to believe you even ventured out."

"We needed to talk and I wanted to do it face-to-face."

"Well, we did, face-to-face, and you know what I think?"

"No."

"That our very own one winter's night should start now," he said, standing and pulling her close to him. "What do you say to that?"

She wrapped her arms around his neck. "I would say start the party."

He swept her off her feet and headed upstairs toward the bedroom, intending on doing just that.

Epilogue

A beautiful day in June

Riley grabbed Alpha's arm when she hurriedly walked by him and pulled her behind a huge planter to steal a quick kiss. "Hey, slow down. How long will I have to be without a date?"

Alpha wrapped her arms around Riley's neck. "Just long enough for Megan and Rico to cut the cake. Don't you think they made a beautiful bridal couple?"

"Yes, and thanks to Imagine, it was a storybook wedding. You truly outdid yourself. I thought everything was perfect."

"I think you're perfect." And she really meant that. Over the course of the past six months, she and Riley had continued to build an even stronger relationship. Somehow he had talked her into that ski trip to Aspen in January and, as promised, he had kept her warm…most of the time. She hadn't gotten the hang of being on skis but the evenings spent in his arms in front of the fireplace had given them plenty more winter nights to cherish.

He had flown home to Daytona Beach with her over Easter weekend to meet her parents. Before that, he had invited Omega and Marlon to a surprise party he'd given for Alpha at the end of February to celebrate her selection as Denver's Small Businesswoman of the Year. She could tell he liked Omega and was one of the few who could tell them apart. And Alpha knew Riley liked Marlon Farmer, Omega's husband. The two had hit it off immediately. Already plans were in the works for her and Riley to visit Omega and Marlon in Paris...especially since Omega was expecting. She had never seen her sister looking so happy and radiant.

She glanced down on the beautiful ring she wore. They had decided on an August wedding, and she was looking forward to becoming Mrs. Riley Westmoreland.

Alpha also knew that while in Daytona, Riley had talked with her parents and let them know that she had his full support in maintaining a close relationship with her twin. He further told them how much family meant to him and that he hoped one day they would be able to repair their relationship with Omega. She had fallen more in love with him at that moment.

The sound of loud laughter made Alpha look in the direction of the wedded couple. They had just cut the cake. After Megan fed Rico a slice it seemed he was still licking the icing off Megan's fingers.

Alpha then glanced around the huge ballroom and her gaze settled on Riley's cousin Zane. He was leaning against the wall and staring hard at Dr. Channing Hastings, the woman he hadn't wanted Megan to invite.

"What are you looking at, baby?" Riley asked her.

She smiled up at him. "Your cousin Zane and how he's staring at Channing Hastings. She's beautiful."

Riley nodded. "Yes, Channing is beautiful both in and out. She and Zane had an affair a couple of years back when she lived here in Denver."

"Now she's engaged to be married to the man with the roving eyes. I bet he's checked out every single woman here today, even a few married ones."

Riley nodded, looking over at the man at Channing's side. "You noticed that, as well? She deserves better, which has me wondering why Channing is marrying the guy. I bet Zane is wondering that, as well. But as far as I'm concerned, when you snooze, you lose, and Zane was definitely snoozing when it came to Channing. I would bet any amount of money that he's feeling the pain of his loss. We always warned him that his womanizing ways would cost him one day. So he won't get any pity from me."

Alpha couldn't help but grin. "How can you talk? You were just as much a womanizer."

Riley shook his head. "Nobody could top Zane when it came to women. And, as far as I'm concerned, you have to admit that when I met the woman I knew was for me, I had no problem making her mine and putting a ring on her finger," he said, reaching out and taking her ringed hand in his. "Zane was too stubborn to do that. And I hate to say it, but he probably has lost the only woman he is capable of loving."

"How sad." She truly meant it. Now that she had Riley, she couldn't imagine not having the person you loved in your life. But she had a feeling, from the way Zane was staring at Channing, that Zane would be changing that soon. Alpha couldn't help wondering why Dr. Hastings would marry a man with wandering eyes.

"I've got to get back," she whispered, before brushing a kiss across his cheeks. "My work isn't completed until I get Megan and Rico off on their honeymoon. I think it's wonderful that they're going to Dubai for two weeks."

"Yes, it is wonderful, isn't it?"

She glanced around at all the Atlanta, Montana and Texas Westmorelands she had met over the past couple of days. The men all favored and the women were ultrafriendly. She felt blessed that she was marrying into such a warm and loving family. She smiled when she glanced over and saw Pam and Dillon with their daughter, who'd been born on Christmas Day. She was definitely a beauty.

She then saw Riley's brother, Bane, whom she had just met earlier that day when he had arrived in town. He was such a handsome man she had to take a second look every time she saw him. Even though he was always smiling, she could detect sadness around his eyes. Now she understood Riley's reasons for not wanting to feel the pain his brother was enduring.

"Alpha?"

She glanced up at Riley. Immediately, he lowered his mouth to hers, swiping any thoughts from her mind and kissing her with a hunger that she couldn't help but reciprocate, capturing her tongue in his and doing all sorts of erotic and scandalous things to it.

Scandalous…

It seeped back into her brain just where they were and what she was supposed to be doing. Dislodging her mouth from his, which wasn't an easy feat, she took a step back and drew in a deep breath. "Has anyone ever told you that you shouldn't mess around with the hired help?" she said playfully.

"No, and I wouldn't listen to them anyway. I have tunnel vision when it comes to you, sweetheart."

He took a step closer to regain the distance she'd put between them, bringing his body to hers. She felt something else he had, an erection that was hard and thick. "I'm going now, and I think you need to stay behind this planter until you get yourself together."

He chuckled. "As long as you're close by, I'll never be together—unless you're sharing my bed. And I've been thinking."

"About what?"

"We've had our one winter's night so what about a summer one?" he asked, leaning down and nibbling her lips.

"Riley…" she whispered in a strained voice, "I do need to get back to the wedding."

"No, you don't," he said, wrapping his arms around her. "Lindsey is a great assistant and has everything under control."

"Megan is going to fire me."

"And I will hire you to plan my wedding," he said as his mouth moved lower to nibble her throat.

"Behave," she said, pulling out of his arms again.

"Only if you promise that as soon as this wedding is over you will meet me at Riley's Station for our own after-wedding party."

She gazed up at him. She had a million things to do, but he was right, Lindsey was a great assistant and Alpha had a fantastic staff. "Okay, I promise."

She quickly moved away but couldn't resist glancing back over her shoulder. She was one lucky woman, and later tonight, when she was through with Riley Westmoreland, he would be convinced he was one lucky man.

* * * * *

She could climb trees, play football, talk cars and quote sports statistics with the best of them. And if the need arose, she knew how to fell a man with one quick move.

What she hadn't quite mastered, though, was how a woman could resist when the man she'd wanted for years was so close she could lift her lips and touch her mouth to his.

With every fiber of her being, she yearned to move against him, rest her head on his shoulder and feel his big masculine arms enfold her. But that was exactly why she couldn't.

Any notion she'd ever had of snagging Sam had disappeared when she'd embarrassed herself with a youthful, impassioned declaration that was ill-timed to say the least. Sam might pretend he'd only been letting her down easy, but she had a hunch that in their charged encounter way back then, he had been speaking the truth.

Sam's perfect woman was not Annalise. Not by a long shot.

Dear Reader,

When I set out to write Annalise's story, I knew she would be someone special. I also realized that her hero needed to be a man who could see past her outer shell of wealth and beauty to the sometimes emotionally fragile woman within.

Annalise fascinated me as she came to life on the page. She and I have very little in common. So I had to stretch my limits to understand this complex sister/daughter/cousin.

After growing up on Wolff Mountain amid an incredible sea of testosterone, Annalise had to learn (as an adult) what it meant to be a woman. Not a carbon copy of anyone else…but simply herself. A still-sore memory from her past puts the lone female Wolff's unexpected chance to find a mate in jeopardy.

Sam and Annalise strike sparks off one another. Come along and see what happens when two strong-willed people go head-to-head and happen to fall in love when they least expect it.

Happy reading,

Janice Maynard

www.JaniceMaynard.com

www.WolffMountain.com

CHOICE OF
TWO
GIFTS!

A **treat**
from us to
thank you
for reading
our books!

Turn over *now*
to find out more

Thanks for reading!

We're treating you to **TWO** fabulous offers...

2 FREE BOOKS

from your favourite Mills & Boon series plus
have books delivered to your door every month!

Find out more and claim your free books at
www.millsandboon.co.uk/bookclub

or call 020 8288 2888 and
quote BOOKCLUB today!

Plus ## 15% OFF **

Your next order online with code
THANKSFEB at **www.millsandboon.co.uk**

*FREE BOOK OFFER TERMS & CONDITIONS

Accepting your free books places you under no obligation to buy anything and you may cancel at any time. If we
do not hear from you we will send you up to 5 stories a month which you may purchase or return to us – the choice
is yours. Offer valid in the UK only and is not available to current Mills & Boon Book Club subscribers to this series.
We reserve the right to refuse an application and applicants must be aged 18 years or over. Only one application
per household. Offer expires 28th February 2013. Terms and prices are subject to change without notice. As a
result of this application you may receive further offers from other carefully selected companies. If you do not wish
to share in this opportunity please write to the Data Manager at PO BOX 676, Richmond, TW9 1WU.

CIFEB13

**WEB OFFER TERMS & CONDITIONS

Offer valid online only at www.millsandboon.co.uk until 31/05/2013. This offer cannot be used in conjunction with
any other offer. Discount excludes delivery charge. Exclusions apply including Offers, subscriptions, sale items and
those with a 40% discount or more. Please see www.millsandboon.co.uk for full terms and conditions.

MILLS &
BOON

ALL GROWN UP

BY
JANICE MAYNARD

MILLS & BOON

All the characters in this book have no existence outside the imagination of the author, and have no relation whatsoever to anyone bearing the same name or names. They are not even distantly inspired by any individual known or unknown to the author, and all the incidents are pure invention.

All Rights Reserved including the right of reproduction in whole or in part in any form. This edition is published by arrangement with Harlequin Enterprises II B.V./S.à.r.l. The text of this publication or any part thereof may not be reproduced or transmitted in any form or by any means, electronic or mechanical, including photocopying, recording, storage in an information retrieval system, or otherwise, without the written permission of the publisher.

This book is sold subject to the condition that it shall not, by way of trade or otherwise, be lent, resold, hired out or otherwise circulated without the prior consent of the publisher in any form of binding or cover other than that in which it is published and without a similar condition including this condition being imposed on the subsequent purchaser.

® and ™ are trademarks owned and used by the trademark owner and/or its licensee. Trademarks marked with ® are registered with the United Kingdom Patent Office and/or the Office for Harmonisation in the Internal Market and in other countries.

Published in Great Britain 2013
by Mills & Boon, an imprint of Harlequin (UK) Limited,
Eton House, 18-24 Paradise Road, Richmond, Surrey TW9 1SR

© Janice Maynard 2013

ISBN: 978 0 263 90465 9
ebook ISBN: 978 1 472 00088 0

51-0213

Harlequin (UK) policy is to use papers that are natural, renewable and recyclable products and made from wood grown in sustainable forests. The logging and manufacturing processes conform to the legal environmental regulations of the country of origin.

Printed and bound in Spain
by Blackprint CPI, Barcelona

Janice Maynard came to writing early in life. When her short story *The Princess and the Robbers* won a red ribbon in her school arts fair, Janice was hooked. She holds a BA from Emory and Henry College and an MA from East Tennessee State University. In 2002 Janice left a fifteen-year career as an infant teacher to pursue writing full-time. Her first love is creating sexy, character-driven, contemporary romance. She has written for Kensington and NAL, and now is so very happy to also be part of the Mills & Boon® family—a lifelong dream, by the way!

Janice and her husband live in beautiful east Tennessee in the shadow of the Great Smoky Mountains. She loves to travel and enjoys using those experiences as settings for books.

Hearing from readers is one of the best perks of the job! Visit her website, www.janicemaynard.com, or email her at JESM13@aol.com. And of course, don't forget Facebook and Twitter. Visit all the men of Wolff Mountain at www.wolffmountain.com.

This book is dedicated to women everywhere
who pave their own way with grace and beauty
and originality. Never apologize for being who you are.
Life has shaped you with experiences both good and
bad. Embrace your unique self and let the world
know what you have to offer. Shine!

One

Annalise Wolff regarded Sam Ely much like she did the IRS. She was forced to deal with him occasionally, but the experience inevitably gave her a bad feeling in the pit of her stomach…thus making her voluntary presence in his office today all the more incomprehensible. She leaned back in her chair, crossed one slim leg over the other and admired the sheen on her soft ebony leather boots. They were Prada, as was her voluminous purse.

Suffering the indignity of face-to-face contact with the ridiculously handsome architect required full body armor. Her crimson cashmere sweater and narrow black wool skirt were designed to show him she was all grown up.

Unfortunately, Sam didn't seem all that impressed.

He lounged against the window frame, his gaze absently focused on the wintry day outside. "Yes or no, Annalise," he said, a faint but unmistakable bite in his voice despite his honeyed drawl. "I'm giving you the courtesy of first refusal, but there are dozens of interior designers who would jump at this opportunity."

He was right, damn his scurvy, sexy, Southern hide. The Shenandoah Valley home and dairy farm that belonged to his grandparents dated back to the time of Thomas Jefferson. The house was listed on the national register. Experts in historic renovation were handling the extensive changes Sam had drawn in detail via the plans rolled out on a nearby table. The project was an interior designer's dream. She stalled, telling herself she could walk away. "And the magazine spread afterward is a done deal?"

"My college roommate's mom is the managing editor of *Architectural Design*. She's salivating at the opportunity to put Sycamore Farm in the earliest possible issue. The only holdup at the moment is you."

He returned to his desk and sat down on the edge of it, his long, muscular legs dangerously close to hers. The position put him above her, and she knew he did it deliberately. She'd known this man for most of her life. His father had done the architectural design for much of Wolff Castle, and Sam and his dad had been frequent visitors to the Wolff home over the years. For an adolescent girl locked away like Rapunzel in her tower, Annalise's interactions with the much older Sam had been her first and only exposure to hormonal-driven, adolescent passion.

"When would I start?" she hedged. "If I agree."

He glanced down at the calendar beside him. "I'm sure you have a few things to wrap up. How about a week from Friday? Gram and Pops want you to live onsite, given the remoteness of the farm. Too much time commuting would eat into the schedule."

She felt her face heat. "Where will you be?"

He put his hands on his thighs, drawing her attention to their size and firmness and the shape of his masculinity nestled where they met. "Don't worry," he muttered, irritation etching a scowl between his eyebrows as he glared at her. "Gram wants me to spend a couple of days at the beginning to orient you to the project, but afterward, I'll return here to my office, far, far away. That should put your mind at rest." He ran a hand through his hair. "For God's sake, I'm not making you a prisoner. Go home whenever you need to, but I want you to give this job a hundred and ten percent. Or nothing."

He sat up, back straight, arms folded, eyes glittering with challenge. "Do I make you nervous, Annalise?"

"Of course not." Her reply was commendably quick, but lamentably false. "I'm just not sure if I have the time to fit you into my schedule." Annalise didn't need the money. But the cachet of having her name on this massive undertaking would take her business and reputation to a whole new level. She was ambitious, damn it. Sam might not think of her as anything more than a family friend, but professionally he had her pegged.

He took her hand and drew her to her feet, cradling her loosely in the vee of his legs. "Make time, Annalise," he said, his gaze locking onto hers like a charlatan preparing to hypnotize an unwary victim. "You know you want to."

Sam was overplaying his hand. Sexual nuance was not his normal mode of doing business. But the God's honest truth was, Annalise made *him* nervous. He'd hurt her badly seven years ago when she'd had a big crush on him, and though he'd like to believe that was water under the bridge, the wariness in her sooty-lashed, pale blue eyes was unmistakable. The adoration she'd showered him with so long ago had changed into fury the instant he'd rejected her, and she had never forgiven him.

The reluctant attraction he battled even now had sim-

mered back then. He'd never been able to forget what
happened, and though he'd tried on several occasions to
apologize over the years, Annalise shut him down time and
again until he finally gave up and avoided her as much as
possible. She did likewise.

But like a stubborn splinter beneath the skin, he couldn't
seem to extract her from his life and his thoughts. So when
his grandparents insisted he offer the job to Annalise, he'd
relished the opportunity to get her alone, to invite her to
his office, to see her face-to-face.

The color of her irises was unusual for a woman with
hair so dark and glossy. But then again, most everything
about Annalise Wolff was extraordinary. Tall and slim and
infinitely confident, her striking looks could have made
her a runway model or a film star. She carried herself
with a boldness that did nothing to minimize her intense
femininity.

For a split second, Sam allowed himself to imagine
all that boundless energy and subtle sexual aggression in
his bed. His sex hardened to the point of pain. This was
why he normally kept a healthy distance. He didn't want
to think of her that way. Cursing his own stupidity, he set
her aside and put the desk between them. "I can't give you
long to make up your mind. Gram wanted you because of
the work you did on the president's home at UVA. She and
my grandfather attended the reception that showcased the
renovations there and they were both very impressed with
your work. But if you don't have the time, just say so."

Annalise folded her arms beneath her breasts. The soft
red sweater she wore delineated her modest curves and
her narrow waist. Sam had big hands, and it was not a far
stretch to imagine himself lifting her and spreading her
legs and—

Oh, hell.

She tilted her chin upward, nose in the air. "You'd like that, wouldn't you? But sorry, Sam Ely, I guess you're stuck with me. If your grandmother wants me to do this project, I'm in."

The jolt of joy that stabbed through his chest was a surprise. Did he really want an excuse to spend time with the prickly, stubborn Annalise Wolff? Apparently, according to his unreasonable but insistent erection, he did.

Sam cleared his throat, making a show of turning the calendar around and jotting a note. "I'll get my attorney to draw up a contract. Do you have any questions?"

Ten days later, Annalise steered her Miata along a narrow paved road that led up to the entrance of Sycamore Farm. In the dead of winter, the property was not all that impressive. Fallow fields crusted with frost flanked both sides of the road. Excessive freezing and thawing had played havoc with the asphalt, leaving the occasional pothole.

Sam's grandparents had been gone for several weeks, searching out warmer climes. But Annalise had been assured that the fridge and pantry were stocked and at least one bedroom outfitted for a long-term guest.

Remembering her last encounter with Sam, she muttered an expletive. Growing up in an all-male household had done unfortunate damage to a ladylike vocabulary. On New Year's Eve she'd made a resolution to give up cursing, but so far, her progress hadn't been stellar.

Sam's last words still rang in her ears. *Do you have any questions?*

Hell, yes, she had questions, one in particular. *Was I so repulsive seven years ago that you couldn't bring yourself to have sex with me when I threw myself at you and acted like a fool?*

The remembered humiliation churned bile in her stomach. Steering with one hand, she rummaged in her purse for an antacid. The intervening days and months had done nothing to blunt the sharpness of the memory....

"Hi, Sam." She was breathless from running downstairs to intercept him before he got in his car. She'd kept a vigil at her bedroom window for the last half hour. Sam and his father had driven separately, because the older man was lingering to play poker with her father and Uncle Victor.

Sam paused, one hand on the top of the car, the other holding a set of keys. "What's up? I thought you weren't feeling well." His slow drawl and lazy hazel-eyed smile took her breath away.

She bit her lip, legs trembling. She'd feigned a headache to get out of dinner. Sitting across the table from Sam would have been torture, because she dared not let her daddy see how much in love she was. Vincent Wolff was very protective of his baby daughter. She lifted her chin, reaching for calm. "Actually, I had some work to do. I'm graduating from college in a few weeks. And I'll start my master's program. Interior design," she added, hoping he would be impressed. She felt like an adult for the first time in her life, with a level playing field, and the resultant adrenaline gave her confidence.

Sam jingled his keys. "Oh." The look on his face wasn't encouraging. If anything he was eager to get on his way. At almost thirty, Sam Ely was in his prime, and just about the hottest thing Annalise had ever seen.

She moved three steps closer. "I thought you might like to take me out to dinner sometime," she said.

The look on his face—as if he'd been poleaxed—was not flattering.

Desperation lent wings to her feet. She moved forward with determination, went up on tiptoe to wrap her arms around his neck and kissed him square on the mouth. His arms went around her reflexively, but his entire body stiffened. "Um, Annalise..."

She scattered kisses from his nose to his chin to his tanned neck revealed by an open-collared dress shirt. "I know you've been waiting for me to grow up," she whispered. "Please tell me you want me. I know you do."

His burgeoning erection gave truth to her words. But at twenty-one, more naive than most, she didn't fully grasp the difference between male reflex and a more romantic motive.

After one heartfelt moment when it seemed as if Sam might return her kiss, he set her away firmly, holding out a hand when she would have embraced him again. "No, Annalise. I think of you as a sister."

Confusion brought her up short. His body had responded...unmistakably. "I think I'm in love with you, Sam," she cried.

He winced. He actually winced. And her heart turned to ashes.

The kindness in his gaze scorched her with humiliation. "You're barely an adult, honey. And I'm years too old for you. I'm flattered. You're an amazing young woman. But both of our dads would string me up if I tried anything with you... And besides..."

He had said enough. Annalise didn't want to hear any more. She was mute with misery.

"Besides," he said slowly, "most guys like to do the chasing. You might want to think about that. I know you've grown up without a mother to teach you these things, but men like gentle, feminine women. Soft, self-effacing. I guess it's the whole caveman thing." He brushed her cheek with the back of his hand. "You're beautiful, Annalise. You don't need to try so hard...."

The front of the car hit a larger-than-normal pothole, and Annalise was jerked back to the present, clutching the steering wheel as she slowed to a crawl. Please, God, let Sam Ely's visit be short. She would listen politely, take notes and bid him a civil goodbye. Then she could get to work.

If she ignored the debacle from the past, surely he would have the decency to do so as well.

As she rounded one last bend in the road and came in sight of the cluster of buildings that comprised Sycamore Farm, she saw a lone, immediately recognizable figure standing on the front porch despite the frigid temperatures. Her heart beat a sluggish rhythm as she put the car in Park and got out.

She was a grown woman, well-traveled. Sophisticated. Sexually experienced to some degree. She had done everything in her power to forget her first love, to deny how much Sam's rejection had wounded her tender heart. Sam Ely was just a man like any other. For thirty-six hours, forty-eight at the most, she would impress him with her calm competence and her utter lack of interest in his sexy smile and masculine charms. By the time he left, all he would remember about Annalise Wolff was that she was damned good at her job.

He lifted a hand in greeting, the habitual smile nowhere in evidence.

Annalise opened her mouth to say hello. But in an instant that felt like the most dreadful slow-motion replay, disaster struck. Her heel hit a patch of ice in the driveway, her feet flew out from under her and she fell flat on her back. Hard.

When she opened her eyes with a groan, Sam Ely's big body crouched over hers as his hands ran lightly over her limbs checking for damage. Gently he lifted her head and felt for a knot.

Annalise shivered inside her warm down coat, but it had nothing to do with the snow flurries swirling around them. All he had to do was touch her and she was that young, desperate woman again.

He brushed her cheek with the back of his hand. "Are you hurt?"

Sam winnowed his fingers through silky black hair that clung to his fingers with static from the cold air. "Say something, damn it. Are you okay?"

Annalise's glare could have melted a snowman at ten paces. She struggled to sit up. "I'm fine," she said shortly. "Quit pawing me."

Though her words were clipped and showed her annoyance, beneath his touch she was warm and soft and womanly. Resisting the urge to touch the curve of her breast, Sam scooped her into his arms and stood, mentally counting to ten. He'd promised himself he wouldn't let her push his buttons. But she was so aggravating, his blood pressure went up immediately whenever they got within sight of each other. Not that such a reaction was anything new. As a friend of the Wolff family, he inevitably ran into her from time to time. Neither of them ever managed more than bare civility.

The animosity was his fault, no doubt. But it wouldn't hurt her to let go of something that happened over half a dozen years ago. Thankfully, she didn't squirm too much. She was a tall woman, and if he slipped on the ice, they'd both go down.

On the porch, he reached with one hand to open the door and stepped inside, ruefully aware that the house held a distinct chill. He sighed. "The heat and air guys will be here in a couple of days to overhaul the vents and put in new units. In the meantime, I hope you've got plenty of warm clothes. The old system is cantankerous."

"Probably learned it from you," Annalise muttered beneath her breath.

He knew she meant for him to hear.

In the kitchen, he lowered her into a chair. A cheery fire crackled in the fireplace, and his grandmother's collection of Fiestaware in the china cabinet brightened the room.

He knelt in front of her. "Tell me the truth. Are you hurt?"

Big eyes stared back at him. And for an instant, he thought her bottom lip might have quivered. But if there had been even a moment of vulnerability, it was gone.

"No," she said bluntly. "I'm fine." She stripped out of her coat, revealing a thin silky blouse in a shade of blue that matched her eyes, and black linen trousers with a knife pleat. "But I'd kill for a cup of coffee."

For a long second, Sam stayed at her feet. She could have stepped off the runway and come straight to him. Vincent Wolff had kept his baby girl locked up like a nun for much of her life, but probably out of guilt, he had indulged her passion for pretty clothes.

Sam sighed. "Don't try to stand up yet. I'll brew a pot." In moments, the aroma of coffee permeated the air. Annalise hadn't moved from the chair where he put her. But she was pointedly ignoring him, smart phone in hand as she scrolled through messages.

He found a china cup, filled it with hot, fragrant liquid and set it on a saucer at her elbow, along with a tiny pitcher of cream and the sugar bowl. He smothered a grin as she frowned at the add-ons and instead put the cup to her berry-colored lips and drained half of it, black and straight, the same way Sam liked it.

He turned a chair around and straddled it, facing her across the table. "How's your dad?"

She paused, the cup halfway to her mouth. "Fine." Her suspicious gaze scanned his face as if searching for a secret agenda.

"And your uncle Vic?"

Annalise set down the cup. "Also fine."

"Lots of weddings in your family in the last year."

Her face softened. "Yes. It's been wonderful. Gracie, Olivia, Ariel, Gillian... I finally have sisters."

"Your family deserves happiness more than any set of people I know. I'm glad the past is behind you." When Annalise was a toddler, her mother and aunt had been kidnapped and murdered. It was a blow that had marked them all, and it had taken years for them to truly recover.

Annalise's eyebrows lifted, a glint of defiance in her expression. "Thank God for that." She laughed, but there was little humor in the sound. And the sideways glance she shot him said louder than any words that a certain moment in their past was definitely *not* forgotten.

He reached across the table and took her hand in his, stroking the back of it, feeling the smooth skin, the delicate bones. "Give me a break, Annalise. We can't work together if we don't hash this out. I'll admit I could have handled things better back then. But I'd known you since you were in kindergarten. And you were still a kid as far as I was concerned."

She jerked her hand away. "I don't know what you're talking about."

Her scowl would have deterred most men. But Sam was tired of being treated like the Ebenezer Scrooge of the romance world. "Your father would have neutered me."

"You said I was like a sister to you."

"Damn it." His clumsy lie was going to haunt him.

"Clearly, I didn't mean that. I was trying to escape with some grace."

"So you were a lily-livered coward. Is that what you're telling me?"

This time he had to count to fifty. Standing abruptly, he tried not to notice the plump curve of her bottom lip or the way dark lashes made feathered crescents on her cheeks when she looked down at her cup.

"Yes," he said, conceding defeat. If she wanted to hold a grudge, there wasn't a damn thing he could do about it. "I was a coward."

His admission seemed to take the wind out of her sails. "Whatever." She sniffed and crossed her legs, picking at a spot of lint on the cuff of one pant leg.

As a comeback, it lacked a certain vocabularic grace, but he was willing to let it slide. "Why don't I show you your room?" he said, trying to live up to Gram's notion of hospitality. "I'll get your bags. Relax and make sure you didn't do any permanent damage."

Her small, wry grin disarmed him. "My butt bone is probably bruised, but I'll live."

Seeing her smile in his presence was such a novelty, he was momentarily stunned. He swallowed. "I'm glad."

Unable to come up with any response more scintillating than that, he turned and executed what might be considered a hasty retreat, striding down the hallway toward the front of the house in order to give himself time to regain his footing. If Annalise Wolff was going to start smiling at him, all bets were off.

He flung open the front door and stopped dead. A string of heartfelt curses brought his lovely guest running. "What is it? What's wrong?"

They stood shoulder-to-shoulder gazing out into a world

of swirling snow. Already Annalise's tire tracks were being erased. And her car was coated in white.

She punched his arm. "Did you know this was going to happen? Why didn't you tell me not to come?"

His eyebrows reached his hairline. "I've been a little busy, damn it. Did *you* even bother to look at a forecast?"

"This is your fault!" They shouted in unison, with two identical expressions of dismay and disbelief.

Sam closed the door and leaned back, his arms folded across his chest. "I can't tell for sure without checking The Weather Channel, but having spent a lot of years in Virginia, I'd say we're in for a big one."

"I'm sure it's not going to be more than a few inches." The unflappable Annalise Wolff was definitely rattled. A pulse beat visibly in the side of her swanlike neck.

The urge to make an inappropriate sexual comment was strong, but he squelched it. "You seem upset," he said mildly.

It was her turn to do the eyebrow thing. "Seriously? Aren't you the man who doesn't leave the office until nine most nights? You could be stuck here. For hours…maybe days…" Her voice ended on a high squeak.

Oddly, the more she freaked, the greater his sense of amusement. "Don't worry, Annalise. At least we have each other."

Two

Glaring, she thrust out her chin and fisted her hands. "I absolutely will not be locked up in this house with you. No way, no how."

He shrugged. "I promised Gram I'd stay the weekend and get you oriented. But if you're worried about being stuck and alone with me, we can leave right now. She'll be really disappointed...."

He was goading her, and not even trying to hide it. Frustration knotted her belly, even as her recalcitrant imagination conjured up images of the two of them entwined beneath one of Gram's handmade quilts. "I'm not worried about myself. You're the one who needs to get back to work."

"What do you propose we do? I drove the Porsche. You're in a Miata. If we stay here any length of time, neither of us has a prayer of making it back out to the interstate."

His expression was veiled, unreadable. Was this some kind of game where Sam waited to see if she would cry uncle? She wouldn't give him the satisfaction.

"Fine," she said abruptly. "The weather doesn't bother me. But I'd like my bags now, if you don't mind. So I can get settled in." She handed him her keys.

She was pretty sure his jaw dropped a millimeter. Clearly he thought she'd go running back to the city. But Annalise Wolff never backed down from a challenge.

He scowled. "Are you sure about this, Princess? If the power goes out, we'll be roughing it."

Annalise gulped inwardly. Her idea of rustic was not staying on the concierge floor at the Four Seasons. "I'm sure there's a generator...right?"

"Of course. But it won't run forever. Did you even bring any warm clothes besides your coat?" His gaze felt like a caress as he did a visual inventory of her silk blouse and thin slacks.

"I have everything I need. Do you want me to *help* you retrieve the suitcases?"

Her snarky question deepened his frown. "I think I can manage."

She watched through the window and grinned as Sam opened the trunk and did a double take. Hiding her smile, she stayed out of the way while he made three trips in a row, grousing audibly at the mounting pile of luggage.

When he was finally finished, he closed the door behind him and locked it, looking for all the world like a sexy abominable snowman. He shrugged out of his thick jacket and ran a hand through his hair, sending droplets of water flying as melting snowflakes dampened the floor.

Annalise leaned against the wall, trying not to go weak in the knees when his muscles flexed beneath the fabric of a thermal weave shirt in a deep rust color that complemented his eyes. "Thank you."

He tossed the wet jacket over the back of a chair. "Does the term *high maintenance* mean anything to you?"

She shrugged. "I plan to be here for several weeks. Am I supposed to write you a check for excess baggage?"

He stared at her, a long, intense clashing of gazes that was unmistakably sexual. "You have a smart mouth."

"You have an arrogant attitude."

The ruddy tinge that colored his cheekbones gave her more satisfaction than it should have. "What's in all those bags?" he asked, his stance combative.

"Books, laptop, snacks, lingerie…" She gestured toward the pieces of her Louis Vuitton matched set. Uncle Victor had given it to her as a graduation present. She was spoiled, she freely admitted it. But that didn't give the insufferable Sam Ely a right to criticize.

"Snacks?" He leaned against the opposite wall, adopting a pose that mirrored hers. Barely three feet separated them, and although the foyer was definitely chilly after Sam had been in and out the door several times, Annalise was not cold at all.

"I have a weakness for chocolate. So sue me. The stuff I picked up in Lucerne after Christmas is better than sex."

"Then you've been having the wrong kind of sex."

This time it was her jaw that dropped. Her thighs tightened, and she was pretty sure her nipples were playing peek-a-boo through the silk of her blouse…though she wasn't about to check. Surreptitiously, she lifted her folded arms. "Is flirtation your default setting? Or do you really expect me to argue the point?"

"You're right," he said smoothly, his voice slow as syrup. "That was an inappropriate remark between colleagues."

"I'm not your colleague," she shot back. "I work for your grandparents."

Sam straightened and closed the distance between them. "You have to forgive me for the past, Annalise. Otherwise we're going to be at each other's throats forever."

She looked at the tanned skin of his jaw and below... saw the way warm, masculine flesh disappeared into the neckline of his henley shirt, revealing a faint dusting of hair where the top two buttons gaped open. Her heart thudded in her chest and her palms were damp.

Licking her lips, she looked past him to the antique grandfather clock that held a place of honor flanking the foot of a curved staircase. "I'm surprised you haven't ever found that paragon of womanhood you described to me. You know, all meek and quiet and docile." Saying the words aloud revived the awful memory of that evening. Her chest hurt.

She heard him curse and felt big, warm hands settle on her shoulders. "Look at me, Princess. I'm sorry. All that crap I said to you that day was just that. I was babbling. Trying to get myself out of a sticky situation. Yes, I was attracted to you. But you had a crush, that's all. That guff I spouted about waiting for a man to make the first move... well, I guess I wanted to make sure you'd never try that stunt again. I didn't want you to end up hurt because some jerk took you up on your offer and then dumped you."

His breath was warm on her face. She dared not look into his eyes. She felt far too fragile, and that really pissed her off, because Annalise Wolff was *not* fragile. She'd grown up in a monster of a house with two brothers, three male cousins, an uncle and a father. Any *girly* ways had been hammered out of her at a young age.

She could climb trees, play football, talk cars and quote

sports statistics with the best of them. And if the need arose, she knew how to fell a man with one quick move.

What she hadn't quite mastered, though, was how a woman could resist when the man she'd wanted for years was so close you could lift your lips and touch your mouth to his.

With every fiber of her being, she yearned to move against him, rest her head on his shoulder and feel his big masculine arms enfold her. But that was exactly why she couldn't.

She was weak when it came to Sam Ely. Weak and dreadfully predictable. So he was handsome, so what? The fact that he was sexy and Southern and so damned funny and smart shouldn't be an issue.

Any notion she'd ever had of snagging Sam had disappeared when she'd embarrassed herself with a youthful, impassioned declaration that was ill-timed to say the least. Sam might pretend he'd only been letting her down easy, but she had a hunch that in their charged encounter way back then, he had been speaking the truth.

Sam's perfect woman was not Annalise. Not by a long shot.

With a strangled mutter of protest, she eluded his embrace, picked up two small bags and headed toward the kitchen. Refusing to look at him, she raised her voice as she walked away. "I'd like another cup of coffee, and then I'd appreciate it if you would show me my room."

Sam grabbed up most of the rest of the bags and followed her, grinding his teeth in frustration. He'd apologized, damn it. What more could he do? He wasn't about to crawl. Especially since he hadn't done anything wrong. In fact, he ought to get a medal for doing the *right* thing. Annalise was one of the most sensual, beautiful women he had ever known. If he'd been a different kind of man—or not suitably intimidated by his father and hers—he would have said *to hell with it* and taken her up on her offer.

He'd certainly thought about it often enough over the years. But he'd been raised to adhere to a gentlemanly code of conduct, and that code precluded a thirty-year-old man from having sex with one not-quite-mature college graduate who'd been sheltered more than most.

He wasn't the bad guy in this scenario. So why did he get the distinct impression that Annalise Wolff would like to consign him to the devil?

Striding through the kitchen and into the hallway beyond, he tried to avoid looking at her. The scent of her perfume, something light and beguiling, mingled with the smell of coffee.

The bedroom that had been prepared for Annalise was as cold as ice. He rolled his eyes in disgust and opened all the vents. Evidently the housekeeping service his grandmother utilized had missed a few key points about dates.

Annalise startled him when she appeared at his side, her arms wrapped around her waist protectively. "It's like a meat locker in here," she said. "Are you sure the heat's working at all?"

He hefted her large suitcase onto a large cedar-lined chest at the foot of the bed. "For now? Yes. But I'll kick the thermostat up a few notches to be sure. It wouldn't kill you to put on a sweater."

"The cold doesn't seem to be bothering you."

"I have a fast metabolism. And quite a few more pounds of insulation than you do." He paused, uncharacteristically uncertain. Of himself. Of her. "Last chance," he said. "If we leave now, I think we can still make it back to town."

Annalise stared at him, eyes wide. "I've cleared my calendar," she said quietly. "This project deserves my full attention. Even with bad weather, there is a lot I can do to keep the ball rolling. Measuring and sketching alone will keep me occupied for several days. But I understand if you need to go back to Charlottesville."

He couldn't read her expression. Weak late-afternoon light, muted by the snow, filtered in through lace sheers, casting dappled shadows on the hardwood floor. "I can't leave you here alone," he said, not really wanting to. "Anything could happen."

She shrugged, glimmers of something disturbing in her eyes. "I'm more resilient than you think. You're not responsible for me."

He allowed himself to touch her briefly, tucking a stray strand of hair behind her ear. "I promised Gram I'd get you started. There's a lot of info I need to share. So I guess we're staying."

He was shocked that she allowed the fleeting touch without protest. A tiny smile kicked up one corner of her mouth. "I guess we are."

At that moment, the lights flickered. Annalise looked at him with apprehension. "Already?"

"It's probably just the wind at this point. Although, to be honest, the power isn't all that reliable on a good week. And by the way, the plans include undergrounding all the utilities. Not only for occasions like today, but to restore the original look of the place."

"Holy cow, Sam. That will cost a fortune."

Coming from the daughter of one of the wealthiest families in America, her amazement was telling. "Yeah," he said, grinning. "But I'm an architectural purist. What can I say?"

The lights flickered a second time, galvanizing him into action. "I need to go bring in as much firewood as I can. If the power goes out, we'll camp out in the living room."

"That's behind the kitchen, right?"

"Yes. The two rooms share a chimney. Fortunately, that section of the house has already been finished. If you don't mind, how about making us a couple of omelets while I get the wood. If we do lose power, it would be nice to have one last hot meal."

Annalise blanched.

"What's wrong?"

"I'm not handy in the kitchen," she said with a wry, self-deprecating twist of her mouth.

"Nothing fancy," he assured her. "There's lunch meat in the fridge. Just chop up some ham."

She grimaced, and for a split second he witnessed in Annalise a shocking vulnerability he had never seen before. "I'm serious, Sam. I don't cook."

The expression on her face seemed to indicate she was awaiting his derision. And although he was certainly incredulous, he tried to hide his surprise. "I guess that makes sense. Growing up without a mother must have been tough."

"I wanted the chef to teach me. When I was thirteen. But Daddy said it was inappropriate for me to spend time in the kitchen when I could be learning Latin and Greek. He has odd ideas about things like that."

"And in college?"

"I lived in the dorm. Ate in the cafeteria. When I got out on my own, it wasn't an issue. I order a lot of take-out, and when I entertain, I hire a caterer."

He was momentarily speechless.

Annalise lifted her chin. "I know your grandmother is a fabulous cook. And I'm sure your mother is, as well. But if that's what you were expecting, you're out of luck. I planned on eating a lot of cereal and canned tuna while I'm here."

Sam inhaled, feeling as though he was stepping through a minefield. "It's not important, Annalise. You caught me off guard, that's all. I have this impression of you as being Superwoman, and I suppose I thought there was nothing you couldn't do."

Her tense shoulders relaxed. "That's a nice thing to say."

He tugged her hair. "I *can* be nice on occasion. When I'm not continually provoked."

"Is that a jab at me?"

He lifted an eyebrow innocently. "Would I do that?"

They laughed softly in unison, and he felt an imperceptible shift in the parameters that had governed the recent cold war between them.

Annalise waved her hands. "Go get the wood. I'll make some sandwiches. And I do know how to heat soup."

"Well, there you go," he said. "What more do we need?"

He found himself whistling as he carried armload after armload of wood into the house from the pile beside the barn. Something inside him felt charged with anticipation, though if he'd been called on to identify the odd feeling, he wouldn't have been able to pin it down. For the moment, he was content to enjoy the prospect of an evening with a beautiful woman.

If they had to rely on the fireplace for everything, the supply of logs would dwindle rapidly. So he labored until his arms ached and his back protested. When he finally was satisfied that they had enough fuel for the immediate future, he replaced the tarp covering the woodpile and prayed they wouldn't need to revisit it anytime soon.

As he returned to the house, a rush of warm air greeted him along with the sound of Adele's voice filling the hallways at high volume. He found Annalise singing along, oblivious to his entrance as she bent over the kitchen table, arranging two place mats at perfect angles and aligning silverware.

It shouldn't have surprised him to see a high-end iPod dock. Those suitcases had been heavy enough to contain a whole range of electronics.

He waved an arm, hoping to catch her peripheral vision, but she jumped anyway, clutching her chest. "You scared me." She turned the volume down several notches. "Are you ready to eat?"

He was still wearing his jacket, which was now really wet, so he hung it over a chair and put the chair near a vent. Annalise set an opened beer and a bowl of tomato soup in front of him and added a small plate laden with a sad-looking grilled cheese. It wasn't exactly burnt, but she had used too much cheese, and the excess had leaked out the side and turned crispy brown.

She hovered until he took a bite of each offering. Then in silence, she brought her own dishes to the table and sat down. With the heat from the stove, the room was finally warm. Out of the corner of his eye, Sam watched her eat. She had tied her hair back in a thick ponytail, revealing a neck begging to be nibbled by some lucky man.

Sam took a swig of beer, swallowed and set the bottle on the table with a muffled *thunk*. Leaning back in his chair, he stared at her. "So tell me, Annalise. Is there some guy back in Charlottesville who's going to be missing you while you're away?"

She gave him a wary, sideways glance. "I'm not seeing anyone at the moment. I've been slammed at work, and frankly, the last man I went out with was a little too needy. I don't have time for all that romantic crap."

He lifted an eyebrow. "Crap?"

"You know. Texting twenty times a day. Long dinners

and hand-holding in the park. Seriously, the man was a walking Hallmark card."

Sam grinned. "A lot of women like that kind of thing."

Annalise frowned at him. "I don't cook and I'm not into romance. Anything else you want to find fault with?"

"Calm down, Princess. I'm not criticizing. I happen to think you're a fantastically talented person. I was impressed with the way you organized that carnival for the new school in Burton." The Wolff family was in the process of funding and building a brand-new school at the foot of Wolff Mountain so the K-8 students wouldn't have to be bussed so far away.

She narrowed her gaze as if trying to discern sarcasm in his words. "I thought I saw you there."

"I didn't speak to you because you were so busy. Like a general in charge of an army. Everything went smoothly as far as I could see."

She nodded, pleasure lighting her face. "The community wanted to be able to invest in the school project financially. And they did…in a big way. The carnival raised a ton of grassroots money."

"You juggle a lot of balls simultaneously. I've noticed that about you." His office and Annalise's were in the same building in downtown Charlottesville. They rarely crossed paths during the day, but they ran in the same social circles and often attended the same charitable events.

"I like to stay busy," she said. She stood and began taking dirty dishes to the sink. Sam had insisted on installing a dishwasher for his grandmother a long time ago, and had even rigged it so that it was virtually unnoticeable in the period kitchen. Annalise loaded the plates and utensils with brisk, efficient movements.

When she was done, she wiped her hands on a gingham dish towel and leaned back against the counter. "Can we do the tour now? I'm eager to get started."

Sam swallowed hard and wished he hadn't finished his beer. Was she doing it on purpose, or was he simply reading into her words his own sexual agenda. "Fine," he croaked.

Annalise grabbed a pen and notebook from the sideboard—she'd obviously been jotting ideas while he'd labored in the snow. "Where do we begin?"

He sighed inwardly, only now beginning to realize what he'd signed on for. Cabin fever, most definitely. And an unfortunately unrequited dose of healthy lust and attraction.

They walked room to room as Sam talked and Annalise scribbled frantically. Once, peeking over her shoulder, he grinned to see that her handwriting resembled a doctor's... sharp and dark and illegible. Every now and then she'd stop and stare, seeming to be visualizing what might be. She talked to herself beneath her breath as she studied angles and walls and lighting.

After an hour, Sam ushered her back to the living room. Holding a match to the already prepared firewood and tinder, he waved Annalise to one of the two leather armchairs that flanked the fireplace. "We might as well be warm and comfortable while we go over the rest of what Gram wanted me to tell you."

Annalise curled up in the comfy seat and tucked her legs beneath her. "You don't know how exciting it is to have carte blanche with a project like this."

He joined her, yawning as the warmth from the fire caught him unawares. He'd headed to bed after one the night before, and the alarm had been set for six. Even though having to stay at Sycamore Farm longer than he had planned would play havoc with his schedule, at this particular moment, he couldn't find it in his heart to care.

Contentment rolled over him in a wave, and his eyes drifted shut.

Annalise was taken aback to hear her host emit a soft snore. She turned to face him and felt a sharp jab in the vicinity of her heart. His legs were propped on an ottoman, and his hands were tucked behind his head. With his big body outstretched, the shirt he was wearing rode up at his belt line, exposing a tantalizing inch of flat, male abdomen.

Annalise was a tall woman, but Sam was taller still, giving her an odd and incomprehensible sensation of delicate femininity. Which was bizarre to say the least, because although she loved fashion and accessories as much or more than the next woman, she wouldn't characterize herself as feminine in the traditional sense.

She was blunt and bold and often spoke her mind when she'd be better served holding her tongue. Arguing came naturally to her, and even as adults, she and her brothers and cousins could go at it at a moment's notice. Not everyone regarded bickering and merciless teasing as an acceptable pastime, though, and with the advent of new family members, the squabbling had been reduced to more socially acceptable standards.

The testosterone-fueled environment Annalise had grown up in had forced her to develop a thick skin. Regrettably, the only person who had ever really had the ability to pierce it at will was presently sitting a few feet away from her.

She wasn't very good at being still, though the house was certainly peaceful. Inactivity provided too much time for introspection, and Annalise was seldom comfortable with that much self-awareness. She preferred to forge ahead and make up the answers along the way.

Gnawing her lip in indecision, she set her notebook on a side table and quietly stood. Already the fire needed another log. Stealthily, she removed the fire screen, lifted a two-foot piece of oak, kneeled and dropped it carefully onto the flaming embers.

Though she'd never had the opportunity to be a Girl Scout, her brothers had taught her all sorts of skills in the forest. As young children they'd tramped around Wolff Mountain and even invented a club, six members strong. The Wolff Mountain gang.

She paused, fire poker in hand, and felt the sting of tears. Where had this sense of melancholy come from? Was it because, one at a time, each member of the old "gang" seemed to be finding happiness? Healing? Peace?

She was thrilled for her cousins and for her big brother, Devlyn. But where did that leave her and Larkin? Would they always be odd men out?

"Do you see something I don't see?" Sam spoke from behind her, startling her so badly she dropped the poker.

She picked it up, rearranged the logs and replaced the screen. At last, she turned to face Sam. Her feelings were too close to the surface, and she feared saying something stupid. "Just enjoying the blaze," she said lightly.

He sat up, yawning. "Sorry to crash on you like that. It's been a long week."

"Since you quizzed me, I suppose it's okay for me to ask if you have a lady friend who will expect you home tomorrow?"

He leaned forward, elbows on his knees, and ran his hands through his hair. "I'm between relationships at the moment," he said, his voice muffled.

Annalise was well aware that Sam Ely was considered

a "catch." Over the years she had noted the stream of females flowing through his life. Noted and been silently
wounded by it. "What happened to the last one?"

His head lifted and he resumed his earlier position. But
although his body language signaled relaxation, his gaze
was guarded. "We differed on some important issues. Politics. Religion."

"And that was enough to forego sex with Diana Sal-
yers?"

He grinned. "You know a lot about me for someone
who hates my guts."

Annalise sniffed. "You paraded her around all over
Charlottesville. Kind of hard to miss. But I'll admit that I
didn't know it was over. You strike me as being the kind
of guy who could overlook things like that."

He grinned. "Touché. All right. If you must know, I
found out she doesn't want to have kids."

Three

Sam took it as a good sign that Annalise was interested in his love life. Not that he had decided to coax his irascible house guest into bed. But it was nice to know there was some level of emotional involvement, despite her determined antipathy.

He crossed one ankle over the other and rubbed his chest with one hand. Annalise's gaze tracked his every move.

She worried her bottom lip. "You want kids?"

Her incredulity nicked him. "I'm on the wrong side of thirty-five. Is that so strange?"

Instead of sitting down, she paced, her nervous energy palpable. "I didn't peg you for the family type. Didn't your parents divorce?"

He nodded. "When I was nine. Dad worked long hours, so Mother got full custody and took me to Alabama, where she was from."

"Hence the accent."

"Yeah. Alabama was great, but I'd visit Dad several times a year, and then every summer, I came here. To Sycamore Farm. Gram and Pops were security. Roots."

"And this farm will all be yours one day."

"I'm in no hurry. It's so far from town I don't know if I'd ever live here full-time. But weekends and vacations certainly. I'd like my sons and daughters to have the same great experiences I remember."

"Kids…plural? I thought children of divorce ended up cynical loners."

"Do I seem like that kind of guy to you?"

She turned to face him, their gazes locking across the room. For long moments the only sound was the pop and crackle of the fire. "No," she said finally. "But I did assume you were a confirmed bachelor."

"Not at all. In fact, when the right woman comes along, I'll snap her up and hopefully give Gram and Pops some great-grandchildren while they're still young enough to enjoy them."

"Interesting." Annalise walked to the window and tugged aside thick brocade draperies. Darkness had fallen and the glass was too frosted to see anything anyway.

He couldn't read her at the moment. "What about you?" he asked. "Are you going to ride the wave of happily-ever-afters that has overtaken the Wolff family?"

She turned, clearly shocked. "Me? Oh, no. And definitely not kids. It wouldn't be fair."

There was no palatable explanation for the leaden block of disappointment in his stomach. "How so?"

Now she paced behind him, meaning that unless he wanted to stand up and join her, he had no way of studying her expression. He stayed seated and gave her the space she seemed to need.

Her voice was almost wistful. "I've never been around children. At all. You know that none of us were allowed to go to school until we were college-aged."

"You had private tutors, right?"

"Yes. And let me tell you, I had a really hard time making friends when I was an eighteen-year-old college freshman. All I knew was how to relate to guys. Girls were a mystery to me, and sororities, giggling confidences, sexual bragging… All of it baffled me."

"What does any of this have to do with having kids?"

"Let's just say I'm not the nurturing type and leave it at that."

Her answer unsettled him. He felt sure there was more to the story. But they didn't have the kind of relationship where he could drag it out of her. After all, he was lucky to be sharing a house without armed hostilities.

He waved a hand over the back of his chair. "Come sit down. Let me tell you what Gram wants." With the cozy fire and the sense of isolation bred by the storm, the room had become far too intimate.

By the time he retrieved his briefcase from the kitchen and extracted a folder, Annalise was sitting with suspect docility in her chair by the hearth. He'd half expected her to change into jeans and a sweatshirt, but then again, he wasn't sure she owned anything that plebian.

Merely looking at her threatened his peace of mind. She was the kind of beautiful that made a man's heart ache. And other parts of him…well, hell. His body reacted predictably.

Trying to ignore the picture she made, he sat back down, clearing his throat. "How much do you know about the house?"

"Not too much, really. I'm all ears."

She had taken her hair down, and now it floated around

her shoulders, black as sin and just as appealing. As he watched, mouth dry, she curled one strand around her finger and played with it absently. The innocently sensuous motion of her hand mesmerized him.

He dragged his gaze away and stared blindly at the papers in his hand.

"Tell me," she said impatiently. "The more I know, the better I'll be able to recreate the past. Every house has a living memory. My job is to find it here at Sycamore Farm."

"Right." He gathered his thoughts and tried to pretend he was talking to a stranger. "Sycamore Farm dates back to the time of Jefferson and Monticello. Some journals even suggest that one of my long ago ancestors was a friend of the Jeffersons, but that hasn't been proven."

"Still, it's fun to think about. And the two properties are not all that far apart as the crow flies."

"True. At any rate, we lost the land for about twenty-five years late in the nineteenth century, after the Civil War. The house suffered some damage and the family experienced financial reversals. But fortunately an enterprising Ely farmer bought it back about 1900, and it's been in the fold ever since."

"I love to think about that lineage. You're very lucky, Sam."

"Your dad and uncle have begun something similar at Wolff Mountain. I know the Wolff legacy was born in darkness, but think about the years ahead. Especially with all the weddings and babies on the way."

"Only one baby so far, and that's a few months away. Little Cammie was already five when we met her, so having a newborn on the mountain really will be different."

"Don't you think *you'll* want a house up there at some point?"

His question seemed to take her by surprise. "I haven't thought about it."

"Liar."

Her head snapped around so fast it was a wonder she didn't have whiplash. "What does that mean?" Indignant and offended, she glared at him. Ah, that was the Annalise he was accustomed to seeing. "It means that I know you, Princess. You're a decorator. You live for color and lighting and creating beautiful spaces. You can't tell me you haven't daydreamed about your own place on the mountain."

Her eyes darkened. "I have such mixed emotions about Wolff Mountain," she said softly. "Whenever I go there, it brings it all back. Tragedy and family and sadness and home. I'm not sure I want to perpetuate that."

"I could help you design it." He wasn't sure where the words came from. They tumbled from his lips uncensored.

She stared, her eyes huge. "You would?"

"Of course. It would be an honor. I feel like my dad's involvement in creating the castle makes me an honorary Wolff, anyway. And even if you build your own place, you could still live in Charlottesville."

A small smile teased her lips. "I may hold you to that."

"I'm a man of my word."

They looked at each other, Sam itchy and aroused and unused to being locked up in a cozy room with a woman who pushed his buttons so successfully. And God knew what the unpredictable Annalise Wolff was thinking. Probably diabolical ways to smother him in his sleep.

He *would* consider seducing her if he wasn't fairly certain she'd go after his private parts with a butcher knife. *Beware a woman scorned.* The old adage rang in his ears, though he hadn't scorned her in the traditional sense. But any softer feelings she felt for him so long ago were clearly dead and buried.

Annalise wrinkled her nose. "We keep getting side-tracked. Tell me what your grandmother is thinking about colors and fabrics."

He leaned forward, handing her several sheets of paper clipped together. When his fingers brushed hers, he felt an unmistakable burst of heat. "She wrote a lot of stuff out for you to go by. I think she trusts you a great deal. She mostly included things she wants kept the same. Other than that, you can do that magic that you do and make Sycamore Farm a showplace."

As Annalise read through what he had given her, Sam added more logs to the fire and went back out onto the front porch to assess the situation. It wasn't good. They were closing in on twelve inches, with no end in sight. He stood there in his shirt sleeves for a moment, feeling the bitter sting of wind and ice crystals on his face.

The frigid air was almost a relief. His reaction to Annalise Wolff had taken him entirely off guard. The attraction was nothing new. He'd watched her grow from a child into a beautiful, vibrant woman over the years. And even when she had thrown herself at him, he'd been tempted. Really tempted.

But at no time since then had he ever really entertained the idea of pursuing her. First and foremost because she had such a damned big chip on her shoulder about him rejecting her. And then there was the almost inevitable awkwardness if they tried something and it didn't work.

Sam and his dad were welcome visitors at Wolff Castle at least on a monthly basis. What would happen if Sam dated Annalise, slept with her and ended things? The fall-out had the potential to disrupt relationships that were years in the making.

For a brief moment he allowed himself to consider the possibility that he and Annalise might be good together.

Really good. Wedding bells and white dress good. He was ready to settle down, more than ready. His own childhood had been decent, but he had always envied the Wolff kids and their invisible but unmistakable bond.

Sam wanted his own children, whenever they came along, to have siblings, to experience the fun and security of knowing that someone always had your back. The Wolffs had been good to him when he visited with his father over the years. But Sam was older even than Gareth, so he hadn't really been able to assimilate into the pack.

As an adult man, he'd forged lasting friendships with all of them. He was particularly close to Jacob and Devlyn. Annalise was the only real holdout, and apparently in her eyes, Sam would always be to blame for their standoff. He was willing to expend the required energy to win her over, but what then? If a romantic liaison went awry, it would be World War III all over again, only this time with no hope of détente.

Shivering hard, he turned his back on the blizzard and went inside.

By the time Annalise finished reading through all the notes Sam's grandmother had made, Sam still had not returned. She added one more log to the blaze and then went to her room to unpack. The antiques spread throughout the house had been lovingly cared for, and it was heartening to know that many of them would be preserved in the newly renovated house.

After filling the narrow closet and most of the drawers in the dresser and armoire, she folded back the covers and tossed her gown and robe on the bed. The beautiful pieces were silk and not very warm. Perhaps she should have thought through the ramifications of sleeping in a drafty farmhouse in the dead of winter.

As she passed by the mirror with its wavy, slightly mottled glass, she stopped and stared at her reflection. What did Sam see when he looked at her? Was she still the socially awkward, love-stricken young woman to him?

Thinking about that dreadful moment in the past was physically painful. It was more than embarrassment. *That* she could have moved beyond. But the hurt that ran deeper was his criticism. Even as he'd said the words aloud, she had recognized the truth of them. She *was* too pushy, too oblivious to other people's feelings at times.

A more experienced woman would have gauged Sam's disinterest and backed off. But all Annalise had been able to recognize was her own desperate longing for the young teenage boy she had adored as a child. The adolescent boy who had gone on to become a breathtakingly handsome man.

"Are you all settled in? Do you need anything?"

Sam lounged in the doorway, effortlessly charming and charismatic. His head nearly brushed the lintel. All of a sudden, the small, delightful bedroom felt claustrophobic.

Annalise felt panic creep into her throat. What if he could see how much he still affected her? Even worse, what if he thought she was pathetic? Lusting after a man who was no more than a family friend.

She cleared her throat. "I think I'll hit the sack. Good night."

He glanced at his watch. "It's eight-thirty, Annalise."

"Oh." Busted. Had she even brought a book to read? "I don't suppose there's internet?"

He chuckled. "Are you kidding? Gram and Pops are pretty much up with the times, but they flatly refused to get a computer. Even though I begged. It might be a different story now that they're in Florida. We'll see. But you've got your phone…you should be able to check email as long as the storm isn't disrupting tower signals."

He paused, shifted from one foot to another, then gave her a lopsided grin. "There's something I could show you… if you're not too tired. But you'll definitely need a coat or sweater, because it's on the third floor."

She nodded slowly. "Okay." Grabbing up a soft suede jacket, she slipped her arms into the sleeves and scooped her hair out of the collar. "I'm ready."

Sam didn't bother with another layer. Apparently he was made of tougher stuff. She followed him up one set of stairs and then another, pausing at a landing as Sam found a key on his key ring and unlocked a rather short door. Ducking to follow him in, she inhaled the scent of history…dust, old paper and the passage of time.

Sam reached up and pulled the chain to illuminate a single lightbulb suspended from the rafters. The space in which they stood ran half the length of the house. It was bone-chillingly cold, and the storm winds shrieked around the gables of the roof with magnified ferocity.

Annalise shuffled from one foot to the other, arms wrapped around her waist. "This better be good."

The grin Sam cast over his shoulder made her weak in the knees. "Follow me." He led her down one side of the room to a section of the attic that had obviously once been walled in. "I imagine this might have been used as servant quarters years ago." Although segments of the wall were nothing more than exposed two-by-fours or whatever the historical equivalent was, part of a single section was still covered in wallpaper. Really old wallpaper.

Annalise bent forward, trying to get close enough to see in the dim light. "Jiminy Christmas, Sam. Is this original?"

She felt his presence, big and warm, at her shoulder. "Jiminy Christmas?"

Heat washed up her throat. "I made a New Year's resolution to give up cussing."

"Ah." He was so close she could inhale his clean, male scent, so close she could hear him breathe.

Doggedly, she focused her attention on the wall. "Has anyone on the historical renovation team seen this?"

Sam pulled a small flashlight out of his hip pocket and handed it to her. "No. But the plan doesn't call for any changes up here. You're one of the only people I know who would get excited about this."

She shone the small beam of light on the edge of the faded paper. Once upon a time it had probably been a cheery yellow. Now, the scattering of small flowers was barely visible on a field of cream. "There's more under here, isn't there?"

She sensed rather than saw him nod. "I've picked at the frayed part enough to tell that there are at least three more layers beneath this. I think that with an X-Acto knife we might be able to extract the various pieces so that you could look at them."

"This is so damn cool!" She clapped her hand over her mouth and heard Sam laugh. "Is there or was there anything like this downstairs?" she asked, hoping to distract him from her failings.

"If so, it's long gone. You'll find Sheetrock and more modern building supplies. But I know Gram would be thrilled if you were able to find a paper similar to one of these and use it in at least one room…just to tie the past to the future."

"I'd love to try. But why do you think they would have gone to the trouble to use wallpaper up here if it was for servants?"

"My guess is that the paper was a way to keep wind

out. Back then, before roofing was really well done, I'm sure this area of the house was almost like living outside."

"Hmmm…" Her brain raced even as she absorbed the fact that she and Sam stood shoulder-to-shoulder. He seemed to be almost deliberately crowding her personal space.

Her jacket was warm, and with Sam in touchable distance her blood was pumping. The cold didn't even register at the moment. Nevertheless, she feigned a shiver. "I'll come back up here one day when I can see better."

"I could show you more treasures. Disintegrating silk dresses with bustles and button-up shoes. Old army uniforms. Collections of sabers and muskets. Even Gram's wedding dress."

She faced him, wondering what he would do if she went up on tiptoe and kissed him. "It will keep, won't it? I think I'm ready for bed. It's been a long day." She handed over the flashlight, and he tucked it in his pocket. But neither of them moved.

"Annalise, I…"

She'd never heard Sam Ely sound unsure of himself. And the scowl that etched tight planes on his face wasn't encouraging.

Sexual tension arced and crackled between them. If it had been any other man, any other situation, Annalise would have initiated a kiss. But the specter of Sam from the past held her back. *Guys like to do the chasing.*

Confused, embarrassed and angry with herself for acting like a 1950s debutante, she turned abruptly. "I'm done here."

She had taken three steps in the direction of the door when the lights went out. Her momentum carried her forward, and she tripped over something on the floor and stumbled to her knees. "Ouch, damn it." Pain shot up her leg to her hip, and her big toe throbbed.

"Hold still. Don't move." Sam rustled behind her, and muttered beneath his breath when something fell to the floor with a loud *thunk*.

"What was that?"

"I dropped the stupid flashlight." He crouched beside her, reaching out in the darkness. "Are you still in one piece?"

"Bruised but functional."

"Let me help you up." His arms went around her and they both froze.

"Sam," she said, her voice unsteady. "That's my boob you're holding."

He released her like a man backing away from a poisonous snake. "Sorry."

She found his hand with hers. "Pull." Gradually, wincing as her knee protested, she made it upright. "Okay then. I can walk."

"Not without me, you can't. Hold on to the back of my belt and I'll get us to the door."

"Are we going to look for the flashlight?"

"No. Who knows how far it rolled, and I have several more downstairs."

She had to touch his waist, brush his hip, to find her way around to his back. And she was pretty sure he inhaled sharply when her fingers curled around his belt and brushed his spine. His skin was smooth and hot to the touch.

A step at a time they made their way through the stygian gloom. What had been a short distance before now became an obstacle course. Suddenly, Annalise yelped and pressed into Sam, wrapping her arms around his waist.

She felt him tense. "What's the matter?"

"Something ran across my foot."

"Probably just a mouse."

"*Just* a mouse?"

"I know you've had the occasional rodent in Wolff Castle."

"I didn't play footsie with them," she complained, shuddering. With all the lights out, who knows how many creatures would come out to play?

"The Annalise Wolff I used to know wasn't afraid of anything. Your brothers and cousins dared you to try all sorts of ridiculous stunts, and you took the bait every time, determined to prove you were as good as they were."

"Well, I've matured since then."

He cursed as they both staggered around some kind of chest. "Too bad...I kind of liked that crazy girl."

Annalise didn't have an answer for that. Was he trying to tell her something, or was this chitchat designed to distract her from the fact that with the electricity out, this old house was going to chill rapidly?

At last Sam located the door, which was rather anticlimactic, because as soon as they stepped through it, they were no better off than they were before. Now they faced two steep flights of stairs.

He ran his palm down her arm, ultimately linking their fingers. "Stay close. I'll follow the stair rail, and you hang on to me."

Annalise wasn't about to argue. Her heart was dancing to some kind of ragged staccato beat and her lung capacity had shrunk to nothing. Not even to herself would she admit that holding hands with Sam Ely rocked her world.

"Works for me," she said, trying to sound matter-of-fact. His grip was firm and warm, unbelievably so, since her own smaller hand was icy.

It was a clumsy sort of ballet, but it worked, albeit

slowly. At the second-floor landing they stopped to catch their breath. Sam squeezed her fingers. "You doing okay, Princess? I know you didn't sign on for this."

It seemed as if he surrounded her, all hard muscle, broad chest and gravelly voice.

She swallowed, her throat dry as the dust that danced in drafts beneath the roof. "Not to worry. I may not have been a Girl Scout, but I can handle you and a dark house."

Four

Sam was disoriented, and it had more to do with having Annalise Wolff clinging to him than it did with the lack of electricity. He was getting definite mixed signals. One wrong move on his part could be disastrous.

Right now, she was silent, seemingly docile. Perhaps regretting her last boastful retort. He was pretty sure she hadn't meant for it to come out sounding like sexual innuendo.

He sighed inwardly. Rarely did he find himself wandering in the dark when it came to a woman, and now he was in the position of doing so both literally and metaphorically. Keeping his voice neutral, he tugged on her hand. "Ready to keep going?"

He felt her nod. "Yes. Won't there at least be some firelight from the kitchen and living room?"

Stepping gingerly down one step and then another, he

led her behind him. "As long as the embers haven't burned too low."

Moments later they made it to the hallway.

She exhaled. "Well, we didn't break a leg. That's something."

He could tell that Annalise was ready to escape into her bedroom and call it a night, but he kept a firm grip on her hand. "We need a snack. Dinner was a long time ago. Can I interest you in a s'more?"

"Served by a roaring fire? Sure."

He steered her to her earlier seat. "Sit here and don't move. We're surrounded by lethal furniture. I'll go find the flashlights." He wasn't gone more than two minutes. Grabbing what he needed out of the kitchen, he returned to find Annalise stoking the fire. The roaring flames danced and crackled, spreading a semicircle of light and warmth.

"What part of *sit still* don't you understand?" Joining her in front of the hearth, he laid two sets of graham crackers and chocolate bars on the mantel and then ripped open a bag of marshmallows. Threading one onto a wire coat hanger, he handed it to her.

She stared at it, a small smile on her face. "I love mine burnt to a nice dark brown."

"Says the woman who doesn't cook. The trick is to get it hot and gooey without involving carcinogens."

"Oh, pooh." She crouched and thrust her marshmallow deep into the flames. "Live a little, Sam."

Again, that odd frisson of awareness. He wasn't convinced she knew how her sharp-edged repartee was affecting him. But maybe he was naive. Perhaps Annalise Wolff was planning sexual revenge and knew exactly what she was doing. He couldn't imagine what that would look like or what her goal could be other than to torment him, but already his body betrayed him.

He wanted to strip her naked and take her there on the rag rug, uncaring that snow drifted deeper and deeper against the windows or that he and Annalise were like oil and water.

Here—and now—he wanted her.

Before he could formulate a suitably masculine retort, Annalise stood abruptly. "Hold this, please."

When he took the coat hanger from her without complaint, she stripped off her jacket and fanned her face. "I think I'm the one melting, not the marshmallow."

Good Lord. That damned silk blouse clung to her arms and breasts with static electricity, outlining pert nipples that riveted his attention even through the evidence of a lacy bra.

He turned away, shocked by how quickly his arousal segued from piqued interest to heavy, molten lust. "Here. Take it back," he croaked. "I'm not going to be responsible for cooking this. Do it your own way."

"Thank you," she mocked. "I will."

As he rotated his coat hanger in precise increments, Annalise laughed when her marshmallow burst into flame. The sound of that husky, sensual chuckle did to his insides what the hot fire had done to puffy white sugar. He was ablaze suddenly, so hungry for her he was actually stunned.

"Blow it out," he said. "Before you ruin it completely."

She waited two clicks—two interminable seconds—and then she did as he commanded. "You just can't stand not to boss me around. That doesn't bode well for our collaboration."

"It's not a collaboration," he insisted. "You're in charge."

She snorted. "Yeah right." Reaching for the rest of her s'more sandwich, she trapped the marshmallow between the other layers and extracted the coat hanger.

"You're gonna burn your tongue."

Annalise bit into her messy s'more and groaned. "Wow. These are amazing. Great idea, Sam."

He pulled his perfectly browned marshmallow from the fire and made his own s'more. He was hungry. And the melted chocolate and marshmallow smelled wonderful. But he couldn't look away from Annalise. Firelight painted her classic features with warm, golden hues. Her mouth was sticky with sugar and chocolate.

"You've got some on your chin," he said gruffly.

She reached up, eyes dancing with laughter, and rubbed a spot. "Did I get it?"

"No. *Lick it. Kiss it. Make her want you like you want her.* The little devil on his shoulder had gotten him into trouble more than once. But something stopped him. A dead certainty that this time he didn't want to screw things up with Annalise Wolff.

He took his thumb and rubbed it across the side of her chin. "There," he said, throat dry. "All clean."

The smile disappeared from her face, and her eyes widened, something unidentifiable flickering in the depths of her wary gaze. "Thank you."

They finished eating in silence. Watching her lick her fingers nearly did him in. "I'll get you a flashlight," he said gruffly. "And there are extra covers in the chest at the foot of your bed."

"Don't worry about me," she said. "Once I burrow under a pile of quilts, I won't come out till morning."

"I'll be sleeping upstairs. Is it going to bother you to be down here alone? If you're worried, I can camp out on the sofa."

Even in the shadowy room he could see her roll her eyes. "Get serious, Sam. Do I strike you as the nervous type? I'll be fine. Besides, there's no way you could stretch out on that couch. You're far too big."

Again, a seemingly innocuous comment with an undercurrent of sexual nuance. "Your choice," he said. And wasn't that the problem? Given their past, for him to make a move on her was risky in the extreme. But in light of his long-ago sins, the likelihood of Annalise Wolff pursuing him a second time was almost nonexistent.

Where did that leave a man who was breathless with wanting and aching for one woman in particular?

"So when do you break out the generator? I assume there is one."

"Yes. But we don't know how long we're going to be stuck, so I suggest we use it sparingly. If you can make it through this one night, we'll power it up tomorrow to cook a decent meal and take showers, anything else we need to do."

"Makes sense."

Annalise was not a whiner. Thank God for that. As soon as he gave her a flashlight, she disappeared with a muttered *good-night*. It didn't escape his notice that when she left him, the novelty and fun of being snowed in vanished. Now he was cold and grumpy and hard…with a long, unpleasant night ahead.

He made sure both of the fires were banked and the screens in place. After clearing up the mess from their bedtime snack, he found his way upstairs. The air was so cold he almost expected to inhale ice crystals.

His bedroom, the one he stayed in when he visited his grandparents, was furnished with more modern items, including a king-size bed. Since he was well over six feet tall, he appreciated the concession. Sleeping in a narrow antique bed had never interested him. At least not until tonight. If Annalise had invited him to share hers, he'd have been more than willing.

In the modern, newly renovated bathroom he made quick work of washing up in the dark. A shower at the moment was out of the question. It might have done him some good considering the fact that he had been semi-aroused for the last three hours. But the house was just too damn cold.

He never used pajamas, and tonight, he bitterly regretted that decision. The sheets felt damp, even though he knew they were not. Huddling into the covers, he tried not to think about what it would be like to have a warm, feminine body curled against his.

Exhaustion claimed him quickly, but he slept in fits and starts. Dreams plagued him. The unrelenting winds rattled the windows and howled around the eaves. At one point he sat up and looked at his phone. Hell, it was only 2:00 a.m.

The cold seeped into his bones. He started worrying about Annalise. But her room was just off the living room and no doubt had benefited to some extent from the fire. And he couldn't imagine that she slept naked. As much as she enjoyed pretty clothes, she probably packed all kinds of sleepwear.

In lieu of counting sheep, he began picturing her in various sexy outfits. Teddies. Football jerseys and knit shorts. Elegant negligees. Camis and thongs.

His imagination was regrettably thorough. Cursing roughly, he cupped his hand around his aching shaft. He didn't want to find relief in that way. He didn't want to be alone.

Another half hour passed. He was more awake than ever. Surely a warm room was preferable to this misery, even if he did have to sleep with his legs hanging off the end of the couch.

Climbing out of bed, he winced when his bare feet met the cold wooden floor. He dressed rapidly in a pair of old, soft jeans and a flannel shirt that he wore when he did chores in the barn. Dragging two pairs of socks over his feet, he grabbed his flashlight and crept downstairs.

Sadly, Annalise's door was firmly closed.

He walked quietly into the living room and shut himself in, away from temptation. His nose detected the faint scent of burnt marshmallow in the air. He had to smile, despite his discomfort. Annalise was never boring.

Crouching on the hearth, he shoved twisted newspaper into the midst of the glowing coals. When a tiny flame erupted, he fed it, using an old-fashioned bellows to encourage the sparks. He thought ruefully of the high-tech gas fireplace in his condo overlooking Charlottesville and the mountains beyond. His home was exactly that— a home. He entertained there, relaxed there, and sometimes when the mood struck him, even worked from home.

He had bought an industrial loft five years ago, torn out almost every wall and redesigned the space exactly the way he wanted it. The resultant living areas were open and roomy, but comfortable and welcoming at the end of a long day.

Like his father, he had a hard time turning down new clients. He loved what he did, and it was both challenging and personally satisfying to give families and small businesses a manifestation of the dreams they carried in their hearts and minds.

Seeing a new structure come to life on paper was a creative and artistic endeavor. Making the reality happen involved hard work and occasionally a dose of informal mediation when a husband wanted a man-cave and his wife a mini-gym.

Sam prided himself on being able to give them both.

He was a problem solver. Unfortunately, one of his biggest problems at the moment lay only a few feet away, fast asleep. It was anyone's guess as to whether or not he and Annalise would reach an understanding…or perhaps even something far more interesting.

Adding a final log to the fire, he rose to his feet, stretched and turned to survey the sofa. It sat farther back in the room at right angles to the fireplace. It wasn't much of a decision to choose the leather chair and ottoman he had occupied earlier. Pulling them even closer to the fire, he grabbed an afghan and prepared to stretch out for what remained of the night.

Before he could sit down, he realized he hadn't replaced the fire screen. He picked up the unwieldy antique and moved it into position, but in doing so, knocked over the bellows, which in turn tumbled into a large brass urn, crashing it to the floor.

He froze, hearing the sound echo through the house. Was Annalise a light sleeper? Ten seconds passed…fifteen…the silence told him he was home free.

With a groan of exhaustion, he settled into the chair, pulled the cover to his chin and crossed his ankles. The position was semicomfortable. His eyelids grew heavy, and he watched the wildly dancing flames through his lashes, remembering bonfires from when he was a kid.

He was almost asleep when a female voice, laden with irritation, spoke not two feet behind him. "Good Lord. What are you doing down here? You scared me to death. I thought an animal had gotten into the house."

Closing his eyes and counting to ten, he tried to assess the situation rationally. But even the sound of her voice turned him on, despite the fact that the tone was more angry than amorous. "I couldn't sleep. That upstairs bedroom is like a morgue during an ice storm."

"Tell me about it."

"I thought you weren't afraid to stay down here by yourself," he taunted. *That's right, Sam. Provoke the beast. Sarcasm will make things better.* He tossed aside the light blanket and stood, only to feel a blow to the chest when he saw her for the first time. In one hand, she brandished a can of pepper spray. With the other she clutched the flashlight he had given her. But what was in between... sweet heaven...

Crimson silk edged in expensive black lace slid sinuously over her body, whispering seduction with every move she made. He scrubbed the heels of his hands over his eyes and yawned, giving himself a chance to swallow the lump of emotion in his throat. Annalise Wolff had grown into an exquisitely beautiful woman.

The stunning view was imprinted on his brain. The gown plunged in front, revealing the swells of soft, creamy-skinned breasts. The thin robe that covered the gown was long-sleeved, but hung open, hiding little. On her feet Annalise wore black satin slippers embroidered in red and gold thread with tiny birds and flowers.

The fact that he could describe her footwear in so much detail only spoke to how hard he was trying not to stare at her chest.

When he finally looked up, she was eyeing him curiously.

"What?" he asked, wondering if he had soot on his face.

She shrugged. "I'm accustomed to seeing you in a suit and tie, or even a tux. This casual 'cowboy' look takes some getting used to."

He might be half-asleep, but he knew interest when he saw it in a woman's eyes. Rounding the chair, he took the flashlight and spray from her hands and set them on a bookcase. "Do you often have animals in the house at

Wolff Mountain?" He was standing so close to her he could see the faint throb of a pulse in her neck.

She flushed. "We've had the occasional bear."

"Inside?"

"I've read stories about such things."

"And you were going to attack a bear with your bare hands? Surely you know that pepper spray makes them more aggressive…and that flashlight is not big enough to do any harm."

"You're insufferable. Has anyone ever told you that?"

Without her habitual three-inch heels, she seemed much smaller…fragile even. And in the middle of the night, with her defenses down, infinitely more approachable. "*You* have," he said, studying her moist, curved lips. "A dozen times. At least when you were willing to speak to me."

He put his hands on her shoulders, waiting to see if she would react, perhaps slap him.

She was heavy-eyed and sleep-rumpled, her thick, shiny black hair hanging almost to her waist. "What are you doing?" she questioned in a husky voice that made him imagine long Saturday mornings in bed.

The room was full of shadows, the hour late. He was tired of reliving the past with this woman. Time to start something new. "I'm going to kiss you."

Her eyes flared wide, but other than that, she made no response. He still had no guarantee this wasn't entrapment. Perhaps he ought to have worn some kind of protective clothing. He knew from hearing Vincent brag that Annalise had a black belt in karate and was fully capable of taking Sam down.

He wanted her to make the first move, craved it, really. But that wasn't going to happen. Not with the painful memory of the last time they both stood on this precipice echoing between them.

Bending his head, he nibbled her neck, inhaling a scent that was so intrinsically *her*. Feminine, yes, but strong, unforgettable. His hands slid down her arms, around her waist, over her butt. She was firm and fit, her soft resilient skin underlain with sleek sexy muscles.

Never had he felt or seen her so still, so submissive. And it worried him. Pulling back, he searched her face. "Touch me," he begged. "Please."

As if his words had broken some kind of weird spell, she moved. With a little murmur that might have signaled any one of a number of emotions, she wrapped one arm around his neck and found his mouth with hers. With her free hand she shoved up the tail of his shirt and stroked his chest. Her touch burned him. It had been years since their first and only kiss, but he remembered the taste of her as if it had been only yesterday.

His tongue plundered the sweet recesses of her mouth, tangling with hers. Gasps and moans were barely audible over the sound of his heartbeat in his ears.

The erection he was unable to hide pulsed between them, thick and hard and ready. When he ground his hips against her belly, she whimpered. Need built and crashed over him, invisible but inescapable. He slid the robe down her arms and let it drop. Lifting her by her ass, he carried her to the chair beside the fire and held her in his lap, bending her back over his arm to kiss her wildly.

Her hair was a silken waterfall. He grabbed handfuls of it, using the grip to guide her mouth to his. Somewhere, deep inside a single rational thought cell, he acknowledged that this was insanity. But the impossible had happened. Annalise, who would normally as soon hiss at him as speak cordially, was actually passionately, eagerly, returning his kiss.

His hands trembled, moving recklessly all over her body.

A nipped-in waist, delicate collarbone, gently curved stomach. Nipples that begged to be touched, pinched, soothed with a kiss. He left the bodice in place. If he stripped her at this point, it was all over. He lifted the hem of her gown and touched her leg, finding nothing but hot skin.

When he moved halfway up her thigh, Annalise clamped her hand over his, blocking further exploration. "Stop," she said hoarsely.

He did, but it cost him dearly. Every sinew in his body throbbed with the need to take, regardless. "I want you, Princess. God knows, I do."

There was a momentary hesitation as if, even for her, the interruption was agonizing. Without warning she slid from his lap and faced him, arms wrapped around her waist, ebony hair a mad tangle. With the firelight behind her, he could see the outline of her slim legs through the thin fabric of her gown. Tears glittered in her eyes, and her distress strafed him with a thousand knives. Why could he never get this right?

He stood as well, but she held up a hand. "Don't come any closer."

"Talk to me," he begged. "Tell me what you want."

Her eyes were tragic, the blue dulled almost to gray. She began to speak. Stopped. Swallowed hard. It almost seemed as if she were holding herself tightly to keep from shattering into irreparable pieces. "Did you have this in mind when you came here this weekend?" she asked, her voice low and broken.

"No," he muttered, staring past her into the fire for a moment and then returning his gaze to her face. "No," he said more forcefully.

His groin ached, his eyes were gritty with lack of sleep and his breath came in great gulps that did nothing to help him relax.

It was the wrong answer. Somehow he knew that instantly. Grief flashed in her eyes and disappeared, leaving nothing but blank, mute misery in its wake. "I know we're snowed in, Sam, but surely you could go without sex for one night. I won't be your easy lay, your sadly predictable one-night stand."

"That's not what this is, damn it." His gut felt like the time he had suffered an appendicitis attack. "You're special. How can you not know that?"

He took her in his arms again, and this time she didn't protest. But the fevered beauty he'd held moments ago had turned to ice. He kissed her again and again...tender kisses, slow drugging kisses. All he accomplished was making himself miserable.

She fit so perfectly in his arms, it was an absolute miracle. How could she not see it?

His own behavior sickened him. Had he told her the truth, or was his subconscious a devious bastard? Had he jumped at Gram's request in order finally to have Annalise where he wanted her?

God, please let that not be true. If it was, he honestly hadn't planned it.

Shocked by his own uncertainty, he released her and stepped back. "I've been attracted to you for years, Annalise, but the timing is always wrong between us. Maybe I did look forward to being here with you, but is that so terrible? You can barely bring yourself to acknowledge me across a crowded room when we cross paths in Charlottesville. We're here now. Alone. For God knows how long. Won't you give me a chance to regain your trust? Please?"

He saw her lower lip wobble before she steadied it with small, even white teeth. "I came here to work for your Gram and Pops. None of this should have happened."

"But it did," Sam said firmly. "And you were right there with me. So don't pretend with me, Annalise. We both stepped into that fire."

Five

If Annalise had ever been more stricken with mortification, she couldn't remember it. In many ways, the ramifications of this moment with Sam were even worse than what had happened years ago. At least back then he had written her girlish passion off to immaturity.

Now, in one mad instant, she had revealed her deep vulnerability where he was concerned. Not only to him, but also to herself. She'd been pretending for years that she hated Sam Ely. The truth was, she was probably in love with him. She wasn't exactly sure what that emotion was supposed to feel like. Surely not this nauseous sensation of impending doom.

At twenty-one she had known what she wanted and gone after it. Sam had crushed her budding attempt to be a sexually confident woman. Now, here he was. Gorgeous. Hungry. And ready to take advantage of propinquity and auld lang syne.

If she overreacted, she risked letting him see straight
into her heart and her soul. Wolffs guarded both those lo-
cations zealously. Too much tragedy and heartache in the
past to be soft. Too much at stake to voluntarily open up
to the possibility of pain and loss.

So she had a choice. She could play this cool, run the
show. Or she could let Sam break her heart. Given that
pairing, it was really no contest.

Gathering the shreds of her composure, she retrieved
her robe, put it on and tied the narrow, ribbonlike belt. The
garment was scarcely a shield against his predatory gaze,
but the operation gave her a few moments to think. Returning to the fire, she put her back to it, warming herself.

"You're right," she said calmly. "I *was* carried away by
the moment. And it does seem as though we share some
kind of basic animal attraction."

He frowned. "I'm not an eighteen-year-old kid, Annalise. Give me credit for at least some discrimination. I
don't have sex with every woman on the street who piques
my interest. You've been part of my life forever. And you're
incredibly warm and lovely."

She forced a smile. "At the moment, the jury's out on
warm, but thank you for the compliment."

"Something happened between us," he said doggedly,
his fierce gaze daring her to disagree.

"Yes." *Understatement of the year.* "Here's the thing,
Sam. I don't really have the time or the inclination to get
involved with anybody right now, much less the grandson
of my most recent client. You were only planning to be
here overnight, two at the most…right?"

"I'd say my schedule is pretty much down the tubes at
the moment. You may be stuck with me for a while."

The weird little happy flutter her heart performed was

too "middle school girl" to take seriously. "That's not a valid reason for doing something stupid."

"Didn't seem stupid to me. It felt pretty damned wonderful."

"There's more to life than feeling good."

"Wow, Annalise. When did you turn into a Puritan?"

He was striking back. Trying to provoke. But the words hurt. She looked at him, really looked at him. The whole package was overwhelming. In Charlottesville she could write him off as just another handsome, successful businessman. Here, alone in a remote house, trapped by a winter storm, he looked like the kind of man who could keep a woman safe, no matter the circumstances.

She didn't need a keeper. As the lone Wolff female, she had grown up strong, resilient, entirely capable of steering her own life. But when it came to understanding the kind of feminine ways that drew a man in for the long haul, Annalise was clueless.

Sam, by his own admission, was looking to settle down, to start a family. Even if he played house with Annalise until the blizzard abated, he'd be going back to Charlottesville soon, trolling for a nice, sweet, amenable kind of gal to cook him meat loaf, defer to his wishes and run his house barefoot and pregnant.

Annalise had grown up in the South. She knew the stereotype. And she knew many wonderful women who could hold down full-time jobs and still be damned good mothers and wives. The problem was, Annalise wasn't one of them.

"I'm not a Puritan," she said. "I love sex."

"Prove it."

"Oh, good Lord. Does that line work for you at your age?"

He grinned. And the sexy flash of white teeth literally made her knees week. When he took two steps in her direction, she was trapped. Flames to the back of her, fire to the front. "Kiss me again, darlin'," he said. "Let me keep you warm."

Impossible. Utterly impossible not to respond this time. He scooped her into his arms and whispered nonsensical endearments as he proceeded to kiss her senseless.

Time. She needed time. How could she formulate a thought when his talented fingers were doing amazing things to her aching breasts? Breathing became problematic. Her lips felt puffy and bruised. All she wanted to do was kiss him more.

He braced one hard, long thigh between her thighs, and the firm pressure there took every last bit of self-control she possessed and tossed it to the winds. She had never been one to second-guess her decisions. Confidence and boldness had taken her far in business and in life.

But holy heck, what was she supposed to do in this situation?

"Sam?" She leaned backward in his tight embrace as far as she could, trying to get his attention.

He took advantage of the position to bend and capture one silk-clad nipple and nip it with his teeth. "Sam!"

The moaning cry finally got through to him. He straightened, his face flushed, his shirt awry thanks to her frantic need to touch his chest. Everything about him was disheveled, earthy, intent on carnal pursuits. Even his eyes were cloudy and unfocused.

"What?" he growled, his sexual frustration palpable.

"We have to agree on something."

He released her, bent at the waist and stared at the floor, clearly in pain. "God give me strength. You are the most ball-busting female I've ever met. Make up your mind, damn it. Do you want me or not?"

She rapped her knuckles on his head. "Don't talk to

me like that. You started this insanity. Yes. I want you. But only for the moment. Only while you're in this house. Got it?"

When he straightened and faced her, a shiver of primal feminine apprehension danced through her veins. Here was a man at the end of his rope. And he looked as if he would as soon strangle her with it than let go.

"Are you seriously negotiating a relationship at this god-damn moment?"

"There is no relationship," she shouted, stung by his incredulity. "All we're going to do is indulge in wild monkey sex. No strings."

"Strings…" He repeated the word, his mouth pursed as he tried to decipher her meaning.

"Tell me you get what I'm saying." She didn't understand exactly why she was pushing so hard. Perhaps because she couldn't bear the thought of another half-dozen years of heartache in the aftermath of an encounter with Sam Ely.

His eyes narrowed, he straightened to his full height and his chest rose and fell with each harsh breath. "Here's what I get," he said softly, the words forced through clenched teeth. "I get that you're crazy. Or maybe this is an act you put on to drive men insane so they'll grovel at your feet. But yes. I get it. Hell, sweetheart, I'll sign over my soul to the devil on the spot if you'll take off that gown."

She licked her lips. "Well, okay then." It was rather heady to have a man so intent on ravishing her. Thank God she wasn't a totally inexperienced virgin. That little detail had been taken care of during a sad and disappointing college encounter that had never been repeated.

She had *wanted* to lose her virginity…so that she could understand what the other girls were talking and giggling about. So that she could be part of their charmed inner circle.

As an eighteen-year-old college freshman, she had thought that becoming a woman in the physical sense would help her understand what it meant to be a girl. But when it was all said and done, she was still Annalise Wolff. Impatient. Driven. And far too confident and assertive for most guys to want a serious relationship.

She dated. A lot. Men liked the external package. And she was not a nun. But no one ever interested her enough to go the distance. Even in bed, she'd felt a sense of failure. Perhaps because the earth never shook and the fireworks never boomed.

Now it had come to this. She waited impatiently for Sam to take her in his arms and undress her. Arousal danced and twisted in her lower abdomen, and her heartbeat skittered out of control. She held out her arms. "Say something, damn it. Or are we going to stand here all night?" She was too agitated to worry about her language at this point.

He shrugged, his expression calculating...like a tiger eyeing a mouse. "Take off the gown."

The blunt words sent moisture blooming between her thighs.

"But I thought you would—"

"Now, Annalise. Slowly. Make me wait. Tease me. Taunt me."

The guttural commands were something new. She didn't know Sam had it in him to be so deliciously barbaric. But she liked it.

Feeling his stare like a hot brand, she shrugged out of the robe and tossed it onto a chair. Now there was no disguising her excitement. Her tightly furled nipples actually hurt. She wanted his hands on her skin, everywhere.

Feeling a bit foolish, but breathless with excitement, she put one hand over her breasts, and with the other hand slid the narrow straps of the gown down first one shoulder and then the other. Releasing each arm completely was a little more awkward than she would have liked, but she gave herself points for bravado.

Sam was transfixed, his entire body tense, hands fisted at his hips. "I want to see your breasts. Lower the top."

For a woman who liked being in charge in almost every situation, it was surprisingly comfortable to cede control. Despite Sam's arrogant demands, she realized that in a deeper sense, she was in the driver's seat.

Feeling faint and giddy, she took the bodice of her gown and dragged it to her waist. Someone gasped. Him? Her? It didn't matter. Sam's gob-smacked response went a long way toward making up for the past. She knew he had seen his fair share of naked women, so his reaction to her no-more-than-average breasts was a balm to her battered ego.

He cocked his head, arms folded across his chest. "You're not done."

The heat from the fire singed her back, warming the silk against her skin. She felt exotic, dangerous. Never in the occasional fantasies she'd allowed herself had Sam looked at her in quite this way.

She put her hands in the sides of the gown and shimmied it down her hips. Stepping out of the pile of ruby cloth and kicking it aside, she removed her exotic slippers and faced him bravely. "I seem to be doing all the work," she said, mesmerized by the enormous bulge beneath his fly.

Sam swallowed, the muscles in his throat rippling, betraying the fact that he was deeply invested in this moment. "Do you want me, Annalise?"

Here it was. A chance for revenge. An opportunity to

take that dreadful memory of his rejection and incinerate it. All she had to do was walk out of the room.

She'd have a better chance of baking cookies and serving tea to the Queen of England. Nothing short of an earthquake could have made her call a halt to this wonderful madness. "Yes," she said. "I believe that I do."

Time began to move in slow motion. Even the sounds of the fire muted to a faint murmur. She held out a hand. "I *would* ask *your room or mine,* but neither sounds appealing at the moment. Do you have any ideas?"

"For you, Princess, always."

With one lingering look at her nudity, he stepped away long enough to rob a nearby cupboard of its stash of throws…a blanket, several afghans and one tattered, faded quilt. As Annalise watched, amused and touched by his urgency, he fashioned a makeshift bed in front of the hearth. Grabbing a pillow from the sofa, he tossed it down on the pile and then added a couple more logs and tinder on top of the coals until the fire blazed hot and orangey-red.

Annalise had scooted out of his way while he worked, but now he dragged her back with a challenging stare that said louder than words what he expected of her. She joined him, limbs trembling, and somewhere found the acting skills to emulate a woman who knew her way around the bedroom. "Put your hands in your back pockets, Sam."

He hesitated, but obeyed. "That's askin' a lot, sweetheart. You're one hell of a temptation."

"We'll get there," she promised. With fumbling fingers, she unfastened the buttons of his shirt. Two years ago she had spent six months in Europe touring every major museum from Paris to Rome. Never had she seen a work of art that rivaled Sam's broad, hard chest.

Hard muscles rippled beneath golden skin. An arrow of dark brown hair bisected his rib cage on the way to his belt buckle. When she had the temerity to taste one cop-per-colored nipple, he cursed.

His hands fisted in her hair, dragging her face up to his for a kiss. "God, you make me burn."

It didn't sound entirely like a compliment.

He ravaged her mouth, left love bites at her throat. She wanted him as naked as she was, but she barely had time to catch her breath, much less make demands. When she tried to open the fly of his jeans, he manacled her wrists with one big hand and held them behind her back.

The overt dominance of the action dragged her more deeply into the spell that swirled around them both. She could have broken the hold. She knew that. And he prob-ably knew it as well. But the force of his hunger demanded her compliance, and her own need fed from his.

"Please, Sam," she begged, arching into him. "I want to touch you."

Finally, reluctantly, he released her long enough to rip off his socks and remove his jeans in a harried, one-footed dance. His sex sprang forth eagerly, its length and girth a thing of beauty. The longer she stared, the more it grew.

"Sam Ely," she breathed, feeling a touch of maidenly vapors. "You're a stud."

He blushed. And the sight of his red throat and ruddy cheekbones hurt something deep inside her chest. He was just so damned cute.

Unfortunately, he didn't give her much time to appre-ciate his masculine attributes. Before she could lodge a protest, he scooped her into his arms and deposited her gently on their makeshift bed. With both living room doors closed, the space had long since warmed up, and even if it hadn't, Annalise was sure she wouldn't have noticed the cold.

He hovered over her on one knee. "I don't know how

long I'll last. You've pushed me pretty close to the edge."
Suddenly, dismay darkened his expression. "Oh, hell. I've
got condoms, but they're upstairs."

She saw him contemplate the long frigid path to protection. And sympathized. "I'm on the pill," she said hopefully, "and I'm okay as far as…well, you know what I
mean." The brazen-woman act fell apart when it came to
discussing such topics.

His face lightened. "I had a physical last month. A-okay.
You can trust me, Annalise. I hope you know that."

"I do," she whispered. Without waiting for an invitation,
she reached out and took him in her hand, measuring the
firm, swollen flesh with inner wonder. If sculptors created
guys like Sam, the museums would be a lot more crowded.

His eyes closed at the first brush of her fingers. He felt
amazingly hard and disarmingly smooth and silky. But
would all that *maleness* fit? Her thighs clenched in something that was a cross between breathless excitement and
genuine apprehension.

Stroking him tentatively, she caught her breath when
he went rigid and found release in her hand, warm liquid
leaking through her fingers and dribbling onto her belly.

He groaned. "Annalise, I'm sorry. Let's try that again."
Very matter-of-factly he used a corner of one thin blanket to clean her and himself. She was abashed, unused to
such easy intimacy. But his tenderness charmed and disarmed her.

His shaft was still mostly erect, definitely firm enough
to get the job done. But instead of moving over and into
her, he knelt between her legs and grinned the kind of
grin that guaranteed a girl in trouble. "You're not saying
anything."

Suddenly, she wanted to cover her breasts with her
hands, but knew that would elicit a hoot of derision from

her beautifully naked lover. "You seem to have everything under control," she said. "Knock yourself out."

The grin broadened, and he stretched out on his side, tucking his torso between her thighs so he could reach what he was after.

Annalise closed her eyes and groaned inwardly. What he was about to do was both terrifying and wickedly wonderful. She'd spent her entire life protecting her deepest emotions. Only once had she dared to wear her heart on her sleeve, and it had been shattered by this very man.

Now she was allowing him the utmost intimacy, and she wasn't at all sure she could separate sexual bliss from a deeper, far more fragile emotion. It was one thing to let him see she desired him. But far more dangerous to expose the reality that she had never stopped loving him.

The first pass of his lips brought her hips off the floor. Her fists gripped the soft covers beneath her to find an anchor. She'd been fastidious and guarded in her few physical relationships up until this moment. Never had she permitted a man to get this close. Never had she imagined how good this would feel. She wasn't naive. She read books. Saw movies. Oral sex was a natural part of lovemaking, even if she'd always drawn a line to hold men at bay.

The oddly clinical commentary in her brain shut down when Sam used his thumbs to part the folds of her sex so his talented tongue could concentrate on the spot that begged for his attention. He tasted her delicately, fine-tuning his technique in reaction to her wiggling hips.

He licked the inside of her thigh, bit gently, laid his head on her belly. The weight of him anchored her in a spinning world. Without volition, one of her hands unclenched and found its way to Sam's hair, sliding into the thick, wavy layers.

She traced the curves of his skull, drunk with the pleasure of being able to touch him at will.

Now he used his fingers, plucking delicately, stroking as if he had all the time in the world. Her belly tightened. An ache coalesced deep inside her. "Stop," she breathed, the word barely audible. "Not like this. I want you inside me when I come."

Lifting his head, he looked at her, eyes solemn, an errant lock of hair falling over his forehead. He looked young and carefree and as tempting as the devil. "Whatever you want, Annalise."

He went to his knees and leaned forward, one hand on either side of her. The heat from his body felt like a warm blanket. Nudging her knees a little wider, he fit the head of his erection to her damp core and pushed.

Her heels dug into the blanket. Eyelids fluttered shut. Neck arched. Breathing halted. The sensation of fullness was both novel and overwhelming. "Sam. Oh, Sam." How many times had she dreamed of this moment? And been foolish enough to let the fantasies keep her from forming relationships with other men.

She hadn't consciously saved herself for Sam. After all, most of the time she was able to convince herself that she despised him.

But not now. Not like this. Her throat burned and her eyes stung. Perfection. Desire met and sated. Damp skin to damp skin. Heart to heart. So badly did she want him to say he loved her that it was a sharp pain squeezing her chest.

His eyes were closed, his face a mask of intensity, of carnal pleasure. The pace increased. His hips pistoned, driving him deeper into her welcoming body.

Her fingernails scored his shoulders. Her legs wrapped

around his waist. He reached beneath her and canted her hips for one last desperate push.

Something exploded inside her, ecstasy and shock and a physical release so deep and utterly breathtaking that she lost a few seconds of reality in the maelstrom.

She heard Sam shout. Seconds later, he slumped on top of her, stealing what little oxygen was left in her lungs. Her arms clung to him automatically. She was beyond rational conversation. Nothing seemed real. Not the place. Not the feelings. Not even the big, raw-boned man smothering her with his hot skin, ragged breath and beautiful body.

As delight winnowed away with the ticking of the clock on the mantel, panic set in. What had she done? It had taken her years to recover from her first romantic debacle with Sam Ely. At twenty-one she had been mature for her age in terms of goal-setting and a life plan. And though some might say in retrospect that she'd had nothing more than a youthful crush on a man much older than she was, Annalise knew the truth.

She had been in love. The real deal. Despite what had happened back then...and even through the intervening years of guarded hostility on her part, based on tonight's utterly unexpected, and unbelievably wonderful events, the truth was impossible to evade.

Annalise Wolff was still in love with Sam Ely.

Six

The power came back on just as faint evidence of dawn chased away dark shadows and painted the room with gray. Annalise yawned, her brain fuzzy. The night before, Sam had gone through the house and turned off all the light switches before they retired, so the only evidence that twenty-first century conveniences had returned was the gentle, reassuring hum of the heat system cranking up.

She allowed herself one last moment to savor the odd but lovely sensation of sleeping with a man. Sam radiated heat. She was curled into his side with one bent leg across his hips and her face tucked against his chest. Sometime during the wee hours he had pulled the covers on top of them.

She didn't know what to do, and that was such an anomaly, she felt mildly claustrophobic. Ordinarily, she *always* knew what to do. Sometimes she mapped out a plan. More often than not, she plunged ahead, full speed, confident that she could handle whatever might be coming down the track.

But that was in business. Her work was her life, a sad thing for a woman her age to admit, but there it was. She loved the challenge of space design, of color, of texture. And she loved helping people create their own nests. Especially since many of her clients had no idea what they really wanted when they signed on.

Recently, she had spent more and more time at Wolff Mountain. It was gratifying to see her family, one at a time, finding happiness after the childhood of tragedy they had shared as a common cup. Even her big brother, Devlyn, had lately managed to lay some of his demons to rest when he reconnected with quiet, patient Gillian.

For Annalise, it wasn't that easy. Her brothers and cousins loved her. She knew that. And her father and uncle did, as well. But despite the close relationships they all shared, Annalise was the only female. How did she say to one of her big, masculine brothers that she was frightened by the specter of never finding her soul mate? How did she ask for advice on becoming a softer, more feminine woman?

Happily, she had a quartet of new in-laws…or at least Gillian would be one soon. But although each of her new-found sisters was extremely gracious and loving, Annalise didn't know them well enough to open a vein and let them see her insecurities.

Sam murmured in his sleep, drawing her attention back to his classic profile and warm-man smell. She would bottle that aroma if she could. His lashes lay dark on his cheeks, and his chest rose and fell with deep, regular breathing.

Slowly, stealthily, she extracted herself from muscular arms and scrambled to her feet. It was no wonder he was dead to the world. He'd been up for hours, either trying to get warm, or later, turning Annalise's world upside down

with a sexual marathon that had included one last coupling
as the fire died. The memory drew a quiet groan of amazement from her throat. At least she had gotten a couple of
hours of sleep *before* creeping through the house to confront a possible intruder.

There had been an intruder, all right. And one equally
as dangerous as a rogue bear. The problem with Sam was
that he seemed on the surface to be the perfect guy.

As long as she overlooked the fact that he was ready to
play daddy. The thought of having Sam's baby both mesmerized and terrified her. That was why she had given
him an ultimatum regarding sex. She had too much self-
preservation to buy into the fiction that she and Sam could
ever work as a couple.

It took every ounce of willpower she possessed to don
her gown and robe instead of waking Sam deliberately
and watching his eyes heat with passion. One of her slippers had slid under a chair, but she finally located it. The
sensible plan was to take a shower, and then pick a room
in which to get started sketching out some ideas.

The fee Sam's grandparents were offering her was extremely generous. But Annalise had enough ego to be
tempted even more by the prospect of the magazine spread.
She'd learned the tenets of ambition and hard work at her
daddy's knee, and one day, if she chose to, she had the
option of joining Devlyn in running the family business.

She doubted she would ever want to…at least not directly, but it was nice to know that no one in the family
would think it odd. She had never faced any kind of discrimination in the Wolff "pack" for being a girl. Well,
except for the fact that her father showered her with gifts
and encouraged her to order a new wardrobe each season.

She was pretty sure he felt guilty for cloistering her
for all those years. An all-access pass to high fashion was

his way of making amends. It was a nice perk. But going to school as a child and making friends would have been even nicer.

Sam never moved as she tiptoed to the door and opened it stealthily. With one last wistful glance at the man in front of the fire, she slipped out across the hall and into the safety of her bedroom.

Sam waited until he heard the door close to sigh deeply and roll onto his back. He had awakened when Annalise was dressing. Rubbing eyes that were gritty from lack of sleep, he forced himself to face the fact that she had run out on him. So much for warm cuddling and perhaps further bonding over morning sex.

Given her behavior in the last sixty seconds, Annalise was not interested. As rejections went, her dismissal was quiet…polite even. Sam weighed the lump of lead in his gut and found it to be a mix of disappointment and hurt. Confidence had never been a problem for him. But if he were dead honest, he would have to acknowledge the fact that he felt embarrassed and at a loss as to how to approach the coming day.

He got to his feet, nude, and was not surprised to find he was still hard. It was inevitable. Annalise, despite her mercurial temperament and frequent antipathy, did it for him. Everything about her appealed to his basic male instincts. Her beauty drew him in, but the challenge of wrangling with her kept him interested.

He'd never been one to use a pretty girl on his arm to shore up his masculinity. He was a guy. Looks mattered. To some extent. But a shallow, self-centered female bored him. And boredom was a buzzkill as far as he was concerned.

It seemed pointless to dress when he was headed upstairs to clean up. But then again, he didn't want to run in to his houseguest while in the buff. Time to regroup and make a plan.

After a long, blessedly hot shower, he dressed rapidly and peeked out the window. Snow as far as the eye could see. Sam had mixed feelings about being stranded. On the one hand, it was an iron-clad excuse to spend more time with Annalise. But conversely, if she proved to be even more prickly than usual in the aftermath of their lovemaking, their living situation was quickly going to become too close for comfort.

When he made his way downstairs, he found evidence of Annalise's presence in the form of an empty mug and cereal bowl tucked away in the dishwasher. He fell on the fresh pot of coffee with a mental hallelujah. Thank God she knew enough not to ruin this. After two cups, he felt marginally more alert.

He had plenty of work to do. And he needed to check in at the office. But all he could think about was finding Annalise.

It wasn't hard to locate her. She had moved her iPod dock to the back of the house where she was working, but this time, the music was dialed down to a far lower volume. He followed the sound to what was known as the library, though in reality, his grandfather used it to house his vintage pool table.

When Sam opened the door that was partially ajar, he found Annalise perched on a ladder photographing small sections of an intricate crown molding.

He frowned, noting the rickety wooden rungs that should have necessitated tossing the thing years ago. "What in the hell are you doing?"

She froze, and then slowly turned her head, casting him a cool, inscrutable look. Full-on ice princess. Damn.

"This is original as far as I can tell. I'm texting a friend of mine who specializes in this kind of thing. He'll let me know what he thinks." She laid the phone she'd been using to take pictures on the top of the ladder. "Did you need something?"

You. The word hovered on his lips. He swallowed it back. "Not really. When will you break for lunch? I thought I'd throw together a pot of chili and some cornbread."

Was it his imagination, or did she pale slightly. "You can do that?"

"Cook, you mean? Well, yeah. I've been a bachelor for a long time."

She gnawed her lower lip. "Noon, then…or later. Your call."

He watched, frustrated, as she returned her attention to the task at hand, effectively dismissing him. She was wearing what for Annalise Wolff were probably casual clothes. Khakis, silver leather ballet flats, a crisp white cotton blouse and a thin black cashmere cardigan tied around her shoulders. Her hair was secured at the nape of her neck, leaving a long, thick ponytail to cascade down her back.

For a split second, he remembered what that hair looked like spread across his chest, his legs, his… He gulped inwardly. "I could teach you," he blurted out.

This time, she half turned her entire body, threatening the stability of her perch. Wariness dueled with interest in her expressive eyes. "Teach me to…"

"Make chili." He felt his neck heat. "If you want to learn. It's not hard." The genesis for his impulsive invitation wasn't clear. But something about the surprised pleasure in her smile made him glad he had asked.

"I'd love to," she said simply. "As long as I can't muck it up too badly."

"Like how?"

She shrugged. "You know. Food poisoning. Too much salt."

He grinned, feeling a return of the euphoria he had experienced in the middle of the night. "Meet me in the kitchen in half an hour. Trust me, Princess. You'll be in good hands."

Annalise worked steadily, one part of her brain dedicated to the disciplines of measuring, calculating, planning. The other hemisphere, the one that acknowledged and ruefully accepted her ill-advised infatuation with Sam Ely, seemed intent on translating each of his statements into a sexual innuendo.

You'll be in good hands. Did he intend the erotic subtext? Probably not. She was hyperaware of the fact that she and Sam Ely had recently become lovers. But such nocturnal calisthenics were no doubt par for the course with Sam. To him, Annalise was nothing more or less than a willing and available woman. Available. Could she be any more of a cliché?

Feeling disgruntled and exhausted and excited in equal measures, she found her way to the kitchen at the appointed time. Sam, standing at the stove, turned to face her. "Ah, there you are. I was just getting started. Come here and supervise the meat."

She hovered in the doorway, all thoughts of food forgotten. Sam was too damned sexy for his own good. He was dressed much as he had been the day before, only with a different shirt. This time, hunter green flannel stretched across the broad contours of his chest and shoulders. It was still hard to get used to his new look.

For years she had known Sam Ely as the sleek, handsome, *über*masculine architect with the expensive Italian tailored suits and the knack for sartorial perfection.

He reeked of money and success from his pricey leather shoes to the high-tech Rolex on his broad masculine wrist.

But this man, well, hell...she didn't know what to make of him at all. He was warm and approachable and nurturing. And about as dangerous as a grizzly bear basking in the sun.

One wrong move, and she'd be toast.

Shoring up her defenses, she crossed to where he stood. "Show me what to do."

Sam stepped back and handed her the wooden spoon he'd been using. "Stir it occasionally and break up the bigger clumps of meat. When all the pink is gone, it will be ready." As she took her position, he flanked her, his arms coming around from behind, his right hand settling over hers as she pushed the meat blindly.

"Like this," he said. The scent of his shower soap muddled her thoughts. She wanted to toss the spoon aside and kiss him senseless. The warmth of him at her back made her hands shake. Gripping the utensil tightly, she tried to pretend it was nothing out of the ordinary to play chef with the man who had seduced her in front of a fire only hours before.

His fingers gripped hers and released, his voice hoarse as he spoke near her ear. "You've got the hang of it."

To her intense disappointment, he stepped away, moving to open cans of tomato soup and sauce. She watched him out of the corner of her eye. The fact that he wasn't producing some exotic sauce from scratch made her feel marginally better.

Suddenly, she realized that the pan was sizzling far more than it had been a few moments before. "Um, Sam?" At about the same moment she said his name, the hot grease popped and crackled. A splatter hit her forearm, and she yelped, dropping the spoon and sending bits of browned ground beef flying everywhere.

Sam grabbed her wrist and pulled it beneath a cooling stream of water from the faucet. Already the sting was subsiding. Leaving her for a moment, he turned the stove off and moved the skillet to another burner.

"Are you all right?" He took her hand and lifted her arm for his inspection.

"It's okay. Just a red spot. Sorry I overreacted." She tugged until he released her.

Sam shook his head. "It had to hurt. My fault for not turning down the heat."

"I told you I'm hopeless in the kitchen." She was mortified to feel the sting of tears.

He cocked his head, studying her face, his whiskey-colored eyes seeing far more than they should. "It's no big deal, Annalise. You've got enough money to *hire* people to cook for you."

"That's not the point."

"Then what *is* the point?"

"Women are supposed to be able to cook."

He opened his mouth, closed it and sighed. "I'm trying not to trivialize your concern," he said, "but that's a ridiculous, outdated stereotype."

"No," she said, sticking out her chin. "It's not. We *say* men and women are equal now that it's the twenty-first century, but when push comes to shove, my sex is supposed to be gentle and kind and proficient in the domestic arts."

"Oh, good Lord, Annalise. Do you hear yourself? So you can't cook. Who the hell cares? If it's that important to you, take lessons. But if you see this as some deficiency in you as a woman, you're nuts."

She stared at him. "I'll bet you a thousand dollars that your mother and grandmother are amazing cooks."

He shook his head in disgust, bending to wipe up the meat she had flung willy-nilly across the floor. "I refuse to get into this."

She nudged his butt with the toe of her shoe. "Because you know I'm right. You've grown up with two generations of women who can plant gardens and make casseroles and bake birthday cakes without a mix."

He straightened, tossing the wad of paper towels in the garbage. "And you didn't. Is that it?"

When he went on the attack, she lost focus. "Not exactly," she muttered. "Forget it. I'm going back to work. Call me when lunch is ready."

"Not so fast." He pulled her into his arms so rapidly, she actually felt dizzy for a moment. Plastered against his chest, she felt every one of his ribs, heard each heartbeat, registered the ragged tenor of his breathing.

When she opened her mouth to protest, he covered it with his.

He went in deep, without apology, staking a claim. Making clear what he wanted. Sam Ely was hungry, but she had a feeling that chili was far down on his list.

"What are you doing?" she gasped, struggling for air between frantic kisses.

He tangled his fist in her ponytail and used the tension to tip back her head so he could nibble her neck. "If you have to ask, I must be doing it wrong."

Before she could assimilate a thought or form a protest, he had scooped her into his arms and was striding out of the kitchen and across the hall to her bedroom. The door was ajar a couple of inches. He kicked it open, endangering ancient hinges.

"Sam!" The single syllable ended on a whimpering sigh as he set her on her feet and cupped her breasts with both hands.

"Don't talk," he begged. "Just let me do this."

This was full-out, desperation-fueled seduction.

And at the moment, Annalise couldn't think of a single reason to quibble about the method. Sam undressed her reverently, but with enough clumsiness to betray his need for haste. His hands found every soft curve, every bit of damp skin, every responsive group of nerves. By the time she was bare-ass naked and flat on her back, Sam was stripping off his clothes.

When he came down beside her, the antique bed squeaked in protest. Manufactured long before the advent of queen-size mattresses, the fit was cozy. He stroked between her legs, finding her damp and ready. "You make me crazy, Annalise."

"The feeling is mutual," she muttered. Tired of waiting, she reached for him and closed her fingers around hard silky flesh. Sam's quick catch of breath elated her. She squeezed gently, tracing the vein on the underside of his shaft with her thumb. Despite what had happened between the two of them in the wee hours, she still felt clumsy and unsure of herself. Lacking domestic skills was one thing, but the specter of possibly being bad in bed took insecurity to a whole new level.

To most people who knew her, Annalise Wolff was a sharp-edged, assertive, take-no-prisoners businesswoman. She'd been told to her face that she intimidated competitors, particularly if they were female. It wasn't something she aspired to or even practiced.

Her family had taught her to be confident and capable in business. Wolff men were all that and more. And they had reared Annalise both by precept and example to be one of the pack.

Though she had mastered the art of "looking" like a sexy female, no one had tutored her in the finer points of

how to transform the essence of who she was from a tom-
boy child into an admirable woman. Except for the female
staff, she had been completely isolated by her sex and from
her sex. Things most girls learned by osmosis had never
registered on Annalise's radar. She had held herself up to
a masculine standard and never realized she was short-
changing an entire part of who she was.

Beneath her touch, Sam's rigid flesh twitched and grew.
Apparently, she was doing something right. He touched
her thigh. "Lift your leg over mine," he said, his voice
rough with sexual intent. She did as he asked, feeling a
momentary frisson of unease at the position. So open. So
unprotected. Sam angled his hips and entered her slowly,
grabbing her hip to thrust deeper.

The penetration was shallower than last night, but conversely, far more risky. Now she and Sam lay face-to-face,
their breaths mingling…her ragged sighs, his groans. His
gaze locked with hers. "I like seeing you like this," he said.

"Like what?" This was why people closed their eyes
during sex. Too much communication was scary.

"Relaxed. Compliant."

"Trust me," she squeaked as he delved farther and hit a
sensitive spot, "I'm not relaxed." The tightly wound spiral
in the base of her abdomen clamored for attention. Sam's
left arm lay curled beneath her neck. With his free hand,
he plucked lazily at her nipple, adding fuel to the inferno
that throbbed between her legs.

His lazy grin made her want to slap him, or kiss him,
or both. "You will be," he promised.

She squeezed him with inner muscles that took over
the reins in naughty intent. "Show me," she whispered,
the words in challenge.

Every trace of humor fled his face to be replaced by
sheer male determination. With one arm, he dragged her

closer for a kiss that was carnal and curious and calami-
tous. With the other, he drew her even more tightly into the
cradle of his thighs, melding their bodies in a frantic hold.
His tongue tangled with hers, his chest heaving, skin damp
with perspiration. "Come for me, Princess. Let go…now."

That he could coax a climax from her at will was both
exhilarating and terrifying. She slammed into the peak
and crashed over it with the force of a speeding train, her
senses all focused on that one perfect moment.

Sam held her in a bruising grip as he shouted and shud-
dered at almost the same instant.

"Sweetheart," he gasped. "You're gonna kill me before
the weekend is out."

Annalise wrote off his dramatic words to postcoital
hyperbole. After all, her hands-on experience with the
erotic arts wouldn't fill a paragraph on a résumé. He was
exaggerating in order to ensure that she would agree to
another round later.

But even as she lectured herself inwardly, she couldn't
help but feel a smug sense of feminine power that she had
satisfied him. Moments later, she winced when he with-
drew, not that it hurt, but because he broke the wonderful feeling of togetherness that was like nothing she had
ever experienced.

Sam made up for the loss by urging her onto her side
and spooning her back, one of his arms cradling her head
and the other tucked beneath her breasts. She allowed herself one dreamy smile, since he couldn't see her face. If
she could maintain the fiction of sex as recreation, she
could protect her heart.

He sighed, the warm puff of air brushing the nape of her
neck like a caress. In the silence, she couldn't tell if he had
drifted off to sleep or was lost in thought. His words, when

they finally came, were totally unexpected, though they were slurred with drowsiness. "Tell me, Annalise, after all these years, what do you remember about your mother?"

Seven

Sam would have to be completely insensitive, or at least a fool, not to note the moment when her body went rigid. And he was neither. Cursing his stupidity, he waited, wishing like hell he could retract the question. He'd spent the better part of an hour coaxing the prickly princess into a warm, malleable mood, and then he'd destroyed it all with his damned curiosity.

Bit by bit, she relaxed. But not like before. Not at all. "Very little," she said in a voice that was suspiciously casual. "I was really young when she died. Most of the memories are from photographs or from things my brothers told me. My father has never really talked about her."

"You missed out on a lot," he said, his heart aching for a bereft little girl who would have been far too young to understand what death meant. The finality. The utter cruelty.

He felt her shrug. "I did fine," she insisted. Did she

realize that her right hand held the sheet in a white-knuckled grip?

He should have dropped the subject. He knew it was the right thing to do. But he was desperate to understand what made Annalise Wolff tick, and his window of opportunity was very narrow. Particularly if the temperatures outside began rising, as predicted.

"I know what it is to be without a parent," he said quietly. "It's not the same as death. I understand the difference, I do. But when my mother took me away from my father, all the way to south Alabama, I felt as if he had died. Phone calls were difficult because of his work schedule and my bedtime. I wanted him to tuck me into bed at night. To read me a story. Divorce was just a word. It meant nothing to me. I was angry for a long time. Screwed up at school on purpose. Gave my mom hell. But in the end, I had to adapt."

She turned her head and kissed the sensitive flesh of his upper arm. "I'm sorry."

"I know they had issues I couldn't understand. I still don't for that matter. Neither of them has ever remarried."

"So why did they separate?"

"Hell if I know. But that's why I'm determined never to do that to my kids. I want a real family. If my parents had stayed together, I might have been lucky enough to have siblings like you do."

Annalise sighed. "My brothers and cousins are everything to me. I can't imagine not having them in my life. We fuss and fight sometimes, even as adults, but they have my back. It must suck being an only child."

"Yeah, well, this conversation wasn't supposed to be all about me. I'm trying to let you know that I experienced a tiny bit of what you went through. And I'm sorry, too. A little girl needs her mother."

"It was no great loss," she said, her voice without in-
flection. "My mother wasn't a very nice person."

The flat, one-dimensional syllables made his scalp tin-
gle and gooseflesh erupt on his arms. Such deliberate lack
of emotion surely hid unimaginable hurt.

Annalise sat up, her narrow, pale-skinned back all he
could see of her. She gathered the quilt to protect her nudity
and stood gracefully. "I need to get back to work. Please
let me know when lunch is ready."

And then she locked herself in the bathroom.

Damn, damn and damn. Pushing her emotionally was
the dumbest idea he'd had in a while. Sam had visited
Wolff Castle enough times over the years to realize that
the family tragedy was kept under lock and key. Neither
the older generation nor their offspring wore their hearts
on their sleeves.

No one discussed the tragic kidnappings, the senseless
shootings, or the move, en masse, to their mountain asy-
lum. It was as if by denying the past, they could pretend
it never happened.

Case in point, Annalise. She had perfected the art of
avoidance. As far as she was concerned, that kiss she gave
him years ago never happened, either. Which pissed off
Sam. He wasn't going to let her forget it. At one time, she
had wanted him. And her body still did, even though her
mind and heart were doing their damnedest to remain
uninvolved.

To put it bluntly, Annalise was having sex with him
like some men would. Strictly physically. With no inten-
tion of entering into any kind of long-term relationship.
Hell, Sam himself had approached sex that way when he
was younger.

But that was then and this was now. Slowly, the light
was beginning to dawn. He might want more from An-

nalise Wolff than he had realized at first glance. He might want it all.

That notion spooked him so badly he bolted from her bedroom, clothes in hand. Was he insane? As he redressed and did his best to salvage the chili, his heart pounded in his chest. He didn't have the luxury of "trying" a relationship with Annalise. If it crashed and burned, he would have to face the music from the older generation. His dad, her father, Uncle Victor. Not to mention five angry brothers and cousins, any one of whom could go head-to-head with him in a fist fight.

As he sliced bread and buttered it, his brain whirled. It was time to back off. The Weather Channel app on his phone said they should see widespread snowmelt by the day after tomorrow. Sam could be back in Charlottesville in time for dinner that night.

Sex with Annalise had been incredible. Possibly the best of his life. But physical intimacy with her came with a lot of baggage. And he wasn't sure it was worth it.

Lunch was awkward and long. Annalise picked at her chili, though she professed it to be delicious. Her careful politeness emulated the demeanor of a reserved young lady. It was weird. And scary.

Sam wolfed down his first bowl and went back for seconds, not so much because he was hungry, but for something to do. When they were done, Annalise offered to help clean up. He declined. When she stared at him briefly, her eyes turbulent with unspoken emotion, he almost cracked.

Instead, he turned toward the sink and held his breath until he heard her leave.

Two hours later, he was ready to climb the walls. He had three young, ambitious paid interns back at the office, any one of whom could run the whole operation given half a chance. That they were all at work on a Saturday morning pointed to their determination to succeed. After a spirited conference call to handle a few pressing matters, he bade them goodbye and hung up. He was itchy, and irritable, and, well…hard.

When he gave in and went in search of his guest, he found Annalise in the same room as earlier, back up on the ladder, picking at a corner of wallpaper with a pocket-knife. This time she didn't give him the courtesy of looking up to note his entrance into the room.

Her gaze was focused on the task at hand, as if by peeling back enough layers she might uncover the secrets of the Rosetta Stone. Sam didn't like being ignored.

"What are you doing now?" he asked, his tone a masterpiece of mild interest.

Still no turn of the head. "Trying to determine how many layers of paper are under here. It's possible that the deepest ones might give us something to go on in terms of color."

"You know that my grandmother doesn't have to have everything exactly like it was…even if you could figure that out. She just wants the decor to be in keeping with the time period of the original house. After all, she's not making Pops get rid of this pool table." He reached in the side pocket and pulled out a striped ball, rolling it in his hand. "I learned to play when I was ten years old. And the old man didn't cut me any slack. It took me four summers to finally win a game."

Finally, Annalise gave him her attention, and a tiny, reluctant smile lifted the edges of her lush lips. "I learned at eight," she said. "And I could beat both Devlyn and Gareth by the time I was nine."

His eyebrows went up. "The devil, you say…."

"I'm always up for a wager."

He felt a kick in his chest and his gut simultaneously. When she forgot to be guarded with him, the luminosity of her smile literally took his breath away. He cleared his throat. "Don't you have work to do?"

She came down two rungs. "Are you chicken?"

His eyes narrowed. He knew when he as being hustled. But he had a competitive streak a mile wide, and he wasn't going to let Annalise get the best of him. "I assume you're going to put your money where your mouth is?"

She cocked her head. "I hate to take your cash."

"A thousand dollars."

That made her blink. But in an instant she was back on track, projecting disdain in her deliberately bored expression. "Ten thousand dollars. To be donated to the new school."

"And if I win? When I win," he amended hastily.

"What do you want?"

Suddenly, every cell in his body hummed with sexual energy. *You.* It was a shocking truth. And one he decided not to give voice to. He rocked back on his heels, hands braced in the door frame. "I want to take you to dinner. Somewhere nice. Linen tablecloths. Roses in crystal vases. Soft lighting."

Suspicion etched her delicate features. "I told you I don't like romantic stuff."

"No romance," he said quietly, trying to gauge her mood. "Just a civilized meal between friends."

"Not in Charlottesville."

"Why?"

"You know why. I don't want anyone to see us together and get the wrong idea."

"Then where?"

"D.C.?"

"We'd have to spend the night."

Her cheeks flushed. "Okay, so Roanoke, maybe."

"We're both grown-ups, Annalise. If we want to have a secretive tryst, it's our business."

She nibbled her lower lip, her gaze moody. "Again with the romance. I said no."

"Every woman likes romance. But the point is, it's up to her partner to decide what that means. If I decide to romance you, darlin', you'll never see it coming. Subtlety is my middle name."

She snorted. "You're about as subtle as a Mack truck. In that case, wager accepted. But dinner only. No funny business."

He held up his hands. "You wound me. I'd never try to seduce you without your permission."

"My permission? That will be a cold day in Hades."

His body tightened. Annalise had the heart of a tease. And she played the game well. The problem was, he was pretty sure it was all instinctive. He doubted she knew what her sass and smart mouth did to him.

Without waiting for an invitation, she started pulling balls out of pockets and setting them on the table, the movements of her hands both graceful and efficient.

"Who gets to break?" he asked.

"We'll flip a coin."

Before he could comment, she pulled a dime out of her pocket, shot it in the air and caught it on her forearm, covering it with her free hand. "You call it."

"Heads."

She showed him the result. Tails. Of course. He sighed audibly.

Annalise smirked. "Too bad."

He slouched against the wall as she gathered the balls, racked them and carefully removed the plastic triangle.

When she leaned over the table, he recognized his basic handicap. Watching Annalise Wolff shoot pool was guaranteed to turn his brain to mush and make other parts of him, well…not mush.

She moved with a confidence that was beautiful to watch. Sam had played pool with other women. Most of them either refused to break or did so with such a weak shot that the balls remained clumped together. It should have come as no surprise to him that Annalise was not like other women.

Ignoring him completely, she chalked her cue, lined up her shot and sent the cue ball slamming into the tightly packed stripes and solids. A trio of the latter slid into three pockets with a precision that made his jaw drop.

She paused to give him one sly, taunting smile over her shoulder before returning to her game and running the table. When nothing remained on the felt but a single white ball, she wiggled her shoulders, stretched her hands over her head and lifted an eyebrow. "Your turn, Mr. Ely."

Muttering beneath his breath, he picked out his own cue and told himself to ignore the fact that a beautiful woman stood watching him. Her gaze tracked his every move. Even so, he managed a creditable break, sinking two shots to her three. He lined up the next few, one after another…and made them.

But when he went for the last one, he made the mistake of looking at his adversary. Her unusual blue eyes sparkled with amusement as if lit from within. His pride suffered a nick. So much so that he bobbled the shot and had to suffer the indignity of having Annalise step up and clean the rest of the table.

When it was over, silence reigned.

She replaced her cue in the rack on the wall and flipped

her ponytail back over her shoulder. "Not bad for an old man," she said. "I guess your reflexes are slowing down."

"Didn't anyone ever teach you that you're supposed to let the guy win?"

It was a smart-aleck comment, a tease, a jab. Certainly not a serious rejoinder. But Annalise blanched. And for the briefest of seconds, he saw real distress in her deep, translucent eyes. "Hey," he said quickly, seeking to temper his blunder. "You know I'm kidding, right? You're amazing. If you weren't already swimming in money, you could play this game professionally. It's true that I don't like losing. But I'll have another shot. You beat me fair and square."

She had turned away during his impulsive backpedaling and was now fiddling with a portfolio of notes she'd been working on earlier. He touched her arm, making her face him. When she wouldn't look at him, he took her chin in his hands. Though several moments ticked by, finally her eyes met his.

He stroked her cheeks with his thumbs. "I… Was… Kidding. Get it? No man worth his salt wants a woman to *let* him win at anything."

"You'd be surprised," she whispered. The single tear that clung to her lower lashes refused to fall.

Feeling like the biggest jerk on the planet, he kissed her forehead. "You can't tell me all those wild Wolffs of yours wanted a fake victory."

She chuckled weakly. "Them? No. Daddy and Uncle Vic used to give me five dollars every time I beat one of the boys. My brothers and cousins hated it, but it made them work harder to improve their game. Unfortunately, when I finally went off to college, no one told me the rules had changed."

"What do you mean?"

"My first week on campus I was invited to a frat party

with five or six other girls. The house had a pool table. One of the pledges offered to teach me the game…I guess to show off to his buddies."

"And you beat him."

"Three games in a row. I was too arrogant for my own good." She paused, as if seeing a painful vision known only to her. "He called me a dyke," she said abruptly. "Everyone laughed."

"Jesus, Annalise." He took her in his arms, despite the fact that she was stiff as a board in his embrace. "College guys are unmitigated jerks for the most part. They check their brains when they walk through those ivy-clad arches and don't reclaim them until four years later. He was thinking with something other than his brain, and you showed him up. It wasn't your fault. Good Lord, you should be proud of your talent."

She sniffed, finally relaxing enough to lay her head on his shoulder. "Mine is more luck than skill. I've always had a knack for geometry. I see the angles. It's no big deal."

He shook her gently. "Be proud of who you are. You're an original. A Wolff daughter. One of a kind."

"Sometimes it's lonely," she said quietly.

He froze, stunned to realize that for perhaps the first time, Annalise was trusting him enough to open that closely guarded heart of hers and let him see a glimpse of the marshmallow center inside the crusty shell. "What about your sisters-in-law?" He stroked her back lightly.

"They're nice women. But we don't have much in common."

"How so?"

"Well, they're all really feminine. Gracie's pregnant and glowing. Olivia already has a daughter, and she's a wonderful mom. Gillian teaches little children and loves

them. And Ariel…well, *People* magazine voted her the
sweetest and most appealing woman on the silver screen."

"I guess I'm missing something. Annalise, you're a
knockout. Killer smile. Fabulous legs. And a personal style
that I'd lay money lots of women try to emulate."

"And yet I've never had a serious boyfriend. Why do
you think that is? I'll tell you," she said, rushing ahead before he could answer. "Men don't want someone like me.
Well, I take that back. In bed, yes. Or as a trophy. They
like the *outside* of me. But…"

"But what?"

She wriggled out of his loose embrace and scrubbed her
hands over her face. He could almost see her withdraw-
ing. "If I need a shrink, I'll pay for one," she said curtly.
"I've got work to do, Sam. Do me a favor and get lost."

He felt his temper boil, despite the fact that he knew she
was goading him deliberately. He had gotten too close, and
she had reverted to her usual antagonistic ways.

"Fine," he said, feeling a real urge to throttle her. "I've
done what Gram asked me to. You know the plan. I'll stay
out of your hair until the snow melts and I can get back to
my real life. But this…" He seized the rickety ladder and
threw it against the wall, feeling a surge of satisfaction
when it splintered into a half-dozen pieces. "This is off
limits. If you really need to get up high, you'll have to ask
for my help. I know it will choke you, but that's the deal."

He stormed out of the room, slamming the door behind
him with as much force as he could muster. Ordinarily
when he was this infuriated, he'd go to the gym and lift
weights or box with the bag. Anything to burn off steam.
But instead, he was being tormented by an advanced case
of cabin fever, exacerbated by lust.

What was he supposed to do with a woman who made
him crazy in bed, and yet did the same thing the rest of

the time in an entirely different, far more maddening way? No man wanted to work this hard for sex.

A flurry of work-related phone calls did nothing to calm him. Instead, he threw on some cold weather gear and went outside to shovel the front steps. After that chore was completed to his satisfaction, he started on the path to the barn until sheer exhaustion forced him to abandon the hopeless endeavor. The storm had dropped at least twelve inches of snow, and the biting wind had turned the top layer to an icy crust that was like chiseling stone.

At last, chest heaving with exertion, he returned to the house. As he walked inside and caught a lingering whiff of what could only be Annalise's signature fragrance, a brilliant plan bloomed in his brain.

His motives were murky, even in his own head. Was he trying to make her mad? Or was he hoping for something more? Annalise had agreed to have sex with him while they were snowed in at the farmhouse. What did it matter if they fought like cats and dogs in between?

Why did he care that guys had hurt her in the past? And why did he still wince when he remembered that he was the first man to break her heart? She'd made it clear that she was no longer interested in any kind of emotional connection between the two of them. Why couldn't he leave well enough alone?

He'd gotten laid twice already. That should be enough for any man indulging a passing fancy. Was it really necessary to play the valiant knight for a woman who so clearly didn't need a hero? Annalise, by her own admission, could take care of herself. She was driven and focused, and fiercely intelligent.

And she hated romance. He grinned as he walked toward the kitchen. She didn't cook. So any meal planning was up to him. He had just the plan to even the scales after that bloodbath of a pool game. Annalise was sharp. But he had an advantage when it came to food. He planned to use every bit of it.

Eight

When Annalise stretched to work the kinks out of her back, it was almost five o'clock. Winter's dark had fallen despicably early, sending her spirits plummeting. She was a runner on occasion, not hard-core-marathon level, but for exercise and stress relief. At the moment, nothing sounded more wonderful.

Unfortunately, she was trapped. And even worse, with a man who made her question everything she knew about herself.

She owed him an apology. The truth stuck in her throat, a huge lump of dismay wrapped in shame. Sam Ely was a nice guy. There. She admitted it. And he'd been doing his best to be kind and understanding when she uncharacter-istically unburdened her soul.

But in return for his gentle, nonjudgmental listening, she'd been bitchy and ungrateful. No wonder he'd heaved a ladder across the room. Why did she have to be so touchy?

Her life would be a lot easier if she had ever learned to be
open to people, to meet them halfway. But she'd grown
up in such an environment of mistrust when it came to the
outside world, it was hard to change her ways.

She ducked into her bedroom to freshen up. Even with
the heat running, the house seemed chilly now that the sun
had gone down. She untied her cardigan from around her
neck and slipped her arms into the sleeves. Taking down
her hair to brush out the dust and tangles, her hands shook
suddenly as she remembered Sam in this room. In her bed.
How would she ever sleep tonight? The image of his big
nude body dwarfing the old-fashioned bed would be impossible to forget.

She had intended to tuck her long unruly hair back into
its hair band at the nape of her neck, but feeling both foolish and hopeful, she left it loose. Looking in the mirror, she
winced. With her hair tumbled around her shoulders, she
looked far more feminine. And vulnerable. Neither of those
were comfortable attributes as far as she was concerned.

When the growling of her stomach drove her to seek out
sustenance, she decided she could hide no longer. Gathering her courage, she went in search of Sam.

The smells from the kitchen took her by surprise, making her mouth water and her nose twitch appreciatively.
Gingerly, she pushed open the door.

Her host looked up, spatula in hand. When he was out
of the room, she could almost convince herself that he was
just another guy. But face-to-face... Her heart stuttered
and then picked up its normal rhythm. He was almost too
much to handle.

She swallowed and bit her lower lip, hovering in the
doorway. "Something smells amazing," she said, offering an unspoken apology in hopes he would hear it and
let her off the hook.

"It's just about ready," he said, his voice neutral. "How about opening that bottle of wine for us? And bring the glasses."

She did as he asked, ridiculously grateful that he wasn't frowning at her. Her nerves were jittery and her stomach unsettled. Though she deserved his censure, perhaps, she was emotional and broody, feeling more like an adolescent girl than a grown woman.

He finished dishing up two plates of pork chops, risotto and home-canned green beans while Annalise watched. Adding a slice of homemade bread to each, he picked up one plate in each hand and nodded his head. "I'll let you go first. We're going to eat in the living room."

She grabbed the crystal and the wine and bumped open the door to the adjoining room with her hip. When she saw what was on the other side, she stopped dead. From the sound of his muttered curse, Sam almost plowed into her from behind.

"Is there a problem?" he asked, his breath brushing her ear.

She swallowed hard, remembering her intent to be conciliatory. "Not at all."

The room was like a movie set. Sam had dragged a small table in front of the hearth and had stoked the fire until it burned merrily, chasing away the cold and cheering the atmosphere immeasurably. He had raided his grandmother's stash of antiques and farm-chic décor. A lace tablecloth set the stage for the brick-red earthenware plates he carried. An old Chianti bottle held a single beeswax candle.

Just behind the table, Sam had positioned the sofa and chairs close enough for post-dinner conversation. Even he couldn't roust up fresh flowers under the circumstances, but he had located a dried nosegay of lavender and heather and tucked it into a squatty china vase.

She set the glasses on the table so he wouldn't hear them rattle against one another. "This looks nice." Clearly, he was making a point. She had professed to dislike romantic gestures. Sam was calling her bluff.

He gently set down the plates and then poured the wine. "Sit and eat," he said, placing a glass filled almost to the brim with Chardonnay at her elbow. "Before it gets cold."

She obeyed reluctantly, feeling her heart race. This wasn't what she had signed on for. She didn't want Sam to be sweet and nice. She didn't want cozy evenings that would make her life feel incomplete when he was gone.

Sam, apparently oblivious to her consternation, dug into his food with the gusto of a hungry man enjoying his dinner. In between bites, he carried on a mostly one-sided conversation in which Annalise mumbled answers only when necessary.

She was fluent in three languages, had dined in four-star restaurants on as many continents and knew the intricacies of cutlery and wine pairings, but on this particular occasion, she was abashed to the point of social ineptitude.

Even Sam, determined to have a pleasant meal, eventually had to address her lack of conviviality. "Cat got your tongue?" he asked, lifting a sardonic eyebrow.

Annalise swallowed. "You've gone to a lot of trouble." Unfortunately, that statement came out sounding far more accusatory than appreciative.

"Don't worry, my little thornbush. This was for my benefit, not yours."

How did one go about calling a man a liar when an earnest apology was already in order? "Meaning what?"

"I was in a bad mood. We have cabin fever. I thought a semblance of civilization might be in order."

"I didn't think you were ever in a bad mood. At least when you're not with me," she amended hastily. "The society editor of the Charlottesville newspaper called you 'Virginia's Consummate Gentleman.'"

He lifted his glass to his lips, eyed her over the brim and drank deeply, the muscles in his throat flexing slightly. The flannel shirt had disappeared. Now he wore a pale blue dress shirt with an open collar and the sleeves rolled up. *Country* Sam was genial and approachable. This recent version, more like the man she knew in the city, was infinitely dangerous.

Twirling the stem of the glass between his fingers, he cocked his head and eyed her reflectively. "Since when do you follow the society columns? I thought Wolffs objected to such journalism on principle."

She stabbed the last bite of her tender pork and waved it at him. "I don't live in a cave. You're quite the celebrity in our corner of the world. I'm sure women line up in droves to be the next flavor of the month."

"Be fair," he said, his eyes narrowing. "I don't flit from flower to flower."

True, damn his hide. She wanted to take potshots at him, wanted it rather badly. But it wasn't that easy to do. He was damned near perfect. "Well, you sure don't show any signs of settling down. Or is all that talk about having kids just a ruse to lure softhearted romantics into your bed?"

"Thank God you're not a romantic," he said grimly. "No telling what would happen."

A ripple of sensation skated down her spine. She had plenty of armor to ward off a lazy, affable Sam. But when he went all dark-eyed and irritated, something about him made her belly flip with feelings that were definitely not wise.

"Are you avoiding the question?" The bite in her words appeared to amuse him.

"Not at all. I don't make any secret of my intentions, but I'm not foolish enough to let a woman think I'm serious when I'm not."

"And you haven't been? Serious, I mean?"

He leaned back in his chair. "Jealous, Annalise?"

She choked on her wine. "Of course not. We'd be a dreadful couple."

"Didn't seem like it last night…or this morning. When you were screaming my name."

Her face turned hot. "Sexual compatibility is nothing more than a fluke of hormones. The only reason I agreed to this temporary arrangement was that I've had a bit of a dry spell."

"How dry?" he shot back.

"None of your business."

"Hmm…"

He seemed to have the terrifying capability of seeing inside her brain. Could he really know how long she had carried a torch for him? She would die of humiliation if he realized.

Sam Ely had rejected her, rather vehemently, a long time ago. Never mind that her heartfelt declaration of love still rang in her ears with sick embarrassment. He had told her she was too young, too forward, too blatant in her pursuit.

Surely he gave her credit for having matured in the meantime.

She gazed into the fire, anything to avoid his laserlike gaze. "Shall I take care of the dishes?"

Sam stood, gathering their plates. "Don't move. Dessert is on the way."

When he left the room, she dropped her head in her hands, only to jerk upright moments later when he re-

turned carrying two bowls of vanilla ice cream topped
with strawberries.

At her look of surprise, Sam grinned. "Gram freezes
dozens of quarts every summer." He had topped each serving with an artistic swirl of whipped cream. "Enjoy," he
said.

She picked up her dessert spoon reluctantly. It was just
ice cream. Nothing sexual about that. No reason for her
palms to sweat and her pulse to do the cha-cha.

After all, strawberries conjured up the memories of
long, hot summer afternoons. And happy times. Her childhood on Wolff Mountain had been idyllic in the beginning.
When she was too young to know she was being held cap-
tive by her father's fears.

Almost as if Sam could hear her thoughts, he tapped
the side of his bowl with the spoon. "Earth to Annalise.
Where did you go?"

She licked a drop of melting ice cream from her upper
lip. "I was thinking about being a kid. How wild and free
it was."

"I envied you your spot on Wolff Mountain. You
wouldn't remember this…because you were probably only
five or six years old when it happened, but your brothers
took me skinny-dipping in the creek one afternoon. You
were the lookout. But you fell asleep, and your dad and
uncle and my dad found us. They read us the riot act, because we had involved you in our escapade."

"My father was and is very protective of me."

"Which makes what we're doing pretty risky."

She frowned. "I'm not five years old anymore. I don't
live on the mountain. My life is my own."

"You're telling me the Wolff men don't keep an eye
on you?"

She wanted to be able to say no, but what was the point?

Sam knew too much about her family. "We all maintain the fiction that I come and go as I please. But yes. I realize that very little I do is completely private."

"And yet you mentioned building your own house on the mountain."

She grinned. "It *is* a conundrum, isn't it?"

"What do you want it to look like? The house, I mean."

"I don't honestly know. I have this hazy image of a screened-in back porch and wicker furniture where I can sit and watch the rain. As far as the house, I haven't nailed down any particular style. But I would want it to be peaceful and uncluttered. A place I could use as a retreat."

"And kid-friendly?"

Unease skittered along her nerve endings. "Maybe a few toys for the nieces and nephews. Perhaps a bunk bed."

"You honestly have no plans to be a mom one day?"

"None," she said flatly. She shoved the bowl aside, though she had eaten less than half of the dessert. "What about you? Are you going to turn your bachelor pad into a baby-proof garret?"

He shrugged. "Doubtful. And I'm not a fan of commuting, so this farmhouse will probably be used for weekends and holidays and a summer getaway. I'm thinking of building a family-sized house just outside of Charlottesville. I've been looking for the right parcel of land for the last couple of years."

"I see." Her dinner sat like lead in her stomach. When Sam didn't say anything more, the silence became oppressive. She struggled to change the subject. "I've ordered a lot of things already. If the weather cooperates, I imagine deliveries will begin to arrive Monday afternoon. I'll start painting a room at a time."

"We can hire people to do that," he said, a tiny line

forming between his brows. "Gram is paying for your expertise, not your muscle."

"I'm picky," Annalise admitted. No point hiding it. "And a bit of a control freak. I'd rather know the work is being done right."

"Then order a ladder," he groused. "I'm not paying for any trips to the emergency room."

Suddenly their earlier fight was the elephant in the room. Not for anything would she admit that his temper had surprised and intrigued her. It indicated a level of emotional involvement that seemed uncharacteristic of a man who managed to make everything in his life look easy and charmed.

Annalise tensed. Almost without knowing it, she had been lulled into a sense of complacency by the good food, Sam's innocuous conversation and the blazing fire. Escape seemed the smart course. "If you won't let me help with the dishes," she said, "I think I'll turn in for the night. I'm reading a good book."

Sam reached across the table and gripped one of her wrists in his big hand. "No."

"Excuse me?" Surely his caveman technique wasn't the reason butterflies tumbled in her chest.

He got up, drawing her to her feet, as well. "I have plans for the evening," he said mildly, although the look in his eyes was anything but. Sexual tension prowled like a dark shadow in the room. "You can cooperate, or I'll persuade you."

"My God, you're an arrogant ass." They were standing so close together she could see a tiny scar on his right cheekbone. His body radiated heat and a scent that was all male. Equal parts soap and sexual determination.

"And you're an aggravating shrew," he said, his gaze on her parted lips. "Lord knows why I want you."

"And yet here we are."

"Indeed." He wrapped a strand of her hair around his finger. "Why do you think that is?"

"You're bored?"

"Not in the least."

"I strike you as some kind of challenge?"

"Like what?"

"I don't know," she said, twisting away to stand in front of the fire. "Maybe you have some deep-seated need to prove you're irresistible."

"I've been rejected on occasion, Annalise. Trust me."

There it was. That tricky word. *Trust*. "What exactly do you want from me?"

"You promised me this weekend. Until the snow melts. I propose we call a truce. Enjoy tonight and tomorrow. And then Monday morning you can decide if you want me to leave. Without you."

"Of course I do. Why would you stay? You'd only get in my way."

He stalked her, backing her toward the corner where the hearth met the alcove. With a flick of his wrist, he reached for the light switch and plunged the room into semidarkness, illumined only by the fire and the single candle. "A truce means you have to pretend you like me."

Her butt smacked into the wall. "I'm not that good an actress."

He grinned, his teeth flashing like a rogue pirate. "You're a spoiled brat, Princess."

"You're a bossy, high-handed pig."

"Kiss me."

The rough command took the starch out of her knees. Her hands flattened on the surface behind her. "I won't."

His arms bracketed her shoulders as his head lowered. "Liar, liar..."

What happened next was like every romantic chick flick she'd ever seen all rolled into one. She was pretty sure an orchestra played somewhere in the background. And Sam's warm, firm lips put any one of a number of leading men to shame as he moved in, surrounded her and took what he wanted. *Oh, Lordy.*

Somehow her arms ended up around his neck, her breasts mashed up against a rock-hard chest. He tasted like sweet berries and cream. The roughness of his tongue tantalized as he intruded ever so gently between lips that trembled. She barely had time to catch her breath before he scooped her into his arms and pressed her against the wall. "You are so damned hot," he said.

"I drive you insane."

He bit the side of her neck. "But I like it."

She giggled. She actually giggled. And that was when she knew she was in trouble. Because Annalise Wolff never giggled. "We already had sex once today." As excuses went, it was pretty pitiful.

Sam snorted. "Then we're way behind."

He hefted her by the ass and skirted the table, knocking over a chair in his haste. She would have giggled again if she had been able to force air from her throat.

Something was strangling her, some desperate, aching realization that her life was never going to be the same after this weekend. "I'm not very good at it," she blurted out, not wanting to pretend with him.

"At what?" He dumped her on the sofa and kneeled beside her to unzip her pants.

"Sex," she moaned, feeling his fingers slip beneath the lacy edge of her panties.

Sam's eyes blazed with hunger, his cheekbones slashed with dark color. "Could have fooled me. Shut up, Princess. Unless you want to say something sensible."

He dragged off her pants, underwear and shoes in one reckless maneuver. Next her sweater, shirt and bra went flying. He opened his jeans and came down between her legs. The denim abraded her inner thighs as he found what he wanted.

"There's no room," she panted. The narrow sofa wasn't made for sexual activity.

"I'll make room." His voice was rough with determination. "Damn, you're wet," he groaned as he tested her readiness with two fingers. The scrape of his fingernail on her delicate flesh sent a keening cry echoing toward the ceiling. But when Sam entered her fully and pushed his way home, the simultaneous cessation of breathing, his and hers, lent magic to the connection.

Five seconds passed. Then ten. She lifted her hips, begging wordlessly. Sam kissed her gently, his mouth firm and sweet. "What is it you do to me?"

Annalise wrapped her legs around his waist. He filled her deliciously. "It's all you," she said, eyes closed with bliss. "I'll hate myself later for saying this, but damn, you're good."

"No cussing, remember?"

He moved his hips, driving deeper. Pinball flashes of pleasure coalesced and ignited at the point where their bodies joined. "Please, please, please," she whispered, voice hoarse, lungs barely able to function.

"Annalise…" His gruff shout sent her over the edge as he hit his own wall, his release coming in a rapid, forceful finish that left her weak and clinging to him like he was the only steady rock in a swirling current.

As their breathing slowed, she became aware of the fact that Sam was heavy, really heavy. And his shirt buttons were making permanent tattoos on her breasts. "Air," she muttered. "I need air."

"Sorry." With patent reluctance, Sam lifted his body off hers and stumbled to his feet.

Suddenly, her nudity in the face of his fully clothed state made her blush. "Will you hand me my shirt and pants, please?"

"No." Again that single, macho negative. Any moment now, she should protest. Instead, she wrapped her arms across her breasts and curled on her side, hiding things he had already seen. "I need my clothes," she said, scrupulously polite.

He threw a couple more logs on the fire and turned to face her. "We're not finished." He shrugged out of his shirt. "I'm just getting started." The sight of his beautiful, masculine chest made her tremble, despite the fact that he had so recently satisfied her. Sam looked different in this light. Like a Viking plunderer...or a wild-eyed barbarian.

It occurred to her that she should show at least a modicum of spunk. Instead of letting him run the show. "What if I object?" Fat chance.

He shrugged, muscles rippling in his arms and torso. "You won't. I promise. Come here, baby."

Nine

Sam had barely touched his wine, yet his head was spinning. The incredible climax he'd experienced moments ago was already fading into the distance, obscured by an urgent need to take her again.

He was not himself. It wasn't false modesty to say he was good at satisfying women sexually. He'd received numerous breathless accolades over the years. But holy hell, the nuclear explosion that triggered when he and Annalise connected was incredible.

At the moment, she was soft, satiated, approachable. It was rapidly becoming apparent to him that the only time he could truly reach her, without the barrier of acerbity she used as a shield, was during sex. When she forgot that she was mad at him…when she forgot that she held a long-standing grudge.

Post-orgasmic amnesia. That's what he should call it. Maybe he had discovered something never before known to science. In another twenty minutes she'd be scowling at him. So the secret was—keep her naked and underneath him. Or on top, or...

As he shed his pants, shoes and socks, his sex reared to attention in increments. Annalise's eyes widened when she took note. He grinned, holding out his hand. "I said, come here."

She stood up, naked and lovely and so very tempting. He knew in his gut that she was right about the two of them. A relationship doomed from the start could only end in messy collateral damage. They weren't living in a vacuum. Their families had been friends for three decades. Whether they liked it or not, their worlds were intertwined.

Which meant that a train wreck on the road to intimacy would affect more than just the two of them.

For a brief moment, he entertained the idea of permanence. He was tired of playing the field. Annalise was smart and beautiful and entertaining both in and out of bed. But she didn't want children. And sadly, that was a deal-breaker for him. Besides, he needed a wife someday who would look at him with adoration, one who believed in romance. Not a termagant who made him want to hide the kitchen knives.

She reached down and took him in her hand, squeezing gently. "I thought you were an old man. It seems I was wrong."

His skin tightened in gooseflesh all over his body. At the moment, babies were the last things on his mind. He closed his eyes, hands fisted at his hips as she caressed the hot length of him. Her fingers curled carefully around his balls, playing with them, testing their weight.

He tried to speak, swallowed hard and tried again. "I have an idea." It had been on his mind ever since that morning when she sat on the edge of the bed, back turned toward him, and he saw the way her slim shoulders and narrow waist flared into a heart-shaped bottom. "Give me a sec."

She frowned when he escaped her light hold. "I'm getting cold."

"Not for long." Grabbing one of the quilts they had used during the night, he folded it carefully and laid it over the wooden arm of the sofa. He snagged her wrist. "That last time was too fast. I want to try slow and easy."

Her eyes widened. "I don't do kinky."

He shrugged, trying to suppress a grin...and failing. "How do you know?"

Her teeth worried her bottom lip. But her raspberry nipples puckered into hard nubs. He brushed them with his thumbs. Annalise shut her eyes, almost as if she couldn't bear to watch.

"I'll repeat the question, darlin', how do you know?"

She swayed toward him, her body lissome and compliant. "I just know. Why did you give me so much wine?" she complained, her arms curling around his neck. "I can't think straight."

"Oh, no, no, no," he said, disentangling himself and holding her at arm's length. "I'm not going to let you blame this craziness on alcohol-induced bad judgment. We're going into this eyes wide open. It's a choice, Annalise. Tell me you want me."

She licked her lips. He was damn sure she had no idea how erotically beautiful she looked. Or how confused. It was the uncertainty in her gaze that slowed him down. "Or tell me you don't want me," he amended, releasing her abruptly and stepping back. "But I won't be accused of taking advantage of you. If you really want to stop, we'll pretend like none of this ever happened."

She shivered hard, as if a ghost had brushed her shoulder. "I *want* you," she said, the words little more than a whisper. "But I know I shouldn't."

He flinched inwardly. He didn't want to be any woman's guilty pleasure, much less Annalise's. "Well, that's honest, at least."

"I hurt your feelings. I didn't mean to."

"I suppose you thought I didn't have any."

She frowned. "Nothing ever seems to bother you."

"You'd be surprised." The ache in his chest was a mixture of arousal and disappointment and a soupçon of Annalise's confusion. God knows, this wasn't what he'd imagined when he drove out to the farm for the weekend. If anything he been dreading a couple of days of armed hostilities as he carried out his grandmother's request to help Annalise settle in.

"Why do you want to have sex with me?"

He rubbed his forehead with the heels of his hands. "Why do women need to have everything analyzed in advance? I just do." He paused, his turn to frown. "Why wouldn't I?"

"I don't know. I've seen the women you date. None of them have much in common with me."

"I can't believe two naked people are standing here having this inane discussion. Only you, Annalise. Suffice it to say that you turn me on. End of story."

"You're getting angry."

"No. I'm getting frustrated. There's a difference. I'll ask you one last time. Do you want me?"

The length of the pause in the conversation was long enough to accommodate an entire symphony...or so it seemed. But at last, she moved, she nodded. A smile would have made him feel better, but at this moment, he wasn't inclined to be picky. "Is that a yes?"

She held out her hand. "It is. I'll never accuse you of anything, Sam. You're an honorable guy. I know that."

Her praise irritated him. "I'm no better or worse than any other man. But I will do my best not to hurt you again. Once in a lifetime was enough."

She managed a small, hesitant smile. "That seems fair."

Feeling his heart thudding against his ribs, he took the hand she offered and drew her into his embrace. "Your skin is like ice," he exclaimed, rubbing his hands up and down her arms. "Come toward the fire for a minute." He faced her toward the flames and stood behind her, wrapping his arms around her beneath her breasts. His erection nestled in the cleft of her bottom. Fine tremors in his limbs reminded him that a baser part of him wanted more than this. But he ignored the insistent pulse of arousal and buried his face in her hair.

She rested her head against his shoulder, her fingers linking with his. "You play dirty," she said, drowsiness in her posture and her voice.

"How so?"

"Romance. It's filled the room. I'm tripping over it." She chuckled. "Maybe it's not so bad after all."

"I'm glad you approve. Are you warmer?" he asked hopefully, about to lose the battle with the constraints he'd placed on his desperate need.

She turned suddenly, taken by surprise. "According to you, I'm hot." Her hands settled on his shoulders and she reached up on tiptoe and gave him a sweet kiss that had a kick to it. "Let's see how kinky you can be."

He'd been hard for so long it was a miracle his brain functioned at all. "We'll start small," he promised, leading her back to the sofa.

With a smile that would have brought any man to his

knees, she brushed his shaft. "Wrong choice of words, Mr. Ely. Not small at all."

Her laughter warmed him from the inside out. If nothing else, he would be grateful that this weekend had eased the pain from the past. He didn't wanted to be at odds with Annalise Wolff. He wanted to be her friend, her very intimate friend.

Without asking for permission, he bent her over the fluffy quilt. The height of the sofa arm was perfect. And as he had suspected, her pert bottom was a sight to see, presented in this position.

"What do you want me to do with my hands?" Her voice was muffled by her hair.

He scooped the thick tresses over her right shoulder so he could see her face. "I'll take care of that." He pulled her arms behind her back and held her wrists. With his other hand, he widened the stance of her legs and reached between her thighs to stroke gently.

Annalise gave a soft exclamation that could have meant any number of things. Her eyes were closed, her face turned toward the fire. He separated the plump folds of her sex and felt the slick moisture that readied her body for his.

It shocked him to realize that his hands were shaking. Badly. Was it arousal or the fear of messing this up? He wanted to show her how sexy she was, how desirable, how perfectly feminine in every way. If later, she chose to take the lead, he had no problem with that. In fact, the thought of Annalise Wolff dominating him in the bedroom had a certain skin-tightening charm.

But he sensed that at the moment she wanted to capitulate, to submit, to revel in the freedom of her sex. To experience the power of driving a man to the point of insanity.

In truth, Sam was almost there.

He fit the head of his shaft to her passage and teased

her with it. She squirmed. Her face was flushed. At least
the part he could see. Wondering if she would consent to
play with him, he decided to test the waters. "I'm going to
release your wrists," he said gruffly. "I want you to stretch
your arms over your head, link your hands, and rest them
on the sofa. Do you understand?"

"Yes." The low, slurred tenor of her reply tapped in him
a primal response.

"Then do it." When he let go of her wrists, she obeyed
his command.

The vision of Annalise stretched out in front of him
like an offering seared his brain...so vivid, he could see
it even when he closed his eyes and sucked in a shaky
breath. With both of his hands now free, he caressed her
butt. Her ass was pale as the moon, curvaceous, perfectly
proportioned to her healthy body.

A small mole, high on her right hip, fascinated him.
When he bent and kissed the tiny beauty mark, Annalise sighed deeply. Once again, he positioned himself for
entry. "You were beautiful as a teenager," he whispered,
fearful of bringing up the past, though beyond dissimula-
tion. "But now you take my breath away. I want you. I'm
going to have you. Again and again until you beg me to
stop. You've bewitched me, seduced me, destroyed me."

Slowly, he pushed into her, painfully stimulated by the
angle of penetration and the caveman position. He wasn't
even sure if this was for him or for her. The fit was tight,
her body squeezing his until his skin dampened and his
eyes stung with the sheer pleasure of it.

"Talk to me," he begged. "Tell me what you want."

She glanced over her shoulder, a sultry, sirenlike gaze.
"Whatever you have to give me, Sam. I want it all."

He drove into her again and again. First slow, then fast,
then slow again. His fingers splayed on her ass, plump-

ing, caressing. "I wish you could see yourself right now. God, you're amazing."

She arched her back, and reared up on her elbows, forehead resting on her clenched hands. "More. Don't stop."

He reached beneath her and caressed the spot where her pleasure centered. Annalise jerked and moaned. Timing the stroke of his finger to the slide of his shaft, he took them both to the edge and hovered there. "Do you want to come?"

She said a word that once again destroyed her resolution.

Sam chuckled, but it was a breathless, weak sound. The air in his lungs had evaporated. Suddenly, his control snapped, and with a groan, he pushed all the way to the core of her and pumped recklessly as he gripped her hips and emptied himself into the warm welcome of his unlikely lover.

Hours later, he rolled over and glanced at the clock. Annalise was in *his* bed this time, in the room that was his whenever his visited his grandparents. The comfortable king mattress accommodated his lanky frame. He held her close, relishing the sweet, trusting way she rested in his embrace.

They had made love for hours, finally abandoning the living room and coming upstairs to collapse into bed. Sighing deeply with repletion and contentment, he succumbed once again to the warm embrace of much-needed sleep.

When he opened his eyes the second time, Annalise was gone. The stone of disappointment that crushed his chest was enormous. Yesterday morning, he had understood her need to flee. But last night he thought they had forged a tenuous understanding, a fledgling truce.

His mouth was fuzzy and his head ached. Reluctantly,

he dialed back his expectations for the remainder of the weekend. Annalise was not like other women. And there was absolutely no way to predict her reactions from one minute to the next.

Perhaps all she wanted from him was sex. For any other guy at any other moment, that would have been a pretty sweet deal. But Sam and Annalise had a past, a connection, an undeniable chemistry. The potential was there to create something wonderful.

He was beginning, however, to have a sinking suspicion that she was determined never to let that happen. Was it because he had rejected her once upon a time? Or did she simply not want anything more from him than one naughty weekend?

Annalise hummed as she worked, her body aching pleasantly, and her cheeks heating as she relived each moment of the incredible night before. Sam Ely was a genius. Even with her limited experience, it was evident that he had devoted a lot of time to learning about women.

Perhaps she should have been jealous. His sexual expertise was no doubt the product of many intimate liaisons. But oddly, she didn't begrudge any of those women their momentary connections to Sam. He wasn't *with* any of those women now. He had moved on.

Despite the painful experience in the past when she threw herself at him and suffered an ignominious rejection, she and Sam had known each other for a very long time. They had a relationship. It might not be the stuff of romantic fiction, but it was something. Even if this weekend turned out to be all she ever had of him in a sexual way, the tentative resurrection of their friendship would be enough.

The essence of that thought rang false, but she ignored

the warning signs. Sam wasn't hers to keep. He deserved someone who wanted the things he wanted. A woman who could create a home and a family with him. Annalise was unable to do either of those things. There were still secrets between them. But that was okay. Because after this weekend, they would be something they hadn't been in many years. Friends.

She pulled out her laptop and perched on a stool in the downstairs room Sam's grandmother had used as a sewing nook. Colors and patterns buzzed in her head, each jockeying for favor. This was her favorite part of the job... choosing palettes, accents, lighting. Already she was falling in love with the farmhouse.

Sam was right. It was too far from the city to be practical as a main residence, but how wonderful it would be to get away on a warm spring weekend, a lazy summer month in August, a crisp, colorful autumn retreat. She could almost see the children playing outside, hear their high-pitched laughter.

Several ancient oaks provided the perfect spot for tire swings. In summer, the generous shade would accommodate impromptu picnics, as well. And the house was big enough for lots of company. Even the burgeoning Wolff clan.

That thought brought her up short. Surely she wasn't weaving improbable daydreams about her and Sam. She hadn't been lying when she told him she didn't really like romance. Romance was what had led her to throw herself at him when she was twenty-one.

Romance made people stupid, and Annalise was not stupid. Besides, even if by some miracle she and Sam fell in love and managed not to drive each other nuts, the truth remained. She was not wife material.

His long-ago words still rang in her ears: *Men like gen-*

tle, feminine women...soft, self-effacing. Perhaps he hadn't really meant that. He said he'd been trying to let her down easy and keep her from doing something stupid with another man who might have accepted her artless invitation and tossed her aside afterward.

But even so, he'd said the words out loud, and their power lingered. Annalise wouldn't change herself even if she could. She liked who she was. But she had to accept that there were some things her upbringing had cost her. And having a family was one of those.

"There you are. Have you had breakfast?"

Sam's voice startled her so badly she nearly dropped her computer. She closed it and stood, clutching it to her chest like armor. "I had some toast and coffee."

"Did you sleep well?" His topaz and chocolate eyes searched her face, his sculpted mouth unsmiling.

She squirmed inwardly. "Yes, thank you." Good Lord. This was a man who had seen her naked, who had done exquisitely intimate things to her and with her. Why was the aftermath so damned difficult?

He lounged in the doorway, his hands shoved in the pockets of faded jeans. Another flannel shirt, this one gold with a navy windowpane pattern, strained across his broad shoulders. His eyelids drooped and his hair was mussed. He looked like a man who had been up all night.

Her prim response amused him. His lips quirked, and he cocked his head, studying her with an intensity that seemed to strip the clothes from her body. "I think we need some exercise."

The color in her face deepened as her thighs clenched. "Well, I...uh..."

"Outside," Sam clarified. "In the fresh air. The temperature has come up considerably. Gram and Pops have all sorts of winter gear in the mudroom. How about it?"

She glanced out the window to the world of white. Suddenly, nothing sounded more appealing. "I'd like that."

In twenty minutes they were bundled up in layers of warm clothing. Fortunately for Annalise, Gram had left behind a pair of yellow galoshes that were close enough to the right size to keep her feet warm and dry.

The first bite of cold air as they stepped outside took her breath away, but when they rounded the house to the side sheltered from the wind, where Sam had scraped a partial path, it wasn't bad at all. The sun shone down valiantly, doing its best to melt the snow. Annalise lifted her face to the sky and inhaled the smell of wood smoke drifting from the chimney.

The farm was somnolent, like Sleeping Beauty's castle. Sam's grandparents had sold off all the livestock years ago when they decided they no longer wanted the responsibility of actually running a dairy farm. Any farmhands had long since been let go. Though the barn was in good shape and the outbuildings were sturdy, the place was a ghost town. Only the house itself showed any signs of life.

Annalise turned to Sam. "Do you think you'll ever turn this back into a working farm? You've talked about how much you loved it as a kid. It seems a shame to use only the house."

He shaded his eyes with one hand and looked out across the fields that had once supported acres of corn and herds of cows. "I'll bring the horses back, at some point. And maybe lease the land so it will be producing as it should. But I doubt the farm will ever be what it once was. Unless one of *my* children takes an interest in agriculture."

The way he said the word *children* hurt something deep in her chest. "How many do you want? Kids, I mean."

He shrugged. "That will depend on my wife, I guess. But at least three. Maybe four."

Four? Annalise felt faint.

When she was silent, he continued. "I have the means to support a big family. And I want a noisy house, not like where I grew up. By the time I was eleven, Mom quit making me go to a babysitter after school. I got off the bus and let myself in with a key we kept hidden under a rock in the backyard. She always left me snacks ready...lemonade in the fridge, fresh fruit and cookies. But I hated the silence when I went inside."

He visibly shrugged off his preoccupation with the past. "I don't want you to think it was a terrible childhood, 'cause it wasn't. My mom is a great person, and she did the best she could with a rambunctious son who was pretty mischievous. I had plenty of friends in the neighborhood. So I spent a lot of time at their houses."

"Tell me something, Sam," she said, touched with compassion by the picture he painted. "How can you be so sure you won't end up divorced like your parents? The statistics aren't in your favor."

He picked up a stick and hurled it into the distance, an almost palpable sense of frustration in the jerky motion. "For one thing, I've learned the difference between lust and love. And how important compatibility is. That's where people go wrong when they marry too young. They ignore the fact that attraction and wild sex are not a sound basis for long-term commitment. I guess I can't be one-hundred-percent certain, but the reason I've waited this long to get married is so I can be sure of as many variables as possible."

"Sure how?" Annalise kicked at a stone with her boot. This was an odd place for a serious conversation, but at least out here they weren't likely to strip off their clothes and attack each other. Just the thought of it made her layers of clothing far too warm.

"My parents weren't a great match from the beginning. I'm going to pick someone who shares my values, who wants what I want."

"No offense, Sam, but you said that your dad's workaholic nature was partly to blame for the divorce. Aren't you like him in that way?" She wasn't being mean. It was a fair question.

He unzipped his coat partway, pulled the hood back and ran his hands through his hair. In the bright sun she could see glints of red in his thick chestnut waves. "It's true," he said. "I work long hours. But that's because I can. If I had a wife and kids at home, things would be different."

"Mmm…"

His eyes snapped with displeasure. "You don't believe me?"

"I think you're pretty set in your ways. Are you expecting this paragon of a wife to stay home with the kids?"

"I hope she'll want to…since finances won't be an issue. The two of us will share responsibility for child-rearing, but it seems to work best when one parent stays home to give the kids security."

She couldn't argue with that. Her mother had not been around, and her dad, though she loved him dearly, wasn't the cuddly type. The Norman Rockwell existence Sam described was very appealing. As long as he acknowledged that his wife would surely have dreams outside of simply being a mother. Somehow, she thought he would. Despite any evidence to the contrary, Sam was not a chauvinist.

"Well," she said, feeling depression settle like a pall over the day, "I wish you luck." Any last glimmer of hope that Sam might care for her in a deeper sense withered and died. The two of them were not compatible. They fought like cats and dogs. She'd be a lousy mother. Even if she were willing to put her career on hold and give him multiple babies, the picture would fall apart rapidly.

When he wasn't looking, she scooped up a handful of snow and shaped it into a ball. Pool wasn't the only game she knew how to play. She wandered a few yards away, ostensibly to look at an old doghouse covered in snow.

Sam was gazing up at the eaves of the farmhouse, probably wondering about things like dry rot and bats and other homeowner headaches. Taking careful aim, remembering everything her brothers had taught her, she reared back and flung the sphere of snow as hard as she could.

Thwack! It couldn't have been a more perfect bull's-eye. The snowball caught the side of Sam's neck, disintegrated from the force of the hit and slid messily into the open collar of his shirt.

"Hey," he shouted indignantly. "No fair."

The childhood rejoinder made her grin. "You're the one who said we needed exercise." Rapidly, she scooped up more handfuls of snow, creating her ammunition and using the doghouse as cover.

Sam's glare promised retribution. He amassed an arsenal as well, only instead of huddling behind a pitiful barrier like her abandoned pet shed, he stacked his snowballs on a windowsill and climbed up beside the house to stand on an old stump. Now he had the advantage of higher ground.

When he turned to put one last projectile on his growing pile, Annalise shot to her feet, threw three snowballs in quick succession and crowed when every one of them hit the intended target. Sam's hair was coated in white, and he had to wipe snow from his mouth.

Revenge was swift and targeted. Too late, she remembered that Sam had pitched for his college baseball team. A hailstorm of snowballs descended on top of her, ricocheting off the roof, the walls and the corners of her shelter. At least half of the shots arced perfectly over the small building and landed smack on her head. She huddled into her coat, pulled the hood down tight and waited him out.

Inevitably, he ran out of ammo. Now it was her turn. Standing with impunity, she mimicked his blitzkrieg, pelting him unmercifully. This time she played dirty, aiming for his masculinity. The snow was too wet and she was too far away to do any real damage, but watching Sam hop and curse and try not to fall off the stump had her laughing until tears ran down her face.

Unfortunately, she, too, eventually ran out of steam and snowballs. Ducking back down, her heart pounding, she waited for the answering volley. Nothing happened. Surely he had managed to make a new pile of ammo by now. Dead silence reigned, broken only by the faraway raucous cry of a crow.

What was happening? Why wasn't he firing back? Tentatively, she peeked around the corner of the doghouse, expecting any moment to be hit in the face with icy, wet snow.

The stump had been abandoned. No sign of Sam anywhere, though messy footprints led in all directions. Surely he wouldn't have gone back into the house without her. Inside her gloves, her fingers started to go numb. And the knees of her pants were getting wet. Where in the hell was he?

Without warning, snow crunched behind her and what felt like a shovelful of snow slithered down her back. She yelled in shock, flailing wildly and knocking Sam's head with hers in the process. He had made a wide circle, sneaking up behind her in a creditable ambush attack.

Before she could recover, he flipped her onto her back

and shoved more snow up under the front of her coat. "Stop, you big goof," she cried. "I'm freezing."

He unzipped her parka and massaged the snow into her chest. "I want to hear you cry uncle," he said, grinning evilly.

She tried to ignore the fact that her body was heading for hypothermia. Smiling sweetly to disarm him, she waited one click…two…and then kneed him dangerously close to the groin before rolling away, reversing their positions and landing on top of him with her forearm over his windpipe.

Sam's eyes crossed and he coughed out a weak imprecation. "I should have known better," he groaned. "Martial arts. Not Barbie dolls. Rookie mistake on my part."

Annalise knew he could overpower her. Despite her considerable skill, he outweighed her by at least seventy pounds. And he was strong and powerful. But for the moment, he allowed her a victory.

He held up a hand. "I surrender."

"Hah."

"You don't believe me?" His lifted eyebrow was all innocence.

She stood up and shivered as melted snow ran down her back and belly. "I don't trust you one tiny bit. You're a schemer and a conniver."

"Only in sports," he said gravely. "Not in real life."

She had been teasing him, nothing more, but his sudden, soft-spoken vow seemed to be aimed at communicating something significant. "Well, duh, I know that," she said. "Eagle Scout. Outstanding young alumnus, president of the United Way campaign. I suppose I'm the only person to ever leave the Sam Ely fan club. Right?"

He stood up and winced when he realized his entire

backside was covered in snow. Brushing himself off, and not even looking at her, he shrugged. "I was rather hoping you'd ask for a new membership card." When she didn't say anything, mainly because her heart had lodged uncomfortably in her throat, he faced her. "Or am I way off base? Do you still hate my guts?"

How had they gone from playful to deadly serious so quickly? The words she wanted to say trembled on her tongue. *I never stopped loving you, Sam.* But good Lord, she couldn't say that. And see the pity and compassion on his face? She'd rather go to her grave an old maid.

"I don't hate you," she said lightly. "But if I catch pneumonia, I hope your workmen's comp is all paid up."

Ten

Sam suffered the tsunami of disappointment stoically. What had he expected? A miracle in less than forty-eight hours? Annalise would never forgive him, not really. And he might as well give up on winning her approval. It was a lost cause.

Swallowing his bitter defeat, a battle she didn't even realize she had won, he waved a hand. "Let's go inside."

On the back porch, they stripped off their outerwear. "Leave it," Sam said. "I'll put it all in the dryer later." He watched her wring water from her hair, and that single, feminine motion made him hard. *What the hell,* he thought. If sex was all that worked between them, he might as well enjoy it. "We shouldn't traipse through the house all wet," he said calmly.

Annalise sat on a stool and tugged off her boots. "What would you suggest?" Her pants were soaked through, and her sweater was not much better.

"Strip naked," he said. "We'll make a dash for the shower."

Her eyes widened and two spots of color bloomed on her cheeks. "Naked?"

"It's the smart thing to do." Not waiting for her to follow his lead, he dragged his shirt over his head, shoved his sodden pants to his feet and stepped out of them. His socks were already balled up inside his boots. In spite of the frigid temperature, his sex reared eagerly, perhaps not at full mast, but headed that way.

When Annalise seemed literally frozen, he lent a hand, undressing her matter-of-factly, not lingering to caress her, or signal seduction in any way.

Now they both stood bare-skinned, their limbs covered in gooseflesh. "After you," he said quietly, unable to tear his gaze away from her nudity. He put a hand at the small of her back and urged her forward. "My shower's bigger. We'll go upstairs."

By the time they made it to his room, he couldn't feel his feet. And Annalise's lips were blue. Leaving her to stand on the bath mat for a moment, he leaned into the shower enclosure, adjusted the water to a warm, steady spray and linked his fingers with hers. "C'mon, honey. Let's get you warmed up."

She was so docile, he worried for a moment that she might actually be in danger of shock from the cold. But as soon as he got her under the steamy water, color returned to her skin, and she moaned in sheer pleasure. The sound she made went straight to the heart of his need, dragging him into insanity without a qualm.

When he stepped behind her, soaped up his hands and reached around to wash her breasts, she didn't make even a token protest. She stood mute, a lifelike statue, allowing him to shampoo her long, raven hair, to tip back her head beneath the water and rinse the bubbles away.

In that position, he couldn't help himself. He had to taste those puckered rosy nipples, his tongue circling them, suckling them one at a time. When her knees gave out, he supported her with one arm behind her back.

He reached for the soap and eased his way down between her legs. Lazily, he slid the wet bar over her sex, back and forth. Annalise came to life, panting, lifting a leg to steady herself against the shower wall.

Laughing softly, Sam dropped the soap and used his fingers to finish the job. She responded to him beautifully, lifting her hips into his touch, arching her neck as she reached for what he wanted to postpone. He wished that she felt comfortable enough with him to initiate sex, but that was asking a lot given their history.

He scraped her hair from her face, drawing it in his fist to the back of her neck. Even wet and bedraggled, she was stunning. He momentarily leaned his forehead against hers, still holding her by the hair. "I know from experience," he said, "that the water is going to run cold in about two minutes. How do you feel about moving this to the bedroom?"

His prosaic question seemed to snap her out of some trancelike state. Her jaw dropped, and she winced, as if only now realizing that she was cavorting with a naked man in the shower. "We've wasted a lot of time playing around. I need to be working."

He gaped at her, his temper rising. She was pretending that she could walk away. That their sexual intimacy meant nothing to her. In his gut, he didn't think she really believed that, but her attempt to shove him to a safe emotional distance infuriated him.

He jerked on the ponytail he had crafted, not hard

enough to hurt her...but with enough force to gain her attention. "Is this where I'm supposed to seduce you against your objections? What kind of game are you playing with me?"

"I'm not," she cried, tears welling in her eyes.

Her genuine distress nicked him. Tears from a woman who never showed weakness indicated a level of involvement that dared give him a flicker of hope. "You could have fooled me," he muttered, but the words held little heat.

She licked her lips, despite the fact that water still pelted down upon them. "I'm sorry if you think that. It's not true. I would never do such a thing, I swear. I know that whatever we're doing here isn't permanent, but you're important to me, Sam."

"Forget it." Now he felt guilty for his outburst. He shut off the water and grabbed two towels, handing her one without comment, using the other for himself. He turned his back, unable to watch the erotic image of his nemesis drying one slender limb at a time. He strode into the bedroom and stepped into a pair of knit boxers. "Do you want me to go downstairs and get you some clothes?" He raised his voice because she was still in the bathroom.

"There's a pair of pajamas and matching slippers in the top drawer of the dresser." The words were subdued. He heard cabinets opening, and then the sound of the hair dryer.

He shivered hard. It was a good thing Gram and Pops were getting the heat and air revamped. This old house was chilly in winter, even when the power *wasn't* out. The trip downstairs and back was accomplished in record time, mainly because he resisted the urge to rummage through the piles of sherbet-colored lingerie. The delicate garments held a faint fragrance that was uniquely Annalise. When he imagined her wearing them, confusion and hunger made him restless.

He took the stairs two at a time, stopping short when he entered the bedroom. She was standing in the doorway to the bathroom wearing one of his shirts she'd found hanging on a chair. Her legs were bare, her eyes huge with vulnerability, her hair mostly dry.

"Do you want to change into these?" he asked.

He saw her chest rise and fall. Her lower lip trembled. "No more pretending from me, Sam. I might as well be honest. What I *want* is to get in bed with you."

It was the most she had ever offered him. The tremulous words socked him in the gut, disarming him even as they aroused. He swallowed his pique and decided to be offended later. "Well, okay then." He dropped her clothing on a chair and approached her. "We're going to talk today…sometime. About why you and I have this weird, screwed-up relationship. But right now…" He scooped her up into his arms and carried her toward the bed.

"Right now, what?"

"Never mind," he sighed, not sure what he'd been about to say. She felt perfect in his arms. As if for the first time, he had found what he was looking for. But it didn't make any sense at all. Annalise was not the kind of woman he wanted for the long haul. She was sharp-tongued and opinionated and bossy. And though her body was sinfully soft, her personality was anything but.

She thrived on confrontation, and she'd rather best him at anything than give an inch. He was convinced that another Annalise lurked inside. A woman who didn't have a chip on her shoulder. A woman who could warm a man with her caring and her courage. But for whatever reason, she had decided to keep the walls in place.

She had granted Sam access to her body this weekend,

but the essence of who she was remained under lock and key. It saddened him, but he was not really in a position to challenge her on it. Not unless he was prepared to go forward with the relationship.

Tossing back the covers, he deposited her on the bed, coming down beside her and covering them both with the blankets. He had forgotten to turn off the overhead light, and the curtains were wide open. On one elbow, leaning over her, he studied her face.

In the clear light of day, her skin was luminous. The blue of her eyes was darker today, perhaps reflecting the navy comforter. She looked at him as she always did, wary, on her guard. As if expecting at any moment to have him lash out at her.

Couldn't she feel how much he needed her...needed this? He'd taken her like a wild man, over and over again this weekend. And as soon as they finished one round, he wanted her again.

Lightly, he mapped her body with his fingertips. She was slender, but not skinny. No ribs protruding, no hollowed-out collarbone. Everything about her was the epitome of life and health. When he cupped her breast, she turned her head away.

He took her chin and made her look at him. "What are you afraid I'll see in your eyes?" he asked quietly.

"Nothing," she said. Long lashes at half-mast cloaked her secrets.

"Tell me, Annalise," he said gently. "We're the ones writing the rules here. I won't make fun of anything you say, I swear."

She moved restlessly, dislodging his hand and sitting up with the sheet pulled to her armpits. Grief darkened her eyes even further as she finally stared straight at him. "You know too much about me," she said, her voice ragged.

"And it scares me that when we're together…sexually…I feel exposed."

"Surely you've been intimate with a number of men."

"Not as many as you think. And besides…"

This time he waited in silence, not prompting her. The honest, unvarnished truth was something he had wanted badly. Now that she was giving it, he had to struggle to sort out his feelings.

Annalise lifted her chin. "I am not an easy woman, Sam. I know that. I have baggage. Both in general, and where you are concerned."

He shrugged. "All of us have baggage."

She frowned. "I don't want to get close to you."

He absorbed the shot, felt it pierce his heart. "I see."

"I don't think you do. Maybe it's just the difference between men and women, or maybe it's my own neuroses. But when we're naked…intimate…it feels as if you take more than I want to give."

"I'm not your enemy," he said, his fists clenched beneath the blanket where she couldn't see. He'd forced himself to remain in a seemingly relaxed position, reclining on his side. But the pretense was wearing thin.

"You're not my anything. That's the problem. We've succumbed to the urge to scratch an itch, probably because we're snowed in and we're both reasonably attractive people, but that's as far as it goes."

He felt the ground shift beneath his feet. "What if it could be more?"

Something flickered in her eyes, a lightning flash of deep emotion that was gone before he could analyze it. He hadn't meant to say the words. They had surprised him as much as her.

"What do you mean?" She was prevaricating…buying time.

"What if we started over? No expectations. A future wide open. Maybe we've both been wrong about what we want. Are you willing to take a chance that we've been too blind to see the truth?"

For a few shimmering seconds, a door into her soul opened. He recognized it without question. He'd stake his life on it. In her eyes he saw the hope and the fear. The dawning realization that things could be different. He was pretty sure he even saw a laughing baby with her eyes and his chin.

He didn't want to push. Not with the chance that she might actually come to him on her own. But he was so damn close to something momentous, it made him ache. "Talk to me, honey," he urged. "Please."

He shouldn't have asked. She wasn't ready. And when she did what he begged of her, the truth hurt more than he could have thought possible.

"You're not making sense, Sam," she said flatly. "I've never known a man more sure of himself, and I told you from the beginning that the weekend was all I was offering."

"God, you're impossible," he shouted. It took a lot, as a rule, for him to lose his temper, but with Annalise, the fuse stayed lit half the time. "How can you be such a coward?"

She went white, and at that exact instant, the front doorbell rang, echoing far away in the house.

Her eyes widened as Sam cursed. "I'll get rid of whoever it is."

He went to the window and peeked out, groaning in disbelief when he read the side of the truck parked in the driveway.

Annalise had scrambled onto her knees. "What is it? What's wrong?"

Sam reached in his suitcase and grabbed a clean pair

of pants and a long-sleeve knit shirt. "Unless I'm mistaken, it's the guy who's going to overhaul the heat and air system."

"But they're not supposed to arrive until tomorrow. How did they get here?"

"A lot of the snow has melted, and they have a heavy gauge vehicle with good tires. What can I say, Annalise? I guess you can consider this your version of saved by the bell. Unless there's something you want to say to me. Right now. Do you, darlin'? Am I really so scary?"

Again that glimpse, that sliver of heaven shining in the darkness. Her lips parted as she started to speak…he felt something tighten in his chest.

But the noise below shattered any last hope of taking a step forward.

Annalise shook her head slowly. "I think we've said it all, Sam. I'm sorry."

He left the room so quickly, she was stunned. Since pajamas were her only option on this floor, she scuttled downstairs wrapped in a sheet and disappeared into her room. By the time she came out fifteen minutes later, fully dressed, Sam was entertaining in the living room. "What have I missed?" she asked, summoning a smile as she assessed the situation.

Sam gave her a chilly smile that perhaps only she realized had an edge to it. "This is Darren Harrell and his wife, Rachel. The little boy is their son, Butch."

Rachel cuddled an infant, her expression anxious. "I'm sorry if we've intruded. Darren called Mrs. Ely and she said it was okay for us to come a day early and to bring the baby. We live in a really rural area, and the heavy wet snow took down all kinds of power lines. If it was just us, we could get by, but I couldn't let the baby stay there. And we only have one vehicle right now."

Annalise took the woman's free hand and squeezed it. "Don't be silly. I'm here to work, as well. And you're not intruding...right, Sam?"

He leaned in the doorway, his smile genuine as he aimed it at the visitors. "Of course not. This old house has tons of bedrooms. I'll help bring in your things. Annalise, do you mind getting them set up in whichever room you ladies decide is best?"

"With pleasure."

While the men were outside, Annalise gave Rachel an abbreviated tour. "How about this bedroom?" she asked, throwing open the door. "It's fairly large and has its own bathroom. The painting hasn't been done yet, and it's missing some finishing touches, but it's serviceable."

Rachel smiled shyly, the baby propped on her hip. "We'll be fine." Though the younger woman was dressed in worn denims and an inexpensive sweatshirt, she had a sunny disposition that proclaimed louder than words that she was happy with her lot in life. While Annalise watched, Rachel put the infant on the bed and efficiently changed a wet diaper. "Butch is such a good baby...he hardly ever cries. You won't even know he's here."

Annalise chuckled. "I'm not worried."

Suddenly, Rachel exclaimed, "Oh, gosh. I promised my mom I'd let her know when we got here. She's a worrier, and the snow was an issue. Hold Butch for me, will you?"

Before Annalise had a chance to protest, Rachel thrust the infant into her arms and disappeared. The sudden change in circumstances put a lump in Annalise's throat. She couldn't remember the last time she'd held a small child. As a rule, she avoided them whenever possible.

Her hands shaky, she held the kid at arm's length and stared at him. "Well, you drew the short straw, kiddo. I'm clueless. Are we supposed to play peek-a-boo? Or maybe I burp you? Do you just hang out when you're not hungry?"

Butch had wild red hair and gorgeous blue eyes. After gazing at her solemnly for several seconds, he smiled, cooing and blowing bubbles that collected on his chubby chin. A single tooth at the bottom of his mouth shone proudly.

Her heart contracted in her chest and her womb quivered. This was why she stayed far away from adorable little rug rats. They made her ache for what she was afraid she could never have. She touched her nose to the baby's, talking silly nonsense syllables to him. When he chortled, she pulled him close, nuzzling his cheek and patting his back as he rooted at her shoulder.

Her blouse was silk, a new offering from an up-and-coming Parisian designer. It never occurred to her that she should keep him away from her expensive outfit. Instead, she held him close, inhaling the precious smells of baby powder and shampoo and a scent unique to small human beings.

She kissed the top of his head. "That's okay, little fella. You and I will do just fine. I promise not to drop you and you try not to poop before your mama gets back."

Eleven

Sam stood stock-still, suitcases in hand, and felt his heart fall somewhere down around his feet. The smile Annalise aimed at Butch—the fabulous, cajoling, entirely unguarded beam of happiness—was one Sam had never witnessed. The look on her face as she bounced her little charge was heartbreaking in its rarity.

Why had Sam never seen her like this? Open, delighted, intensely feminine in her gentle care of another woman's child.

"He likes you," Sam said, setting the luggage just inside the door and lingering there.

Annalise whirled to face him, her cheeks pink. "Isn't he cute?"

Butch was wearing John Deere overalls and a yellow onesie with long sleeves. On his tiny feet were soft cloth tennis shoes that matched his outfit.

Sam grinned, enjoying the show. "He could use a barber, but yeah, he's a peach."

Annalise held him out. "You want to take a turn?"

It hit him in that moment that she had been hiding herself from him the entire weekend. Never once had he seen this side of her, the soft, nurturing affection, the unself-conscious pleasure.

The knowledge grieved him, for it spelled doom to any fledgling dreams he might have been weaving. Annalise didn't want to be in a relationship with him. She didn't want intimacy, roots, commitment. She was afraid of what he made her feel. Of what they both felt. Because she didn't trust the feelings and she didn't trust Sam. Seeing her now, with a baby, made him face the unspoken yearnings that had sprung up deep in his gut.

He tasted the bitter bile of failure and found it to be more painful to swallow than he could have imagined. Watching Annalise hold a small child reminded him of everything he didn't yet have in his life. And it also pointed out that a woman who could show two such different faces to him was someone with issues.

He had his own demons to fight...the specter of statistical marital failure, the possibility that he might be no better a father than his own dad had been. But at least he knew in those instances what battles he faced. When it came to Annalise, there were depths he'd been unable to reach in her, secrets she wouldn't share. And the fact that he had only now realized he was perilously close to falling ass over heels in love with her didn't help in the least.

He shook his head, backing out into the hall, feeling appalled and clumsy and off balance. "You keep him. Darren needs my help."

When he went back outside, he found Rachel wrapping up a phone call. Sam lowered his voice. "The kitchen is stocked. But Annalise doesn't cook and she's self-conscious about it. Feel free to take over the meal planning for as long as you're here."

Rachel nodded. "It's the least I can do."

Over dinner, the conversation between four very different adults was helped along by little Butch's antics. His parents had brought every conceivable baby conveyance, including a high chair. Rachel had matter-of-factly prepared country ham and hash brown potatoes for dinner, along with a simple serving of applesauce.

Annalise was subdued, but held her own in the odd social setting. Sam had no appetite at all, because all he could think about was that he had missed his last chance this afternoon. He couldn't stay any longer. He wouldn't. It was too painful.

As soon as it was polite, he stood and carried his plate to the sink. "Thanks for the dinner. I'm going to head back to Charlottesville. Tomorrow will be a full day."

When he turned around, Annalise's face was the color of milk. "You're leaving now?"

He nodded tersely. "I have a business to run, and now that Darren and Rachel are here to keep you company, there's no reason for me to stay."

"But what about the snow and your car?"

"I checked the forecast. The temperature is still above freezing...and will stay that way. I'll follow the truck tracks Darren made until I get back out to the highway. He said all the main roads have been plowed and salted."

"But..." Her eyes shimmered with anguish.

Seeing her reaction almost made his resolution buckle. Perhaps if he stayed, they could continue their aborted conversation. "But what, Annalise? Can you think of a reason I should hang around?" Their guests had disappeared seconds before to the back of the house to change a poopy diaper.

She stood and faced him, her arms wrapped around her waist. "You're angry with me."

He shrugged. "Maybe."

"For what?"

His jaw worked as he filtered through the words that wanted to tumble forth uncensored. "You told me that this weekend was as far as you were willing to go. Have you changed your mind?"

Annalise was no fool. She heard the question behind the question. *Are you willing to take a chance and see where we end up?*

With every cell and sinew in his body he willed her to say yes, to come to him with a smile and hug and tell him she wanted him to stay. But she didn't.

At that moment, the Harrells returned. Darren held Butch as Rachel started cleaning up. With a baseball cap on backward and a scraggly mustache that was almost too blond to be noticeable, the skinny young contractor barely looked old enough to be a dad.

He held Butch easily, tucked in his left arm like a football. "I hate to inconvenience you, Miss Annalise, but you'll probably need to leave here Wednesday morning. By that time I'll be done with the preliminary stuff, and my crew will arrive to start ripping out the old duct work."

"What about Rachel and the baby?" Sam asked.

"My mom's coming from Roanoke to pick them up that morning. She and my dad have been asking for a long visit with Butch, and this seemed like the perfect time. Me and the boys will have sleeping bags and a few electric heaters, 'cause the furnace won't be online at all until Friday night or Saturday morning. Maybe Monday if we run into any hitches. After that y'all can come and go as you please, warm as toast."

Annalise nodded. "That makes sense. But you'll have to sign for any shipments that arrive before I get back. I've started ordering a lot of the paint and wallpaper and draperies."

"No problem. And you don't have to worry. My guys will leave everything as nice as when they found it. We'll camp out in the living room...won't even need to mess up the bedrooms."

Sam frowned. "That's not necessary. I know my grandmother would expect you to make yourselves at home. Especially since commuting each day isn't a viable option."

Rachel wiped her hands on a dish towel, grinning. "Don't worry, Mr. Ely. He's been looking forward to this for days."

The younger couple left, ready to get settled in their room and put the baby down for the night.

Sam exhaled slowly. "I'm going to head upstairs and pack. If it's not too much trouble, why don't you put all our wet snow clothes in the dryer."

He brought up the subject on purpose, curious to see how she would react.

Annalise nodded, not meeting his eyes. "Of course."

Drawing this out was futile. He ground his teeth together, fighting almost irresistible temptation. "Goodbye, Princess. I'll see you around."

Feeling like an old man, he turned to leave.

"Wait," she said urgently, her voice breathless. "Won't you at least come tell me goodbye before you go?"

He turned back, though he knew he shouldn't. She stood there tall and poised and yet with a hint of melancholy. "If you want me to."

"I do."

Upstairs in his bedroom, he threw things haphazardly into his large bag. He didn't want to go into the bathroom, couldn't bear to look at the shower and remember. He grabbed his toiletries, stopping dead when he saw his face in the mirror. Where had those lines on his forehead come from? Or the evidence of stress in his posture and on his jaw? He looked as if he were at the end of his rope.

Cursing roughly, he returned to the bedroom, gave one last sweeping glance at the bureau and then stopped dead. Piled on a straight-back chair in the corner were Annalise's pretty feminine pajamas. He picked up the top and held it to his face, his eyes stinging. God, he was a fool.

For seven years…seven long, damn years. Beautiful, sexy Annalise Wolff had tormented him with her icy silences and her cool, accusing gaze. Now…finally, she had given him a taste of what it could be like between them. She had connected with Sam in a way he'd only dreamed about. They were damned near perfect in bed together.

In two short days, he had second-guessed everything he thought he knew about his goals for the future, had even tried to convince himself that he and Annalise might have what it took to be a couple, in spite of their differences. But she wasn't going to let it happen. And he didn't know why.

The reason didn't really matter. He dropped the soft cloth as if it had burned his hand, and scrubbed both palms over his face. He was finished. It was over.

He loaded the car and sat in the front seat to call his grandparents and update them on what was going on. His grandmother asked a few seemingly innocent questions, and Sam had to wonder, at least for a moment, if she had hired Annalise with some kind of matchmaking in mind.

When he hung up, he looked at the house, warm light gleaming through Gram's lace curtains. Some of the happiest times of his life had been spent in that house, this weekend included. Would he ever be able to bring a wife and family here without encountering the memory of Annalise's sex-rumpled hair and sparkling eyes?

He rubbed his chest, feeling an ache that wouldn't go away. If he could understand where he'd screwed up, he'd be able to fix things. Surely Annalise wasn't still holding on to the past. No way could she doubt the sincerity of his apology or the intensity of his attraction to her. They'd damn near burned up the sheets.

But it hit him then that perhaps he didn't know her at all. Maybe she enjoyed luring men into her web and destroying them. The black-widow analogy disturbed him. She wasn't cold or calculating. The worst he could say about her was that she was insecure.

The sheer absurdity of that thought forced a laugh. He was probably the only person on the planet who would describe her that way. The woman was hell on wheels, kicking ass and taking names on a daily basis. She was full of life and sass and enthusiasm.

Except where Sam was concerned. Around him, she acted like she wanted him and hated herself for doing so. Maybe that was harsh. At times he had felt a softening in her, a simple pleasure in the heat they generated together. He felt as if they had lived a lifetime in the last forty-eight hours, the past and the present coming together in a cataclysm of epic proportion.

Drumming his fingers on the steering wheel, he debated taking the easy way out and simply driving away. But as Annalise had so helpfully pointed out on a number of occasions, the world expected Sam Ely to do the honorable thing.

He'd told Annalise he would say goodbye. No way around it.

She was standing in the foyer when he opened the front door. "I thought you'd left," she said, her voice subdued.

The wind caught the door, jerking it out of his hand and slamming it. "Sorry," he said. "I told you I would say goodbye. I'm not a liar."

"You could have forgotten. You have a lot on your mind."

He shoved his hands in his pockets to keep from grabbing her. "I'll tell Gram you have everything under control."

"I'll send you email updates with photos. You can forward them to her."

So polite, so bloody polite. He hadn't planned to ask, but the question wouldn't be ignored any longer. "Have you forgiven me for what happened when you were twenty-one?"

She shrugged. "Of course."

"No *of course* about it. We've barely spoken in seven years."

"True."

"Is that what we're going back to?" he asked bluntly. "Veiled hostility?"

"I doubt I'll have much occasion to speak to you when you're with your wife and kids."

The sentence held equal measures of sarcasm and stoicism. He searched her face. What the hell did she want from him? "In that case," he said, feeling the dual punches of anger and need, "I'd better take what I can get right now."

Perhaps he grabbed her or maybe she launched herself at him, but whichever way it happened, she whispered his name as they ended up desperate in each other's arms. She kissed him as wildly as he kissed her. Tongues thrust and mated, breathing harshened.

Beneath her thin blouse her nipples were hard pebbles. His sex was equally firm, pushing urgently at her belly.

"Do you want me to stay?" he asked, giving her one more chance to claim what was hers. It didn't matter that she was nothing like the image of a woman he'd always imagined building a life with. He *wanted* her...not in spite of the difference, but because of it. She was perfect for him.

She laid her head against his collarbone, squeezed her arms around his waist and then released him, outwardly calm but for the rise and fall of her chest. "I don't need you to stay," she said. "With Rachel and Darren here, I'll be fine."

She hadn't answered his question. She'd talked about *need,* not want. "God, you're stubborn." He said it quietly, no accusation in his words. Only sadness. "See you around, Princess."

When he walked out the door and closed it behind him, he could see her silhouette...tall, slim, alone.

Annalise didn't know it was possible to have your heart ripped from your chest and still function as a living, breathing human. For two hours, she sat with the Harrells in the living room, playing Monopoly, talking about current events, speculating about the economy. She couldn't bear to go to her room and see the bed where Sam had made love to her.

The baby woke up around nine. Rachel fetched him, his little face blotchy from crying. "Poor thing is teething," she said, "and this is a strange house to him. But it's okay, isn't it, darlin'?" She smooched the top of his head and held him to her breast.

Before he left, Sam had brought down a rocking chair from his grandparents' bedroom. Annalise looked at the infant with barely concealed longing. "May I rock him for a bit? Do you mind?"

Rachel and Darren laughed in unison. Rachel tucked a thin blanket around Butch's legs and handed him over. "Believe me, hon, we'll take all the help we can get."

For a while, silence reigned in the room. Again, a warm fire crackled. Rachel found a pencil and a book of sudoku. Darren brought in a beautiful guitar from his truck and began to sing old ballads.

Annalise rocked slowly, immersing herself in the exquisite, bone-deep peace of holding the tiny body that very quickly went limp against her shoulder. She looked over Butch's head at his parents. "How do you know what to do?" she asked.

Rachel looked up, nibbling the end of the pencil. "What do you mean?"

"How did you learn to be a mother?"

"Oh, Lord, honey. It's called trial and error. No two babies are alike. We got lucky on this one, but my best friend has a kid with colic. They haven't slept in six months. There's no manual. I call my mother if I really get spooked. And Darren, here, is a rock in the middle of the night when we're both at our wit's end. But it all comes down to loving Butch. We do *what* we have to *when* we have to. That's all there is to parenting. It's no secret formula."

Annalise nodded, not that she really understood. It had to be more complicated than that. Otherwise, there wouldn't be so many awful parents.

Rachel, for all her youth, and she couldn't be much more than nineteen, seemed mature beyond her years. She eyed Annalise gravely. "Haven't you ever been around any babies, Miss Annalise?"

"No. Not really. I was the youngest in my family."

"Are you one of the Wolffs? Darren said he thought he recognized you from your pictures in the paper."

Oh, hell. Make that *crap*. She couldn't even give up cussing in her own head. And no matter what she did, she could never escape the notoriety of being a Wolff. "I am. The only girl in the bunch." She said it lightly, but she wondered what Rachel was thinking.

"It must have been hard…growing up around all that testosterone."

Annalise grimaced. "You could say that. They couldn't decide whether to coddle me or to toughen me up."

Darren stopped playing momentarily, curiosity written on his raw-boned face. "Which won out?"

Annalise thought about it for a moment. She'd never really analyzed how her family treated her, but oddly enough, it dawned on her that it was a mixture of both. "Depends on the day," she whispered, not wanting to wake the baby. "They act like I'm one of them when it comes to sports or arguing politics. But when we hit on the subject of my adult life and my ability to run it as I see fit, we sometimes break ranks."

Rachel nodded slowly. "They want to wrap you in cotton. I know the feeling. There are three of us girls, and my daddy thinks we're still ten years old and wearing pigtails."

Darren lit into a lullaby, his rough tenor slightly off-key, but pleasing nevertheless. "If I ever have a girl," he said, pausing as the guitar wandered through the chorus, "it will be the same. Daddies and their daughters have something special."

Annalise and Rachel laughed, ruefully acknowledging a universal truth.

Rachel stood and reached for the baby. "He'll go down for the night now. I'd better turn in, too. The little rascal will be up at dawn."

As Annalise watched, Darren tucked his guitar away and went to put his arm around his wife and son. "Thanks for the hospitality, ma'am. I know Rachel will be glad of the company."

"Me, too," Annalise said. "Me, too."

She went through the house, extinguishing all the lights. Everywhere she looked, she saw Sam. Laughing, frowning, teasing, seducing. He'd filled the house with his charm and his personality, and now, even with the advent of three visitors, the rooms felt empty and forlorn.

Her bedroom was even worse. The second time he'd made love to her was right here...on this mattress, face-to-face. Now, with Sam long gone, it was hard to believe it had happened. Maybe this weekend was all a dream.

She'd fantasized plenty about Sam Ely over the years. And wondered, if she hadn't thrown herself at him so blatantly, whether she might have had a chance later...when she was older.

Well, she was older now. And Sam...wow. Sam was in his prime. And still unattached. As she climbed into bed, she thought about all the women she had seen him date over the years. Each relationship, no matter how long or short, had broken her heart. And when each one ended, a tiny flicker of hope had valiantly remained lit in her heart.

She had believed, with incredible naïveté, that as long as Sam was still on the market, there was a chance.

Now, thanks to her job, she had stumbled upon her opportunity. She'd been locked up, all alone with Sam for forty-eight hours, give or take a few. And the sparks had flown. So much so, that she felt singed by the fire. She and Sam were sexually compatible, that much was clear. A man couldn't fake pleasure to that extent. Sam wanted her.

But wanting wasn't enough.

Though he had begged her to give them a chance—with

every seeming evidence of sincerity—his words had to be weighed in the context of forced proximity, sexual excess and the cold light of day. Annalise wanted to say yes...so much that it hurt her chest to hold back. But she had to be strong enough for both of them. Strong enough to say no.

Sam deserved to have his perfect woman. He was too good a man to settle for less than that. And she cared about him too much to begin something that would disappoint him in the end.

After finally falling into a fitful sleep, she awakened abruptly sometime around 3:00 a.m. Her heart pounding, she listened for whatever sound had disturbed her. Unfortunately, this time she wasn't going to find Sam huddled in front of the fire trying to get warm.

Pulling on her robe and slippers, she stepped into the hall and saw light coming from beneath the living room door. A baby's cry disturbed the silence of the sleeping house.

Rachel looked up when Annalise entered the room. "I'm so sorry," she said. "I was trying to calm him in our bedroom. But Darren has so much work to do tomorrow, and he needs his rest."

Annalise pulled an ottoman close to the rocking chair and sat down. "Don't be silly. I sometimes prowl around the house at night. Most women I know are light sleepers."

"I've always thought that was God's way of making us ready for motherhood."

That one simple statement struck Annalise with the force of a lightning bolt. Could it be that easy? Were women born with an inherent capability for nurturing? She reached for hazy memories of her mother, trying to catch a vision of bedtime songs, snuggly hugs, storybooks read together. Nothing came to mind except an uneasy feeling in the pit of her stomach.

"Why don't you let me tend to him for the rest of the night? You must be exhausted. If you trust me, that is," she said hurriedly. "Don't feel like you have to. I know I'm a stranger."

Rachel closed her eyes and sighed. "I shouldn't say yes. Butch is my baby, not yours. But Lord knows, the thought of a few uninterrupted hours of sleep sounds like heaven right now."

"Then do it. I swear I'll guard him with my life, and if he's inconsolable, I'll come get you."

"You talked me into it. Let me go change him, and I'll bring the diaper bag back with me."

As mom and baby departed, Annalise added logs to the simmering coals in the fireplace, and soon a cheery blaze roared. She dragged the generous-sized sofa in front of the hearth, her cheeks heating as she thought of what she and Sam had done on this very piece of furniture. It was humbling to realize that he lived in her thoughts constantly. Even though he had physically left the premises, the memories remained, tantalizing and vivid.

Butch was still fussing when Rachel returned. She handed Annalise a teether. "Let him suck on the hard side. It might help." She paused, her nose crinkling. "Are you sure about this? It might be a long night."

"Don't worry about me," Annalise said, taking Butch from her arms. "Consider it a show of support from one woman to another. We females have to stick together."

Rachel's grin was tired. "I'll owe you one."

When she left, Annalise stared down at Butch. His eyes were puffy from crying. His nose was snotty, and his cheeks were cherry-red. "Poor darlin'. We'll get by. You'll see."

She sat down in the rocker, trying to get him to latch on to the teether, but he was having none of that. At last, she cradled him on her breast, stroking his downy-soft head as he snuffled and squirmed. At least he wasn't full-out bawling. That might have rattled a novice like Annalise. But this she could handle.

When he simply wouldn't be still, even with the rocker moving to and fro in a steady motion, Annalise began to sing. An old Billy Joel ballad her father liked, a Sheryl Crow song about soaking up the sun, several Adele numbers. At last little Butch sighed deeply and began to relax.

Annalise's own eyes were heavy. She wondered why she had always been so scared of this. Rachel was right. Much of it was instinctive. Of course, that was easy to say with the child's parents just down the hall. It might be a whole different story if she held her own fussy baby.

But then again, with the right man for help and support, how bad could it be?

Idly patting the little boy's back, she felt the smooth nap of his pajamas. Soft, so soft. And Sam wanted three or four of these. A family, a bulwark against the world, a unit bound by love and belonging.

Soon, Gracie and Gareth's baby would arrive. Annalise had a feeling that other little ones wouldn't be far behind. Wolff Mountain would once again echo with childish laughter.

Her hands trembled as a wave of longing swept through her, leaving her spent and weak. She had sent Sam away. Because she was afraid of failing. Failing as a woman. Sam's kind of woman. Motherhood didn't offer do-overs. And Sam wanted babies. Plural.

But what if she were wrong? What if her unconventional past was no longer relevant? Sam seemed to like her the way she was. Were her insecurities about her femininity nothing more than habit? What if Annalise Wolff had a maternal instinct despite all odds? And not just that…what if she had the ability to be the kind of woman Sam needed, the kind of woman who trusted in herself, believed in herself and opened her heart to share love?

Butch was sound asleep now, his tiny snore a miracle in itself. Carefully, she stood, moving toward the sofa. Laying him down for a brief instant, she stoked the fire and replaced the screen. Grabbing the pile of covers she had gathered earlier, she eased down oh-so-carefully, positioning her body with her back to the fire and Butch tucked carefully between her and the back cushion.

Their little nest was surprisingly comfortable. She wanted to savor the experience, to file it away to pull out and remember on another day. But her eyes were heavy, and she succumbed to sleep.

Twelve

Sam wasn't worth a damn when he got back from the country. It was business as usual in his office Monday morning, and for the first time in years he didn't care about any of it. The interns were patently disappointed to see him. They had been looking forward to their sanctioned reign. Too bad the weather hadn't cooperated and kept Sam stranded.

The late January warm-up and a dose of undiluted sunshine appeared to be making everyone happy and cheerful. Everyone but Sam. A man known for his easygoing disposition, he shocked himself and most of his staff by snapping and growling. At last he resorted to hiding out in his inner office to keep from doing bodily harm to anyone who dared cross him.

He ached with missing Annalise. Memories of their lovemaking taunted him, keeping him hard and frustrated. The days and nights he'd spent with her seemed like a dream…except for the fact that he could still smell her perfume on his clothes.

Like a lovesick schoolboy, he'd kept those flannel shirts out of the laundry hamper, unable to erase her presence from his life. She was difficult and challenging and sexy as hell. More than any woman he had ever known, Annalise Wolff satisfied the hunger in him, a need that was as much emotional as physical.

The only thing keeping him sane was the knowledge that on Wednesday morning she would be coming back to the city, and he'd at least be able to see her at the office. Thank God for Darren and his crew.

From the moment Sam drove away from the farm, his brain had wrestled with a problem that had no answer. For years he'd been trying to find the perfect woman, the one who would give him his perfect family. And now, in one of fate's perverse games of chance, he'd fallen in love with the one woman who not only didn't trust him, but who also was the antithesis of everything he thought he wanted.

He could move on…keep looking for a suitable candidate. The trouble was, he was pretty sure he couldn't live without Annalise Wolff. Which meant he had some big decisions to make. He'd give her until Wednesday evening to miss him, and then he was going to claim what was his.

Annalise loved him. He had to believe that. Because the alternative was simply unacceptable.

Annalise loved having the Harrells underfoot. The house buzzed with noise and laughter, Darren measured and crawled into the basement and ordered parts. Rachel cooked and entertained the baby, and was well on the way to being a new, honest-to-goodness friend. Annalise felt comfortable around her. And despite their differences in lifestyle and finances, Rachel was not intimidated by Annalise.

Monday, before dinner, something odd struck Annalise. So much so that she marched into the kitchen and asked, "It only now occurred to me that you took over the meal preparation duties when you arrived. Not that I mind... I've loved it, but how did that happen? You don't strike me as the kind of woman who would waltz in and take over someone else's kitchen."

Butch was tucked into a high chair gobbling Cheerios. Rachel's face turned pink. "Well, um..."

"Spill it, woman, I won't bite."

Rachel shrugged. "Mr. Ely pulled me aside and asked me, soon after we arrived. He said you couldn't cook and that you were self-conscious about it. He didn't want you to feel uncomfortable."

"I see." Annalise digested that, feeling a little fillip of warmth in her chest. Sam really was a gentleman. But it seemed thoughtfulness was simply his default setting. It didn't mean he cared about Annalise. "Well, he's right. About the not cooking, I mean. Carry on with my blessing and my gratitude."

"Do you not like to cook?" Rachel asked, her gentle smile curious.

"It's a long story. And pretty boring. Let's just chalk it up to growing up with in an all-male household."

"I get it. The culinary arts weren't high on the list."

"More like repairing foreign cars and learning to fly a helicopter."

Rachel's eyes rounded. "You can really do that?"

"Yeah. If someone put a gun to my head. My father and uncle use one for both business and pleasure. I stopped riding in it a long time ago...and have lobbied fiercely for them to get rid of it. But no one listens to me."

"Wow. You're really something, Annalise. I'm glad we got to know each other."

The compliment was heartfelt, sincere. Annalise accepted it as such, realizing with a sort of dazed puzzlement that perhaps other people were not as dismissive of her accomplishments as she was.

Clearing her throat of some emotion that constricted her words, she said, "Thank you. You're pretty amazing, as well."

By the time Wednesday morning arrived, Annalise had a good grasp of which rooms would require the most work and which furniture needed to be donated, pending Mrs. Ely's approval. The weather was fabulous, and though the ground was muddy in the wake of the snowmelt, it felt good to be outside.

After breakfast, in preparation for leaving, she wandered the perimeter of the house, trying to imagine Sam and his mythical family staying there. Already she hated the woman in the picture. Annalise wanted to be her.

She stopped dead, her toes curling in her borrowed rubber boots as the truth hit her. *Holy hell. She wanted to have Sam's babies. All of them...however many the good Lord chose to send their way.*

Swaying on her feet, she told herself to snap out of it. Sam didn't want her. Well, that wasn't exactly true. He enjoyed her body. *He enjoyed her body.* That's all it was. Sex. Plain and simple.

Only, with Sam, sex was the furthest thing from simple. It was world-altering, unprecedented. In his arms, she felt complete, she felt feminine, desired. And that feeling of fulfillment allowed her for the first time in her life to see another choice, another way.

Sam had opened the door to possibilities. Had practically begged her to take a chance, to be the daring, adventuresome woman the world thought she was. Sprawled in his bed after their last, erotic shower, he had laid his cards on the table. *Are you willing to take a chance that we've been too blind to see the truth?* Sam had been brave enough to take the first step, to initiate a shift toward something far more profound even than physical pleasure.

But she had fallen into old habits of self-protection. And in doing so, had sent him away. Afraid to be hurt again, terrified of the idea of bringing children into the world. Scared that Sam would look at her with disappointment and regret. She deserved the pain that made her chest ache with grief too deep for tears.

She might have been brought up in a household of men, true. And yes, she had many skills not typically regarded as "womanly." But Sam liked her the way she was. He'd said so on more than one occasion. And surprisingly, he'd taught her to see herself as he did...and to accept and appreciate what she saw.

A man like that was rare and wonderful. So it was about time she got her act together and went after him.

A couple of hours later, she stopped at a Walmart in a suburb outside of Charlottesville. It was a safe choice, with little likelihood that she would run into anyone she knew. Jittery and anxious, she knew she wouldn't be able to tolerate small talk. Plus, she didn't want to have to explain what she was doing.

Grabbing a shopping cart, feeling more than a little self-conscious, she headed for the housewares department and began throwing things in the basket. Twenty-five minutes later, she scoured the grocery aisles. All in all, "Project Sam" took just under an hour.

She shook her head in self-derision as she headed back

out to her car. Grand gestures were more expensive than she realized. It was a good thing she had money to burn. Which reminded her, she needed to send Rachel and Darren a really nice baby gift, even if it was a bit belated.

When she arrived in Charlottesville, her condo welcomed her with stale air and half-dead plants. She'd forgotten to water them…again. For a moment, the old insecurity surfaced. How could she take care of a baby? She'd been reared by a bad mother for a brief period of her life, and then no mother at all. Her formative years had been influenced by air rifles, fist fights and playing army ambush in the forest surrounding Wolff Castle.

Her brain whirled while, on autopilot, she put away the cold groceries and unloaded her luggage from the car. After her fourth trip, she shook her head in disgust. Maybe Sam was right. Maybe she *was* high-maintenance. It had never been a problem. Her father had indulged her every wish. But in any situation when a baby came into the picture, everything had to change.

She didn't want to think of herself as a selfish person. Charity, both via her checkbook and her volunteer hours, was important to her. And she cared deeply about her family. But being a mother was so much more. It involved self-sacrifice and a consistent determination to put another person's needs first.

Could she be that woman for Sam? For herself? For a newborn?

She sat down hard, clutching a bag of flour. Terror and exhilaration squeezed her chest in equal measures. Suddenly, the future taunted her with bright possibilities. But she was not so naive as to ignore the flip side of the coin. If she tried to change and failed, the consequences were unthinkable.

* * *

Sam left work Wednesday night before 6:00 p.m. His relatively prompt homecoming was such an anomaly, he knew he was in trouble. All day, he had imagined Annalise in her car, driving the interstate, heading back to him.

His hand shook as he put a key in the lock of his loft-turned-condo. All he wanted during the next half hour was a shower, a change of clothes and a few quiet minutes to decide if the plan he was contemplating was total suicide.

As soon as he opened the door, he groaned inwardly, cursing life's capricious sense of humor. His mother was in residence, God help him.

"Hi, sweet pea," she said, enveloping him in a cloud of Obsession, a tight hug and a Southern accent so thick it took him back in time for an instant.

"Mom," he said, grimacing inwardly and fiercely regretting that he had ever given her a key. "What are you doing here?" He loved her dearly, but after he'd hit his mid-thirties, she'd been at DEFCON 1 in her campaign to marry him off. Her pop-in visits, often with some co-conspirator in tow, were usually poorly disguised match-making attempts.

Charlaine Ely smiled broadly, clad in a stylish winter suit that belied her age. "Can't a momma visit her baby? Come in the kitchen and see Daphne. You're gonna love what she's fixin' for us."

Annalise had broken her New Year's Eve resolution so many times and in so many ways, she probably should have her mouth washed out with soap. Cooking was damned hard. The FCC needed to take a bunch of those Cooking Channel chefs to court for false advertising.

At long last, her creation was finished. She stared at the cake on her trashed kitchen counter with misgivings.

Although it was supposed to be round and two-layered, it had ended up more of a free-form shape with a distinct dip in the middle. Disguising it the best she could with icing, she finally gave up and decided it was the thought that counted. The cake was resting on a cardboard circle she'd bought when she got the groceries. Hell, she didn't even own any Tupperware. She'd had to buy a knockoff.

Getting the cake into the carrier was a bit like forcing a beloved pet into a cage for a trip to the vet. The cake didn't want to go. In the end, she had to use her bare hands, which unfortunately meant ripping off part of the icing in the process, and thus having to make another half batch to cover up her boo-boos.

She decided to clean up the kitchen when she got back. Nobody was going to be around to see the disaster anyway. Her outfit was ruined, so she dashed into the bedroom and grabbed a pair of designer jeans and a winter-white cashmere turtleneck. One dash of eyeliner, a fillip of mascara and a swish of lip gloss, and she was ready. High-maintenance indeed.

The trip to Sam's condo was less than ten miles, but the drive felt like it took an eternity. She hadn't exactly worked out what she was going to say when she saw him. She was hoping that her peace offering and perhaps some quick and kinky sex might ease the way.

Tapping her fingers on the steering wheel as she idled at a red light, her thighs quivered and her breasts grew heavy and tight as she contemplated his welcome. *Please, God, don't let him be mad.*

He was well within his rights to be furious. The last time they'd been together, he'd asked *her* to ask *him* to stay. But instead of meeting his overture halfway, she had practically shoved him out the door in a futile effort to prove to herself that she didn't need Sam.

What an idiot she was.

Thank God she had come to her senses. But what if it was too late? The prospect of seeing condemnation in his eyes—disgust, even—shriveled her soul. Sam's opinion mattered to her. It always had. Which was why she was prepared to grovel today if necessary. She had a big speech to make and she wanted desperately for it to go well. Maybe Sam would be in a forgiving mood.

Ruefully, she realized that the last time she had been this nervous was the evening she propositioned Sam when she was twenty-one. That day had ended in disaster. Though her stomach clenched and twisted, she refused to dwell on the negative. Sam cared about her. And this time, she knew beyond the shadow of a doubt that he wanted her sexually.

Relationships were founded on far less all the time. But she had really screwed up with Sam.

Was he going to believe the truth? That she had changed her entire world view on the basis of one magical weekend? That she was willing to consider the possibility of a grown-up relationship...of children?

She found a parking spot on the street, got out on shaky legs and locked the car with a flip of the button on the door. Unfortunately, her keys were on the seat beside the cake box.

Damn, damn, damn...

She would *not* cry. Tears were girly and weak and unworthy of her new resolve. Thankfully, she had her cell phone in her hand. She called her automobile club service, and because she was downtown, the helpful service tech was at her side in fifteen minutes.

Annalise shifted restlessly from foot to foot as he slid a device down inside the glass, popped the lock and opened her door. "Thank you," she said fervently. She handed him a fifty-dollar tip. "Take your wife out to dinner on me."

With the man's excited thanks still ringing in her ears, she sprinted for the building and boarded the elevator. She'd been in Sam's condo once before…at a fund-raising reception for the Alzheimer's Foundation. But on that evening, she and Sam had never even exchanged words, even though she'd been aware of him all night.

The elevator clanged to a stop. Annalise stepped out into a hallway carpeted in pewter and burgundy color blocks. Clutching the cake carrier and her purse like a lifeline, she rang the doorbell.

When Sam opened the door, she gaped. Never had she seen him like this…wild-eyed, harried, suspiciously unsurprised. She frowned. "May I come in?" She didn't mention the offering and he didn't seem to notice that she carried an odd accessory.

He kept the door closed except for a barely polite twelve inches. "I saw you park on the street," he said. "Now's not really a good time. I've got—"

A woman appeared at his shoulder, peering into the hall. "Who is it, Sammy? Dinner's almost ready."

Sammy? Dear God. Surely Sam hadn't taken to dating cougars.

He closed his eyes momentarily, a crease forming between his eyebrows. "Annalise, this is my mother, Charlaine Ely. Mom, Annalise Wolff."

"Wolff? Oh, my goodness, come in. I've heard about your family for years, but you know that since my husband and I divorced when Sammy was little, I've rarely been in Charlottesville. It's a pleasure to meet you. One of Sam's old high school friends is here. She's opening a new restaurant soon back in Alabama, and I thought it would be fun to try the menu out on Sam. We're having a casual bite to eat. You're welcome to join us."

With Sam and Annalise acting like cardboard cutouts, the talkative Charlaine ushered them into the kitchen. It was then that Annalise's heart stopped. Because there, standing in front of the stove, and wearing an apron, no less, was Sam's perfect woman.

She was shorter than Annalise, and curvier. Her smile was open and generous, and she seemed right at home in Sam's ultramodern, state-of-the-art kitchen.

After a flurry of introductions, all orchestrated by Sam's mother, *Daphne* spoke up. "The rolls will be ready in five minutes. I hope everyone is hungry."

"Rolls?" The question came from deep inside Annalise's nauseated tummy.

Daphne beamed. "Yeast rolls. My grandma's recipe."

"Oh, goody." Annalise felt her temper rise. Sam had barely left her bed, and already this cross between Martha Stewart and Angelina Jolie was ensconced in his condo. *Jerk.*

Charlaine noticed the cake box. "Oh, lovely. Did you bring dessert? I bought some ice cream, but it will keep. Let me put it on a plate."

Annalise gripped the carrier with all her might. "Um, no. This is for my grandmother. I didn't mean to bring it in."

Sam frowned. "All your grandparents are dead."

"Sam!" Charlaine was shocked. "That was rude." She patted Annalise on the shoulder. "Now don't be intimidated by Daphne. She's a professional, so we can't hope to compete with that. But I'm sure your cake is lovely."

While Annalise watched, mute with mortification, the insistent Charlaine loosened Annalise's fingers one by one and took possession of the cake box. When she set it on the counter and removed the lid, you could have heard a pin drop in the room.

The smell of warm yeast permeated the air, and Annalise wanted to die. All eyes were locked on the chocolate-covered blob. She bit her lip. "Sam mentioned how he always loved white cake with chocolate icing," she mumbled. "When he was growing up. I wanted to thank him for putting me in touch with his grandmother and helping me get the new job."

Daphne leaned over, a lingering horrified fascination in her eyes as she assessed Annalise's very first effort at baking. "I'm sure it tastes good," she said, her cheery voice consoling.

It was the last straw. "I have to go," Annalise croaked. "Sorry to miss dinner." She made a dash for the door, blinking back stupid feminine tears. Her hand was on the knob when Sam stopped her by the sheer expedient of putting his body between her and the exit.

"It's not what you think," he said urgently. "I didn't know they were coming."

She searched his face, trying to read the truth, summoning her courage and refusing to remember the last time she had poured out her heart to this man. "I really need to talk to you," she said. "Tonight."

Sam hesitated. And in that split second, her heart shriveled. Her soul turned to ice.

With all her might, she shoved him out of the way, ripped open the door and ran like hell.

Thirteen

Sam might have had worse days, but he couldn't remember when. With his mother and her guest in his house and a very nice dinner that Daphne had labored over for several hours ready to serve, how could he run out and leave them?

But dear God, Annalise had come to him…of her own free will. And she wanted to talk…tonight. That had to be good. Right? He would gobble down dinner and then go find her. A forty-five-minute delay to satisfy his social obligation was all that stood between him and holding the woman he loved in his arms again.

By the time the dessert course rolled around, Sam knew he had screwed up big-time. All he could think about was the stricken look in Annalise's eyes. It hit him with sick certainty that she must have seen his hesitation to drop everything and follow her as a second rejection.

His mom brought a bowl of ice cream from the kitchen and set it in front of him.

Sam glared at the offending dessert. "I want cake," he said, the words blunt and to the point.

Daphne leapt to her feet. "Of course," she said brightly. "Let me cut you a piece." She returned moments later, carrying a small china dish. "Here you go."

He took his fork, cut off a big bite and shoved it into his mouth. What happened next made his eyes water. The icing tasted like bitter mud, the cake itself was dry and gritty and he found a piece of eggshell that he was forced to spit into a napkin.

The two women stared at him expectantly.

Sam studied his dessert and sighed. He laid down his fork, and stood up. As an afterthought, he picked up his cup of coffee and took a long swig, trying to rinse the taste from his mouth.

"I have to go," he said firmly. "You both are welcome to stay until tomorrow. The guest rooms are ready. But I have other plans tonight. You'll need to excuse me."

Daphne glared at Charlaine. "I told you this was a bad idea." She smiled wryly at her reluctant host. "Sorry, Sam. Your mother can be very persuasive." She walked around the table and kissed him on his cheek. "It was nice to see you. Good luck with your girl."

Charlaine pouted, but she, too, apologized. "Sometimes I get carried away. Please don't tell your dad. Go find that nice Annalise and smooth things out."

Sam gave them a weary smile. "I'll try. But if you don't hear from me by noon tomorrow, you might want to start dragging the river."

The dark humor was a reflection of the knot in his gut. How in the hell had he managed to repeat the biggest mistake of his life? And with the same woman? The last time he had rejected an overture from Annalise Wolff, she hadn't spoken to him for over half a decade. This debacle was infinitely worse. He'd made love to her, fought with her, left her unwillingly and now this. Annalise had come to him to "talk," and he'd let her think that his mother and her guest were more important.

He grabbed his keys and coat and ran downstairs to his car. Annalise could be anywhere, but she had been upset when she left his place, so he was guessing she headed home to hide out.

The building Annalise lived in was high-end and very classy. The doorman and the concierge were both men in their sixties. Fortunately for Sam, he had gone to college with each of their sons. After an exchange of pleasantries, he laid his cards on the table.

"Annalise and I have been seeing each other. We had a fight. I'm pretty sure she's upstairs planning my demise. I would consider it a deep personal favor if you could give me the spare key."

The two older men exchanged glances. The concierge frowned. "I saw her go up. She looked like she'd been crying."

Sam felt about two inches tall. His heart contracted. "It's a long story, but my mom meddled and made Annalise think I was interested in someone else."

The grizzled man muttered. "Mothers. They're amazing, but damn, they can cramp a guy's style. Sorry, Mr. Ely. I know you don't mean any harm. But I could lose my job."

"At least call upstairs and tell her I'm here," Sam urged.

"Okay. I can do that." He picked up the house phone and dialed two digits. His face was unreadable as he carried on a brief conversation.

Still holding the phone in his hand, he looked at Sam. "She said to tell you she doesn't care about her New Year's resolution. You're a lying, cheating, two-faced…"

Sam held up a hand. "I get the picture. Can I talk to her?"

The concierge handed over the phone.

"Hey, Princess. Please let me come upstairs."

It killed him that her voice was hoarse from crying. "No."

"I was going to call you this evening."

"Ha."

"But when I got home, my mom was there with Daphne. I had no idea they were coming, I swear."

"Did you eat her rolls?"

The weird question took him off guard. "Yes."

"They were delicious, right?"

"Yes."

"And my cake?"

An enormous crevasse opened up at his feet. His heart pounding, he wondered what he should say.

The concierge grabbed the phone from his hand. "Oh, for pity's sake, Ms. Annalise. I'm giving him the spare key. You two are on your own."

He hung up and rummaged under the desk for the correct fob. "Good luck, man."

Sam was pretty sure he should have made a plan before he confronted Annalise. Despite the fact that he was known for his diplomatic abilities, he'd sooner face a mountain lion than a pissed-off Wolff daughter.

It would have been nice if her door had been unlocked... perhaps signaling a softening of her anger. But he had to use the key. Quietly, he stepped inside, laying his things on a table near the door. In front of him, the living room and kitchen opened into each other. The mess caused by the cake creation was painfully visible. He gulped and wiped the back of his hand across his damp forehead.

"Where are you, Princess?"

He jumped when she appeared at his elbow. "Where do you think I am? I live here."

She walked past him to the sofa and waved a hand at a nearby chair. "Since you so rudely burst into my home, you might as well say what you came to say. I don't have all evening."

"I'm guessing you do."

She gaped at him. "I beg your pardon?"

He shrugged. "You came over to my house with a peace offering. And you must have known I wouldn't throw you out. Thus, you must not have plans."

Annalise was wearing an old pair of jeans and a UVA sweatshirt. He didn't even know she owned such clothing. Her hair was hanging loose and wavy down her back, and her feet were tucked into thick woolen socks.

She stared at him, eyes cool with disdain. "I dropped off a thank-you gift. Wasn't planning to stay. No big deal."

He got to his feet and paced, unable to be still. "It *is* a big deal. A very big deal." He waved a hand at the kitchen. "You cooked for me."

Color tinted her cheeks. Wariness veiled her true emotions. "An experiment, nothing more. A messy one, at that."

"I did not reject you tonight," he said firmly. "This is nothing like what happened seven years ago."

"Could have fooled me."

He closed his eyes and counted to thirty. Ten was not nearly enough. "You took me by surprise. I had unexpected company. I handled it badly. Besides, you're not exactly blameless in all this. You sent me away, Annalise. Rather coldly. So, I'm sorry about tonight, but I was angry and I didn't expect to see you. Let's call it even."

"Sure," she said carelessly.

Her easy dismissal was suspect, but he decided to take

it at face value since he had a far more complex agenda to get to. "Why did you really come to see me?" he asked, wanting to take her in his arms, but not sure if she was ready to hear what he had to say.

"It was an impulse. You know how I am. I can't really remember."

He took a deep breath. "In that case, I'll do the talking. Whether you believe it or not, I was coming to see you this evening."

Her total lack of expression indicated boredom or disinterest or maybe both. She was mute.

"Don't you want to know why?"

"Will you leave if I say yes?"

His temper snapped. "I wanted to tell you that I love you, damn it…and ask you to marry me."

He'd never imagined yelling those words at a woman in just that way, but his suave, debonair manners had deserted him. Clearly, he should have dressed up his declaration. He might as well have said the weather was nice for all the reaction he got from Annalise.

"Well," he growled between clenched teeth. "It's customary for a woman to respond with something appropriate at this point."

She bent her head, her face obscured by a fall of hair. "Please don't," she said, her voice almost inaudible. "It's no use."

"You have to talk to me, Annalise. Or we'll never find our way out of this mess." He sat down beside her and pulled her into his arms, her head buried on his shoulder. "I promised I would never hurt you again, and today I made you cry. You have no idea how wretched that makes me feel."

Her slender fingers played with one of his buttons. "I

worked up my courage," she said softly. "So I could tell you the truth. And then I saw Daphne."

He hugged her more tightly. "I haven't set eyes on Daphne since we were in high school. She doesn't matter."

"I believe you, but I saw her, Sam. She's your perfect woman. It was blindingly clear to me. Even if you don't want *her,* there will be another Daphne."

"And that's why you came to my house today?"

"No."

He waited, keeping the chains on his impatience. This was too important to screw up now. "Then why?"

A deep sigh made her chest lift and fall. Beneath his touch, her body was warm and pliant. She sat up, scrubbing the hair from her face. Her eyes were puffy and her nose was red. She was still the most beautiful thing he had ever seen.

"Sam, I…"

"What, darlin'? You can tell me anything."

She shrugged, her eyes suspiciously bright. "I love you. I think I always have. You thought I was too young to know my own mind, but I did."

"You don't sound too excited about it," he said, trying to lighten the mood with humor. She looked tragic rather than happy. Perhaps because he had spouted off so much nonsense in the last week. All about his dreams and plans and never once taking into account that to love Annalise Wolff was to love the whole package, a package that didn't fit his requirements and yet somehow was so much more.

He put his hand over her mouth. "Don't say anything else. Not yet." Brushing her cheek with his thumb, he felt his heart seize up in terror at the thought he might have lost her. "If this is about having children, forget it. I want *you,* my love. Nobody else. I don't have to have two-point-five kids and a dog in the country to be happy. All I need is you."

He kissed her softly, a fleeting brush of his lips on hers. "That's why I'm still single at thirty-six. Turns out I wasn't waiting for you to grow up, I was waiting for you to forgive me and offer me another chance."

Tears welled in bright blue eyes, but didn't fall. "I won't let you give up your dream for me, Sam." She cupped his face in her hands. "I want to give you babies. If I can. But you'll have to help me, you'll have to tell me if I do things wrong. If I'm too impatient, or if I'm neglectful of our child."

"Where is this coming from?" She was drawing a scenario that was literally impossible.

Shaking, her face chalky white, she bit her lip. "My mother was a child abuser."

Six words. Six horrible, dreadful words. The stark syllables fell from her lips like stones.

"Oh, my God." This time she was stiff in his arms, too stiff. Fine tremors continued to shiver through her body.

Her whisper was almost inaudible. "She didn't do anything to me. Or if she did, I don't really recall," she said brokenly. "I think Devlyn took the brunt of it. But I remember hiding with my brothers. That was before we went to the mountain, of course. She would drink and she would yell."

"No one interceded?"

"I don't think anyone knew."

"Not even your dad?"

"Maybe. I don't know. But don't you see, it's not just that I grew up without a mother. Even when she was still alive, she was poisoning my mind about what it means to be a loving parent. It's possible that I have inherited her shortcomings."

"That's a load of crap," he said, pushing her away and leaping up from the couch as anger coursed through his veins. The image of a toddler Annalise being knocked around, or even being to scared to come out of hiding, ate at him, curdling his stomach.

He bowed his head. "I know what you're trying to tell me. And it's okay, I swear. The only family I need is you. Not that I think you wouldn't be an amazing mother, but I won't put you through that. Holy hell, Annalise, you've been carrying this around for years. And yet you turned into a beautiful, caring, capable woman. I'm so proud of you, I don't even know how to express it in words."

"Then show me." She stood and joined him. "Tell me that part about loving me again."

He was sick with regret, furious with pain for this delicate and yet incredibly strong Wolff child. "I adore you," he said, the words choked. He held her so tightly, she protested. Relaxing his grip only a bit, he laid his forehead on hers. "I want to marry you. And if we have babies or we don't have babies, it will be a decision we make together. I love you, Annalise."

She reached up to kiss him. The aching hunger that had built inside him since the moment he drove away, leaving her at the farm, coalesced into a white-hot desire that hardened his erection to the point of pain.

Kissing wasn't enough. Feeling her body against his wasn't enough. He had to be in her, on her, devouring her. He stripped her clothes with mad abandon. Annalise sobbed once, her hands ripping at his shirt. "I need you, Sam. So much."

They were naked and tumbled onto the couch before he could speak. "I won't ever let you walk away again. You're mine, Annalise. I'll spend the rest of my life protecting you." He stroked her breasts one at a time, reverently, hungrily. "I know that sounds strange. Since you could probably kick my ass if you wanted to. But just because you've been taught to be tough doesn't mean you can't let down your guard with me. Everyone deserves a safe place...a shelter from the world. I want to be that for you."

He watched her eyes close when he slid inside her body, the fit tight enough to make him catch his breath. "Princess... Tell me you love me. Tell me again."

"I do," she moaned, her legs wrapped about his waist. "Forever. Always."

The sex was different this time, deeper, more powerful, forging a connection that would never be broken. He wouldn't allow it. His climax bore down on him, impossible to resist. "Come for me, my love." He kissed her hard, grinding his hips until he heard her cry out. After that, nothing mattered but Annalise, always Annalise....

When he could breathe again, he lifted her in his arms and carried her down the hall until he found her bedroom. It was bright and eye-catching and unconventional. Much like its owner.

The bed was not made, so he dropped her on the magenta sheet and sprawled beside her. "Can I spend the night?" he asked, yawning.

Annalise grinned. "Your house too full?"

"You could say that."

"Poor Sam."

He skated his fingers over her flat belly, headed south. "I noticed that you didn't answer my marriage proposal."

"You need to be sure, Sam. We've only had one weekend. That's hardly a foundation for a future."

"I've known you my entire life, honey. If things had played out differently, we might have hooked up a long time ago. I probably know more about you than any of the men you've dated. And as for our one naughty weekend, that just seals the deal. A sexual connection like that is rare, Princess. So I'll ask you again. Will. You. Marry me."

She curled onto her side, head propped on her hand. "One question first."

His roving hand stilled, halting just beneath her ribs. The steady beat of her heart reassured him. "Ask me anything."

"How did my cake taste?"

There it was again, that brutally dangerous, gaping hole at his feet. Taking a deep breath, reminding himself of all he knew about his wife-to-be, he grimaced. "It was awful."

She burst into laughter, her vibrant face alight with happiness. "In that case, yes…I'll marry you. Because such brave honesty is rare," she teased. "And I'd be a fool to let you go."

Epilogue

Eighteen months later

Annalise leaned over the counter, putting the finishes touches on a birthday cake for her dad. He'd been thrilled when she and Sam married, and happier still when they'd built Annalise's dream house on Wolff Mountain.

In fact, today was the first official function in the new abode. She gazed around her, seeing Sam's skill and caring in every detail. He'd been absolutely determined to give her everything she wanted.

"Come taste the icing," she called out. "I know the cake part is okay, because I made two just to be sure."

Sam walked in, still buttoning his cuff links. They had decided to do a formal dinner for the entire Wolff clan. "Okay," he said, his face doleful. "Guinea pig reporting for service."

She pinched his arm. "Don't be mean." She scooped her

finger through the icing left in the bowl. "Be honest. I've got a frozen cheesecake I can use as a backup."

Her handsome husband took her hand, sucking two of her fingers into his mouth and licking them clean. "It's perfect." He paused, eyes alight with mischief. "I know how you hate wasting anything. I imagine we could put that leftover icing to good use."

"Behave yourself, Sam." Knees weak, she swallowed hard, reminding herself that their guests were on the way. But the temptation to take up Sam on his wicked offer was almost irresistible.

He released her long enough to dry his hand on a dish towel. "So what did you end up getting him for a present?"

"I didn't." Her mouth dry, she watched his face.

"Why not? I know the old man can buy anything he wants, but he always loves the gifts you pick out for him."

"I thought I'd go nontraditional this year." She pressed her hand to her stomach. "And you helped."

Sam went white as incredulity, joy and fierce triumph raced across his face in quick succession. He scooped her up, whirling her around in a circle. "A baby? You're sure?"

She ruffled his hair, smiling down at him, feeling a wellspring of happiness that never seemed to fade. "In about seven and a half months you're going to be a daddy."

His eyes glistened. "Thank you, Princess." His voice was hoarse. He lowered her to her feet and kissed her with aching sweetness.

She laid her head on his shoulder, chuckling as her arms slid around his waist and squeezed. "In all fairness, you did most of the work."

"I'm hoping for a girl," he confessed softly, stroking her hair in a way that brought tears to Annalise's eyes, tears of inexpressible wonder at the goodness of life.

"Can you handle two of us?" she teased.

"God, I hope so. " He took her hand and lifted her fingers to his lips, kissing them tenderly. "Such news requires a very private celebration. Later. When I have you alone. But for now, my love, please know this. You're my perfect woman. In every way."

* * * * *

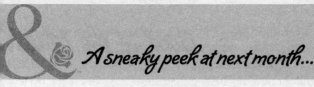

A sneaky peek at next month...

Desire

PASSIONATE AND DRAMATIC LOVE STORIES

My wish list for next month's titles...

In stores from 15th February 2013:

2 stories in each book - only £5.49!

☐ All or Nothing – Catherine Mann

& A Conflict of Interest – Barbara Dunlop

☐ Sunset Surrender – Charlene Sands

& Undeniable Demands – Andrea Laurence

☐ Bachelor Unclaimed – Brenda Jackson

& In His Brother's Place – Elizabeth Lane

Available at WHSmith, Tesco, Asda, Eason, Amazon and Apple

Just can't wait?

Visit us Online

You can buy our books online a month before they hit the shops! **www.millsandboon.co.uk**

0213/51

Book of the Month

MILLS & BOON

We love this book because...

A dramatic, gloriously sensual family saga. Descendants of a proud warrior Viking, the Brunson brothers and their sheltered sister rule the Scottish borders. It's a time of danger and treachery—and emotions run high!

On sale 1st March

Visit us Online

Find out more at
www.millsandboon.co.uk/BOTM

0213/BOTM

Special Offers

Every month we put together collections and longer reads written by your favourite authors.

Here are some of next month's highlights— and don't miss our fabulous discount online!

On sale 15th February

On sale 15th February

On sale 1st March

Save 20% on all Special Releases

Find out more at
www.millsandboon.co.uk/specialreleases

Visit us Online

0313/ST/MB407

Join the Mills & Boon Book Club

Want to read more **Desire**™ stories?
We're offering you **2 more**
absolutely **FREE!**

We'll also treat you to these fabulous extras:

- 🌹 **Books up to 2 months ahead of shops**
- 🌹 **FREE home delivery**
- 🌹 **Bonus books with our special rewards scheme**
- 🌹 **Exclusive offers... and much more!**

Treat yourself now!

Visit us Online

Get your FREE stories now at
www.millsandboon.co.uk/freebookoffer

0113/D3XE

MILLS & BOON® Book Club

2 Free Stories!

Get your free stories now at
www.millsandboon.co.uk/freebookoffer

Or fill in the form below and post it back to us

THE MILLS & BOON® BOOK CLUB™—HERE'S HOW IT WORKS: Accepting your free stories places you under no obligation to buy anything. You may keep the stories and return the despatch note marked 'Cancel'. If we do not hear from you, about a month later we'll send you 2 Desire™ 2-in-1 books priced at £5.49* each. There is no extra charge for post and packaging. You may cancel at any time, otherwise we will send you 4 stories a month which you may purchase or return to us—the choice is yours. *Terms and prices subject to change without notice. Offer valid in UK only. Applicants must be 18 or over. Offer expires 31st July 2013. **For full terms and conditions, please go to www.millsandboon.co.uk/freebookoffer**

Mrs/Miss/Ms/Mr (please circle) _____

First Name _____

Surname _____

Address _____

_____

_____ Postcode _____

E-mail _____

Send this completed page to: Mills & Boon Book Club, Free Book Offer, FREEPOST NAT 10298, Richmond, Surrey, TW9 1BR

Find out more at
www.millsandboon.co.uk/freebookoffer

Visit us Online

0113/D3XEb

The World of Mills & Boon®

There's a Mills & Boon® series that's perfect for you. We publish ten series and, with new titles every month, you never have to wait long for your favourite to come along.

Blaze.

Scorching hot, sexy reads
4 new stories every month

By Request

Relive the romance with the best of the best
9 new stories every month

Cherish™

Romance to melt the heart every time
12 new stories every month

Desire™

Passionate and dramatic love stories
8 new stories every month

Visit us Online

Try something new with our Book Club offer
www.millsandboon.co.uk/freebookoffer

M&B/WORLD

What will you treat yourself to next?

Ignite your imagination, step into the past...
6 new stories every month

INTRIGUE...

Breathtaking romantic suspense
Up to 8 new stories every month

Captivating medical drama – with heart
6 new stories every month

MODERN™

International affairs, seduction & passion guaranteed
9 new stories every month

n o c t u r n e™

Deliciously wicked paranormal romance
Up to 4 new stories every month

RIVA™

Live life to the full – give in to temptation
3 new stories every month available exclusively via our Book Club

You can also buy Mills & Boon eBooks at
www.millsandboon.co.uk

Visit us Online

M&B/WORLD2

Mills & Boon® Online

Discover more romance at
www.millsandboon.co.uk

- 🌹 **FREE** online reads
- 🌹 **Books** up to one month before shops
- 🌹 **Browse our books** before you buy

...and much more!

For exclusive competitions and instant updates:

 Like us on **facebook.com/romancehq**

 Follow us on **twitter.com/millsandboonuk**

 Join us on **community.millsandboon.co.uk**

Visit us Online   Sign up for our FREE eNewsletter at **www.millsandboon.co.uk**

WEB/M&B/RTL